CW01511841

DAUGHTER
OF THE
DARK
SEA

DAUGHTER OF THE DARK SEA

Copyright © 2025 by G. E. Smith.

All rights reserved. Printed in the United Kingdom. No part of this book may be used or reproduced in any manner whatsoever without written permission except in the case of brief quotations embedded in critical articles or reviews. The author and publisher do not permit any company, group or individual to use any part of this publication for the purposes of training any form of AI software, generative or otherwise.

This book is a work of fiction. Names, characters, businesses, organisations, places, events and incidents either are the product of the author's imagination or are used fictitiously. Any resemblance to actual persons, living or dead, events or locales is entirely coincidental.

For more information, please contact:

gesmithauthor@outlook.com

https://gesmithauthor.my.canva.site

Cover design by April Ward Graphics @april.wardesigns.

Edited by Wonderporium Ink.

Map designed with Inkarnate.

Formatting and Chapter Headers by Humble Author Services.

ISBN: 978-1-0682440-2-5

First Edition: September 2025

10 9 8 7 6 5 4 3 2 1

DAUGHTER
OF THE
DARK
SEA

THE AZARIAN SAGA

G. E. SMITH

To those who ever feel unheard, your voice smothered and disregarded. To those who drown in their anxiety and grief, unable to catch a breath.

To those who believe they are weak . . . you are strong.

You are powerful.

You will not be conquered.

AUTHOR'S NOTE

Dear Reader,

Daughter of the Dark Sea is a fantasy novel with mature or upsetting themes that are intended for ages 18+. It includes content such as oppression, sexual assault, death, blood, war, violence, sexual themes, and grief. Reader discretion is advised.

For a comprehensive sensitivity list, please visit https://gesmithauthor.my.canva.site

THE AZARIAN ISLANDS

IRONWHARF
OUTPOST

TALMON

EMERALD
FOREST

THE
CITADEL

SHANNARA
TERRITORY

SOUTH WHARF
STATION

LIFELESS WATERS

CALYPSO
ISLANDS

PERIL COVE

GALEN

SHAUROCK SEA

LIFELESS WATERS

OTROVIA

FANG
HARBOUR

SULFIRE SEA

THE BLACK ABYSS

EBONMOOR
MOUNTAINS

BLACKSTONE
REEF

NARROWFEN
PASS

STORMKEEP
FORTRESS

ALDARA

BELLMOOR
TERRITORY

SOUTHERN
OASIS

SILENT
TUNDRA

WHITESTONE
BAY

ACHLYS CHANNEL

KING'S COVE
GUARD

THE DEAD
ISLANDS

DEADWATER
PRISON

TO AZARIA ⟶

Prologue

Finlay

P romise me you won't die."

"It's a bit hard to promise that." Finlay cautiously glanced down the cobbled street before placing a comforting hand on his partner's cheek. It was risky, and he tried memorising the smooth planes of John's features; the way his brow furrowed at the surprisingly gentle gesture.

Orange dazzled the sky, like sparkling citrine. The sun hung low in the horizon, and a warm, summer breeze entwined their bodies, with a promise of adventure—and urgency—awaiting Finlay. He *needed* to do this, but gods' darn it, his heart was breaking at leaving.

"Then promise me you'll come back." John shifted, his heels rocking on the wooden porch of his tavern. Finlay's chest tightened at the familiar squeak of wood, his breathing restricted, and he stared into his partner's striking blue eyes.

"You're all I've got," John's voice strained, and he cleared his throat.

"I'll always come back to you, John," Finlay spoke quietly, dark eyes darting around at their surroundings. "I promise I *will* always find you. Together, *ayterni*—right?"

John's eyes widened in alarm at the old language rolling off Finlay's tongue, followed by a tentative smile at their endearment for *eternal*.

A soft whine sounded, and Finlay glanced down to his loyal hound sat beside John's side. He stroked the gossamer-black fur, fingers shakily brushing over the collared chain, and placed a soft kiss on the dog's head. The pooch reeked of stale ale, cigar ash and aged wood, the scent of home curling up Finlay's nose, and he inhaled deeply.

"Conan, take care of John for me." Finlay winked at his partner, before straightening his black-and-green uniform. He brushed his long hair out of his eyes with a trembling hand and flicked his wrists, warding off the persistent shakes. *That's going to be a problem.*

"Aye, you know he will." John smiled tightly but his eyes were alight with worry. "*Temporarily*—because you'll be coming home. Alive."

Finlay swallowed a panicked laugh and grasped his partner's slender hand. "I need to find her . . . we're running out of time, John. She's everything we've been working towards."

John only nodded once, his stare wary of the bustling life in the street passing them by. They were blessed by the gods to own a tavern on the main street, with a constant influx of sailors and weary souls to fill their coffers. It was much needed after Finlay had estranged from his family . . . if he could even call them *that*.

"Two weeks," John spoke, his sharp voice cutting through Finlay's bitterness. "Come back with the girl. Then we can get the clan ready to move."

Another reason for Finlay's estrangement. He descended from pioneers of malice, hardship, and *judgement*, who thrived under the empire's reign of these islands. The clan he'd built with John was the opposite. Survivors in a world recovering from war— *two* wars in fact—who sought to eliminate the infestation of the Talmon Empire.

"If it even is her." Finlay sheathed his family's broadsword behind his back. Its weight was a continuous burden; a mark of shame running down his spine. Hatred filled him at what—*who*— the sword represented.

Sun rays bounced off a shining gleam of Talmon silver parading down the street, stopping cloaked civilians, searching their baskets, and confiscating weaponry. Their clan had caused a stir lately and, as a result, searches and surveillance had increased, and rebellions were lighting in people's hearts. Only small embers, but it was enough to spark unrest amongst nobility.

"We can only hope." John took Finlay's trembling hands into his steady, rough palms, chapped from years of bartending at their tavern. "Remember the plan. The *story*. And don't. Get. Caught."

Finlay shook out a wavering breath, rolling his shoulders. "And don't die."

"Aye, that would be nice. We'd like you back in one piece."

John flashed a grim smile of sharp teeth, and the heavy weight on Finlay's back burrowed into his chest. A horn blared from the nearby harbour and John let out a gasp, woeful blue eyes shimmering with tears. He released Finlay's trembling hands.

"I have to go." Gods, it was *really* happening. Ten long, hard years finally coming to an inevitable end. Finlay's pulse fluttered as he slung a knapsack of minor belongings over his shoulder, the strap biting into his slender frame.

"We'll be waiting for you." John gestured to Conan, his dual tails wagging between his two owners, unaware of what was unfolding. "Be careful, Finlay, *please.*"

"Always. I'll miss you."

John opened his mouth, but quickly shut it as a nearby guard shouldered his way past them to the entrance of the tavern.

"If you're joining the ship I think you are, you'd better hurry," the guard grunted, his gruff tone directed at Finlay. "The captain's in a foul mood and she's casting off early, eager to set sail." His expression was pinched with irritation. "Bloody woman-captain, what's this world coming to?" He ducked into the tavern, bellowing at the barmaid for an ale.

John tightly nodded, his mouth settling into a thin line as he retreated into the shadows of their haven, despite the *guests.*

With a tear in his eye, Finlay turned his back on his small, *true* family, and ventured down the main cobbled street towards the thrumming heart of the port, which was crawling with citizens, all rushing to bid farewell to their loved ones. Throngs of women and children waved and cried, and Finlay bitterly scoffed. No one was here to bid him farewell. The empire quashed anything *different* to their values, and he'd had no choice but to become an expert at hiding in plain sight.

Each step was an eternity, his feet dragging like stone through mud. He couldn't mess this up. This was his last chance to right his wrongs—to right this messed up world.

As he stepped onto the wooden deck of the port, his dark eyes squinted against the low, dusky sun setting behind a formidable black ship. Teems of sailors boarded the gangplank, all wearing the same identical uniform as himself. Good. He'd swiped this from a sailor when he'd fled his family's estate, in the hope it was the correct uniform, and it was a little big on his slender, bony frame.

Finlay had promised John he'd return home, but with everything at stake . . . he would lay down his life, if it meant saving hers. The sting of the false promise made him wince, that burrowed heaviness in his chest imploding into a scattering of shards, crystalising into his bones, and fortifying his resolve to make this sacrifice.

I'm sorry, John.

He wiped his clammy hands on his breeches as he filed into the stream of sailors boarding the ship, the heat of bodies causing beads of sweat to drip from his brow. Up ahead, he spotted a being with a head of gleaming white hair, donning a black leather jerkin, and two daggers strapped to her back. She stomped across the deck, barking orders at her crew.

With a deep breath, ash and ale swirling around his mind, the rebel leader took his first step onto the mighty *Hell's Serpent*.

PART ONE

THE DEMON SEA SIREN

Kora

Kora Cadell had been tracking the pirates for three days. Her heartbeat thundered in time with the rocking of her ship on the cresting ocean waves of the expanse of the Shaurock Sea, her eyes fixed on the horizon, scouting for signs of unruly sails. She'd been staring for so long that the endless blue swirled her vision, but she would not stop. Not with the thrill of the hunt sizzling beneath her skin.

A breeze ruffled her hair, short strands of sea-foam white fluttering into her gaze as she gripped the helm, keeping her ship steady against the persistent current. Kora inhaled deeply, savouring the cool, briny southern winds as the midday sun blazed down on her crew.

Three blisteringly hot days they'd been sailing off-course from their scouting mission near Scarlet Bay. They were royally fucked. But she wouldn't admit that.

Before their return voyage from the bay, she'd caught wind of pirates gathering in Peril Cove, and her trusty, unknown voice—that wasn't her own—had compelled her to hunt them down. She often listened to the mysterious voice inside her mind, not that she'd admit it to anyone. She wasn't insane! But it'd kept her alive the past ten years, and was the sandy foundation to her whirlpool mind.

Now, it'd driven her to the notorious homeland of pirates—Peril Cove. At least, it *was* their homeland, until a brutal war raged over two hundred years ago, scattering pirates across the seas whilst their home was desecrated. Good bloody riddance. Kora would ensure *all* pirates were wiped from the world they'd stained, like an ink splotch on a map.

What else was a pirate-hunter meant to do?

The cove's unique sharp, horseshoe shape loomed ahead, surrounded by reefs and archipelagos. It was troublesome territory to sail and navigate, and many shipwrecks happened in these southern waters. Northern towers guarding the pointed tips, armed to the teeth, making it impossible to enter. Except for Captain Kora Cadell.

Her eyes flickered to the deck. Exhaustion laid heavy on her sailing crew, and dehydration was rapidly setting in. Supplies were dangerously dwindling, and rumours circled that she wasn't fit to be captain. But those were only rumours. It was fine. No big deal.

The stench alone of the lower decks was eye watering. They'd been out at sea for too long, and she tugged at the sweat-damp collar of her black jerkin. It'd be another mark against her carefully crafted reputation.

Kora cast her eyes to the port side of *Hell's Serpent*. A few miles away, she could spot the edge of *the Mist*, lingering like a shade.

It spanned for miles, consuming the entirety of the western island, Galen. A mystery among these god-abandoned lands, the Mist was untouchable, and impenetrable, and no one had been able to contact Galen since it appeared ten years ago.

Shortly after the empire united the islands, ending the two-hundred-year war, Galen lit the fire for a secondary war when they'd refused to bow. But the Mist arrived as a blessing, and the hostile enemy the empire feared had met their demise, contained in a prison of nature's creation.

Being this close to it unnerved Kora, and chills ran down her spine, snaking into her weakened limbs. She'd nearly lost her life in these waters, succumbing to an attack nearby the Mist. Luckily, the commodore had saved her life from—

"*Go . . . keep going*," the deep, inviting voice whispered, dragging Kora from the depths of her mind.

The voice travelled on the ocean winds, it sang to her in her dreams, and it soothed her raging, vengeful heart. She steered the ship away from a rocky reef patch and paused to fill her lungs, tasting the thrill of sailing the barrens of the Shaurock Sea.

The night-black sails of *Hell's Serpent* whipped in the air, propelling them forward. Thick, dark-green ropes looped around the base of the central main mast, with rigging and shrouds dyed the same dreadful colour. An envious malachite stone, shaped like a diamond, and embedded in the heart of the wheel, sparkled at her. The colours of the Talmon Empire followed Kora everywhere.

The crew worked relentlessly hard, muscles stretching and straining, slick with ocean spray and sweat. Black-and-dark-forest-green uniforms, lined with golden buttons and stitching, were discarded in the heat of the sun. Kora absentmindedly scratched the embroidered insignia over her chest—a sharp four-pointed star, connected by an inner loop. The empire claimed it was a symbol of unity, or some bullshit like that. Kora scoffed as she eyed the isolated, shrouded Galen Island.

"Captain Cadell." A familiar, deep drawl sounded from the stairs leading from the main deck.

Blake Marwood rounded the corner, his dark hair blending in with the ebony wood of her fearsome ship. He prowled with a predatory stalk in his gait, and a tight smile stretched his handsome face, causing Kora's stomach to sink to the depths of the brig.

"The crew are beginning to wonder whether you're of . . ." he paused, ". . . unsound mind, with these *impulsive* plunders. We've sailed too far." His deep, green eyes fixated on her face as he stood close to her side. Close enough to feel his warmth radiating from him.

"Ah, but my *crazy* plans always pay off. They always end up with treasure," Kora replied, angling her head up to meet his keen gaze. "Rewards *I* am willing to hide from the empire," she added, fixing him *that* look. She put her neck on the line by amending the ledgers of their plunders. But her crew's families were starving, and struggling to survive in the streets of Aldara's lower districts.

It was the least she could do in her position.

Blake's hair ruffled in the breeze, damp strands hanging over his glinting eyes. Compared to the sun-beaten skin of most naval officers, he was lightly tanned, with *muscled* broad shoulders, and a comfortable yet powerful authority he wielded effortlessly. So different from when they first met, all those years ago.

His uniform mirrored her own, and it suited him well, matching his hair and eyes like it'd been made for him. A thick, dark-brown leather belt hugged his hips, with a gleaming cutlass sword sheathed at his side. Gold thread trailed around the black hilt, connecting to a golden pommel that arched round and protected his hand. A dainty green-and-black tassel completed the weapon.

Everything about Blake *screamed* the Talmon Empire—Kora personally preferred to *play* with daggers—but good gods, was he handsome.

"They're aware of your previous successes. But this latest venture of yours . . ." Blake glanced past the bow of the ship towards the open, endless ocean. Kora adored the sight of it.

"Then why are they moaning?" Kora snapped. She'd worked her fingers to the bone to achieve her status. Fought harder than anyone. Endured too many horrors.

Blake inhaled sharply, his hands hovering near her calloused and scarred ones, from the many years of working as a low-level sailor. A whisper of a touch. She inspected the dirt crusting her fingernails. She really needed a bath.

"It's been an extra three days, Kora. We still need to sail back. Supplies are low—no, they're *non-existent*. The crew are close to fainting, or even dying." His assessing gaze raked across her. "So are you. We won't make it back to Aldara alive."

They were having this conversation now, then.

"*Ignore him . . . keep sailing.*"

She grimaced and wiped sweat from her brow. It was no lie that Kora had kept rooted to the helm lately, using it to steady her legs that swayed in time with the ocean waves. Once she'd realised they were running out of water, food, and *grog*, she was the first to ration her portions. She didn't dare admit that all she'd eaten for three days were tiny nibbles of cured meats, the taste so bland she'd barely chewed, gulping down the contents to line the gnawing hole inside.

She couldn't show any form of weakness. The first sign of it, she'd be removed from her position, losing the respect and authority she'd wrestled for under the scrutinous judgement of society.

"Are you sure it's not what's between my legs that's stirring them?" she asked saccharinely, distracting him from her quivering stance.

As the only female captain in the armada, Kora was a prize circus act to males—something she felt strongly about challenging as a captain. A small ember blazed within her at the vision in her mind of female captains leading an entire fleet. She'd poured her blood, sweat, and tears into clawing her way into the armada, and rapidly ascended to the empire's best-ranking captain within two years.

Now, she needed to claw her way up higher, and avoid making *any* mistakes.

Just like the one she was making now.

Blake stilled, his eyes pointedly roaming her body, taking in her slender frame that was packed with muscle from working on ships. Not that she could feel the benefit. Her limbs were ready to give way any moment. Years of working on ships under the hot sun had imbued her freckled skin with a golden kiss, and his eyes skimmed across her rounded face, finally settling on her pouted mouth. Kora's toes curled in her boots from his piercing stare.

Gods-damn it with that stare. It undid her every time.

He cleared his throat. "I'd say—"

"Captain!"

She whipped her gaze northwards, to the top of the foremast, as a sailor frantically pointed ahead. Her eyes refocused on the horizon. Red sails peaked in the distance.

Thank the gods.

They'd found the pirates.

Y ou were saying?" Kora asked Blake with a smug grin. Adrenaline coursed through her, strengthening her weak legs, and he rolled his eyes.

"Just don't get too close to the Mist. I'll get the crew ready." He sauntered to the main deck with that annoying prowl in his gait. Kora hesitated, a strangeness tugging at her from the shimmering, grey expanse drifting on the rolling waves.

The short war that had raged between Galen and the remaining islands ten years ago left a scorched mark upon the islands. Countless lives lost from of the brutality of Galen because they believed they should've been the rightful rulers instead of Talmon.

Endless epic tales, spoken in hushed tones to her over the years, caused shivers to snake down her spine. Tales of the mountainous piles of bodies Galen left in their wake as they cleaved through the young empire, jealous of the unity they had achieved after the two-hundred-year war with pirates and rebels devoted to the *old ways*. Galenites had showed no mercy to innocents, wives, and children.

Before the Mist, Galenites were infamous for stringing up their victims and staking them on the shores of their island for ships to witness. The victim's backs were split open, and their lungs strung out behind their corpses like a colony of blood eagles.

They were *bloody barbarians*.

Kora had never been this close to the Mist before, or Galen, for that matter. It was thick, grey, and lifeless and, the longer she stared at it, the more she thought she could see shadows dancing within. Erick had forbidden her from venturing too far into the western waters. Her gut twisted at the intrusive thought of her adoptive father *and* her commodore. She never disobeyed him. Ever.

At least, that's what she told herself.

He'd saved her from a ship wreckage, her presumed family slaughtered by pirates, around the time the Mist had manifested. She didn't remember anything from before that, but a strong belief powered her resolution that she *had* a family. A warmth, deep in her core, stirred as she conjured blank faces with sweeping white hair matching her own, framing the same round, lapis-lazuli eyes she possessed.

Kora had a nasty bash on the head, from murderous pirates, to thank for her missing family and broken memory. She traced the jagged scar on her left temple as it arched over her ear and hid below her short hair, following it as unfavourably forked from her temple. The two, wavy, pink lines drifted apart, one ending just by her eyebrow, the other curling over her cheekbone.

Erick had said she'd been close to losing her left eye in the accident, and it was a blessing she thanked the gods for everyday that he'd saved her when he did.

The chilling Mist trailing beside them, and the jagged sharpness of Peril Cove ahead, set her teeth on edge, and a trickle of a dark memory haunted her mind. The sounds of screams, the crash of waves, the splitting pain of her skull cracking open. She hissed as she wondered whether the bodies of her parents rested beneath the deep ocean's surface.

She'd sworn vengeance on *every* pirate for what they did to her. What they took from her. And she wouldn't stop until they'd crumbled, disintegrated, *vanished*, like her previous life had. Like her family had. Like her identity and memory had.

"Ahead, you're almost there," the voice brushed against her ears and shivers rippled down her spine. It normally uttered only a word or two, never more, but now it was so vocal it practically shouted. Sometimes, Kora doubted whether it truly *was* a voice, or if it was simply her intuition? She couldn't speak of it to anyone. That'd be a one-way ticket to an asylum, or exile to the desert.

She'd never been able to speak back to the voice; always a one-way system in her mind. Even if she screamed her thoughts, there'd be no response. She'd become a master at hiding her reactions to it. At first, she'd been panicked, screaming to Erick she was hearing things. But he instantly knew what to say, how to reassure her. That her injury had caused minor damage and, over time, her mind would settle and adapt.

But it never did. So Kora had to learn the art of poker faces. Swapping one mask for another, and keeping her expression in neutrality, whilst the voice ravaged her mind, telling her where to go and what to do . . . albeit in a minimal number of words.

Blake barked orders at the crew to get into offensive positions, and the stamping thunder of boots vibrated on the ship as they descended below deck to prepare the cannons. Lancers armed themselves with jet-black, sharp spears that were long, lethal, and capable of impaling bodies from a great distance. Archers climbed the shrouds up to the several masts for a better vantage point, longbows slung over their shoulders as Kora's head archer hollered instructions at his squadron.

Sailors with shining silver shields raced to her and inclined their heads as they stationed around the quarterdeck. No sign of any mutiny or discontent in their faces, but shadows lined their eyes. One of them openly stared at her, shock plastering his slender face as his dark eyes tunnelled onto her scar. His uniform was too big for him, the jerkin held together by the scabbard attached to his back, containing a unique broadsword.

"What are you staring at?" she snapped, rolling her eyes. The sailor averted his gaze, a blush creeping up his neck. A waver trembled in his step, vibrating up into his hands, causing a sliver of guilt to slice through her. He must be starving.

Forged from the hardest silver, black bolts adorned the edges of the shields, with a golden insignia plastered on the front. Kora swallowed her distaste for it, and firmly gripped the helm as they ventured closer to the red pirate ship.

This was it. The thrill of battle crested within her as their ship raced on the southwestern winds. Another pirate ship to hunt and destroy, another one marked off her list—

No . . . it can't be.

Kora frowned as a picture formed in the distance, and the wood of the wheel spokes bit into her skin, her grip so tight her callouses cracked.

"Blake!" her voice rang.

He whipped his head up to meet her panicked stare and scanned ahead. Five sets of sails. All different colours and patterns. They hadn't stumbled on a couple pirates, but a full flotilla.

"Shit," she whispered. This wasn't an *ordinary* pirate meeting.

Blake raced up to the quarterdeck, taking two steps at a time. "We're not prepared for this," he breathed. "Turn around, now.

Before it's too late."

The sailors shuffled in wariness, but something in her core urged her forward. "No," she replied sternly. "We've battled this many before. We can do it again." By the gods, she wouldn't miss this chance.

Miss her chance at *five* ships full of filthy pirates. These might be the last pirates left. By her record, she'd decimated over half of the pirate scum, the majority of them now locked up in the dreaded Deadwater Prison. Or sunken to the bottom of the ocean, along with their victims.

"Kora," Blake grabbed her wrist, pulling her left hand from the wheel, her nerves heating at the contact. A sailor's gasp cut through the air and she glared at Blake. She would have to reprimand him later for the informal address. Kora forcefully tugged her wrist from his firm grip, her skin smarting.

"Kora!" Blake repeated, ignoring the shock from the sailors that he'd addressed her so casually. "These aren't *normal* pirates."

A chill settled in Kora's bones as she took in the pirate ships a few miles ahead, preparing for warfare. Their ships were grand, with mighty sails billowing in the wind, and masses of sturdy, *hydrated* crew members.

"Where did they get those ships?" she spoke quietly.

Pirates normally had run-down, pathetic little vessels that could barely survive a few rounds of cannon fire before they were destroyed. Their crews usually in a panic at the presence of the empire flag. The red-sailed ship had taken the forefront of the five. It was large, with deep mahogany wood and green shrouds.

"They're *our* ships," she hissed. She recognised unmistakable accents of green across the flotilla, signature embellishments of jewels and carved wood exclusive to the empire. Her mind raced. When had the admiral's ships been raided? Had they missed an attack whilst venturing across the Shaurock Sea? Worst yet, had Aldara, her *home*, been attacked? Dread surfaced in Kora's chest and she squashed it down, maintaining her mask.

"They're *our* ships," Kora repeated confidently. "We know their weaknesses."

Shock raged on Blake's face; his knuckles clenched white at pirates using their prized fleet ships. Vengeance coursed through her body, propelling her into action.

"See there," Kora pointed to a small archipelago of rocks southwest of Peril Cove. "We can lure them in there and use the reef and rocks to slow down and break apart their ships."

Blake's gaze followed as he surveyed the reef, before his face hardened and he nodded. "We're faster than them." He ran his hand through his hair, pushing it out of his eyes. "If we can trap them, they won't realise until it's too late."

A little spark ignited within Kora as their plan knitted together. It felt like old times—working together to achieve the best outcome for *them*. It'd be so long since their duality had surfaced, and she vibrated with anticipation. Blood pounded in her veins with a rush and the ship rocked, the ocean waves cresting along with her heart.

Blake met her gaze once last time, studying her face, before sprinting down to the main deck to deliver new orders. The sailors behind Kora quivered, their longbows and swords armed in their hands, shields hoisted against their backs. She lingered on the nearest sailor, his broadsword slack in his grip, as if he couldn't bear the touch. He returned Kora's inquisitive gaze, his own sparkling stare reflecting curiosity, and a hint of fear.

Once the ships were close enough that Kora could count the feathers of the fallen-angel figurehead of the red ship, its eyes made of malachite stone, she braced her legs as she deftly spun the wheel of *Hell's Serpent*. Her nostrils flared, heat consuming her. She knew that figurehead anywhere. The empire's navy prided themselves on their uniquely tailored ships. Each one purposefully designed to be lethal; reflected in their figureheads.

"*Come about!*" She gritted her teeth against the rough turn, her ship swiftly avoiding colliding with *Fallen Angel*, and a sudden, warm southern wind propelled them towards the archipelago. Kora sent a prayer up to the gods as they narrowly avoided a round of cannon fire.

Hell's Serpent was the fastest ship in the armada, and she patted the helm in appreciation as they gained speed. "Atta girl." Adventure speared through Kora, and she grinned as they sailed away from the jaws of evil—until a foghorn sounded behind them.

The sound of war.

The sound of pirates.

Cold crept up her neck, around her skull, as an echo of a memory crashed through her body and she faltered, losing her grip against the currents. *Hell's Serpent* rocked aggressively, and sailors cried out as they stumbled, their lances skittering across the deck.

The foghorn roared in her ears, murky ocean mixed with blood swirling in her mind as an unforgiving pain swept through her. The Mist filled her vision . . . beckoning her . . . inviting her . .

. to succumb to its inky depths. She reached out, her mask falling away as she cried out from the agony.

What in the gods was happening?

"Captain!" the sailors yelled, and they braced her body as she sucked in a breath, her mind clutching at fragments of a memory fading as quickly as it appeared. She regained her composure, remembering she was the infamous Captain Kora Cadell. The fiercest captain in King Staghart's armada.

And she would not be conquered.

T hey destroyed the first ship. An all-black small vessel, with a similar serpent figurehead as *Hell's Serpent*. A pitiful attempt at replication. It bewildered her as to why the pirates had brought along an imposter; the vessel clearly made of shoddy woodwork. They didn't even fire a cannon or launch any arrows. It was horrifically laughable—and satisfying—when the ship had exploded into pieces, shattering into the high coastal cliffs of Peril Cove. But it was an easy win, and Kora desired a challenge.

The archers of *Hell's Serpent* were swift and lethal, their arrows raining down in quick, waved succession onto *Fallen Angel*, causing it to fall back for protection behind its remaining flotilla. The ship was a staple in the empire's armada, and how it was *here* was a mystery.

A new ship commanded the front, with golden-yellow patchwork sails, and a harpy creature figurehead featuring an eagle-bodied female. Malachite stones embedded her wings, but her eyes had been removed, altering her usual serene face into one of sorrow.

Golden Harpy.

Kora winced, she'd once stood on that ship, prowled its chambers when she'd achieved her captain rank, searching for her dream vessel. She'd nearly chosen that ship, but the bare bosom on the figurehead didn't scream *terrifying female captain*, and elicited the wrong kind of attention.

To the right, a ship with torn grey sails defied the odds of sailing on the winds. Cannon blasts scattered across the weathered, peeling wood, which was constricted by shredded, ashen-green ropes, as if they'd never bothered repairing it from battles.

A misted grey aura, that even sunlight couldn't pierce,

shrouded its deck. Kora strained, rubbing her eyes. It must be dehydration . . . *right?* A laughing-skeleton figurehead, clutching an unlit iron lantern with a malachite stone in its iron candle wick, stormed the front.

Bone Rattler.

A reject in the empire's armada, used only once in battle before it was deemed a failure. It'd been abandoned in a shipyard years ago, its purpose reduced to spare parts for other vessels.

Lastly, to the left, sailed a magnificent ship with royal blue sails. It was the second largest of them all, and in the most pristine condition. It gained on *Golden Harpy*, the crew in uniformed formation, never missing a beat as they armed their lances and cannons.

Kora swerved her ship as a cannon blast flew past them starboard side, the sound ringing in her ears. She panted, glancing to the blue-sailed ship, eyeing its mermaid figurehead. Her face was stretched into a tortured scream, exposing fanged teeth made of the malachite stone the Talmon Empire favoured.

Demon Sea Siren.

The fiercest ship the empire had ever built—and it was now commanded by filthy pirates, threatening the world and murdering innocents . . . like her forgotten family.

Kora's blood boiled, and her anger rose with the ocean waves as she swerved around the small, sharp archipelagos, navigating the trickiest way through possible. Her smaller ship was deft, and easier to manoeuvre.

"*Fire!*" Blake's voice thundered, and a rain of arrows, tips alight with fire, soared above them. He briefly appeared at the top of the steps to the quarterdeck and signalled Kora, his fingers brushing over the side of his face in the pattern of her scar. It was simplistic, and something they'd perfected together. To anyone else, they'd think he was mocking her marred face, but truly, it was an unspoken language between them.

"I need you to tell me what's happening back there," Kora commanded the sailor hovering close to her. His dark eyes widened, full of fear. Not an ounce of curiosity remained on his paled, stricken face. "Update me on their formation. If they make any moves."

"Our archers missed most of the pirates. They avoided the fire," he replied, his broadsword hanging limp at his side. Kora smiled devilishly. Her archers were not trained to miss. But they had, as they planned.

She peered ahead, spotting a break in the archipelago that was only big enough for *Hell's Serpent* to pass through. Well . . . most of it.

"It's *Demon Sea Siren*," his face grew shocked, his tremor increasing. "Oh *no*! It . . . it's really here." He blinked. "She's gaining on us!" his voice reached a fervent pitch as he backed up, bumping Kora's shoulder.

His stale, bitter stench stuffed her senses and she wrinkled her nose. Like old burnt wood, ash, and dried, fermented wheat. Long, dirty-brown hair, damp with sweat, was tied at the nape of his neck with a leather strap, strands plastered to his forehead and face.

"The other two are hiding behind it. I'm not sure why." He must be a newbie, still gaining his sea legs. He irritatingly drifted closer, their shoulders continuously brushing, the flat edge of his sword catching her legs.

"You better hold that sword properly before I use it on you, sailor," Kora snapped, and he stiffened, shifting his blade to his other side. A cross-work pattern covered the pommel, and a symbol beneath the hilt had been scratched, marring the metal.

The fire arrows disbanded the flotilla as planned, forcing them to break their formation to avoid catching on fire, allowing Kora to lead them deeper into the archipelago—and pick them off one by one.

She gritted her teeth and sent a prayer up to whomever was listening as she motioned with her right hand, signalling back to Blake, who was running around the main deck with an intense purpose, hollering orders at the crew. The leader of the archer squadron commanded the archers to descend from the masts, whilst lancers headed to the starboard side.

They were in position. She angled her ship towards the small pass in the east. The cracking *boom* of another cannon swept across the deck. It was a whip of a sound, smacking Kora's senses across the face.

The pirates were so close—*too* close.

Ocean waves devoured the sides of *Hell's Serpent*. A large boulder shattered to Kora's left, chunks of rock flying across the watery deck. Shields instantly rushed up, protecting her from the explosion as debris showered from above after a third cannon fire, narrowly missing the main mast.

"They're getting closer!" the sailor shouted, peering around his shield. Blood oozed from a small cut on his head, mixing with his sweat.

"Good, let them come." She didn't stop to think as she yelled to her crew to drop to the deck. Sailors fell to the floor like a black wave, covering their heads with hands and shields as they approached the pass at rapid pace.

Two large jagged rocks formed the small pass, arching up to meet at a pointed curve. Barely tall or wide enough to fit her masts through. Kora winced. Her ship would suffer significant damage, but it was the only way through. She had to get to the other side.

Boom. Another cannon fired, breaking the peaked pass apart as chunks of moss-covered rock plummeted into the ocean.

"How'd they miss us?" The sailor frowned, his shield vibrating with nerves.

Hell's Serpent sailed through, the jagged, crusted mass scraping against the sides of Kora's precious ship. She shuddered as it creaked, panels cracking and breaking off. The rigging caught and tugged against the rocks, and Blake ordered the lancers to cut it free.

Their speed slowed and her heart thumped wildly. *Boom.* A cannon scraped the stern. These pirates certainly had lousy aim.

The top of the main mast snapped against the cresting peak and wood shattered, raining down and mixing with rock infested puddles. Another cannon blasted from *Demon Sea Siren* and rocky nature exploded, allowing more space in the pass for *Hell's Serpent* to sail through.

Another cannon fired on the left. Right. Left.

"No," Kora replied, realisation dawning. "They're trying to fit through the pass."

Almighty Thanos.

Kora released a sigh of relief once they cleared the edge of the archipelago, and she spun the wheel with her captain flair.

"*Anchor!*" she cried.

With quick precision, the crew descended the anchor as they passed over a reef patch, anchoring *Hell's Serpent* port side. The ship whipped around, wind blowing in their favour.

The crew grabbed on to the right-side railing as it creaked and rocked heavily towards the anchored side, nearly sending them all overboard. She hooked her arm through the spokes of the wheel, crying out as ocean water sprayed onto the deck, soaking her legs as they slipped beneath her.

Jet-black sails fluttered in the wind as her ship aligned sideways with the narrow pass. Lancers were armed at the starboard side, black spears glistening in the sun, along with archers, their bowstrings taut and arrows nocked. The thunder of cannons loaded by the gunners reverberated throughout the ship.

Demon Sea Siren struggled to sail through, its masts splintering and shattering completely all the way down. The main sail tore in half and listlessly hung, no longer able to catch a breeze. Cracks splintered the wood, the side sails catching on the rocks and tearing holes in the fabric. Satisfaction filled Kora as the pirates broke their uniformity, yelling at *Hell's Serpent*, who aimed at them with the full might of their artillery.

"*Fire!*" Kora bellowed, her voice straining as it ripped from her throat with vengeance. The ocean's surface crested, like a tunnel spearing for their foe, and her core lurched with the movement, as if an extension of herself shot from her flesh before vanishing.

Blake echoed her command to the brig and the archers fired first, their movements powerful yet fluid, effortlessly volleying arrows. The pirates scattered like cockroaches as they sprinted away from the forecastle deck, cries ringing out.

The lancers swiftly followed, their lethal, sharp spears tearing the wood and foremast sails. Guts of pirates spilled as they were pierced by dark spears, their ribboned entrails pinned to their doomed ship. Blood exploded, splattering across the deck, stark against the royal-blue clothing and rich mahogany wood. Finally, the cannons blasted. Rocks broke apart, and the pass crumbled, collapsing onto *Demon Sea Siren*.

Her crew were relentless, firing one after the other in trained, tactical succession, all perfectly timed, giving the other a chance to reload.

Yet . . . something stirred deep inside her as the massacre of *Demon Sea Siren* unfurled. A tingle snaked across her skin, filling her with apprehension. This was what she'd been trained for. Why did she feel like something was wrong?

"*Look,*" the voice stroked Kora's mind, and she released a shuddering breath as *Demon Sea Siren* was demolished, pirates' screams submerged beneath the sea. She shoved her doubt to the back of her mind as something pulled her gaze to the west. The three remaining ships were sailing directly towards . . . Galen. *Why were they sailing there*? She hurried to the edge, placing her hands on the wide railing and squinting against the harsh light of the sun.

No.

Surely they wouldn't sail into the Mist? They'd be caught in its tendrils, unable to proceed or return, suspended in a cloak of nothing. Kora leaned forward, straining to see across the vast blue miles. Heat shimmered off the ocean surface, and sweat, dust, and dirt coated her body, hair, and clothes.

Gods, she was so hot. She was so thirsty. She'd drink the ocean water at this point.

This had to be a mirage. The remaining pirates *had* to be in the archipelago preparing for another attack. Her heart pounded with adrenaline, her uncertain fear wallowing in the depths of her stomach, not daring to reveal itself to her crew. This couldn't be over already. They were *pirates*, driven by murderous bloodlust.

"They're going into the Mist," Blake appeared beside her, his walk near silent. "It's suicide."

Shock slackened his face, as the elegantly built rear of *Fallen Angel* disappeared into the vapid Mist. They would be lost forever, wandering the endless grey void. His hands, a hair's breadth away from Kora's, were coated in dust from the rock explosions, and slick with oil from helping archers light their arrows.

"I don't understand," Kora spoke in hushed tones, the steady course of adrenaline draining away, as exhaustion crept in. "If they sail into the Mist, they'll die. No vessel can pass the barrier."

The Mist was a blessing, but also a curse. It kept the enemy in, but it kept the empire out, too. Her head pounded and she licked her dry lips, tasting blood. She gently brushed her fingers over her mouth, where a small, stinging cut was already clotting.

"We don't *really* know that for sure. We'll need to report this," Blake said roughly. "If the pirates are allying with Galen. There must be a reason for sailing into *that*."

At least it confirmed she wasn't hallucinating. But pirates forging an alliance with *Galen*? This meant trouble, and not the fun kind.

Erick's tales about the Galenite War swirled around in her mind. The Galenites had captured countless Azarian innocents, dragging them to their lifeless island to torture. To turn them against their own families, who remained devoted to the Talmon Empire. To turn them into weapons of destruction.

When the Mist came, trapping them in their soulless wasteland of an island, the conflicts instantly ceased, and the Galenite War ended. Peace returned after two long wars. All that remained were rebels in favour of Galen—and pirates. And soon, Kora would eradicate them all.

She had a personal stake in this. Her new life depended on it. She wanted peace and comfort, and to know she did all she could to avenge her previous life in order to move on with her new one. To ensure what happened to her, would never happen to anyone else.

It'd been ten years. Her memory was never coming back, of that she was sure. What mattered now was the present. Why else would Erick spend countless hours training her? Honing her into the ultimate weapon on the sea. The drive to follow in his footsteps, as a formidable force against the rebels, was all-consuming. A raging red haze sometimes blanketed her mind, and she would lose herself in grief for people, and a life, she couldn't remember.

A totally, super normal response to her '*trauma*,' as Erick liked to call it.

Erick had taken her in, and shaped her anger into something tangible. Ten years of gruelling training, and endless readings about the history of the wars and islands until her eyeballs spun in their sockets. Each day, she was one step closer to her goal, but now it had sailed away.

"Maybe they didn't want to face the wrath of the armada's *most fearsome* ship." A grin lit up her face.

Blake rolled his eyes, but a smile tugged the corner of his mouth. Kora drank him in, noticing the smile didn't reach his eyes. Wet hair framed his gaunt face from rationing, and dust covered his ripped shirt, along with a thin, bloody gash on his forearm.

"Blake! Why didn't you say anything? You, there!" She snapped her fingers at the sailor with the bleeding forehead and he stepped forward, a slight tremor still shaking him. "Fetch some healing supplies quickly, and something for yourself." She pointedly glanced at his head. His gaze flickered at Blake before nodding as he hurried to locate the healer.

"I'll be fine," Blake sighed. "It's just a scratch."

"A scratch, my arse. Sit down. Now."

Blake thudded down at the top of the steps as the sailor returned with supplies, a bandage haphazardly placed on his head, presumably by the healer. Muscled flesh peeked through Blake's torn jerkin, and she admired his strong frame as he unbelted his cutlass sword and carefully placed it beside him.

The sailor hovered behind Kora, watching her curiously, his dark eyes lingering on her scar. It wasn't uncommon for Kora to be stared at, but it felt as though he was boring a hole into the side of her head.

"You can go now. Check on the others," she ordered, her attention trained on her first mate.

The sailor hesitantly scarpered off as Kora tended to Blake, who didn't wince or moan once as she cleansed his wound and dressed it.

"You should be nicer to them more often," he gestured to the nervous sailor. "This job is dangerous. They never know which voyage will be their last."

"Being captain means playing a certain role. Besides, he was *staring* too much." Her mask snapped firmly back into place, smoothing her features out.

Kora nibbled her bottom lip as she focused, ignoring the sudden guilt at how little she knew about her crew, including most of their names. But she'd been captain of *Hell's Serpent* for a year, and couldn't afford to lose the authority she'd worked so hard to gain. The slightest slip up and the viceroys would dismiss her, revoking her status as captain. Even after all this time, she still walked on eggshells.

"Come," Blake's familiar drawl soothed her inner rage from the battle. His hand lightly brushed hers and her body fluttered at the spark as she finished tying off the bandage. "Let's get our reward."

Oh, he was *divine* to stare at.

His eyes darkened mischievously as Kora followed him towards the bow, where uninjured crew members prepared small boats. She cast a curious glance back towards the bereft Mist.

"Look," the voice repeated once again, clanging through her already-pounding head.

Look at *what* exactly, she wondered.

The shattered remains of *Demon Sea Siren* surrounded Kora. Swaths of royal-blue sails shredded into ribbons trailed in the sea, entwining with the limbs of scattered bodies. It reminded her of mermaids, swimming in the ocean depths, dragging sailors to their demise in the dark seas.

Panels of wood were torn clean off in the hull, courtesy of her crew's deadly cannon fire, and the entire bowsprit and masts were blown to pieces, along with the main deck. Only the quarterdeck and the captain's quarters remained intact, arrows and lancers' spears decorating the once-remarkable woodwork. She admired her crew's handiwork, and the sheer force and might of *Hell's Serpent.*

The pirates' attempt to replicate her ship irritated her. No one could impersonate *Hell's Serpent*—or her. Kora's reputation was as a cold, fearless captain, accompanied by an even colder and brutal first mate with an annoying drawl.

She was also a highly sought-after pirate-hunter.

She kicked debris and rocks out of her path as her crew picked their way across the hold, scavenging for supplies and survivors. Why would pirates impersonate a pirate-hunter? It didn't make sense. Kora's notoriety made her a target in the open ocean, away from the safety of the islands—something Erick incessantly fretted about. The meeting was strange, too. Two ships were a surprise, but not uncommon . . . but *five*, and in their centuries-old homeland*?* That was suspicious. Pirates were solitary creatures, driven by greed and lust. They'd kill each other if it resulted in a reward.

And why did they sail into the Mist?

Sailors collected arrows and spears still intact to stock up their artillery, whilst others rummaged for ration supplies. A cheer sounded in the distance and Kora smiled, her mind clearing—they'd found grog that'd survived the battle. After what felt like hours, they'd salvaged grog, water, and food—enough to last the two hundred sailors aboard her ship the weeklong trip home with minor rationing.

Blake summoned Kora to a golden weapons chest. He brushed away the rocks and debris coating it with a grunt and flipped open the unlocked lid, which was embedded with gleaming moonstones and pearls. High-level-grade cutlass swords, daggers, and an ancient-looking claymore greeted them. They were expertly crafted, and better than anything she'd seen in Aldara.

"Where did they find these?" Goosebumps pimpled her flesh as she fingered the curved, sharp edges of one of the gleaming silver daggers. Swirling silver patterns embellished the hilt, the continuous, evolving shapes connecting to an unfamiliar archaic symbol etched into the star shaped pommel. Blake knelt beside her and studied the chest's contents with brisk attention.

"I don't recognise these weapons, or the symbols." Kora reluctantly placed the beautiful dagger back in the chest. Damn, it was exquisite. "The stones on the chest . . . it's from Galen." She glanced sideways at Blake, arching a brow. Moonstone was Galen's preferred gem, and their castle in Skybell was rumoured to be made of it. Something so dazzling didn't belong to a place so cruel.

Blake's mouth formed a grim line. "We'll take it with us. This could be payment from Galen to the pirates. It'd explain why they'd willingly sail into the Mist. Maybe the pirates can reach their shores."

"That's impossible. Why would Galen want pirates to work for them? And no one has ever been able to survive the Mist," Kora pointed out. "If pirates have found some way in . . . does that mean Galen have found a way out?"

Blake abruptly stood and slammed the chest shut, his body tense. He shook his head, denying her question. It was unfathomable. If Galen could escape the Mist, the Galenite War would reignite, blazing until it consumed the islands, disintegrating them into ash. He signalled for three nearby sailors to haul the chest to the boats, and Kora's shoulders slumped as her favoured dagger was carried away.

Shame it'd been crafted at the sinister island.

"They attacked us because that's all pirates *do*. Galen is up to something. Somehow, they're contacting the world," he spat, before helping her up. Their bodies hovered close together, mere inches between their entwining heats. Blake's green gaze captured hers, sparkling like emeralds in a sea of death, and he released a breath, loosening his shoulders.

"We need to head back soon. Don't get lost, I don't want to have to rescue you," he whispered with a teasing wink.

"I think you'll find, it's normally *me* rescuing *you*." Kora tapped his bandaged arm, and Blake retreated to the boats with a chuckle, overseeing the remaining plunder. She weaved around piles of debris, missing the balance of her daggers strapped to her back. Swept away by the thrill of the hunt, she'd left them in her quarters on *Hell's Serpent*.

The fragmented hull was silent and void of life, aside from the occasional arm or leg buried underneath the desecrated debris, and she eyed the suspicious door below the quarterdeck, leading to the captain's quarters. No one had searched it yet. Kora motioned to the nearest sailor and stifled a moan as the trembling newbie approached.

"I thought you stayed on the ship." Her tone dripped with irritation.

"No ma'am." Blood seeped through his head bandage as he wiped his hair from his lean face.

Kora grimaced. She was by no means old enough to be addressed as *ma'am*. Erick had guessed her age as fifteen when he'd recovered her from the wreckage, and now she was approaching her presumed twenty-fifth birthday. They'd decided the day of her rescue would be her birthday. It was at the end of summer, before cool air swept in for autumn, soothing the raging heat.

"You may address me as Captain," she reminded him.

He gaped with worry, shaking his head, but his eyes sparkled. "Please accept my apologies, Captain, I—"

Kora held up a hand, his sparkling eyes irking her. Did he think this was a joke? "It's fine. I need you to help me reach the captain's quarters," she paused, remembering Blake's suggestion, "please."

The sailor stilled, glancing to the heavy-set mahogany door lined with dark iron bolts. He surveyed their demolished surroundings, dark eyes turning quizzical. Open space loomed between them and the captain's door, decking strewn around in obliterated shards. Kora rubbed her chin, casting her stare over piles of rubble.

"We need to find a ladder, or barrels to stack." She began searching, dust collecting on her clammy hands. Nodding at her command, the sailor silently picked through the debris, face paling at the fingers and limbs peeking through the wreckage. She curiously studied him as the sense of purpose eased the tremble persisting in his body.

"What's your name?" Kora enquired reluctantly. *Damn it, Blake.*

"Finlay," he replied without looking, "Finlay Blackstone, Captain." His shoulders hunched, squishing the broadsword strapped to his back between his bony blades.

"As in the House of Blackstone?" Surprise tinted Kora's voice. What was a son of a noble house doing on her ship? And how did *she* not know? Had Blake authorised his draft into the crew? She would certainly remember seeing *Blackstone* on the recruitment list.

Finlay tensed, his hair falling over the side of his damp neck. This close, Kora could see it was dark blonde, the dirt and sweat from over a week at sea hiding its true colour. He met Kora's inquisitive gaze, face pinching.

"Yes, I hail from Aldara, like you." His voice cooled, and his dark eyes seemingly stared off into the distance, as if remembering his home haunted him. Black eyes, like the black-stoned shores of the north-west of Aldara.

"Why are you here? A son of a noble house shouldn't be out here hunting pirates." *Not that he'd done much hunting.* Sons of noble houses were destined to rule in politics, or become consults to the royal family, ensuring their families married into wealth, and carrying the legacy on entitled shoulders.

Kora's stomach knotted. It couldn't be a coincidence that a son of a prestigious noble house, known for its huge contributions to the navy, was here. Drafted for the first time to join the same voyage that was ambushed by pirates sailing stolen empire ships.

Had the Blackstone family organised this? Had they sent their son to spy on the empire? Her spine tingled, skin prickling from the humidity. What if they'd reviewed her plunders and discovered a chunk of wealth missing? Was Finlay here to investigate?

Finlay straightened and sighed at Kora's intensity, clasping his shaky hands together. "Joining the armada gave my family certain . . . advantages." His bitterness leaked through, coating his voice. It was thick, and he cleared his throat. "What better ship to be placed on than *Hell's Serpent*?"

She narrowed her eyes and a blush crept up his neck. It was a double-edged truth, hidden behind deceit, and her gut gnawed. He was hiding something.

Kora probed, "Why would your family force you to enlist?"

"They didn't approve of my . . . lifestyle." Something sparkled in Finlay's dark gaze.

Before she could push further, he suddenly pointed behind her and Kora whirled, expecting an attack, her hands raised to fight. Her breath whooshed out of her system as she faced a partially broken ladder, tucked away in a dark, damp corner.

"The ladder won't hurt you," Finlay chuckled as he brushed the cobwebs off it. Her hands dropped to her side, shaking the tension out of her. *Gods,* she was so tired, her nerves fried from the pirate ambush. Adrenaline had abandoned her, and Kora's body screamed at her to rest. They positioned the ladder against the broken deck panelling, precariously placed at the foot of the captain's bolted door.

"Just about fits," she mused as Finlay held it steady, his tremble now non-existent.

"It's your lucky day. Time to claim what's yours." He smiled, and *gods-damn* he was a pretty male. Kora returned the smile, and a light danced in his fathomless dark eyes as she ascended the ladder.

H eavy, royal-blue drapes shrouded the room in darkness, blanketing the rear cracked windows. Sweat, damp, and something *else* lingered, permeating the air. Kora wrinkled her nose, peering around the thick edge of the door. Darkness moulded itself around large chunky furniture, bolted to the floor.

Finlay hauled himself onto the thin panel of decking and stepped forward, motioning to let him pass, and he nudged the door ajar. Was he being protective? Brown-nosing the captain on his first voyage? Smart lad. Light sliced through the room, revealing a four-poster bed to the right and a desk to the left. A large chest, covered in rubies in the centre, sparkled, casting a red starry sky on the low-beamed ceiling.

"Bingo!" Kora strode towards it, shouldering past Finlay.

"Wait!" he whispered harshly.

Silence smothered them and the sounds of her crew grew distant. She reached for the beckoning ruby chest, treasure dancing in her vision, but a dark bumpy shape in the corner snagged her attention. She halted, turning to inspect the lump at the base of the bed.

"Captain!" Finlay cried in warning.

Kora stumbled as a figure sprang from the exquisite gold covers. Finlay leapt between them, broadsword drawn in his shaky hands as the pirate lunged. She staggered back in surprise, knocking into the desk, papers and trinkets that littered it flying onto the floor.

"Stop where ye are!" the pirate bellowed. A mottled, grey unruly beard, tied with blue string, framed a darkly tanned, chapped face. His eyes were the deepest brown, matching his slicked hair covered with a dark blue bandana.

Finlay swiped wildly with his marred heavy blade as the pirate attempted to shove him away. The pirate yelled, dodging the attack, drawing his cutlass sword and aiming for Finlay's frantically heaving chest.

"Get out of me way, lad." His long coat and breeches matched the royal-blue sails of *Demon Sea Siren*, with a thick, black leather belt and a silver buckle, to sheath his even larger cutlass sword. Kora eyed it cautiously. It was wide, curving to a sharp point, capable of slicing through an arm, or leg . . . or two. Three more males emerged from underneath the bed, covered in dust, debris, and blood. So, *that* was the stench. Their venomous glares fixated on Finlay and his trembling sword.

Filthy pirates.

Kora's blood boiled anew with hatred, and she spared a glance at the desk. A thick, silver envelope knife glinted at her. Its handle, with an intricate vine pattern woven around it, captured her gaze.

"I suppose you're the captain." Kora shuffled forward, obscuring the desk behind her.

"Captain James Cannon." His deep, rough voice bounced through the quarters as he lifted his curved blade level with Finlay's throat, a threat poised on his weather-beaten face.

"Quite the spectacle. You must've fired enough cannons to kill a kraken," she smirked, lips tugged into a lazy smile. "Captain Kora Cadell, at your service." She bowed low and mockingly, and as she straightened, her hand swiftly stroked the surface of the desk in a casual caress.

Krakens were common legend amongst pirates. A mythical creature capable of capsizing the largest of vessels in *minutes*. Consuming sailors and chomping through boats with rows of pointed teeth, their tentacles dragging them to the crushing depths of the ocean. Shame they were only myths. She could do with a kraken in her artillery.

Cannon's face flashed at the mention of her name and he shook his head. "Aye, we know of ye," he snapped, glowering at her insult. His pirate comrades crept out at the edges of the quarters, closing the space between Kora, Finlay, and Cannon.

"Attacking us is pointless," she addressed his crew, glaring at them individually. "Four of you against my ship of sailors."

"We don't see no crew," one to the right sneered.

She refused to look towards the open-door entrance. Had the boats already departed back to *Hell's Serpent*? They wouldn't leave her. Blake wouldn't leave her. She inhaled deeply, repeating the thought over.

A blood-soaked pirate advanced. His white shirt clung to his bony frame, revealing a wound in his side. Blood trickled from his busted lips, and he spat on the floor, his saliva traced with speckles of red.

"You may come on board with us," Kora said slowly, edging closer to Finlay, his sword still raised at their captain. "We won't harm you."

"Lies!" White Shirt snarled as he limped closer. "Ye murder our kind for sport!"

"Aye," Cannon repeated. "It'll be ye that'll be coming with us. Enough of this bloodshed."

"You're the liars. We're not going anywhere with you!" Finlay's voice rose, grimacing as he violently trembled. Kora stilled. He wouldn't make the kill. It was plain as day on his face.

Cannon barked a husky laugh. "Lad, ye'll be at the bottom of the ocean in Davy Jones' Locker. We want the lass." He motioned the wicked blade to Kora, its end nicking her throat.

They wanted her alive, and they didn't intend to send her to the Locker with Finlay. How . . . *confusing*. Pirates were murderous thieves, and nothing more. Finlay blanched at the mention of the Locker, and something protective surged within her.

"No," Kora placed her hand on Finlay's shoulder in comfort. "He won't be."

With a hard warning squeeze, she dragged Finlay away from Cannon and flung the envelope knife with precision. It shot through the air, embedding into Cannon's right shoulder, forcing him back onto the golden bed with a painful yell. His cutlass sword scattered across the floor and Kora leapt, her hands scrambling before the limping, white-shirt pirate could snatch it first.

Drawing herself onto her knees, she clutched the sword, its hilt too big to grapple. *Damn it!* The white-shirt pirate clasped her shoulders, shoving her onto her back before she could draw the weapon up in defence. Her head smacked against the polished floor, pain exploding behind her eyes, and stars danced in her vision. Her ears rang, drowning out Finlay's cries for help.

Finlay.

She'd be gods-damned if she'd let the pirates win. *Move, move now!*

"It's to the Locker with ye now, lad." White Shirt hauled Finlay up by the lapel of his dark jerkin. The bandage around his head unravelled, his blood matting his hair.

"N-no, please!" his voice wavered.

Kora pushed to her feet, the room swaying, and violently drove the cutlass blade through White Shirt's lower back, gutting him. He released Finlay with a shocked splutter, blood dripping from his mouth as Finlay tumbled to the floor with a sickening *thud.*

"Not before I send *you* to the Locker," Kora snarled viciously in his ear.

She plunged the magnificent blade in deeper, all the way to its silver, decorated hilt, pouring all her revenge, hatred, and distaste into the strike until she withdrew it with a horrifying, killing twist. Blood splattered across her jerkin and face and the pirate collapsed in a bloody heap, his guts tumbling out of his stomach.

Finlay gasped, placing a shaking hand over his gaped mouth, blood spraying over him in a decorative crimson streak. The remaining two pirates froze, warily eyeing their crewmate crumpled at Kora's feet as she gripped Cannon's sword, dripping with blood. Finlay scrambled to his feet next to her, clutching his clean broadsword, panting with shock. *Poor lad.*

"Stop!" Cannon yelled, raising a red-stained hand. He'd propped himself against the wooden pillar of the four-poster bed, his bandana removed, staunching the wound soaking into his long blue coat.

"Kora," Cannon's tone was familiar, but her lips curled hearing her name rolling off a pirate's foul tongue. "We've been lookin' for ye for a long time." Desperation flashed in his eyes.

"Well, it's not every day you catch a pirate-hunter." Kora twirled Cannon's cutlass sword in her hand, aiming at his chest. He released a frustrated sigh that turned into a low, wheezing chuckle, shaking his head in disbelief.

"Ye have no idea who ye are, do ye lass?" He bravely squared up to his own blade, the lethal tip brushing apart his torn shirt to his exposed heart.

"I'm Captain Cadell," Kora said each word slowly and offered her most feral smile. Finlay inhaled sharply as a tall dark shadow prowled behind Cannon.

"No, *cildbah.*" The roughness in Cannon's voice softened. Kora's stomach flipped at the old language, her skin crawling at the affectionate term for *kid.* How did a pirate know the language of the ancients? It originated from the old world, Devania, before the empire united the islands, creating Azaria.

"Who ye *really* are." He edged closer, the razor-sharp tip

pressing into his skin enough to draw a thin line of blood. "This wasn't meant to be ye life. Ye need to come with me. I need to take ye to them. Show ye the truth, where *they* stole—"

Blake charged in from the light of the sun, barrelling into Cannon, the force pushing Cannon onto his own sword, and it tore through his chest as easily as ripping bread. Cannon smiled sadly at Kora as the life faded from his eyes.

He was dead instantly.

She dropped the sword in shock, Cannon's hot blood staining her hands, and her crew barged into the quarters, forcing the remaining two pirates to their knees, shackling their wrists with thick, iron cuffs.

"Captain?" Blake appeared before her, his hands resting lightly on her shoulders. "Kora . . . look at me." She blinked up at him dazedly.

"He knew. About me," she whispered. Blake peered at Cannon's body, shifting to Finlay beside her. Realisation flooded his face and he gently squeezed her shoulders.

"Take the prisoners to Hell," Blake ordered the crew. He winked at the prisoners, their fury mirrored on their grimy faces. "We'll meet you there. I need to speak to the captain," he added, clearly dismissing Finlay.

The sailor stiffened at Blake's dismissal, and looked to his captain for confirmation, but Kora's gaze was firmly fixated on Cannon's body, disbelief consuming her. Cannon knew about her past . . . and now he was dead. Did he know the pirates who had attacked her, stealing her life away? Was that where he was going to take her? Were they trying to finish off the job? Was she somehow . . . a loose end?

Finlay touched her forearm in comfort and reluctantly left, grimly glancing at the bloodshed coating the quarters.

Once the crew dragged the pirates kicking and screaming to the boats, Blake released a sigh and wrapped his arms around Kora, crushing her to his chest. He buried his face into her hair, inhaling deeply. His petrichor and leather scent washed over her, and she closed the remaining space, their bodies colliding.

Gods, he smelt good.

"You silly woman," he muttered. "We had no idea where you were."

Kora's arms tightened before she released Blake, taking a step back with a shaky exhale. His expression was tight, his body tense.

"Don't tell me you were worried." Kora let out a small laugh, smothering her unease. Blake's mouth firmly stayed in a disapproving line. "I'm fine!" She smiled and twirled around. He raised an eyebrow, jaw twitching as his eyes roamed over her stained clothing. "It's not my blood," she added.

"What happened?" His voice lowered as he caught sight of the gutted pirate by the desk. Kora filled Blake in, right up to the point of Cannon beginning to reveal information of her past. A shudder crept down her spine. A pirate knew *intimate* secrets about her. Blake listened thoughtfully with his arms crossed as he surveyed the quarters.

"He knew, Blake," Kora matched his lowered tone. "How does a pirate know I have no memory of my life?"

He grasped her hands, leading her away from the bodies towards the far edge of the desk. His rough, calloused thumb stroking her palm, whilst his other hand brushed the flaking, dried blood off her cheek.

"Only a select few know the truth," he said firmly. "Someone must've been feeding them information. Did he say why they were after you?" His hand settled on her right shoulder, his thumb caressing her throat.

Kora shook her head. If only Blake had waited a little longer, Cannon might have spilled more secrets. Drawers lined the mahogany desk and she pulled on the latches, the wood screeching as she rifled through the desk's contents. Blake mirrored her movements, his brows shooting up into his hairline in surprise as he opened a drawer near the bottom.

"Did you find something?"

He shook his head. "If you mean *something* like this." He revealed a pipe, its end dusted with purple powder. Black soot stained the edges, coating the simple brown woodwork.

"I'm not surprised, I'd need to be high to be a pirate," Kora scoffed at the alkaloid pipe. "Being a killer takes its toll on the soul. He probably smoked iridweed every day."

Blake snickered, placing the pipe on the top of the desk. "Actually," he picked it back up, "probably best to leave this here. Erick will only blame me if he finds iridweed powder on the ship." He placed it back in the drawer, slamming it shut, and she winced at his reaction.

It was a mystery where the drug was being funnelled from, or where it was grown, and no one knew what plant it resulted from, only that it spread through pirate vessels like wildfire. The empire didn't care, as long as it didn't reach their lands.

She flipped through multiple drawers as Blake shifted to the ruby chest, inspecting it.

What in the—

Every drawer was clean, aside from the pipe and a small bag of silvers. Not even a ledger, or a weapon. Gods, not even a crumb of a sea biscuit. Kora collected the blood-stained papers on the floor. *Was that . . . poetry?* Who *was* this pirate captain?

Frustration boiled beneath her skin, and she peered at Blake by the beautifully crafted chest. Intricately woven rubies of various sizes and cuts covered the gold, the lid fastened shut with a golden, heart-shaped lock.

"Have you ever seen so many rubies before?" She joined Blake, grasping the lock, turning it over.

"No," he mused, "nor ones this . . . exquisite." He shuffled to her right and rifled through Cannon's still body. "Aha!"

He retrieved a dual-pronged golden key from Cannon's inner breast pocket. A twisted heart-shaped bow, with a solid ruby held in its centre—and it was coated in Cannon's blood. Kora paled as Blake unlocked the chest, wiping the blood absentmindedly on his jerkin. The chest lid creaked open and she peered inside, eager to see what treasures would be hidden in a pirate captain's quarters.

Gold. So much gold.

A rare metal in these lands. The chest was filled to the brim with wealth from *Demon Sea Siren*'s plunders. Trinkets and jewels from both Aldara and Talmon, and even dark stones from the far-off marshlands of Otrovia.

"Oh . . . my," Kora whispered in awe. Blake audibly swallowed as he picked up a gleaming silver goblet hidden amongst the gold. Its stem and bowl were lined with swirling moonstones and pearls.

"Galen," Kora observed. These riches and treasures had come from Galen. "But why is it in a ruby chest? That's the witches' stone." The witches kept to themselves in the Shannara Territory, threatening any who dared to enter. The empire had secured a treaty with them during the Galenite War, ensuring neither party could disturb the other.

"This isn't a coincidence, if the wenches are involved," Blake grunted. He could never call them *witches*, referring to them instead as wenches, because of their savage nature. They roamed through the remaining pieces, picking out anything that remotely resembled the mysteriously misted island of Galen.

"What should we do with this? We can't give our crew bounty from Galen."

Kora's head pounded at the thought of amending the ledgers over this. She'd certainly be caught if her ledgers indicated Galen wealth. The empire would leap to check her plunder records and discover a year of missing treasures. Blake assembled a third of the treasure containing the Galenite moonstone in a pile on the floor, and ripped golden fabric from the bed to conceal it in.

"We'll hide this. We need to show it to Erick when we return. He'll know what to do." He tied the craftily made knapsack into a knot, hiding the silver treasure inside. Kora curtly nodded and went to close the lid of the chest when something dark and glimmering caught her eye.

She gingerly picked up the trinket and studied it. A talisman necklace, with a thin, dark-steel chain and a delicate oval-shaped pendant. Like a teardrop, with a hollow centre. Individual, spiralled columns intricately connected around the pendant, and light glinted off the midnight-blue hue, stark against the rubied chest. A small smile formed on Kora's lips as she traced the curves and spirals. It reminded her of the dark depths of the ocean.

"Take it," Blake studied her, and she blushed. "You never keep anything for yourself."

Kora shook her head. It could go to one of the crew. They needed it more than she did, and could sell it to feed their family for a few weeks. He strode over and gently took her wrist, unfurling her fingers.

"If you won't take it for yourself," he placed it over her head, his green eyes glinting, "then please, do me the honour of accepting it as a gift." The metal cooled her flushed neck as it settled on her pimpled skin, and the metal teardrop nestled comfortably between her breasts.

"Well, if you insist," Kora smiled.

Her breath caught at the intensity of his green-eyed gaze against the red hue from the glittering, ruby chest. She nibbled her lower lip and Blake's stare snagged from where the talisman lay snug on her chest, to her pert lips. His hands glided from the chain to her throat, gently stroking her flushed skin, up to her jaw, tracing her lips.

His mouth swiftly followed as he tugged Kora into a passionate kiss, his stubble tickling her skin. One hand cupped her jaw whilst the other pressed against the small of her back, pulling her closer to him. Her hands ravaged the obsidian lengths of his hair, making him moan. His lips parted, inviting her in, and her tongue flicked out, savouring the taste of him.

It'd been too long. Hot, tiring days out at sea together, unable to touch yet always in proximity. It'd been torture for her, and stealing moments like this stirred a fire deep within her core. Their passion burned in the shadows, filled with secret glances, light kisses, and subtle caresses. Romance was forbidden between officers, yet their hearts longed for each other. Not to mention Erick's insistence on separating them, stating Blake was dangerous, and would get Kora into trouble.

It only spurred her on, and a defiant ember sizzled between her legs. "Blake," she groaned his name against his mouth and a visible shiver ran through him. "We can't . . . not now . . . not *here.*"

She reluctantly pulled away, her hands resting on his sculpted chest, and his heart pounded underneath her fingertips. She pointed at the two bodies and he sighed with frustration.

"My timing is never great." He rested his forehead against hers. "Soon, my *asterya.*"

Kora rolled her eyes at Blake's infuriating nickname for her from the old language. His *shining star.* Despite its disappearance, a few words from the old world of Devania had survived history.

"Let's head back before the crew suspect something. I don't want them getting any ideas about us."

"I'll give them something to be suspicious about tonight," he whispered against her ear, and her toes curled in her boots at the dangerous promise. It was her lucky day, indeed.

The prisoners had refused to talk, eat, or drink for three agonisingly slow days. Kora didn't mind the latter, it meant more rations could be spread amongst the crew, but it was infuriating they'd not been able to break the prisoners out of their stony silence.

She sat, with her legs crossed before her, on the ebony main deck, aggressively polishing her dual-sabre daggers. The briny wind of the Shaurock Sea whipped against her short, now curling hair, tickling the nape of her neck and curve of her ears.

Galen and Peril Cove had faded into the western horizon, and endless, glittering-blue ocean surrounded them, greeting sunset orange skies. It was heavenly.

Blake had taken a temporary reprieve of interrogating the prisoners and stood at the helm. His body tense, and his face thunderous, steering them home. Kora knew better than to approach him when he was in one of his *moods*, and she'd sent Finlay down to the prisoners to coax them into drinking water. They couldn't die before they reached Stormkeep Fortress. She would *not* arrive empty-handed. Her reputation depended on it.

Exhaling a long sigh, she poured her frustrations into polishing a single speck on her gleaming silver daggers. Stormkeep Fortress was four days away if the winds remained on their side. They were making good time, and would likely see the dusty maroon coast of Scarlet Bay once again in a day's journey.

The mighty fortress—the beating heart of Aldara—had been Kora's home for the past ten years since Erick rescued her. Yet, the thought of being on land for too long made her feel trapped, her skin crawling with reluctance at returning. She didn't know where her real home was, or *who* she was, and it fuelled her eternal rage from having her life ripped away.

Even Erick wasn't sure, seeing as he'd discovered her, half-dead on a piece of floating driftwood in the Shaurock Sea. He'd said it had happened around the time Galen had vanished from the world, causing pirates to grow bold with the absence of the ruthless barbarians. They began attacking more vessels—including the one Kora and her presumed family had been sailing on.

Erick had assured her they'd scouted every inch of the vast Shaurock Sea for survivors, to unify Kora with her lost ones. But the ocean was wicked, endless, and deadly. One wrong move, and sailors succumbed to its dark depths, their lives snared by currents of death.

It was the sea she intended to tame. To make hers to command—and that would start with working her way up in the empire. Even if it meant accepting she was an outsider in this god-forsaken world.

But Admiral Kora Cadell had a nice ring to it.

"I don't think they can get any shinier."

A tall, lean shadow appeared by her side, interrupting her thoughts, and Kora suspended her polishing as Finlay plopped down beside her, his back resting against the railing. His bony shoulder brushed hers, and he wiped his hand across his sweaty brow, smearing dirt across his face. The healer had removed his bandage, and the wound to his forehead was knitting together, forming a pink and scabbed scar.

"Any luck?" Kora quietly murmured, placing her daggers down gently beside her, beams of dazzling sunset bouncing off the shining metal.

Finlay nodded, taking a swig from his waterskin before offering it to her. "They eventually caved."

She patted his knee in appreciation, the water blissfully quenching her parched throat. "Good. I need them alive."

The azure ocean drew her gaze. She'd not heard her comforting, windful voice since destroying *Demon Sea Siren* three days ago and she kept finding herself repeatedly gazing towards the west, as if her soul longed to venture towards the Mist.

But that couldn't be true. No one longed for the Mist. She was just tired, that was all.

"He's not been the same since *Demon Sea Siren*." Finlay inclined his head towards Blake. Sailors kept a wide berth around him as he handed the helm over to Kora's best sailing master and strode towards them like a walking black thundercloud.

"You could say that," she muttered, bumping his bony shoulder back.

Blake hadn't fulfilled his promise the night they'd returned to *Hell's Serpent*. He'd been focused on interrogating the prisoners around the clock, to Kora's chagrin. In fact, since they'd set sail from Peril Cove, Blake had frequently found other things more *important* to handle, and she was sure he was avoiding her. He'd even stopped sharing their bed.

Her core ached with longing and loneliness, and it pained her whenever his dazzling charm evaporated, replaced with a crushing dark weight on his shoulders. Blake's mood swings were an intermittent dilemma in their dynamic, and whenever she probed, he'd lash out and storm off to release his pained past in physical combat.

Whether that was sparring, or barrelling his knuckles into the faces of their enemies.

To distract herself, she'd spent more time with Finlay, training him to wield his family's broadsword. His grip was always slack, the sword tumbling from his hand, and sometimes he'd flat out drop it, nearly severing his toes. Finlay had been hesitant at training, pain consuming his face whenever he gripped the broadsword. But recently, that pain had hardened into strength.

Blake's large leather boots stomped to a halt in front of them, unlike his usual silent predatory grace. "What do you think you're doing?" he snapped at Finlay with a glare. Annoyance sliced through Kora, heat rising to her cheeks.

"I-er, I was just updating Captain Cadell on the prisoners." Finlay heaved himself up to address Blake face-to-face, black eyes narrowing. His dark, blonde hair gleamed in the afternoon sun, absorbing the orange tones painting the sky.

"You can get to work. We don't pay you to sit around." Blake clapped his shoulder, sending Finlay scurrying away. Kora threw Finlay an apologetic glance as he headed towards the lancers scrubbing the main deck and organising the recently stocked artillery.

"Blake," Kora sighed again, lightly rubbing the sore scar by her temple. She gripped the thick railing, swiftly rising, and sheathed her daggers into the scabbard attached to her back. "Don't speak to him like that!"

"What?" Blake scoffed. "You're the one who likes to act cold and distant. I'm just following your example, *Captain*." His green eyes glinted wickedly—a challenge.

She stilled, sensing the brimming heat between them, a tension so thick Cannon's sword couldn't sever it. He possessed a troubled past; one Kora was still trying to coax out of him patiently. Nights spent together as she spilled her deepest, darkest worries, baring her soul open to him, only to receive scraps in return.

She'd treasured each vital piece of his past he offered, holding them close to her heart. Minute details of growing up in the lower districts, clawing to escape his abusive upbringing. But to hell with patience. This male irked her with his senseless bravado. Kora glared back. "If you have a problem, Blake, then just say it."

Sailors glanced up from their posts, pausing to listen to the fight building between their patient captain and *irritating* first mate.

"You need to do your job," Blake's voice lowered, "not fraternise with the crew."

Fraternise? Was he joking? Did he really think that, or was he jealous? He'd never displayed a possessive streak before, and he was the one to suggest she get to know the crew more and reveal a more personable, *warm* side. She'd been enjoying it, not having to pretend all the time to be someone so cold and heartless. Gods, it'd been *exhausting.*

Multiple pairs of eyes ogled them. They couldn't do this here and now. There was only one, easy way to dissipate his mood. By doing what they did best.

"Do you think *you* can do better?" Kora raised her voice for all to hear. "Are you challenging me to be captain?"

Blake's eyes flared in shock, until he noticed the growing audience gathering. His stare slid to the hidden daggers attached to her back, and a dark smile bloomed on his handsome face.

"Oh! Yes." His hand tightened around the golden hilt of his sword, understanding their new game. "*I challenge you*, Kora Cadell."

A gasp waved through the crowd, and sailors poured in from all corners to watch the fight unfurl, shouting for their comrades to come witness the combat. Kora retrieved her polished-to-perfection dual daggers and chose a defensive stance, arms poised in the air. *Come and get me.*

Constructed from the finest Talmon silver, and as long as her forearms, the weapons balanced perfectly in her hands. Embossed with the golden symbol of the empire, below the dark, dazzling hilts made of smooth malachite stone. Enemies cowered in her presence whenever their eyes feasted on the serrated blades.

Blake withdrew his cutlass sword from its scabbard, his

muscles rippling beneath his shirt. His teasing, dark smile seemed to say, *be careful what you wish for.*

Kora swallowed. The wound on his arm peeked through the rolled-up sleeve of his shirt. It had healed quickly, nothing more than a thick, red scar. Lucky bastard, he was always swift at healing. A natural gift from his family, he'd say, the only good thing they'd bestowed upon him. A gift, to survive the torrents of his father's punches, and his mother's wickedness.

His blade was similar size to Cannon's, and the memory of his death sliced through her—the expression on his face as he was impaled on his own weapon, seared into her retinas.

Blake charged with a subtle warning yell, and Kora parried, swiftly darting around him, and driving her elbow between his lower shoulder blades. The crew laughed as he tumbled, spun around, and raised his sword to deflect her next attack. She leapt with surprising force, her blades crossed over the other to slice his neck.

She bounced back, her movements nimble, as Blake lunged again. His dark smile spreading as she deflected, twirling in the air, followed by a parry, slicing the edge of his black jerkin, but not injuring him. They'd done this many times before. Fighting for the audience. Showing off their moves. Telling the world they hated each other, when deep down . . . it was quite the opposite.

Love was forbidden in the armada.

As their weapons clashed, Blake leaned in with a grin. "If you wanted me out of my clothes so badly, all you had to do was say." Her cheeks heated at his whisper, and his mood dissipated, replaced with a new kind of hunger.

They continued their deadly dance of ducking and sparring, their attacks missing *slightly*, to give the impression they matched each other in combat, when really, Blake was stronger. His weapon was impressive—she would know, she'd bought the damned thing as a gift—and could easily spear her to the deck in one lethal movement, ending her life. But Kora had speed and agility on her side.

She narrowly ducked Blake's next attack. His blade a hair's breadth from slicing her torso, and a shocked murmur rippled through the crowd. Kora whirled on her knees, whipping her daggers up as Blake swiped his weapon down to her head in a deadly blow, hovering by her thrumming scar. A move they'd perfected over the years.

Metal upon metal clanged, the force vibrating up their arms

as they sprawled onto their backs, legs tangling together. Her body smarted with pain and sweat dripped down her back onto the warm deck. She pushed up onto her elbows and Blake smirked. She laughed as the crew stood in stunned silence.

Finlay shouldered through the crowd, concern and confusion clouding his slim, tanned face. As Kora stood, heading to Blake to shake hands over the friendly skirmish, she could feel Finlay's curious eyes pinned on her back.

"Maybe next time, Mr Marwood." Kora flashed him a cunning smile.

Blake's thumb slightly caressed the back of her hand. "It would be my honour, Captain."

He bowed his head and silently strode to the brig—or, as they liked to call it, Hell's Pit—to resume his prisoner interrogation. Kora retreated to her quarters located beneath the helm with a spring in her step, sensing Finlay wasn't far behind.

K ora's quarters were spacious and cosy. Warm, inviting cream bedding, with bright blue throw pillows, adorned a sturdy large bed, hidden behind a tall wooden divider she used for privacy. Heaps of identical jerkins, tunics, leathers, and breeches were casually draped over the top.

A stunning view of the ocean from the rear bay windows peeked through heavy, dark-blue drapes, lined with cream silk. A matching exquisite, cream chaise longue, with black claw-feet, stood before the windows. It was Kora's favourite place to be alone when at sea, surrounded by stacks of books and an assortment of favoured weapons she hadn't bothered to place on the rack.

A large desk, big enough for eight people, centred towards the entrance, was littered with maps and navigational charts of the Azarian Islands. The drawers stuffed to the brim with ledgers of their escapades from the past year. Nearby the chaise lounge, the two suspicious—yet stunning—ruby and moonstone chests were hidden under a swath of torn sail from *Demon Sea Siren*, their contents safely locked from prying eyes.

Kora quickly brushed one of Blake's discarded shirts under the wooden frame of the bed with her foot, obscuring the makeshift knapsack containing Galen's bribery hidden underneath.

She eyed the rumpled bed from where she'd tossed and turned all night from the absence of Blake. They'd never *done the deed*, so to say. As Blake regularly mentioned to her, their timing was never *quite right*, but it hadn't prevented them from exploring each other's bodies. She yearned for his touch, and his warmth.

Finlay stopped by the desk. "That was all for show, wasn't it?" *Damn, he was perceptive.* His eyes took in her snug quarters, landing on the obscenely large brass tub located in the far corner.

His nostrils flared, his mouth thinning. The tub possessed a clever contraption to drain water through an openable window, back into the sea, but she'd never used it. Water was valuable for her crew's survival. It wasn't for a captain to take luxurious, *unnecessary* baths.

Although, she *was* filthy, and probably reeked.

Kora sat behind her desk and propped her legs up, crossing one ankle over the other. The muscles in her legs and arms ached from the sparring she'd done since they'd been sailing home, especially against Blake's strength. Her hand drifted to the cool talisman resting beneath her shirt, her heart fluttering that it'd been gifted by him.

Finlay arched a brow, waiting for a response. He'd grown confident recently since their friendship blossomed, but his scepticism remained.

"Yes," Kora replied.

Finlay exhaled sharply. "I honestly thought he was challenging you for captain."

"*Trust him*," the calming voice drifted through her mind, but it was quiet and faint—barely a whisper. It soothed her tension, and a wave of relief washed over her at its return.

"It's something we've done for a long time to . . . maintain appearances." She placed her daggers on the desk and motioned for him to take a seat.

"Appearances? Why would you need to?" His brows knitted as he sat in a chair across the desk, rubbing his thickly stubbled chin. He scanned the room once again, gaze settling on the large bed with enough room for two people. A twinkle in his dark eyes sparked, and his mouth gaped. "You and Blake?"

There was that perception again. This male was intriguing. Kora picked up one of her daggers and twirled it in her hands as she explained. The light cascading through the rear bank of windows caught the shining surface and Finlay winced.

"We met nearly two years ago at the end of our participation in the Darkoning Trials, when we were both low-level sailors trying to find our paths in this world."

Finlay's face paled with horror at the mention of the Darkoning Trials—a famous, gruelling, militant training programme, that only the finest and most lethal *males* were subjected to. It contained physical, mental, and emotional feats, and not everyone survived. The trials weeded out the weak, producing only the strongest for the Talmon Empire to use at their will in their armies and armadas.

The programme had been created and named in honour after Admiral Darkon, who had campaigned for the Staghart royal family across the hostile islands during the Devanian Conquest that lasted two hundred years. He won the territory with admirable feats of strength and resilience, uniting the lands, and creating the Azarian Islands as Devania faded into history.

"The attraction to Blake was instant. But I hated him at first. He was so arrogant," Kora continued, rolling her eyes. "But he grew on me, and we eventually allied together to make sure we both made it through the trials alive."

It'd been incredibly tough. The trials were designed to break participants past their limits. To dispose of their fear and create soldiers of war. Males born and bred for violence in the north were pre-selected to participate, the trials fixed so they'd win, ensuring the prize money returned to line the noble houses' overflowing pockets.

Blake had been a scrawny, penniless young male, with minimal chances of escaping the lower districts . . . or surviving them. The trials were the only way for him to ascend to something greater, and he smashed expectations by becoming the latest victor.

Citizens subjected to living in poverty, or as a servant to one of the noble houses, participated in the trials to achieve a new life. It was a cruel injustice. Weak, innocent civilians forced into trials designed to kill them, and meeting the sharp-tipped end of a sword wielded by those who were bred for it. Who lived for the kill.

How Blake had survived—and *won*—was a testament to his strength and his will.

And Kora was a female. A female with no past. But the first female to enter the trials and live, all because she was too stubborn to listen to Erick. And it'd changed her. She was a weapon, as cold and sharp as the blade in her hand.

"We were pitted against each other a lot, forced to become a skirmish duo in the fighting rings. We raked in audiences, creating large sums of bets for the trials. Coins filled the nobles' pockets faster than they could spend them—all because of us. We learned to stage fights, pretending to wound each other, and became the favoured to win. People were fascinated to see a woman wielding a weapon, and a man from the slums fighting off multiple assailants. It was a circus act to them. We started infiltrating the bookers, to see what the punters were betting on us. We thought if we could ensure it won in the punters favour then—" Kora stopped suddenly.

The memory of the tormenting requests that'd been asked of her surged like a terrorising, sickening wave.

They had been sadistic. No one had been interested in her fighting. Punters had betted on her dying every time, and special *guests* had requested an audience to observe her chained up and violated. Once they'd discovered the bookers intentions, Blake had seen to it that every single of them met their demise . . . by slaughtering them all in the final conquest of the trials.

"*Breathe,*" the voice caressed her, and Kora loosened a tense breath, regaining her focus.

"What you saw today was a *simpler* version of that. Word spread of us, the champion and the 'woman survivor', and the armada took interest, seeing our potential," she swallowed. Those had been their darkest times together, and they both had scars— physically and mentally—to prove it. "We became junior officers on separate fleets, and spent several months apart. During that time, we realised . . ." Kora twirled the dagger again, "what we felt for each other."

Finlay nodded, following along. "And then you were stationed together on *Hell's Serpent.*"

"I requested Blake to join my crew a year ago. I had some help getting him appointed."

She'd pleaded with Erick, desperately convincing him Blake would bolster her crew and make them a formidable force. Erick had been furiously reluctant at first, stating Blake was pre-destined to advance the ranks of the empire's army as their latest champion.

The trials happened every two years, and soon, Blake's title would be stolen from him. Being stuck as a first mate was detrimental for a champion. By now, he should be a commander, or a commodore in the armada. But instead, he was *here.* Serving under a female. Because Kora couldn't let go of him. Because she couldn't live without him. Because he was the only one who understood the scars haunting her mind. Who truly understood what the Darkoning Trials had done to her inside.

Aside from the fact having a *champion* as her first mate made her pretty ruthless.

"So, what was *that* earlier then? Why keep up these appearances?" Finlay warily eyed the continuously twirling sabre blade in her hands.

"To maintain the illusion," she stopped twirling the dagger. "It's a constant push and pull to show that we're *both* running the show. Without one of us, the whole thing falls apart."

She slammed the weapon down into the desk, piercing the wood, and left it standing upright. Finlay stared at the vibrating dagger, his gaze flickering to the wooden surface of the obsidian desk. Dents and scratches covered it from Kora repeatedly using it as target practise during long voyages.

"Relationships between crew members are forbidden in the armada," Finlay whispered, his eyes glancing over the shuddering dagger to her. She lowered her head. After the Devanian Conquest, the viceroys had enforced that relationships were a distraction and a weakness that would cost them everything.

They may have won the war. But the enemy remained.

"Can I trust you, Finlay?" The malachite dagger between them stilled, and a palpable silence fell over the large cabin.

His dark gaze bored into her, as black as *Hell's Serpent*. The colour haunted her. Maybe she should request for the ship to be repainted. She maintained his stare, praying to the gods it wouldn't come to using the lethal blade between them.

"A truth, for a truth," Finlay finally spoke, and Kora gestured for him to continue, relieved. "I know you're curious about why I'm here," he paused. "I had no choice. My family told me it was either join your crew or face exile to the Silent Tundra."

Kora was stunned. Joining *Hell's Serpent* was a *punishment*, and not a tactical move from the imposing Blackstone family.

"My lifestyle," Finlay wiped a shaky hand across his face, "is not acceptable to them. I bring shame to my family." He hung his head, lips trembling. Kora silently skimmed round the desk to crouch beside him, her hand gently placed on his knee. "You see, I . . ." His gaze met hers and she nodded in comfort, a silent friend to lean on. "I *prefer* the company of men. A lot."

Kora's face broke into a warm smile, and she let out a small laugh. "I was *so* worried you were a spy!" She squeezed his knee and Finlay stared at her shocked, his fists clenching.

"You . . . you're not going to gut me with your dagger?"

His tremor became intense, so much so she paused. It was an unnatural tremor, and he flicked his wrists, settling the shake, as his jaw ticked at her stare.

She took his quivering hands in hers. He had every right to be afraid. Such relations were frowned upon in Azarian society— not illegal, but for the son of a noble house, it was unwarranted. He was expected to marry and continue the noble bloodline.

"No. Why would I hurt a friend?"

Finlay's beaming smile melted the depths of Kora's cool

heart. The twinkle in his dark eyes suggested he knew what she was asking for. A friend, a companion, in this fucked up world. He released a shaky breath and thanked her for understanding. "If I was a spy, I wouldn't be hanging around you," he teased. "Hey! Why not?" Kora twirled. "Am I not spy-worthy?" "You're worthy of many things." She blushed at his genuine words. "But that tall, dark drink of water you like so much would be far more interesting to stalk."

Kora pretended to grab her dagger and Finlay chuckled at her jealousy. "I can't disagree, I'd stalk him all day if I could."

"Maybe you should try it, you might learn something interesting." Finlay's stare glinted.

"Why send you here though?" She directed the conversation away from Blake's mysterious nature.

"They believed the armada could teach me a thing or two." He fiddled with his tied-back hair, pushing loose strands out of his eyes. "You know, magically turn me into a womaniser. Or a heartless warrior."

Kora rolled her eyes. "Are we as dreadful as being exiled to the desert?"

"No," Finlay winked, "you're much more horrifying."

H ell's Pit was exactly as it sounded.

Mould was growing, multiplying, and creeping up the festering, black-stained walls of the pit. A stench of acrid damp, along with the hideous odour of waste from the two prisoners shackled to the walls, permeated the air. *Almighty Thanos, they reeked.*

Blake had tossed them into the smallest cell, their legs bent up to their chests to add to their discomfort. They only had the tattered scraps from the sails of the wasted *Demon Sea Siren* for blankets, and a small, dented cup of water to share between them. It remained untouched at their bare feet.

The bars of their cell were thick, black iron, and offered no reprieve on their aching, hunched backs. In fact, the entire pit was black, with no light penetrating it, blinding their senses, making them unsure how long they'd been caged in Hell.

Kora perched on a small wooden stool in the walkway between the two rows of cells. A large, candle-lit iron lantern illuminated beside her on a rounded, rickety wooden table splattered with old, dried blood. It cast a daunting red hue in the pit, shadowing the prisoners. A ladder ascending to the secured, light-proof hatch lingered at the end of the walkway.

Heavy, robust shackles clamped their ankles together. Connected to impenetrable chains leading to bolts in the hull walls, reinforced with Talmon-grade steel. She lightly fingered her dual-sabre blades delicately placed on the table.

Kora drew a deep breath before speaking, the memory of their previous pirate hunts rising from the individual cells surrounding her. She remembered every single one . . . and they all had begged for their lives.

Unlike these two.

"You boys lost some weight since I last saw you."

A harsh, cold, and indifferent persona consumed her, the mask for her role as captain sliding over her face. No matter how long she tried to put this off, she eventually had to come down here and question the prisoners—and hoped that was all she had to do.

Blake had unsuccessfully pried any information from them, and they'd sailed past the scorching coast of Scarlet Bay half a day ago. Time was running out. Stormkeep Fortress was less than a few days away. A few more days of freedom.

Stony silence greeted Kora.

The pirates blinked rapidly, adjusting to the small light from the lantern. Their white shirts and navy pants were filthy, their bare feet wallowing in puddles of urine. She wrinkled her nose at the disgusting smell. The males had lost *a lot* of weight, in fact *too* much weight from a few days of starvation. Matching brown eyes, sunken deep into their sockets, were lined by gaunt cheeks and ringed with shadows. She shifted the lantern, squinting into the darkness, devouring their features.

"Separate them," she ordered.

Blake's dark, brooding presence emerged from the shadows of the opposite cells, and the prisoners' eyes widened simultaneously, suddenly clutching at each other in despair.

"No!" they screamed over and over. "Don't come near us!" Their voices were hoarse from dehydration and silence.

As Blake unlocked the cell, with two of his favoured guards hovering close behind, the pirates kicked back violently, clasping at each other's thin frames.

"Put one in the cells near the hold. They can't see or speak to each other."

Kora casually sat back as the guards unshackled the closest prisoner, dragging him towards the hold adjacent to the ladder. His wide, grog-blossomed face twisted; rotten teeth surrounded by ginger stubble gnashing at their hands. He screamed and clawed, spitting curses at Kora, Blake, and her crew until his voice was a faint echo from the brig, eventually silenced with the creak of iron bars. Blake melted back into the shadows behind her with a menacing stare at the remaining pirate.

"How did ye know we were brethren?" His raspy voice set Kora's teeth on edge.

"Not just brothers," Kora leaned forward. "Twins."

The pirate mirrored her, leaning on his knees in curiosity,

narrowing his soil-brown eyes. His features were sharp and angular. A chiselled jaw lined with a short, thick, ginger beard. Matching long hair was slicked back with sweat and dirt, and matted into thick locks, adorned with wooden charms.

"You both have a tattoo on your arm in the native language, meaning *twin*." Kora motioned to the smattering of ink on his left forearm. A singular letter from the old Devanian language glared against the red welts on his wrist.

"You speak Devanian?" he asked in the native tongue in which he was expertly fluent. Kora waved him off, pretending not to understand.

"Let's not get sidetracked," she replied, in the common language.

Blake simmered with intensity, and she was sure he was brooding over his inability to notice they were brothers—identical ones at that. Although . . . his torture techniques took place in the darkness, where he thrived most. So, she'd let him off this time.

"We arrive at Stormkeep Fortress in three days," she announced. The pirate scoffed and sat back, half his body hidden in the shadows of the pit. "It'd be in your best interest to answer our questions before we make port."

The pirate blankly stared, his mouth a tight grim line, his right hand lightly tracing the twin tattoo.

"Have you been in contact with Galen?"

Silence continued.

They stared each other down for several minutes in deafening quiet. The stench of him made her eyes water, and his body was black and blue, peppered with lance burns. Signs Blake had attempted torturous tactics to force him to sing. Kora grinded her teeth in irritation.

After a few more moments of infuriating silence, she retrieved a circular cloth-bound shape on the table and unwrapped it carefully. The pirate's attention was drawn to it instantly, and he expressed ravenous desperation as Kora revealed an enticing red apple.

She plucked one of her precious daggers, and began slicing pieces off, popping them into her mouth slowly. She savoured every bite, and the pirate swallowed audibly.

"Well, we can assume you've been in contact with them," she murmured between bites. "We saw the treasure payment. The more important question is *how*."

"And *why*," Blake added from the shadows.

The scent of the sweet juices from the apple wafted into the air and the prisoner lunged forward, his hands gripping the bars of the cell so tightly his knuckles turned deathly white. Kora cut another slice and placed it into her mouth with a satisfying, loud moan.

Yet . . . silence persisted.

"Let's make a deal." She hovered the half-eaten apple out of the pirate's reach. "A piece of food for every *truthful* answer." She gestured beside her, and the pirate drooled at the second apple and small loaf of bread also present on the table, a whimper escaping his lips.

"And me brethren?" he asked quietly.

"If he accepts the same deal, he will eat." Kora placed her hand on her chest in a silent oath.

"We don't know much." His eyes nervously darted from her to the food. She sliced her dagger down the apple once again and offered the piece of fruit.

"Tell us what you can."

He snatched the apple slice from her calloused fingers, shoving it into his mouth and chewing sloppily. She prepared another slice as he groaned, his hands immediately returning to clutch at the bars.

"We joined the crew late," he spoke rapidly. "Cannon already had the booty from Galen." Kora dropped another piece of apple into his filthy hands and reached for the loaf of bread. "All I know is, we were goin' to an important meetin' at Peril Cove. From the north. Cannon said we was to grab somethin' special there. Next thin' I knew, all the pirate lords showed up."

"The pirate lords?" She froze cutting the loaf of bread. "What do you mean the pirate lords were there?"

A sly smile broke on the pirate's face. "The four ships."

"There were five . . ." she whispered.

"They always brin' a spare. A diversion."

"*Shit*," Blake cursed from the darkness. "Cannon is—*was*—a pirate lord?"

The pirate nodded solemnly.

"He didn't put up much of a good fight," Kora scoffed, remembering the countless poorly aimed cannons from his vessel.

"Who's to say he was fightin'?" the pirate countered.

Kora frowned, and she opened her mouth to speak but the pirate grasped for the bread in her hands. "Ye swore!" She chucked a small piece at him, and he scrambled for it hysterically before it landed in a puddle of piss.

"You've still not explained the connections to Galen," Blake pushed, emerging from the dark gloom, his arms crossed. "We saw the ships retreat into the Mist. No one goes into it, not even scum like you." He cast a cautious glance towards Kora. If those ships were truly the pirate lords, the situation was more dire than they'd thought—and they'd *killed* one of them. It was grounds for another war.

"Aye, I don't know how Cannon got the booty from Galen." His lips smacked from eating, and Kora exhaled to quash her rising nausea. "But there were rumours on the *Demon*. They say the Mist was made. By a man."

Blake let out a short, disbelieving laugh. "That's ridiculous, a man can't *make* mist—especially one that can kill you."

"Tis what I heard. A man made the Mist, and he can control it. Who goes in," he motioned with his hands, weaving them into the shadows. "And who goes out." He withdrew his hand from the darkness and flexed his palm open once again, demanding his payment of food. Blake whipped out his hand, preventing Kora from passing over another piece of bread. She glared at him.

"That's a lie. Magic doesn't exist," Blake's voice frosted.

The pirate ignored Blake, his stare meeting Kora's, and his tone turned serious and eloquent as he spoke in the Devanian language, "You know it does."

Her heart stopped.

"Stop that," Blake snapped. "No one speaks that gibberish anymore."

Kora flinched internally but kept her face neutral. It was a beautiful language, and their world still used a few of the words when convenient. Blake frequently called her his *asterya,* but it was one of the few words she pretended to understand.

"It used to exist," he said to Blake. "Ye should learn ye history, lad."

The talisman nestled between her breasts warmed and she rubbed her chest, willing her heart to settle back into its normal rhythm.

"Liar! He just wants the food, Kor—Captain," Blake corrected himself, but it didn't go unnoticed. Kora had pinned him down to chastise him about referring to her as Kora—not Captain— in front of their crew a few days ago. She handed the pirate his final piece of bread and stepped away, mulling the information over.

"Complete bullshit!" Blake slammed his hand against the

cell, his face furious. "I hope your brother is smarter than you are, or at least a better liar." He stormed off into the darkness towards the other cells.

Before she left, Kora paused and glanced over her shoulder at the pirate. "What's your name?" she asked in Devanian.

The pirate smiled devilishly. "Jack Flint."

A guard rounded the corner from the hull passage, his face grim and hardened. A foul odour wafted from him, and she gagged at the stench of the other Flint twin's excrement coating the guard's legs. Gross.

"You can keep the lantern," she said, and he nodded with gratitude for the extra illumination. A small reprieve for being in the pit.

Kora climbed the ladder, her skin tingling from the talisman, as if it'd awoken after that conversation. Daylight blinded her after the bleak black of Hell's Pit, and she hunted for a sparring partner, leaving secrets buried in the shadows of the cells.

A whole day passed, and the pirates refused to crack. Their unwavering stubbornness was a thorn in Kora's side, and Blake's mood swings were erratic, his knuckles consistently bloody and sore from his interrogations, intent on disproving Jack Flint's reveal. About the Mist made by *man*.

And the pirate lord they'd slaughtered.

Hell's Serpent had been at sea a total of three weeks, and she took a deep, clear breath before entering the crew's quarters—because it certainly smelled like it—leaving her worries behind in the moon-kissed night.

Iron oil lanterns decorated the vast space, stretching across the forecastle, and small, starry shapes lined the lantern's glass windows, casting beautiful patterns across the low-beamed ceiling. Makeshift tables, created from barrels and crates, interspersed hammocks suspended by thick ropes, with bottles of rum, sea biscuits, and playing cards littering every surface.

The crew were excited to make port in two days, to see their families, and take home their latest lucrative treasure from plunders, thanks to Kora's crime she rinsed on repeat.

"Captain!" Finlay waved her over with a welcoming smile, and she approached a small group of sailors huddled around a low crate playing Cribbage. He patted the stool beside him with a lopsided grin. "Be my partner."

Two other males sat with him, one of which was *Hell's Serpent's* sailing master—Samuel Rommier. He inclined his head in respect towards her, whilst the other eyed her curiously, clearly surprised at her presence in their quarters.

Her head archer, although his name eluded her. Her brow

creased as a fog blanketed her mind, suppressing the name of the lean, youthful male. A thin, dual-lined tattoo inked his cheek, and her vision tunnelled on it, sparking her attention. It was an unnatural tattoo, and simplistic, as if dirt simply streaked across his face.

A hushed silence fell across the room as sailors glanced up at Kora whilst she observed the archer dealing out cards, his hands deft. She plastered on her brightest smile, picked up a bottle of dark rum, and took a huge swig.

"Who's going to take me for a run of my silver then?"

A loud cheer echoed across the quarters as she plopped down beside Finlay and he passed her a sea biscuit. It was moist, and lightly flavoured with vanilla and cinnamon. She gently nibbled it, the spices warming her gullet. Her stomach still roiled from her conversation with Jack.

A rebellious alliance was growing against the Talmon Empire . . . and magic had returned.

Music cut through her swirling thoughts, rising her from the depths of her murky mind. Several sailors had small, flute-based wooden instruments, and played a hearty melody in the far corner, whilst another used a crate as a drum.

"Sam's bleeding me dry, you *have* to help me win," Finlay pleaded. His words slurred, and his usual ash and malt scent had a hint of grog.

Samuel chuckled. Double the size of most crew members on her ship, a stoic air radiated from him, yet he preferred navigation over weaponry. Samuel's build would've made him a perfect soldier.

Compared to Finlay's darker and straighter mane, Samuel flaunted bright, wavy blonde hair, half-tied up, revealing his deeply golden squared face. His long fair beard was impressively groomed, despite being at sea, and fastened at the bottom with a thin green-and-black strap.

Was being devastatingly handsome a requirement to join the armada? Apparently so.

"Face it, lad, you're awful at this game. Stop while you're ahead." Samuel winked an enchanting grey eye at Kora.

Finlay only had a few coins left, but a large pile of silver coins gleamed by Samuel's elbow. Interlacing navigational tattoos covered his exposed forearms, dark sea lines cutting through the artwork on his rippling muscles. He pushed his shirt sleeves up to his elbows, his biceps flexing with the movement.

"Do you know how to play?" the archer asked casually once

he finished dealing the cards. His voice sounded wiser beyond his years, with a slight accent hidden within his words—one Kora couldn't place, yet it sounded too familiar. Perhaps he was from the north?

She nodded and placed pieces of eight in the middle of the crate. Their eyes bulged out of their sockets. Why couldn't she remember his name? Their paths had crossed on her ship—gods, she even remembered approving his draft months ago, gleeful to hire a professional archer to lead the archery squadron.

He'd even bandaged her wounded hand once, after a battle with pirates in the spring. Had she not asked his name? Her gut twisted. Was she an awful captain? So far removed from her crew she never bothered to acknowledge them? With a deep breath, Kora let her mask slip, her face softening as the taunting from Samuel continued.

"Aye!" Samuel laughed. "You're on." He matched her bet excitedly. "Aryn, put your lot in."

Aryn.

Aryn rolled his eyes, pushing his small pile of silver two-bits forward. Next to Samuel, he looked tiny, and his name tingled the deep recesses of her mind. His dark brown hair flicked out at the ends, curling around his charm-adorned ears. He must be no older than eighteen.

He still wore his brown leather archer tabs on his right fingers, and the edge of a longbow peaked out behind the crate by his feet. Aryn collected his cards, his almond-shaped hazel eyes studying them, surrounded by thick dark lashes. His face gave nothing away, but as he absentmindedly brushed his fingers over his tattoo, his name slammed into her.

"Aryn Di Largo," Kora spoke in awe. Astonishment crept onto his wheat-toned face. "My head archer."

The astonishment quickly faded, but her memory snapped back into place. She had seen his name on the recruitment list, and the voice urged her to hire him on the spot. Aryn Di Largo, the world's best archer, renowned for an aim that could never miss.

How in the gods did I forget him? It must have been the stress of everything. She'd barely slept the entire voyage, her body aching and smarting from the hours of sparring with Finlay, and other brave crew members who dared to fight her.

Samuel rubbed his hands together excitedly. "I'm feeling lucky!"

He placed a wooden board with holes and pegs beside the pot

of winnings, and Kora peeked at her hand of cards. She had a poor first deal, equalling less than ten points.

"Captain can go first," Aryn nudged. His hazel eyes peered over his deck of six cards, and a challenge flashed in them. He was a wise boy, indeed. Aryn placed the starting card down—a jack. Her throat tightened.

They played a few rounds, both teams rapidly approaching the one-hundred-and-twenty-point goal. The pegs on the board were consistently neck and neck, and Finlay grew more agitated as the prized pot of silvers enviously increased in the middle.

Their group had amassed a live audience, all watching intensely as Aryn and Samuel tried to overtake their captain. Finlay had steadily drunk through another bottle of rum, and he suddenly smacked the table in delight as he placed a card—the king of hearts—on the pile.

"Blimey! We've won!" Finlay exclaimed.

Samuel groaned, placing his head in his large hands as the audience of sailors cheered for their captain. Some clapped Samuel on the back for attempting the challenge, and resumed their own activities, jovially drinking grog, and the swell of band music rumbled through the quarters.

"Better luck next time." Kora smiled sheepishly as Aryn sat back with a sigh, accepting his defeat. His head hung back in the chair, and he gazed up at the ceiling.

"Those were my last bits, Sam," he muttered.

"Let's play again." Samuel's hands fluttered over the makeshift table, collecting cards to pass to Aryn to reshuffle. "We can win it back."

Kora glanced to Finlay, who was heavily leant over the crate, swaying as he peered at his noble-worthy pile of silver coins and bits. His reddened nose was mere inches away from the pile, and he began sorting the winnings into neat, shining silver piles of ten.

"Maybe that's enough for tonight." She inclined her head to where Finlay mumbled quietly.

Samuel shook his head, fondness consuming his face. They both bid Kora farewell, and retreated to the far side of the quarters with stacked barrels of grog to refill their silver steins.

Her focus returned to Finlay, as he continued stacking his piles of silver in neat rows—with steady hands. After a couple minutes, he looked up to meet her observant gaze as she sipped from her sweet rum, letting herself relax. Her body felt woozy, and her mind hazy, but her soul was merry.

"You're not trembling," she regarded.

"Drinking grog stops the shakes," he spoke bluntly.

"Does it ever go away?" She gently placed a hand on his shoulder. Kora had noticed his tremor since they'd met when evading *Demon Sea Siren*, but she'd always assumed it was his nervous disposition. He shook his head.

"Sometimes when I'm tired, or when I have something to focus on," his voice was woeful. "I have a *curse*. An ailment my family believes I deserve. My great-grandfather also had it. The shakes, as they call it, will haunt me for the rest of my life." Finlay stopped counting and flexed his fingers, marvelling at his steady hands. "My great-grandfather chose to become a heavy drinker so that he may have use of his hands, and his body. His provocative nature was deemed the cause of the 'Blackstone Curse'."

Her grip on his shoulder tightened. "Your family think you're cursed? Will it spread?"

Lowering his head back to the crate, he wiped a single escaped tear from his cheek. His bony shoulders hunched over, and he spread his fingers wide, as if savouring the ability to control them.

"If I don't drink, it'll eventually take over my whole body. I'll be unable to walk or feed myself. I won't even be able to take a piss! I'll become debilitated," he stumbled over the last word.

"Have you seen any healers? I can find you the best in Aldara—"

Finlay abruptly stood, pocketing his winnings, and his gaze darkened, the shadow of his shame haunting him as tears threatened to spill.

"Please . . . please don't try. There's no cure." He stumbled on his footing. "We tried everything already. But without a miracle, there's nothing to be done."

He attempted to storm out, ungracefully knocking into tables, and sailors who yelled back, and eventually tripped through the door onto the main deck.

Kora hurriedly followed him, nodding to sailors who waved at her as she left, and hauled Finlay to his feet, helping him stumble to the side of the deck. *Gods,* he was drunk—and heavy. The cold evening breeze soothed her grog-flushed skin, and they both inhaled deeply, side by side.

It was peaceful. Moonlight bathed them from the cloudless sky, stars twinkling against the black abyss of the night. Ocean waves lapped at the edges of *Hell's Serpent,* and she wished she could reach out to brush her fingers against the water.

Finlay morosely stared at the endless expanse of dark ocean, his hands gripping the railing.

"I wanted to be an artist," he blurted out. "Imagine . . . the eldest son of the House of Blackstone—a gay, incapacitated, penniless artist. I can't paint or sculpt with these hands, and I can't be inspired when on the grog." He looked down at his hands in disgust.

"I will help you in any way I can," Kora promised. "We can find a cure. Together."

"So that I can fall in love with a woman?" he asked bitterly.

Kora pulled him into a sudden embrace, her heart overflowing with compassion. This was a new side of Finlay, with his suppressed nature, hiding his true self yet trying to discover where he belonged.

Something she knew all too well.

"So that you can follow your dream *and* your heart."

Finlay's steady strong arms tightened around her at the hint of promise, and the new strength in his shoulders and back was impressive. He'd gained muscle from their days of sparring.

"I'm so glad I found you," she continued, her heart fluttering with vulnerability.

"Me too . . . and I'm flattered," he patted her back, "but you're not my type."

Kora's laugh muffled against his shoulder. "Don't get hot-headed now, I'm not into blondes."

"No," Finlay chuckled. "You like them dark and brooding."

She playfully swatted his arm in response. And they stood like that. Comforting each other in the quiet calm of the night for several minutes, an eastern breeze circling them.

"Maybe exile would've been better," he said quietly, and Kora tensed. How were the endless hot, barren dunes of the desert better than her ship and her crew?

"How so?"

Finlay suddenly tore from her embrace and hurtled over the side of the railing, and she grabbed the back of his black shirt as he violently vomited rum and sea biscuits.

"There's no rum in the desert," he groaned.

K ora had amusedly helped Finlay drunkenly stagger back
to the crew quarters and collapse into a hammock.
Samuel had guffawed at the sight, spilling his grog
everywhere and earned several snickers amongst the
crew, to Finlay's chagrin.

"I know this great ta-tavern near the fortress," Finlay had
slurred. "Go there with me, please."

"If it'll make you go to sleep, then yes." She'd tucked him in
to his hammock, placing a bucket nearby for him to chunder in.

Now, Kora studied the ledgers on her desk, her soul
brimming with possibilities of making a life-long friend in Finlay.
She skimmed a few trinkets, silver bits, and coins off the top of the
coffers, marking it in the ledger. Barely enough for the crew to
survive on, but it'd have to do.

Once she was satisfied with the amendments, she placed the
black, leather-bound book of deceits back in its designated rickety
drawer and strode to the cream bed to undress. Her muscles sharply
protested as she stiffly removed her jerkin and shirt before
proceeding with her breeches. Gods, she was looking forward to
some decent sleep.

The door to her quarters flew open, a gust of cool eastern air
rushing in, and she squeaked, darting behind her privacy partition.
A deep, dark familiar chuckle echoed from the entrance, and a thrill
raced through her.

"Blake!" She peered round the divider, glaring at him.
"Knock before you enter, you heathen."

"Why? It's my room, too." He prowled, his glinting green
eyes hungrily devouring her bare chest like a predator stalking his
prey. Good gods, *that stare.* The talisman hung from her neck and

bounced between her pert breasts. There was a chill in the room, indeed.

"You could've been anyone," Kora huffed as she stomped to him. Half-naked and all.

"Well . . . I certainly wouldn't want *anyone* seeing this." His warm hands encircled her body, gently tugging her close as he planted soft kisses along her golden shoulder. He grasped the nape of her neck, his thumb stroking the column of her throat.

"Where have you been?" She willed herself not to give in to the temptation of him as petrichor and leather filled her senses. "You've been avoiding me for days. You haven't slept in here for a few nights."

Blake's mouth paused just below her ear. A sigh tickled her neck, and he reluctantly straightened, meeting her defiant gaze. His jaw twitched in amusement, and heat collected between her thighs. Floppy obsidian hair cascaded around his face with a gentle wave. Her hands ached to touch it.

"We must pretend, Kora. People were beginning to suspect something between us." He ran a hand through his hair—a sign he was frustrated. "I heard rumours about it among the guards. It could jeopardise *your* position."

Kora placed her hands on her hips, staring up at her first mate. Rumours had travelled through her crew before. She'd easily quashed them, and she could do the same again. His inquisitive gaze lingered on her body, and a bulge began growing below his waist. The air was suddenly, suffocatingly hot.

"Even so, doesn't explain your . . . absence." She glanced towards the bed, and Blake hung his head apologetically.

"I'm sorry, my *asterya*. Once we had the prisoners, I became so focused on questioning them. There's so much happening that we don't understand. Something's stirring in Galen, and we need to find out what." He flung his arms up in exasperation.

Dark circles loomed under his beautiful green eyes—he hadn't been sleeping. A smattering of dirt lined his jaw and neck. She studied his face, drinking in his strong, prominent features, haunted by dark shadows.

She nodded solemnly in response. Blake had been trying to find any reason other than magic to explain the Mist, and Galen's allegiance with the pirate lords. Kora didn't dare tell him she believed otherwise. If Galen and magic were returning, it'd mean certain death for them all. The empire had outlawed magic when they amassed control, deeming it far too volatile and dangerous for the islands, and any remaining mages were sentenced to exile or death. If Galen could wield magic, they would overpower the empire. A fully stocked army couldn't survive magic.

She shuddered at the thought of her loved ones dragged into the Mist, becoming as soulless as the island lurking behind it.

"Please, forgive me," he whispered. His rough, large palms reached out, leading her towards the enticing bed, and her core simmered deliciously.

"We'll figure it out, Blake," she murmured, distracted by his growing member as she perched on the edge of the cream bed.

His fingers lightly grazed her scar, following it to her high cheekbone, before tracing her jaw, and brushing down to her collarbone where the dark chain of the talisman rested. Kora trembled under his touch, his fingers leaving a blazing trail of sensation. She needed this. She needed him.

The swath of blue pillows cushioned her white head as she fell back and Blake continued tracing her upper body. Memorising every curve. Smiling at the talisman, he hovered over her body, brushing the edge of her waistband, teasing her flushed skin. In one fluid movement, he removed her breeches, exposing her entire bare body to him.

Her heart raced, her legs shaking in anticipation.

"You're beautiful, my *asterya.*"

His mouth greedily explored her body, planting hot kisses on the scars between her thighs from the Darkoning Trials. He followed the trail of horrific memories up her abdomen to the smooth curve of her breasts. Kora shivered from his touch.

"This suits you." He admired the talisman necklace, gently tracing the intricately curved midnight blue edges. "I like seeing you wearing nothing but it." His hand moved to her breast, and she gasped as his tongue flicked her erect nipple.

Kora tugged at his black shirt in silent demand, and Blake chuckled as they removed it together. He settled his body above hers, his strong, muscle-toned arms either side of her head. She roamed her hands over his broad back, feeling the ridges of his own traumatic scars from the trials, and he shuddered in response.

His emerald gaze captured her, sharing the same memory that painfully danced behind their eyes, deep within their souls.

Blake seized her mouth with his, and her hands fisted in his hair as he ground his hips, letting Kora feel his sizable, hard length. Excitement fluttered through her, parting her mouth open for him, and his tongue expertly caressed hers, making her moan.

"Blake," she panted, their legs tangling, bodies melding together. They suited perfectly. This was meant to be. Kora had never been more certain. Their bodies simply *fit*, like a puzzle.

"I know. *Fuck*. I know, *asterya*." He nuzzled her neck, and uttered the words she didn't want to hear. "We can't. Not here."

Disappointment flooded her. She removed her hands from his hair and pushed up on his smooth, bare chest as a frosted current of air swept between their separated bodies.

"Why?" She hated that she sounded so desperate.

"Because . . ." Blake smiled wickedly, "when I finally take you, I will make you scream."

Heat lanced through Kora, her cheeks blushing wildly.

"I also don't want an audience," he murmured against her ear, nibbling her lobe. "Trust me, I want to. There's nothing I want more than this."

There was no such thing as soundproofing on a ship, and she knew she would moan until the gods heard her. Kora smiled up at him and kissed along his jaw and down his neck, brushing specks of dirt away, nipping his skin and making him hiss.

Blake shifted his weight to the side and lazily stroked up and down her stomach, tracing the edges of earned scars before his fingers navigated to the quivering apex of her thighs. Her breathing hitched at the unspoken promise between them.

This male had saved her life countless times. He'd been to hell and back with her in the Darkoning Trials, and Kora had professed herself to him when they'd finally reunited a year ago. Not quite an admission of love, but she'd promised to give her whole self, and he'd vowed to serve her to the end.

If we do this, you give me everything, Kora. Your heart, your soul.

Everything?

Everything. You're the light in my life—a shining star. An asterya.

Everything then.

I will follow you to the ends of the earth.

And Kora would never let him go.

Those three dangerous words lingered on her tongue, as Blake's fingers grazed her slick wetness, and she gasped in pleasure. Circling her entrance, he groaned her name and she bit her lip, holding in her moans, gripping his strong, toned shoulder as his fingers plunged—

CLANG—the alarm bell rang from the centre of the ship.

They froze. The bell continued trilling erratically in the distance, followed by bellowing shouts of her crew. Kora leapt off the bed. Blake rolled to the side in surprise, and she frantically began putting her clothes back on. He hastily dressed, his movements rapid and fluid as he chucked her boots towards her and sheathed his blade to his hip with unnerving speed.

"PRISONERS ESCAPING!" a familiar voice screeched from outside. The ringing intensified.

"Shit!" Kora grabbed her daggers and back holster, briskly securing it around herself as they sprinted from her quarters onto the main deck.

11

An unsettling silence fell upon *Hell's Serpent.*

A splattering of blood streaked across the deck, and Kora quietly followed it. Her boots were near silent on the wood, until she discovered one of the guards from the pit, lifeless on the ground, his throat slit.

"Damn it, William," Blake hissed, anger radiating from him.

Kora's stomach churned as she peered at a shadowy figure by the main mast, near the alarm bell. Fog had fallen during the night, and she strained to see against the faint illumination of iron lanterns at each end of the ship. The light of the moon barely pierced the grey veil coating the body of *Hell's Serpent.*

She signalled to Blake in their code. *Move in, but stay hidden.*

As they neared the mast, a current of smoky air curled from the crew's quarters, their door broken, the wood splintered. The dark smoke wafting out thickened the fog, and her brow furrowed. What in the gods had happened?

"Where is everyone?" Kora whispered sharply to Blake.

He shook his head, motioning to lower themselves into a hunting crouch. They quietly approached the heart of the ship, and the moving shadow hissed, followed by a pained yelp. Using the darkness as a cloak, they raced forward. Dread coiled in Kora's stomach, and a foreboding chill crept into her bones as the fog thinned, repreiving her blindness.

Covered in blood, Jack panted as he threatened a sailor with a cleaver knife to their stubbled throat, and an arm tightly pinning their lean torso.

"Finlay!" Kora gasped.

Jack whipped his wild gaze to her as she revealed herself from the shadows, and her heart thundered as Finlay trembled, his tremor worse than ever. The knife pressed deeper against his throat. *Shit. Shit. Shit.*

She held up her hands as Jack eyed her suspiciously, spitting on the floor near her boots.

"Jack, what are you doing?"

"Guess again, lassie." His features twisted into a hideous smile.

A tattoo blazed on his *right* arm, paired with a red grog-blossomed nose from excessive drinking, spreading across a squared, menacing face.

The other Flint brother.

He looked identical to Jack in ways, but his foul nature distinguished them apart.

"Just let him go." Thank gods her tone was calm. "You're surrounded." She gestured to the bereft ship. Eerie silence answered, sending Kora's mind flying as she scrambled for sight of her crew through the thickening mist. The alarm had been so loud, why weren't any of them here?

"Nah, don't think I will, missy." The twin's shoulder oozed thick, darkened blood, soaking his tattered, filthy shirt.

It spilled onto Finlay, as his foot flexed for his broadsword behind them, by the pit entrance. Blood soaked the blade, and a small seed of pride bloomed with Kora. They had fought. Her pride quickly extinguished as Finlay's head wound spurted, dripping down the side of his ashen face.

"Don't see any of ye here to stop me," the pirate sneered.

Blake had disappeared, melting into the shadows, becoming one with darkness, and she swallowed, praying he was circling the ship to capture the pirate from behind.

"Ye see, I think ye like this lad," he continued, laughing sinisterly in Finlay's ear. Kora grimaced at his rotten teeth. Finlay's sparkling dark eyes pleaded with her as his tremor became violent. "Ye be wantin' him alive."

She ground her teeth. "What do you want?"

"Me and me brethren will be gettin' off ye ship now," he grinned. "With our booty, and ye coffers—as interest." He winked, and she nearly launched herself at him. *Bilge-sucking scum.*

Kora edged closer, and the pirate tutted as he pressed the thick, sharp knife against Finlay's stubbled throat, spilling precious drops of blood.

Where were the crew? She tried to suppress the rising anxiety within her.

"Stop!" She raised her hands higher, desperate to save Finlay. "Where's Jack?"

A dark predatory shadow weaved through the equally dark gloom of *Hell's Serpent*.

"He be here soon. With our treasure." The pirate's gaze flickered, and it was enough of a sign. Kora twisted and froze in horror. A warm light beamed from the open door to her quarters, slicing through the fog, and Jack silently shuffled out of the cabin, dragging something behind him.

This was a diversion.

Blake slithered up behind the rotten pirate with disturbing calmness. He hesitated, glancing towards her with concern, and swept his leg under the twin's. Blake's fist pummelled down into his chest, knocking him down, and he mercifully lost his grasp on Finlay.

Finlay careened to Kora, and she caught him before he hit the deck. *Thank the gods.* His shaking hands gripped onto her as he cried out with fear—fear of death circling him once again. Blake wrestled with the pirate, his hand reaching for the cutlass sword sheathed at his side.

"We need him alive!" Kora ordered. She was determined these pirates would meet their demise in the courts of the Aldara Council.

"Silas!" Jack cried from the quarterdeck. He staggered from her quarters, his right shoulder bleeding, the arm hanging limp, hauling the makeshift knapsack of Galen's wealth with his left arm. He froze at Blake pinning Silas to the floor, his sword drawn in an execution.

"Jack! Don't move!" Kora shouted.

Jack dropped the knapsack, swiftly sprinting for the steps up to the quarterdeck, and she chased after him, with Finlay hot on her heels.

"Don't kill Silas!" she called to Blake over her shoulder, and he growled in response.

They'd absconded from their cells, and she knew Blake saw death as a fit punishment, but she wanted a crueller hand of justice. Kora wanted to see them rot in the worst place on earth—

Aryn suddenly stumbled out of her quarters as they raced for the ebony steps, and he collapsed to his knees, the fog wrapping around him like a blanket.

"Aryn!" She diverted towards his crumpled figure and Finlay hoarsely cursed. Aryn groaned, clutching his head, which was peppered with bruises, and clogged with thick blood. Kora crouched beside him.

"I'm sorry," he mumbled, his body sagging. "I saw him go in. I-I tried to stop him."

Kora braced Aryn by his shoulders, helping him sit back against the outside wall of her quarters. "Do you know where the crew are?"

Aryn pointed weakly towards the crew quarters at the bow end. "The smoke," he wheezed, and her eyes widened. Jack's boots pounded against the wood above them.

"Finlay, stay here with Aryn," she quipped. "Keep an eye on Blake. Don't let him kill Silas."

Finlay sharply nodded as Kora took off to the wide steps, and she rounded the corner, her hand following the smooth curve of the ebony balustrade railing. The fog was thinner up here, and Jack stood defiantly at the helm, his left hand gripping the wheel.

His dark brown eyes tracked her stalking across the deck, and she kept her palms open and up, offering a false sense of parley. "Jack, stop this now," she spoke in Devanian. "It's over. You can't win this."

He released an exasperated laugh, and his long ginger hair wafted in the gentle night breeze. "We're getting off this *gods-damned* ship alive." He spoke in the common tongue, without his pirate dialect.

Who were these pirate twins?

He sucked in moistened air, sweat plastering his face and body, holding himself well despite the obvious wound to his shoulder from one of Aryn's arrows.

"You know I can't allow that." Kora shuffled closer.

"You don't *know* what's happening." His deep breaths became shaky. "We are *not* your enemy!" She paused her hunting stalk, a few feet away from the helm. Her fingers itched to reach behind for one of her hidden curved sabres.

"Don't feed me that drivel." Her lips curled in repulsion.

Jack's eyes pleaded and her stomach coiled. She narrowed in on his grimy hand clutching at the wheel of *Hell's Serpent*.

Her ship.

"We are not your enemy," he repeated, switching to Devanian.

Kora's temper flared. She was angry at pirates for taking her life and her family away, but she was now angry at herself. She'd been foolish, letting Jack use their connection of Devanian to soften her and bring her guard down. The breeze turned into a gust of wind, circling around them with strange warmth, and his face broke into a mystic smile.

"Listen," Jack spoke softly. "Listen to the voice that carries on the wind. I know you can hear it."

Kora's world froze. *How did he know?*

She'd never told anyone about the guiding hand of the wind that followed and whispered carefully to her mind. He laughed, smiling up at the dark, night sky. He was mocking her. A low, animalistic growl ripped from her throat. He had to be lying. He was tricking her once again, and she silently reached for her daggers.

"Jack! *Help me!*" Silas roared.

Returning the yell, Jack suddenly spun the wheel, turning the ship starboard side. The ship violently rocked, and Kora's legs slid as she fell to the deck, her side slamming into the weathered wood.

Jack dashed around the helm, darting to the balustrade and hurling himself over. She scrambled to the railing, unsheathing one of her daggers, ready to impale it into his back. Jack tucked his body in, shielding his injured shoulder from the fall as he expertly rolled onto the deck, disappearing into the thick of the fog in a matter of seconds.

He was no ordinary pirate, and Kora smiled—it was time for a hunt.

Racing down the steps to her left, she gripped her dagger. Aryn lay unconscious by the entrance to her quarters. His body was slumped in the amber light, the exquisite cream makeshift of treasure discarded and forgotten by his feet, and Finlay was nowhere to be seen.

The fog was so thick she could barely see a few feet in front of her, but she carefully stalked to the edge of the ship, keeping her back to the open air of the ocean as she followed the thick railing. It'd become rough over the years from sea exposure, and the number of arrows embedded into it during warfare created various dips and grooves in the wood.

She'd spent so much of her time upon *Hell's Serpent*, she could navigate it blind. Once Kora was sure she was adjacent to the main mast, her hand flung out and thankfully grabbed onto the shrouds. She couldn't charge into the fight hidden within the fog and risk harming Finlay, Blake, or herself.

So, she began to climb.

Once the sound of blades clashing, males shouting, and boots stomping against the wood were directly below her, she paused. The honey glow of the lantern pierced the misted veil enough for her to make out a collection of shadows fighting each other.

It was easy to spot Blake. She knew his body as well as she knew her own, his movements a mirror of hers when they fought. He was a strong opponent against Silas, with Finlay defending the rear. Until Jack's shadow arrived, and they became an undistinguishable frenzy.

A crash sounded to her right, and Kora sighed with relief as Samuel emerged from the crew's quarters, his shoulder leaning against the broken doorway, and he stumbled towards the scuffle mere feet below her.

"No! Don't!" Finlay cried. "What are you doing? Why? Pl-please don't do this! NO!" he wept, followed by a heavy *thud* against the deck. Silas' laugh rang in her ears, as Finlay cried a male's name over and over.

"*Save him*," the reliable voice pressed on her shoulder, and she relaxed her grip on the shroud, letting her body fall silently towards the grey abyss of her ship.

Kora had fallen many times before.

The fog rushed up to greet her—and a memory flashed from the darkest depths of her mind.

She'd once savoured the wind on her face. Had enjoyed it immensely as she'd gently plummeted through the lavender and blue skies. Laughter filled her ears, her body caressed and protected by the wind, as though it were alive with the warming presence from—

Her knees collided with Jack, his body collapsing to the deck as she landed on his back. Her right arm lifted to defend herself with her lethal dagger as her left hand whipped down to grip his neck like a vice, pinning him down.

"Can't get away from me that easily," she purred. He wrestled against her.

"Silas—don't do it!"

Jack heaved against her weight, and Kora tightened her claw-like grip. Her head whipped towards Silas, who stood holding Finlay by the neck with inhuman strength. His feet dangling as he desperately clawed at Silas' hands wrapped around his throat.

And behind them, laid Blake's . . . body—*his body.*

A gaping wound gushed through his torn jerkin on his side. Kora froze, unable to tear her eyes from Blake's unbreathing, still body. His blood steadily flowed, stark against the onyx deck.

Finlay choked, spit flying from his mouth as his face turned crimson.

"Let go of the lad." Samuel emerged through the fog. Anger hardened his expression, deepening taut lines across his brow. He seemed unaware of Blake shrouded a few feet away—or did he refuse to acknowledge . . . *Blake's body?*

Kora shook vehemently. This *could not* be happening. She *could not* have lost control this quickly. She *could not* lose Blake.

Samuel edged closer to Silas. Twice the width of the pirate, he towered over him, as he did with everyone. "Aye, listen to me. Let go of the lad. You've put yourself in a sticky spot here."

A growl vibrated from Silas, and he tightened his fist around Finlay, who violently kicked his legs, clutching for air—for life. Kora's focus tunnelled on Blake, his chest unmoving, his face deathly pale.

"What are you doing?" Jack wheezed beneath her pressing knees. "This isn't the plan!"

"Fuck the plan!" Silas snapped.

"Captain!" Samuel's rough voice penetrated her shock and she vacantly blinked in response, reluctantly dragging her eyes away. "I'll say it one more time," he threatened Silas. "Drop him, before it gets messy."

Silas laughed, the sound grating against Kora's ears.

Jack violently pushed up, heaving her off with an unnatural strength like his twin. She catapulted to the side, crashing on top of the brig hatch, pain reverberating through her bones. Jack scrambled for Blake's sword, discarded by his motionless side, and Samuel leapt towards him, wrestling for the weapon.

"*Save him!*" the voice invaded Kora's mind with force, and she gasped at the vociferous sound and overwhelming urge swelling within her. For the first time, it was urgent, desperate, and *loud*. She unsheathed her second dagger. "*Save him, now!*"

Jack wielded the empire-branded blade in his hands, cutting through the fog like liquid flame as the lantern's golden illumination reflected off the lethal curve. Samuel grunted, rolling away from the blade, as Finlay thrashed in Silas' chokehold, suffocation branding him purple.

Who am I supposed to save?

Her heart hammered as she rapidly glanced between her comrades, with Blake's deafening, *still* presence between them. Roaring rushed in her ears, drowning out the sounds of the struggles.

Samuel dodged Jack with a roaring shout towards Kora, trying to bring her around, and Jack lunged forward, the sword slicing Samuel's braided beard and chest. She aimed her daggers at Jack's back, the fog and her overwhelming grief threatening to hinder her senses. She had to save Samuel before he was killed.

That's who the voice meant.

"Silas, stop this now! Enough!" Jack pleaded as Samuel dodged another attack.

For a second, Finlay locked eyes with her, and the veins in his head throbbed as he mouthed two words from his swollen lips.

"I'm sorry."

"Fine." Silas casually shrugged. "Let's stop." He squeezed—snapping Finlay's neck, and the sound cracked through Kora's skull.

Finlay's dazzling dark eyes faded into a black lifeless void within a second. Silas opened his hand, dropping Finlay, his lips curled in disgust as if her friend were no more than a bilge rat. His limp body landed with a sickening *crunch*.

A heat consumed Kora so bright, and her veins felt like they were on fire. With a sob wreaking from her breaking chest, she launched her twin blades through the air. They sank into Silas' back, impaling him through the heart and shoulders. She screamed her burning rage—her grief—as she ripped her blades from his back. She repeatedly stabbed him until Silas sagged to the floor, with her on top, tearing her despair into his flesh until the flames banked into cold hatred.

"NO!" Jack whirled as his twin collapsed.

A painful roar tore from his throat as he clawed behind him, his back arching. Tears brimmed his eyes, and he kicked Samuel in the stomach, his abnormal strength winding Samuel as he flew into the thick of the fog. He stalked towards her, with Blake's sword shaking in his grip.

"*Do you know what you've done!*" he raged.

Kora released a deep, perishing breath, and she prepared to embrace death by Blake's blade. She couldn't fight Jack. Even she wasn't skilled enough against a mighty cutlass sword wielded by his supernatural strength. The ocean stilled, the water so calm that her ship froze in time.

She would join Blake, Finlay, and her unknown family in the spirit realm—or would she end up in the Locker? Either way, she was ready. She was so tired of fighting.

A whisper of a shadow caressed her, cold breath tickling her neck. Thanos had come—

An arrow ricocheted through the air.

Its force parted the fog as it speared towards Jack. It struck his hand and he dropped the sword with a pained yelp. The sound of it clattering across the wood shook Kora awake, and she jumped to her feet in a flash.

Her life was spared.

Aryn sprinted through the fog, his longbow armed and raised between his skilled hands as he cautiously approached. "Get on your knees, Flint."

He aimed another arrow at Jack, and Samuel stormed over, yanking Jack's arms behind him. He produced a thick pair of shackles to bound his wrists, with Aryn's arrow still pierced through his bloody palm.

"This is all wrong," Jack mumbled through his tears, his brown eyes glued to Silas' stiff body. "It wasn't supposed to happen this way." He hung his head in defeat.

Anger consuming her, Kora whipped her palm against Jack's cheek with such force it made Samuel wince.

"What wasn't supposed to happen?" she seethed, her palm smarting. She welcomed the pain.

Jack kept his head lowered, and Kora cried out in frustration, pouring her grief into harsh blows across his face, a red haze numbing her mind as Jack remained unresponsive.

"Look at my friend!" she cried. "Look at what you fucking did!"

It wasn't Jack's face, bloody and bruised, but Silas' menacing smile as he snapped Finlay's neck, staring back at her. Jack winced, as if he knew what she was thinking, what she was feeling.

Kora sobbed again, and she collapsed beside Finlay. Her hands hovered over his body, unsure of what to do, or say. His devoid, dark eyes endlessly stared at the night sky, and she bit her lip, holding in her tears as she lightly brushed her fingers over his lids, closing them shut. They were never to sparkle again.

Her promise to him was broken.

"Captain," Samuel's melancholy tone washed over her. "What'd you want us to do?"

She bristled. In times like this, she could lean on Blake's strong character to see them through.

Blake.

"Who killed Blake?" her tone was flat, distant, and cold. Her mask practically suctioned to her face like a kraken's sucker. Jack audibly swallowed, fear leaking into his gaunt face, his cheeks red and already swelling from her punches.

"You . . . you don't understand," he stammered. "He was going to—"

Blake groaned.

Kora startled, sprinting over to him, her mind in chaos. His body was still motionless, blood pooling around him. Had she imagined the sound?

His fingers twitched and her heart lurched, tears pouring down her face as she reached for one of Blake's cold, limp hands. Gods-damned the appearances they had to make. Samuel raised an eyebrow—his only indication of surprise.

"Blake?" she whispered. He groaned again and hope bloomed in her chest. "Aryn, see if you can find the healer!"

Aryn took off, but not before he ripped his arrow from Jack's hand. The hope in her chest withered as the pool of blood beneath Blake spread, dripping through the wooden cracks.

"What happened to the crew?" She clutched his hand tightly, not daring to move him in fear of him fully bleeding out.

"We'd settled in for the night," Samuel spoke hoarsely, and he coughed. "Then this smoke appeared out of nowhere. It knocked us all out—most of us."

Jack's brown gaze hooked on Silas, not daring to look anywhere else other than his twin. A splattering of dark blood materialised on the back of Jack's white shirt, but he didn't react.

Aryn approached through the fading fog, holding up the swaying ship healer with his arm. The healer was aged, his skin weathered, with a skinny frame and long grey hair. Kora stepped back, allowing the healer room to observe Blake, and clasped her hands together to prevent them from shaking. As he inspected him with slender, aged hands, Blake groaned a third time, his eyes fluttering open.

"Any longer, he would've been dead," the healer announced. Kora's throat clenched. "But he'll live, with my help."

She sent a silent prayer to Thanos, the god of death.

The crew spilled out of their hazy quarters, rubbing their sore heads as they peered around with bleary eyes. Dark smoke emanated from their bodies, clutching at remnants of their consciousness. Once their eyes landed on Blake's bleeding body, and the battered pirate, they began yelling, waking each other up.

Several sailors knelt beside him, producing a wooden stretcher with taut fabric between two beams. Kora looked away when Blake cried out in pain as they shifted him onto it and carried him to the medical bay.

"Get him out of my sight!" Kora snarled at Jack, and Samuel and Aryn shouldered his limp, hopeless body between them as they dragged him back to Hell's Pit alone.

T he healer had declared no one could visit Blake for the remainder of the evening—and most of the next day.

Kora paced around her quarters. Her blades were clean of tainted blood, and permanently attached to her back, hidden away in their scabbards in anticipation of another attack. But her soul remained marked, marred by the pirates' continuous onslaught. Their cruelty never ended.

The dual chests they recovered from *Demon Sea Siren* had remained untouched by Jack Flint's odious hands. However, he'd ransacked her quarters, hunting for the Galenite wealth—which she'd safely stashed away again.

Why the Flint twins specifically sought the Galenite wealth eluded her. This potential alliance had to end. Galen's return would destroy everything the Talmon Empire had worked for—everything Kora had worked for. She'd rather end up in Deadwater Prison than at the hands of Galen. Her marred soul would disintegrate in their presence, fading to a wisp, ready to be moulded into a creature of darkness, of torture and mindless slaughter.

A knock sounded at her door and Samuel shouldered through the slim doorway, his face set in a stony grimace. Aryn promptly followed, his attentive, hazel eyes surveying the wrecked chamber, his quiver and longbow strapped across his shoulder and chest. She inclined her head towards him, neither of them were taking any chances after last night.

She appreciated the archer's hindsight. In fact, if it weren't for Aryn, she'd be amongst the piles of dead in the hull, her carcass wrapped in abandoned hammocks. He'd spared her life from Jack's fury . . . even if she *had* been willing to die by his hand. To join the blank faces, surrounded by the moonlight-kissed hair her mind clung to, in Thanos' realm.

She wasn't sure what it meant. Years of hardship, years of gruelling pain, for her to suddenly throw it all away in one night. To accept defeat and surrender to the god's obvious intention on making her suffer. At least, that's what it felt like.

To Kora's surprise, the ship's healer entered the wrecked space. She vaguely remembered his name was Koji Sanatorre, along with the knowledge that he had a reputation for favouring wealth over aiding the infirm.

Long grey hair was balanced in a knot atop his head, and in the daylight, his face was pale and wan, wrinkled skin scrunching as he smiled tentatively. But the smile didn't reach his slanted eyes. Light brown trousers and an oversized white shirt lined his slender frame. The sleeves were rolled up, with an unbuttoned brown waistcoat hugging his chest.

If he was here, it had to be bad news, and Kora tensed as Koji opened his thin mouth to speak, his bony hands clasped before him. "Before you worry," his voice was rough, "he's progressing well."

She closed her eyes for a moment, thanking the gods—especially Thanos. "Thank you."

"I'm here to check on you."

Fan-fucking-tastic. She twitched, her skin crawling with an itch that had persisted since the twin's attack.

The healer motioned for her to sit in one of the onyx chairs by the desk. Luckily, she'd recovered everything from the workspace, returning items to their trusty drawers—more importantly, the ledgers. The rest of her quarters laid in tatters. Her precious books of fiction and seafaring torn to streams as if they held a valuable secret, the pages scattered.

Her heart felt the same. Ribbons of muscle shredded within her.

Her favoured assortment of blades glistened across the floor, and several throwing knives were still embedded in the ebony woodwork of the walls. Aryn's stare snagged on them, his body jerking. The bedding was tossed all over the room, creating waves of cream and blue, smothered in white feathers from ripped open pillows.

Kora had slept on the chaise longue last night, with her mattress propped against the bay window, too tired to put anything back together. Even now, exhaustion rimmed her eyes. Her body was fatigued, her heart bruised and aching. Her mind had gone into overdrive, incessantly worrying about Blake, Galen, and the pirates.

Anything to keep her mind off . . . what happened.

"I'm fine," she waved Koji off. "Just some light bruising."

Indeed, she had woken up to her entire side bruised and battered from Jack. Her back ached unforgivingly from sleeping on the stiff-backed chaise longue. The pain was a welcomed distraction.

Koji hesitated and Samuel smirked at him.

"Very well," the healer swallowed. "About the boy . . ."

Kora's chest tightened. "What are we doing with the body?" His tone was matter-of-fact. Void and emotionless. All three males looked towards her expectantly. It was *her* decision. The weight of it crushed her shoulders, and she rubbed her hand over her face.

"We'll do a sea-fire burial at dusk, near the coast of Blackstone Reef. Before we make port tomorrow."

"You don't wish to return Mr Blackstone to his family?" Confusion clouded the healer. "It's the correct procedure for sailors—"

"Sea-fire burial," Kora interrupted, "at dusk."

Finlay wouldn't have wanted his eternal corpse abandoned to his putrid, unforgiving family. She'd spent nights with Finlay on the quarterdeck, listening to the tales of the infamous noble Blackstone family. How cold and harsh they were, how dark their minds and ideals had become—as dark as their famous black shores. All that mattered to them was power and their titles—so much so that they would exile their eldest son to the Silent Tundra for the sake of *appearances.*

Kora planned to set Finlay free, on the eastern shallows of the Shaurock Sea, where he first experienced freedom on her ship. Conveniently beyond the hallow clutches of Blackstone Reef. There was no greater place than the expanse of the ocean.

And a great *fuck you* to the Blackstones.

Samuel and Aryn hovered in uncomfortable silence as Koji keenly observed her, seemingly focusing on her eyes. She supposed they were a unique colour, a blue so vibrant it bordered upon unnatural. Many males became entranced in her stare, until they realised what lurked between her legs and asserted their own annoying dominance.

"You may visit Mr Marwood tonight." The healer turned on his heel and shuffled away.

"Those healers can be so uppity," Samuel quipped as he sat at the desk, the chair groaning under his impressive weight.

Aryn silently sank into a chair to Kora's left, after dusting some feathers from it, whilst she placed herself opposite Samuel, the entrance to her quarters in her sight.

"They believe in forces that are above the empire," she replied, as she tried to force her body to relax, lightly scratching her wrist.

"Ach! You don't believe in that gods nonsense, do you?" Samuel tutted.

Aryn's curious gaze slanted towards her.

"Of course not," she shrugged with her nonchalant lie, and Aryn's shoulders pinched. She frequently conversed with the sea goddess, Calypso, in her mind—albeit one-sided conversing—praying for good voyages and seas. "How's our . . . guest?" Her tone dripped with venom.

"Aye, he won't speak no more." Samuel sifted through the small, silver platter of food laid on top of the navigational charts. "I think Silas' death broke him."

He inspected Kora through blonde lashes as he helped himself to dried meats, fruit, and sea biscuits. She refused to meet his stare. She also refused to acknowledge the stirring of shame within her.

"They had a unique bond," Aryn spoke, his voice hoarse, "and were incredibly strong."

So she wasn't the only one who'd noticed. The Flint twins had surprising strength, surpassing the brute force of males like Samuel. Silas' scrawny arms had delivered a death blow so severe the *crack* of bones still scraped against the inside of her skull.

"Suppose you'll say that's the gods as well?" Samuel joked, but a flash fleeted across Aryn's gaze before it was replaced with muted amusement.

"Whatever it is," Kora interjected, "two pirates escaped the pit, hijacked my ship, killed Finlay—nearly killed Blake! What happened out there?"

Samuel sighed, tracing his shortened beard. His thick fingers trailed down, past its blunt end, absentmindedly playing with the space where his original beard ended. A white bandage peeked through the edge of his half-unbuttoned black shirt.

"As I said before . . . we'd settled in for sleep. We received orders the ship was anchoring for the night and didn't need as many crewmen stationed."

She'd given no such order.

"Next thing, this dark sleep smoke exploded in the quarters, knocking everyone out. I grabbed a cloth and covered my face in time, and passed out only momentarily compared to the others." His tattoos stretched across his flexed, large muscles, making his point.

"Exploded?" she asked. "Smoke doesn't *explode*."

"I don't know how else to describe it." Samuel motioned with his hands. "It filled the room within a second . . . and *silently*."

"How did you avoid it?" Kora shifted her scrutinising stare to Aryn.

"I'm fast," he replied flatly.

She scoffed her disbelief, but Samuel nodded excitedly. "Aye, Captain. I've never seen anyone move faster than the lad."

"I saw Finlay leave the quarters." Aryn drank from the waterskin beside the food platter, quenching his hoarse throat. "He looked like he was going to be sick. I guess from all the grog. I went to follow but heard a yell outside, and then the sleep smoke exploded, as Sam said. I escaped out of the quarters, breaking the door in the process. Someone had locked it. I ended up collapsing on the far side of the deck away from the brig."

Kora glanced to the bruise at the side of Aryn's head, and he nodded in confirmation.

"I knocked my head from the fall. When I came to, the fog had become dense, but I could see Jack skulking around. I followed him here . . ." His slanted gaze searched for the mysterious treasure the Flint twins desired. "Jack didn't go down without a fight." Aryn tapped the top of his skull where, sure enough, dried blood matted his thick hair.

"If you hadn't broken the door, I don't think everyone would've woken up in time," she deciphered. It was a stroke of luck, the open doorway allowing the sleep smoke to drift into the open air.

Samuel's eyes widened. "That'd explain it, I was closest to the door. Where was Blake when this was happening?"

"He was giving me a debrief." She pressed her lips together to prevent the smile threatening to surface. "On the prisoners."

Samuel's mouth curved. "How'd they escape the pit in the first place? The guard rotation is iron-locked."

"They killed most of the guards with Cook's cleaver knife." She placed the weapon on the table, stained with Finlay's blood. "I think Finlay rang the alarm, and it's why Silas went after him. I think that's why you saw Finlay leave the crew quarters. He must've seen something."

After Jack had been locked in his cell, Kora had discovered a trail of mangled guards in the hold, and several disposed near the bowsprit. Her crew whittled down to one hundred and fifty, from its usual two-hundred capacity after the battle with *Demon Sea Siren*, and the Flint twins' rampage.

"Shit. He was trying to warn us. You don't think Cook would ...?" Samuel wondered out loud.

"Cook was with you in the quarters, right?" They both nodded. "So, either one of the guards happened to be carrying a cleaver knife and was overpowered by the twins ... or someone was helping them. Maybe it *was* Cook."

"Well, shit," Samuel cursed again, and sat back in his chair, exhaling deeply.

Aryn rubbed his rounded chin in contemplative silence. A light shadow of stubble lined his jawline. "They seem strong enough to break through the cells," he observed. "I'm surprised Jack's not tried to again, with the limited guards we have now."

"Maybe it was a twin thing," Kora considered. The Devanian tattoo was unmistakable. A clear-cut sign of the *old ways*. But magic had faded long before the two-hundred-year war. It no longer existed.

Until now.

"Forget the twin thing." Samuel clenched his oversized fists. "We have a rat!"

Aryn's eyes flared, understanding seeping in. "That's why you summoned us here."

Kora rubbed her aching scarred temple with a tired sigh. "There're only three people I trust on this ship. One of them is in the med bay, and one is ... gone."

"I wouldn't trust the healer," Samuel winked, trying to lighten the mood. "But ... Captain, if I may? You can trust Aryn. I vouch for him with every fibre of myself."

Aryn startled at Samuel's sincerity, his cheeks blushing.

Samuel had joined her crew when *Hell's Serpent* was founded. He'd dazzled her with his sailing knowledge and navigational expertise, daring to sail routes across the sea that'd never been attempted before, and swiftly earning them the title of the fastest ship in the armada. He enjoyed it immensely, stating it was the best ship he'd worked on, and would do so until he retired.

He appreciated the simple life, and continuously sought a bride—to Kora's annoyance. There'd been too many times when she'd walked in on Samuel and a barmaid tangled in the sheets. He desired a mother for his future children, and a partner to build a home with. Countless barmaids and females had fallen to his charms, but none yet had snared his heart. Beneath that boulder-like exterior was a male as soft as a sea biscuit. And she liked sea biscuits.

Aryn on the other hand, was far more cryptic. His recruitment commenced several months ago, his reputation renowned before he joined. Despite his name drenched in inky shadows, she absorbed his youthful face. How could she ever forget him? Had he been hiding in the darkness, avoiding her path whenever necessary?

Yet, his demeanour, his skills, they flickered a faint light in the deep recesses of her mind. A firefly, in the blackness of tar tormenting her memory. Something about him was comforting to Kora. As well as becoming thick as thieves with Samuel, an aged kindness and resilience radiated from Aryn. She stared down the two males, accepting she wholeheartedly trusted one, and was warming to the other.

"I need you both to help me," she begrudgingly admitted. "Investigate the crew. Talk to Cook. See what you can find out."

"Aye! If there's a rat, I'll catch it." Samuel banged his fist against the desk and scoffed another sea biscuit.

"We won't have long," Kora warned. "We make port tomorrow morning. Whoever did this will escape the ship and flee into the lands of Aldara."

"We should interrogate the pirate again." Samuel wiped his mouth before filling his stein with rum. She agreed, but she wanted to speak to Jack alone . . . to learn about what he knew of her secrets.

"I'll speak to the crew." Aryn's mouth settled into a grim line. "I can use my position with the archers to gain information." Her warmth for him increased.

"Jack's mine," she spoke with cold quiet. Both males beheld her apprehensively, but she returned their looks with a steely, unwavering gaze.

"Guess I'll have a chat with Cook, then." Samuel rolled his shoulders, lifting his stein to his mouth. "He's a stubborn, tough bastard." He heartily gulped, draining half of the drink in one mouthful. Ripping a top drawer open in the desk, he retrieved paper and a quill, jotting down notes, as drops of rum splashed onto the parchment from his beard.

"Is that a problem?" Kora asked saccharinely.

His smile dazzled her. "Certainly not, Captain. Just noting questions so I don't get distracted. By food." And with that, Samuel helped himself to the final dregs of food on the platter.

The setting orange sun dazzled against the onyx-stone shore of Blackstone Reef. Even from a distance, Kora reluctantly admitted the reef was stunning. A mile or so from the coast, *Hell's Serpent* had anchored, and the crew gathered starboard side.

Beyond the glittering pebbled ebony shores laid a grand keep made entirely of black basalt. She imagined the Blackstone family hobbling around the grounds, their backs hunched, limbs twisted, living in the eternal darkness of their pitiful souls.

A black leather harness clung to her chest, overlaying a white shirt. The crew had forgone the traditional black and green of the empire, and a sea of brown-and-white clothed bodies washed the deck. She hung precariously close to the edge of the railing, where Finlay had vomited the previous evening. Curling her hand around the green shroud, she used the biting sting of the rope to centre herself.

A hundred feet in front bobbed a wooden boat, listing over the gentle current. Upon it laid a long cloth-wrapped shape, tied with brown leather straps and ropes. A silver broadsword rested on top of the figure, its metal marred.

Kora turned to her crew, their solemn faces basking in the warm, titian sun. At the rear of the crowd, Aryn held a lit iron torch. A faultless, straight line of archers flowed next to him, their mighty longbows in their hands, and lethal arrows dripping with oil.

"Today, we mourn the loss of a good sailor," her voice travelled on the gentle breeze. "Finlay Blackstone was brave, and he fought with his life against the scum of pirates."

A crew member spat on the deck at the mention of pirates, and Kora's eyes cast over the crew. None of them *knew* Finlay.

None of them knew about his inner demons. They were angry at the Flint twins, and at losing several of their crewmates. But *she* would give Finlay the send-off he deserved.

"Finlay . . ." she paused. "Finlay . . ." her voice trembled, her grip tightening on the shroud until the rope grazed her palm. The crew murmured at her wobble, frowning at her emotional exposure. *Hell's Serpent* rocked in time with the bobbing boat, and her core steadied with the comfort of the ocean sea, soothing her aching soul.

"Finlay had been looking for his true home," Kora raised her voice, her captain-tone taking the reins. "He was looking for somewhere to belong, and I believe he found it with us on *Hell's Serpent*. His future—his hopes—were torn away from him. Just as pirates tear apart families, dreams, and lives. Now . . . we will set him free!"

She thumped her fist on her chest in a steady, beating rhythm, and cries of grief rang from the crew as they joined in unison, humming the tune of a farewell sea shanty. They created a wave of sound with their feet, hands, and weapons, yelling for their fallen comrades. The formidable beat of *Hell's Serpent* grew, until she was sure the Blackstone family could hear it from their obsidian castle.

Aryn lit the arrows of his squad, and flaming arrows soared above Kora, landing on their mark without missing. The boat ignited, becoming a roaring flame on the surface of the darkening water.

As the flames flickered, blending into the deepening orange-toned sky, more wooden boats floated along the ocean surface, away from *Hell's Serpent*, carrying the deceased guards. Silver brimmed her eyes as she breathed out her waves of grief, until all that remained was her endless well of loss.

It was a respected naval ritual to be buried by sea-fire. In Devania, they believed the dead would be ferried to the spirit realm of Umbra by Thanos. Instead, the empire encouraged the lore of Davy Jones escorting souls across to the Locker, forever in the ocean where they belonged. What had started as a tale soon turned into a nightmare, using Davy Jones as a tactic to spread fear amongst subordinates.

Someday, Kora would be reunited with her forgotten lost family, in Umbra. It was a comforting solace to know *something* awaited her on the other side. Resolve seared through her. She didn't come from *nothing*. A family existed for her somewhere, whether in this realm, or the next. And she would find them and fill their blank faces with wondrous detail.

A second wave of burning arrows volleyed, and four giant flames danced on the undulating ocean, in the shape of a diamond. Bottles of grog passed amongst the crew. Some cried, some laughed, as they all dispersed, muttering their prayers and despairs.

A large, blonde male weaved through the crowd towards the equally large and threatening dark-haired Cook. Aryn silently appeared at her side, expertly balancing on the railing with delicate ease, whilst her gaze pinned to Finlay's drifting boat.

"The crew didn't know much," he murmured quietly, passing her a metal stein of dark liquid. Kora pressed it to her lips, savouring the warm burn as it travelled down her throat, loosening the tight knot within her. She wasn't sure what type of grog it was, but she welcomed it. "Most don't remember last night. Sleep smoke impairs memories as well."

"How convenient," she muttered. She knew the feeling all too well. "What about who gave the orders for the crew to stand down last night?"

Aryn cut her a curious glance. "That wasn't you?"

This close, flecks of gold shone in his hazel eyes. He was youthfully handsome, with rounded, unreadable, yet familiar features. A comforting warmth stirred within her, and she shook her head, taking another spiced sip.

"There was a letter signed by you and Blake, pinned to the wall of the quarters. It had the empire's seal."

Kora stiffened. "Do you have this letter?" Only two people on this entire ship had access to the empire's seal, and they had both been swept away with each other's bodies last night.

"I can try to find it." Aryn cautiously peeped at the crew. "But I think it might have been thrown away in the aftermath, when we cleared out the bodies."

"Well, thank you anyway, Aryn." Kora passed the stein back, her tone distant and cold, and he nimbly leapt down to the deck, slipping through the crowd to his archers.

Finlay's flames raged and the air shifted. A weaving, glittering, smoky current, speckled with ash, curled, and circled up towards the looming, black, twinkling sky.

A small smile lifted Kora's lips, and her head tipped back as the sun set beyond the horizon. She waited until she was met with the dazzling black night. A small laugh escaped her, as the stars twinkled back at her, and she sent a silent prayer to Thanos, and whoever now rested with him.

15

The guards hadn't bothered shackling Jack to the festering, mouldy walls of Hell's Pit. He laid on his side, knees clasped to his chest, gormlessly staring at the darkness lingering by the side of his cell with red, tired eyes. Kora studied him. Blood stained the back of his torn white shirt, but there wasn't a single wound on his freckled back.

Koji the healer had been here. A white bandage encased Jack's right shoulder, which was no longer hanging limp or disconnected from his lean body. A small platter of bread and dried meat, and a fresh cup of water, had been left for him, along with the lingering scent of disinfectant salve.

Jack's breaths were slow and shallow, his chest barely moving. Gingery strands fell across his face, which he painstakingly brushed away with a bandaged hand. Blood seeped through the gauze, resulting in a dark, red spot on his palm. Thick, sore welts cuffed his wrists, and she crouched by the iron door of his cell. Luckily, it wasn't the same rancid one from before.

She placed a large lantern at her side, illuminating more of the pit. Deep scratches marred the walls from previous prisoners, along with short, scored lines, recounting their days captured in the dark abyss.

Gently knocking on the bars of the cell, Kora shifted her weight so that she sat with her legs crossed, scratching her waist to relieve an itch. She'd ordered the guard on duty to have a short break; to mingle with the mourning crowd jovially drinking above.

Jack's silence was deafening in comparison.

"Jack," she spoke in hushed tones. "We need to talk."

He curled tighter into himself.

"Look . . . it's obvious you were lying before. You know more than you're letting on about Galen. We arrive at the fortress tomorrow, and after last night, you'll most likely be hanged." Kora swallowed. "Speak to me. Tell me what's going on. I might be able to ensure a better sentence."

He shuffled an inch further into the darkness.

"Is that what you want? To be hanged? To join Silas in death—"

"Don't you say his name," Jack's voice strained, as if he'd been screaming until his throat turned raw. Slowly, he unfurled with a venomous gaze. "You have no right to say his name." His eyes were fathomless, and she grimaced at the empty husk of a male before her.

"He attacked Blake and killed Finlay." The cold captain surged within, consuming her. "You escaped these cells, brutally slaughtered my guards, and hatched a plan to steal from the empire. *Silas* would've been dead within minutes once his feet touched Aldarian soil."

The cup of water fizzed, pockets of air bubbling to the surface, and Kora shifted the lantern away from it, suspecting the heat caused it to boil. Her fingers tingled with rage as the massacre replayed in her mind. Raging brown eyes met her cool, calm stare.

"So you thought you'd give him a mercy killing instead?"

"He murdered my friend. It was justice."

Jack hysterically laughed. "Justice? What justice? That wasn't justice, it was fucking *revenge!*"

Kora's blood simmered. There was no wafting breeze down here to cool her temperament, and Hell's Pit felt as hot as the flames of Finlay's burning body. Her palms turned clammy as she pushed the thought of Finlay's lifeless corpse from her mind.

"Justice. For my family . . . for everyone, and *everything.*" For everyone she'd lost, and continued to lose to filthy pirates. How dare he insinuate she'd killed him without cause. She'd silenced a murderer, benefitting society with his death.

He frowned. "What—"

"Pirates destroyed my life, and I'll see to it that every last one of *you* is hunted down."

Jack stilled, studying her closely with unnerving familiarity. He lingered on the scar peeking through her short hair, and followed the curve round the sculpted smooth planes of her face. She felt exposed and vulnerable, like a raw nerve.

"Is that what they told you?"

Kora avoided looking at his swollen, bruised cheek. An echo

of her scar. She'd battered him. Rubbing her fingers together, she collected her thoughts. Jack was trying to divert her, and make her doubt that the empire had saved her . . . when *pirates* had branded her with that malicious scar. *Pirates* had shipwrecked her and killed her family, resulting in a child lost in this confusing, degrading world.

"The empire doesn't lie." But her voice wavered, uncertainty tainted the edges of her fortified mind.

"You don't remember," he observed. "You blindly believe a tyrant." She bristled at the truth, and her mask clung to her pores, sealing off her emotions. The empire wasn't tyranny. They were unification, prosperity, and innovation.

The noble houses were richer than ever, raking in profit from the fleet's voyages. Deals with the continent boosted the economy, allowing imported goods to spread across the land. The empire had devised modern waste systems, creating plumbing, clean drinking water, and *warm* baths.

It wasn't tyranny, it was the *future*. Yet . . . the lower districts still suffered. Still participated in the trials as their only path to salvation. Kora stole from plunders, spreading thin layers of wealth like a silver blanket over her crew.

But the empire had saved her life. Erick had saved her life. What was the alternative? Let pirates run amok, brutalising the islands, and pillaging innocent civilians? Anger blazed within her. Once she had eradicated pirates, the islands would settle. Galen was still trapped behind their Mist, and hopefully the pirate lords were trapped in there, too. That was the only way.

"Don't distract me with putrid lies. You will answer my questions, and I'll secure a lighter sentence at Stormkeep. It's more than you bloody deserve."

Jack hesitated, his gaze snagging on her scar once more. He was inspecting her, like he was searching for something within her face or soul. Slowly, he hung his head in defeat, and Kora quashed the rising feeling of discontent at the broken male.

"What was your plan last night?"

"We were going to escape, to a small port town between Scarlet Bay and Blackstone Reef . . . with the treasure."

"You knew about the Galenite bribes," Kora assumed. "You pretended to be simple backwards pirates who joined *Demon Sea Siren* recently."

"I acted the way you expected of us," he shot back. "We saw the treasure Cannon had amounted. We planned to steal it, but we were *interrupted.*"

His glare churned her stomach. So much death in a matter of days. It was no use pushing Jack, not when he blamed her for everything. He sipped the water, wincing at the pain of his ruined face. Cold, damp silence wrapped around them, and she waited in the shadows, as the events of Silas' death haunted him.

"Something was wrong last night. Silas said the plan had changed, and suddenly started killing everyone." Jack's gaze shuttered, as he seemingly stared at nothing. "I followed him up to the deck, and he was already brawling with that sailor."

Kora's chest ached, and her breathing hitched as the sound of Finlay's neck snapping echoed through her mind.

"I thought, if I got the treasure, he'd stop, and we'd jump ship . . ." He sucked in a shuddering breath as tears lined his eyes. Jack traced the faded tattoo on his left arm, its vibrancy muted and grey against his skin.

"Tell me how you know Devanian," she whispered. "Are you in favour of the *old world?*"

He continued to stare into oblivion, repeatedly tracing the tattoo. Precious seconds ticked by, and the shuffling of boots echoed above, followed by the sound of a guard approaching the hatch to the pit. She had to go—soon.

"Do you know anything about magic, or mages?" she pressed, her hushed whisper straining. Their abnormal strength had made her mind tick. Was it possible that magic was returning? If the pirates could sail into the supposed magical Mist, then was Jack's claim true?

Or maybe that was a lie too . . . and it was just *Mist.* Not made by man.

"Are you a mage?" Her skin crawled, veins bubbling beneath the surface. She needed to know. "Answer me!"

Silence. The guard's voice rang from the entrance to the pit.

"Did you send the letter?" she hissed, frustration pushing her closer to the bars.

Jack furrowed his ginger brows. "What letter?"

"Did Silas mention anything about forging a letter?"

He tensed at the mention of his twin's name. "I don't know who he was last night," Jack whispered to the darkness surrounding them, withdrawing into his inner pit of grief. Ready to await his uncertain fate.

Kora sighed, rubbing the constant dull ache in the side of her head. She got to her feet and stalked to the end of the row of cells, leaving the lantern with Jack.

"We are not your enemy!" Jack hoarsely called in Devanian. "Remember what's real."

She paused by the ladder to the deck hatch. "I'm sorry. But I don't," she replied in the ancient tongue.

16

Samuel met Kora in the shadows of the bowsprit. Brimming with merriment, he smelled like half a barrel of grog, and stuck out like a large, blonde boulder amongst the sea of slender, lithe males. He hummed a sea shanty under his breath as they ducked into a small coving away from prying eyes.

"Captain!" Samuel's broad face broke into a gleeful smile, and she steadied his drunken sway with her hands. They looked so tiny against his chest. "I love this ship," he crooned, his stein sloshing with spiced liquid. *Good gods.*

"Sam," she commanded his attention. "Did you speak to Cook?"

He nodded eagerly. "Aye, he knew nothing. I had to help make dinner to get any information from him." Samuel patted his stomach, which was spectacularly muscled—and full of food.

"He said the knife disappeared two days ago. He's been using a sword to cut meat from our raid instead." Samuel shrugged, swigging from his rapidly emptying stein.

"Did he have any idea who might've stolen it? Anyone suspicious seen around his kitchen?"

Kora placed two fingers on the rim of Samuel's stein, lowering it away from his grog-blushed face. Drips of liquid coated his beard and soaked his shirt as his sharp, grey eyes focused.

"Nah, I asked. Some of the pit guards spent a lunch in his kitchen two days ago, but nothing seemed out of the ordinary."

The day before the Flint twins escaped Hell's Pit, and three days after their capture on *Demon Sea Siren.* She had to find this rat, and fast, before her secrets leaked.

Kora patted Samuel's shoulder, and he drunkenly staggered to a circle of sailors, ready to sing more sea shanties. She could still hear the jovial melodies as she meandered to the med bay. Pausing before the crooked door, she raised her knuckles.

What if Blake *was* the rat?

He was the only other who had access to the empire's seal in her quarters. If only they still had the letter, she'd be able to recognise the handwriting. But what would he gain from releasing the twins from their cells? He'd been ready to kill Silas for absconding. It didn't make sense. If Silas could steal a cleaver knife, then he could steal a wax seal.

But *how?*

Her heart thudded unpleasantly with shame for thinking Blake could be the rat, and she wondered about his condition on the other side of the wooden door as it flew open. Koji appeared through the slanted frame, his brows raised questioningly. His hair was falling out of its top knot, and wild grey strands framed his long, aged face. Kora wrinkled her nose at the waft of disinfectant and herbs permeating the room.

Every Talmon Empire capital vessel contained a med bay, built into the port side above the hull. In their case, as far away from the mouldy, acrid starboard side of Hell's Pit as possible.

"Can I see him?" She folded her hands serenely in front of her.

He curtly nodded, motioning to enter. Kora silently stepped across the threshold and the overwhelming scent of herbal remedies washed over her, stuffing her nose. Her chest tightened, and she let out a hacked cough, causing Koji to throw her an irked glance.

The room was rectangular—like the pit, but slanted from a kick of wind knocking it when the ship had been built. Several bolted-down beds lined the far wall—enough for eight people, two of which were occupied. One was Blake's dark form, the other a nameless sailor, his laboured, wet breathing filling the silence. Three brass portholes interspersed the wall above them, and shafts of moonlight beamed through the room.

Chests and cabinets lined the remaining walls, filled with varying bottles and tins of gods-knew-what, with a small desk beside the entrance, covered in scribbled, thick papers. She couldn't make out the writing under the dim lantern illumination. Large stacks of thick-spined books towered by the desk, all intricately detailed. Some had gold embossed into their covers. *Gold.* Koji shuffled forward, blocking her view of the curious collection.

"He's very tired," he explained. "But he's healing well. Try not to disturb him too much." Irritation flashed through Kora and she narrowed her eyes. *This damn healer.* "He'll need to sleep soon. Rest is important for recovery," Koji continued, in his factual manner.

"Then why let me visit at all?" She braced her hands on her hips to give them something to do beside throttling the healer, and scratching the relentless itch on her shoulder. *Gods,* what if she'd caught fleas from the pirates?

Koji glanced back at the occupied bed in the corner. "Because," he lowered his voice before meeting her gaze, "he's been asking for his blue-eyed beauty."

Red stained Kora's cheeks as she faltered, sputtering, trying to think of something to tell Koji—that they were *not* together. That they hadn't promised their selves to each other. That they weren't each other's *everything.*

That they hadn't committed a forbidden act in the eyes of the law.

The healer raised his bony hands, his attempt at comfort causing her to cringe. "I'm not the empire," he assured. "I go where the coins are."

Fatigue consumed his seasoned wise face, and he silently trudged out of the med bay, his pointy shoulders hunched. Indeed, healers were notoriously money-driven in the empire, their allegiance leaning towards the wealth they could attain rather than the infirm. They worked wherever they obtained contracts, and Koji had a long-standing one with *Hell's Serpent.* Whenever they set sail, he had to be onboard.

Once the leaning door shut with a gentle tug, Kora exhaled, forcing the stench of disinfectant and herbs from her nose. Gods, it smelled awful. Like lavender soaked in lethal levels of grog and left in the sun to rot.

She sat on a small, cracked stool by Blake's narrow cot. A candle burned brightly beside the bed, black wax dripping down into a plain brass holder. Unsurprisingly, the whole room was the same ebony colour as the rest of *Hell's Serpent,* and Blake eerily blended into the darkness.

His raven hair hung limp in his ashen face, and a bandage covered his abdomen, rising and falling with strained, shallow breaths. The wound on his arm was stark against his paled skin. Koji had pulled back the white sheets down to his waist, and the scent of disinfectant was so strong, Kora's eyes watered.

"I think he's addicted to that salve," Blake mused, his voice weak as his eyes fluttered open.

"Oh!" Her watering eyes threatened to spill into tears, and she wiped her face before clutching his clammy hand. He squeezed her fingers. As their flesh touched, all her doubts about him faded away, her faith in him solidifying within her heart.

"I was so worried!" Kora's pulse fluttered at his emerald gleam.

"You're not getting rid of me that easily," he joked, wincing as he shifted in the bed.

"Blake . . . I thought you'd died," she whispered, barely able to sound the words out. A world without him was unimaginable. His eyes softened, and he gently reached up to stroke her hair.

"Hey," he soothed as Kora's lip trembled. "You will never lose me, *asterya*. I'll follow you to the ends of the earth, and beyond."

Her wobbling lips curled into a smile as their silent promise coursed through the air, and she leaned over, placing a kiss on his cheek.

A hacking cough grated her, and she glanced over to the sailor, several beds down. He wheezed, coughing repeatedly, and gasping for breath before he settled back down. His breathing was scarily faint yet raspy. The male was deathly pale, his cheeks sunken, his skeletal frame protruding through paper-thin skin. How did he get so skinny? Several vials of varying amber liquids had been left beside the bed.

"I think he won't be with us much longer," Blake murmured.

Kora sat down, her body deflating at another crew member fading away.

"He's what's left of the casualties with *Demon Sea Siren*. He was badly wounded by their archers." Blake tugged on her hand, pulling her gaze from the heavily bandaged sailor. "Koji's just keeping him comfortable . . . until it's time."

Her decisions had caused this. He was probably so thin from starvation, only to meet his demise after she believed she could crusade against *four pirate lords*.

Hindsight was a beautifully painful thing.

They wouldn't have lost so many crew members, and would never have discovered the Flint twins. Finlay would still be alive. Blake wouldn't be here, in the med bay. She rubbed at her ever-aching chest and nodded glumly. So much death, and all because she wanted to hunt pirates.

Because her revenge, was everyone's revenge.

"It's all my fault," Kora snivelled.

"Don't," Blake's voice strained. "You did everything you could. Those twins planned this. They . . . they could *do* things, Kora. Things I've never seen before. If you blame yourself, the pirates will win, and they've already taken so much from you. Don't let them take this." He clasped her hands.

"What happened last night?" Her voice cracked as the intensely strong-smelling salves attacked her senses and she wiped her nose, scratching at her cheek.

Blake winced, as if remembering ignited the pain of the physical wound. "I don't fully remember. It's all hazy to me now. I remember darkness, and feeling cold. Before that, I was fighting the twins with Finlay, and one of them grabbed a sword—gutting me. Just like that." His eyes shuttered, as he attempted to snap his fingers, but only managed a small brush of his fingertips.

"Which one did it?"

"I'm not sure. They're fast, strong, lethal," Blake sighed. "They easily bested me. I *should* be dead."

She stilled. Kora had witnessed the full might of Blake Marwood, as he tore through a hundred soldiers during the Darkoning Trials with a single sword, enforcing his revenge on her behalf for the fighting pits. He was one of the most skilled swordsmen in the entire empire, as well as a powerful commanding officer in the armada. If anyone could match Blake's sheer might and strength, or even surpass it, they had to be something else entirely.

Something unnatural. Inhuman.

Another wheezing cough broke through the room, followed by a sharp gasp for air. The sailor didn't have long left.

"*Asterya*, tell me how things are faring up above."

The threat of slumber lurked in the shadows of Blake's forest-green eyes, but she propped her chin on her hand as she stroked her thumb across his rough palm, divulging the events since Finlay's death—excluding her secret chats with Jack Flint.

Blake cursed before she reached the part of the forged letter. "Sam's right. We have a rat," he hissed.

"Whoever it is, I bet they're still on this ship, hiding amongst the crew," Kora summarised, Finlay's death burning a hole in her heart.

The traitor had to be here. And why would they help the Flint twins? Was it a coincidence two unlikely events happened so close together? Pirate lords never worked together, yet they'd stumbled onto the meeting, just for the survivors to escape Hell's Pit. Were the Flint twins . . . spies?

Realisation dawned on Blake's face, and he tried pushing his body up, his teeth clenching at the effort.

"What are you doing?"

"Getting up, we've got a rat to catch." He sat up and gasped with pain, clutching at his side. "On second thoughts, maybe this is a task for the morning. But don't do anything without me. Not when it could endanger you."

Kora smiled wryly as she helped him settle back into the bed. She pulled the covers up to combat the evening chill in the room and pushed his hair out of his eyes as his lids slowly drooped. Blake suddenly caught her wrist as she leaned forward to brush her lips against his flushed forehead.

"Stay," he pleaded softly.

"Koji wants you to sleep."

"I'll sleep better knowing you're here. I . . . I don't like being in here."

"Well, if it'll improve your health." Her smile grew as she sat, resting her upper body on the bed by Blake's legs. "Is Koji not entertaining enough for you?" she teased.

He laughed once, wincing to control the pain. "I've spent enough days in an infirmary. Countless nights sweating from infections from my . . . father's *training*. He liked to think it built character, branding me with wounds, just for me to suffer on the precipice of dying. It made me fearful, of my own family."

She stilled. Another insight to his past. Her entire being pulsed, elated with receiving information about his life, but also with a deep hatred that someone could harm Blake, especially as a child.

"I'm sorry. That's awful. What kind of training did he make you do?"

As she reached out her arm, her fingertips brushing Blake's, his eyes slid shut, exhaustion overpowering him, and he fell into a deep slumber, leaving her question unanswered. Her skin prickled, the itch clawing up her neck and across her scalp. She followed it, her nails scratching until her skin was raw.

For a while, Kora watched his chest rise and fall, as he breathed deeply, making sure those breaths never stopped.

Falling.

Falling through the air—no, the sky.

Laughter bubbled out of her, the sound escaping her lips and carrying on the current of the winds.

She was so free. So . . . alive.

She smiled up at the bright, cobalt, and lavender endless sky. Little tufts of pearlescent clouds drifted around her, and she reached out, gently brushing through the puffs, beads of water clinging to her golden skin. She twirled her fingers, weaving them through the sky as she soared.

Soared downwards, to the glimmering azure ocean.

She was not afraid.

As she approached the welcoming sea, she exhaled an elated sigh, bringing her hands above her flowing, long hair, shimmering like moonlight.

Following the curving sweep of her arms, a thick stream of warm, ocean water rushed out to greet her. It swept under her body, cascading around her, wrapping around her curves until she floated above the surface of fathomless blue.

A gust of briny wind ruffled her hair and she smiled, sensing a presence behind her. She whipped her hand up, palm extended out, sending a blast of water at—

Kora jolted awake, gasping for air as she *choked* on water, violently retching on the floor. Salted water pooled on the wooden slats of the med bay, and a shuddering gasp wrecked through her as she ran a shaky hand through her short hair.

What. The. Fuck.

Blake was still asleep, his pale face taut with pain and a sheen of sweat. She sat back in bewilderment. Her black breeches and white shirt were damp, and salt residue coated her harness. Her skin was clammy, her hair curling from moisture, and she could *taste* salt.

The talisman had escaped from under her shirt, now exposed over her heart. Kora tentatively held it up to the dawning light from the porthole. It was changing colour.

Whispering shades of purple, blended with silken midnight blue, transformed into shimmering teal in the teardrop-shape end.

She lightly traced it, as the rising sun shone into the med bay, reflecting off the peculiar, metal pendant. Her fingers tingled at the touch, and the sensation travelled up her arms, into the curves of her shoulders, and down into her core.

Where *something* rumbled in response.

"You're still here," the healer's unimpressed voice made her jump, and Kora shoved the talisman back under her shirt before turning to face Koji.

His hair was freshly tied upon the crown of his head, not a strand out of place, and he donned the traditional empire attire of black and green. The tunic wrapped around him, tied off with a golden twisted cord. A high collar encircled his neck, with intricate black embroidery of the empire's insignia.

Attire fit for a renowned healer. They were considered equal to the noble houses for their abilities and knowledge. A priceless skill. Kora nodded silently, her throat tense from choking on mysterious water.

How did that even happen?

Koji's eyes roamed over her. She was a dishevelled mess. How would she explain the water all over the floor? Or why all her clothes were damp? She stood abruptly, knocking the stool, meaning to block his view of the puddle . . . only to discover the floor was bone dry.

She rapidly blinked. Had she imagined it? Kora almost knelt to touch the parched wood until she realised the room was silent. To her right were seven empty beds.

"He passed during the night," the healer commented. "His body will be returned to his family."

His golden sloping eyes gave her a deliberate look. This healer was so irksome. "I suggest you get cleaned up." Koji began packing books and vials into a brown leather portmanteau bag with brass clips. "We'll be at Narrowfen Pass within the hour."

Kora nodded again, unsure whether she was capable of speaking. She worried if she opened her mouth, the ocean would pour out of her, so she squeezed Blake's hand, before hurrying out of the med bay and back to her quarters.

The talisman hummed against her chest the whole way.

PART TWO

THE ROYAL HOUND

N
arrowfen Pass was as deadly as it was beautiful.
A lethal sea stack of razor-sharp towering rocks denizened the entrance of the pass leading to the bay of Stormkeep Fortress. Only natives of Aldara could navigate the rapidly shallowing waters and, even then, many ships risked being wrecked upon the geode-crusted formations if they were a metre off course.

Samuel stood at the helm, his large hands firmly gripping the wheel as Kora peered through her brass spyglass. Sparkling hues of amethyst, rose quartz, and white crystal dazzled her vision as she carefully navigated Samuel around the dark sea stacks, interspersed with magnificent colour.

It was the perfect defence.

Stormkeep Fortress was impossible to attack from the northern sea, and to the north-west they were protected by the noble Blackstone family, who possessed an abundance of naval military, guards, and soldiers at their disposal.

To the north-east of Aldara laid the ancient and mighty Ebonmoor Mountains, too steep to scale or cross without plummeting to death. To the south was the vast, torturingly hot Silent Tundra desert, filled with raiders and convicts, with little hope of survival from either threat.

Even if assailants survived navigating the shallow waters of Narrowfen Pass they'd soon learn the fortress had formidable defences of their own. Two watch towers made of thick limestone, their bases encased in warped steel, protected either side of the pass. Sunlight glinted off the silvery bases, and the Talmon Empire flag was hoisted at the top of a pole, flapping in the coastal breeze.

Between them, a thick, spiked, iron chain secretly lurked

below the surface of the water, with the capability of shredding ships in two. As they neared the pass, both towers aimed destructive harpoons at *Hell's Serpent.*

Samuel raised his tattooed arm, signalling to Aryn, who was perched in the foremast's nest. He replicated the covert signal to the guards at the watch towers, who promptly lowered the blockade chain and swivelled their harpoons to the horizon beyond the sea stacks.

"They like to make a fuss," Samuel muttered.

Hell's Serpent sailed through Narrowfen Pass, the edges of the sails mere feet from colliding with the watch towers. Kora nodded to the stone-faced guards, lances and longbows gripped in their beefy hands.

"Can't take any chances," she murmured quietly to Samuel as he cruised the ship across the crystal-clear waters of the bay. "Pirates are stirring in the oceans. They've obtained our ships. We can't let them raid Stormkeep as well."

"That'll never happen, Captain. This is *the unbreakable fortress.*"

As they approached the port, Kora's body pinched, her pores tightening at the encroaching land whilst the glittering ocean faded behind them. *Goodbye, sweet ocean.*

"We never found the informant who helped the twins." Disappointment crushed her shoulders.

"Aye. My guess is one of the dead pit guards. They *always* ate in Cook's kitchen. One of them could've seen the chests from the *Demon* and planned to use the twins to get more of his share. Only for the Flint twin to kill him. It's a pirate's style to double-cross. Cover their tracks."

An insightful guess from Samuel. He wasn't just a pretty face. His gaze shifted to the hatch entrance to Hell's Pit on the main deck, and Kora bit her lip, refraining from admitting about the forged letter. If the twins weren't involved in that, then there was another party at play. Another piece of the puzzle she couldn't see.

Maybe a guard *could* have forged the letter? They'd been on this ship long enough to know what her and Blake's handwriting looked like, *and* the empire's seal. Had she been chasing a ghost this whole time?

Kora mulled the thought over as they docked at the busy, mighty port. Wide enough to fit up to thirty capital ships within the concave bay, it bustled with life.

Her crew cheered as *Hell's Serpent* anchored, and descended the walkway planks to the docks with a spring in their steps. Some sprinted to their gleeful families and wives waiting with open arms—or to the local brothels.

Samuel reunited with Aryn, clapping his slender shoulders, and Kora hovered at the edge of the ship as they disappeared into the fortified port town, joining crew members beelining towards the nearest grog establishment.

Samuel's vouch for Aryn settled in her gut. They'd always been joined at the hip, yet Aryn had kept a wide berth around her, until now. His name was no longer stained in inky, dark tendrils in her mind, but shone at the forefront like a beacon, breaking through her broken memory.

"Well done, girl." Kora stroked the railing, her fingers dipping into the grooves of the wood.

In one solid movement, she joisted over the railing, landing on the dock with a *thump*, her legs absorbing the impact of solid ground. She clutched her brown satchel bag strapped over her shoulder, peering round to make sure no one noticed she'd leapt off a ship without breaking her legs.

It was something she'd discovered in early spring, when she'd leapt from the mast, desperate to evade death by a pirate's sword, and landed on the deck unscathed. It'd been near the Dead Islands, during a convict shipment to the prison. She must've inherited sturdy bones from her family.

As she stretched, she took in the mighty, sky-reaching fortress.

The heart of Aldara.

Her home.

Beyond the docks, a grey, stone wall loomed on the pale sand, stretching the length of the bay. Battlements lined the top, with patrolling soldiers armed to the teeth dotted across in gleaming Talmon silver armour. Behind it, nestled the port town of Stormkeep, filled with taverns, inns, stores, and brothels. Anything a sailor could need after a long time out at sea.

Kora strolled down the dock, her head tipping back as she soaked in the elevated fortress protecting the town on the other side. Made of thick, near-indestructible ivory stone, it was three times the size of the town, and rose higher than the watch towers at Narrowfen Pass.

Green and black banners, emblazoned with the elongated, four-pointed star insignia, hung from various windows, wafting in the high breeze. Pernicious turrets lined the corners, with archers and harpoons peeking through the slits.

"No! Let go of me!"

A small group of pit guards hauled a writhing, chained figure down the walkway plank onto the dock. Jack Flint whipped his head up, his damp, filthy hair flicking behind him, and horror leaked into his face at the sight of Stormkeep Fortress. He erratically kicked his spindly legs out, the iron chains flying up in the air as he resisted the guards.

"What's all this?" Kora stopped them by the sandy bay.

"He's resisting, Captain."

She frowned at the pirate. "You seemed so ready to die yesterday."

"Death is not what awaits him," a guard replied, his voice gravelly.

"Ah, yes. He'll be sent to trial in the courts of the fortress—"

"No, Captain," the guard interrupted, his grip tightening on Jack's shaking body. "He's going straight to Deadwater Prison."

Jack thrashed at the mention of the prison, and Kora froze in shock.

"With no trial?"

The guard shook his head.

"On whose authority was this decided?" Kora snapped.

"That'll be mine." A strong voice drifted from the arched, iron-doored entrance of the fortress wall. Flanked by several silver-armoured soldiers branded with the golden insignia, strode a broad, athletically built male.

He wore dark, tarnished silver armour, with a flowing, dark-forest-green cape clipped to his shoulders. A mighty sword, with a fully golden hilt and pommel, entwined with malachite stone, was sheathed at his side.

Grey strands flecked the sides of his short, wavy, chestnut brown hair—when did he start going grey? Dark stubble lined his strong jaw, and his tanned skin wrinkled as he smiled warmly at only her, displaying a gleaming set of white teeth. Years of training succumbed her to bow in his presence, and the pit guards straightened, hoisting Jack up abruptly. His chains clinked together in the sudden stunned silence that had fallen over the group.

"Commodore." They all respectfully saluted him, eyes widening in surprise that the esteemed commodore of the empire's armada was present.

Jack warily gazed at him as he attempted tugging at his shackles, trying to loosen their dooming hold. The commodore halted before Kora, and she peeped through lowered lashes, meeting his warm, brown eyes as he raised a brow curiously.

"Erick," she spoke smoothly. She could be informal, to an extent, with her adoptive father.

As she straightened, he held out his silver-braced arm, and she clutched it at his elbow as they shook firmly, just as he'd taught her.

"Captain Cadell." He squeezed her arm gently, and his stare conducted an assessing rake over her.

She knew with *that look* he was probing for clues as to her whereabouts when they hadn't returned from their mission scouting Scarlet Bay. A small drop of shame pooled in her depths for causing him worry, for abandoning the mission that'd been granted to her.

"What's happening with my prisoner?" she enquired as they released each other.

"The Aldara Council have already agreed his crimes are too great." Erick cast a loathed glare at Jack. "Nor do they have time— or resources right now—to waste with pirate scum. He'll be incarcerated to Deadwater Prison, without trial."

Erick produced a small, branded letter from the folds of his armour, and Kora whipped it from his grasp, her eyes absorbing the familiar handwriting on the envelope. Brown stained the edges, and the wax seal had been removed, leaving a red splodge on the closure.

"Blake sent you a hawk," she gritted the words.

Messenger hawks were the only way to communicate to land, or other fleets, once they were out at sea. When did Blake have time to send a hawk after *that* night? And where had he stored the bird upon the ship? The faintest whiff of medicinal herbs drifted from the paper.

"No, no, no . . ." Jack repeatedly moaned. "Anywhere but there!"

"You can try your luck out in the desert, but I'd say you'd last two days." Erick's calculating gaze absorbed Jack's dishevelled, weakened state and he shrugged.

"Kora," Jack begged. "Please, you know I-I didn't do anything. It was all Silas—"

"How do we know you're not Silas?" Erick posed.

"What?" Jack whispered, his jaw dropping.

"You are identical twins. You could be *pretending* to be Jack Flint."

Kora dragged her stare away from Jack's sickeningly pleading face. The face identical to Silas'. Silas, who'd murdered

Finlay with a simple snap. The sound still haunted her mind.

Erick tapped his foot on the edge of the wooden dock, counting down the seconds to Jack's sentence. He read Blake's note out loud. It stated Silas had attacked him, murdered several guards—including Finlay—and his own brother Jack Flint, in a fit of pirate-driven rage.

Her chest pinched at the twist of truth. Blake had orchestrated it well, ensuring both brothers would meet their untimely demise, as deserving of any pirate, and absolved her of any involvement in what happened. It was an unfortunate accident. A wild, vicious pirate set loose on the loyal crew of *Hell's Serpent*—so wild that he killed his own kind.

"That . . . that's not true," Jack stammered. "I'm Jack!" He desperately tried to capture Kora's gaze, and she prayed that he wouldn't begin speaking Devanian. "Kora, please! I did what you asked."

Erick's observant stare swivelled to her, a question lingering within it. The weight of it was crushing, of the years of training her into the person she was today. The depth of the debt she owed this male, for saving her life from the kind that snivelled beside her, was an infinite pool.

"You killed Silas! Tell them—tell them what you did you murderous little bi—"

"Quiet!" A guard backhanded Jack, and his pleas ceased as he spat blood. It mixed with the pure, pale sand by near her feet, and she edged away from the tainted grains.

"Are you calling an honourable, commanding officer of the armada . . . a liar?" Erick's tone turned bone-chillingly cold.

Jack's jaw twitched, focusing his blazing brown hateful stare on her. Their pact bounced through her skull. Another promise broken. Another failure. After moments of agonising silence passing between them, Jack opened his mouth, his gums bloody, and drawled one sentence in Devanian. "This isn't you."

The guards attacked, jostling him for speaking the forbidden tongue of the ancients, and Erick's attention curiously shifted to Kora. It was time for her to show where she stood, within the face of the council's decision.

"Someone has to pay for his crimes." She swallowed, meeting Erick's eyes, and he nodded at her approvingly. The crushing weight on her shoulders smothered her so much it drowned out the pain. A cool numbness sweeping over her as her expression schooled into neutrality.

Jack cried out as Erick ordered him to be taken to a prison wagon, to begin the long journey southwards to King's Cove Guard, crossing Achlys Channel to the small, barren Dead Islands housing Deadwater Prison.

"You'll regret this!" Jack brokenly yelled, as the guards dragged him towards the horse-drawn, iron-barred wagon, stationed by the arched fortress entrance. As they slammed the door, locking Jack within, he cried out once more, his voice cracking. "Don't trust them! They're lying to you! Find me when you no longer believe!"

Something within Kora cracked along with him, and the droplet of shame threatened to slither in and turn into something *else*, but she held it at bay in Erick's presence.

Jack's ranting cries faded into the distance as the prison wagon pulled away, the clip-clop of hooves drowning out any other horrible sounds, and Erick placed a comforting hand on her shoulder. She exhaled, letting the tension flow out of her like an ocean wave. The sea waters gently lapped up at the edge of the docks, splashing onto her boots.

"You've been gone a while," he murmured as they faced her ship. Soldiers and crew worked together, hauling the cargo off. Shortly afterwards, the two gleaming golden chests from Kora's quarters appeared.

"I had reasons," she replied, as the moonstone and ruby chests were carried past them towards the fortress vaults. She suspected they were lighter than expected, after her crew had been granted their small share to secretly take home.

"It appears so." Erick curiously gazed after the chests, and Kora retrieved her ledgers from her brown satchel slung over her shoulder. She passed them to Erick, keeping her satchel open for him to peer inside and glimpse several shining Galenite trinkets. His brows shot up instantly.

"We have some *things* to discuss," she spoke in hushed tones. "Not here, though."

Erick revered *Hell's Serpent*, huffing at the broken main mast, torn sails, cracked wooden panels across the hull, and new scars from arrows and lances smattering across the body.

Two figures stumbled down the walkway plank. One with raven-black hair, the other a gleaming grey. Blake hunched over, supported by Koji, as he helped him down onto the dock, his face tense with pain as he attempted to straighten in Erick's presence. His jerkin was half buttoned, allowing his wound to breathe, but he still had his cutlass sword sheathed at his side, causing him to lean from the weight.

"Yes, it seems we do," Erick observed, as a wounded Blake hobbled towards them, leaving Koji behind to assemble his medicinal belongings from the ship.

"Commodore Cadell." Blake halted, weakly attempting a half bow, gritting his teeth from the exertion. The urge to reach out and help him was so overpowering, that Kora had to clench one hand over the other to prevent herself from rushing to his aid.

"Don't harm yourself more, Marwood."

Blake paused, gingerly straightened, and adjusted his loose jerkin in the process, his pale face flushing. Erick's weighing stare passed between his daughter and her first mate. So many previously spoken words laid thick in the air.

He's not good enough for you.

How would you know? You never let anyone come near me!

Kora—listen to me. Do not go near Marwood. No good will come of it.

Blake nodded respectfully, and his quick emerald gaze homed in on the letter peeking from Erick's grasp.

"You received my message."

"Yes, the prisoner—Silas Flint—has been dealt with. He's on his way to Deadwater Prison as we speak."

Kora chewed the inside of her cheek as cautious green eyes met hers. She willed her face to remain in neutrality, the edges pinching with worry. She wasn't sure whether to be thankful or mad at Blake for the missive.

"I suggest you acquire some overdue rest." Erick casually placed his hand on her arm, but it didn't go unnoticed by Blake. "We'll be meeting tomorrow at first light to discuss your latest . . . voyage. Amongst other *things.*"

"Yes, sir." Blake dipped his dark head, and Erick ordered two of his soldiers to assist Blake to the barracks within the fortress, whilst keeping his firm grip on Kora's arm. She meekly murmured a farewell to Blake as he begrudgingly shuffled away towards the port town, his shoulders hunched once again.

Kora tugged her arm out of Erick's grasp with a glare once they'd disappeared down the narrow street. "You know he looks up to you."

A wry smile danced on Erick's lips as he chuckled. "Just makes it all the more fun."

"Why can't you be more accepting? He's a good first mate."

The smile faded and Erick's face turned serious, those rich, brown eyes frosting. "*You know* what I think of him," he solemnly replied. "He's a reputable soldier, and can protect *Hell's Serpent*— and that's all he can and *will do*. Now, head home. Rest up."

Kora sighed as he strode towards *Hell's Serpent*, his minions following closely behind, to oversee the remainder of the capital vessel. Erick had voiced his opinion many times of her beloved Blake Marwood, and his *personal* connections to her.

She wasn't sure whether his keen observations had noticed their lingering touches, prolonged stares, and ghostly smiles. Whenever they docked, they had to increase their distance to each other. Another reason she hated being on land.

But she prayed Erick's opinions weren't true.

E rick had informed Kora that *Hell's Serpent* would be repaired within two weeks.

Two weeks away from the vast ocean seas, from the winds blasting her face with the sheer freedom sailing offered her. She was stuck behind the towering fortress wall, with nowhere to go, nowhere to discover, nowhere to plunder, and no pirates to hunt. Two weeks of pretending to be indifferent to Blake, struggling to capture moments alone together, unable to let their desires run rampant.

It had driven her to the nearest tavern. Her sex life may be as dry as the desert, but her throat didn't need to be.

The Abandoned Barnacle was rife with noise and bodies, as sailors from various ships filled the room. Kora perched on a high stool by the bar, a hooded cloak draped over her, obscuring her infamous white hair. Finlay had wanted to visit a tavern with her once they docked, and her heart ached as she glanced at the empty stool beside her.

She recognised many faces, clustered around high tables and booths. People from her crew, other fleets, and the trials. She refused to meet the lingering gazes of those from the trials, their memory a shadowing darkness lurking in the corners of the tavern.

Her slender hands gripped a stein full of golden ale, and she slowly sipped, ears pricking at the sounds of cheering and jokes from the sea of males around her. The tavern reeked of stale ale, followed by a bitter, smoky scent that clung to the furnishings.

Low wooden beams cut across the ceiling, and a set of rickety stairs in the far-left corner circled behind the bar, leading to an assorted taste of *service*. Netting lined the walls, with clams and shells woven throughout, and splotches of dried seaweed coated the crevices, filling cracks and holes from previous brawls.

A large bloodhound peacefully snored behind the counter of the bar, a thin chain collared around his thick neck. Kora admired his gossamer black fur, as his two-pronged tail gently wagged in his sleep, creating a steady soft drumbeat against the tiled floor. Drool leaked from his jowls and pooled on the floor as his droopy red eyes suddenly sprang open at a resounding *crash*.

"Oi!" the barkeep shouted, waving his thin hand at the commotion.

Two sailors brawled with two soldiers over a pot of silver bits in the middle of their table. Their glass steins of grog plummeted to the tiled floor, smashing to pieces as they swung for each other.

Kora quickly picked up her stein, nimbly shifting off the stool as one sailor sprawled into the bar, the wind knocked out of him. Bottles of grog and numerous glass steins rattled from the impact, teetering on the edge of the shelves.

"They started it!" he wheezed to the barkeep.

"I don't care who started it. I'll finish it if the lot of you don't get outta here now!"

The bloodhound emerged from the bar and snarled at the group, his maw drawn back to reveal a set of huge, sharp canine teeth. His drool splashed on his oversized paws, lined with extended claws. The brawlers paled at the beast and scarpered, falling through the porch entrance and abandoning their money.

A barmaid scurried from a door near the stairs, and swept up the mess as the barkeep pocketed the bits and coins. He ruffled the bloodhound's ears, patting him on the back, before returning to polishing the glass steins behind the counter. The formidable hound happily trotted to his owner's side, lapping water from a small bowl.

"You keep interesting company," Kora mused as she settled, legs dangling around the foot of the stool.

"Ah, Conan's a softie at heart." He smiled at the bloodhound, who snorted in return. "He's good at keeping the vermin out." The barkeep was gangly, with pale skin and slicked-back hair matching Conan's colouring. When he smiled, his own teeth were as sharp as the hound's.

"I've never seen one that colour before."

"Aye, poor Conan was cast out of his litter for it. The breeder thought he'd turn out to be a runt." The male chuckled. "Look at you now, boy."

Bloodhounds were unique dogs, used within armies for

seeking out enemies. The empire had bred them so that they were now the size of mountain wolves—with sharper fangs, and retractable claws. The red eyes were the telling sign of noble houses breeding them, resulting in a premier breed with heightened vision and senses, so they could hunt in the dark. Those exact red eyes were drawn to Kora now, capturing her gaze unblinkingly. Conan sniffed, letting out a small, low whine.

"What's the matter, boy?" The barkeep leaned towards Conan, stroking his long back. "Are you hungry?"

As he pottered about, fetching Conan food, a foreboding sense overwhelmed her to leave as those red eyes bored into her. His large snout rapidly snuffled, absorbing her scent, and he whined again.

"I best be off," she murmured, placing a silver bit on the counter.

Conan raised up on his haunches, placing his large, front paws on top of the counter as he eagerly leaned towards Kora, drool splashing into her stein. His head was a foot away from brushing the low-beamed ceiling. *Almighty gods, he was massive.*

"Conan! Get off there, you mutt." The barkeep gently swatted his paws with a cloth. "We don't need you drooling into people's drinks."

She stumbled back in surprise as Conan eventually dropped to the floor, his paws thudding on the tiles, followed by his chops smacking as he devoured his food.

"Sorry about that," he said sheepishly. "I'm looking after Conan for someone else. Still getting used to him." His dark blue eyes flashed, and he scanned the crowd, his gaze lost in the endless males.

"Say, don't suppose you know if a ship named—"

"Captain!" a deep voice boomed from the crowd, and the barkeep startled as Samuel shouldered his way through the throng of males. "Fancy seeing you here."

The barkeep snapped his sharp gaze to her as she pulled down her hood to greet Samuel, and an impish Aryn lingering behind him. The barkeep's eyes flared at her hair and scar, his mouth gaping, and he dropped his rag.

Several sailors' eyes ogled at the mention of her title, and she quickly ushered Samuel and Aryn into an empty booth near the entrance of the tavern. She glanced back to the bar. The barkeep had vanished, leaving the barmaid in his stead to polish glass steins.

Samuel waved at the barmaid to bring a round of drinks to

the table, and she hurried across the room, expertly holding three full, heavy steins in her tiny hands. Her simple grey dress clung to her body, accentuating her curves, with a burgundy, tied corset cinching her waist. It was low-cut, revealing a full bosom which bounced as she walked.

As she placed the steins on the table, Samuel shot her a dazzling smile that made her round cheeks blush. Her brown hair was braided, and curled on top of her head. Kora placed a couple silver bits before the barmaid on the table, her fingers hovering on the coins.

"Where'd the barkeep go?"

"Oh, John?" The barmaid glimpsed round the thriving room and shrugged. The motion made Samuel suck in a breath. "Said he's gone to collect a brewery shipment from the harbour."

"When will he be back?"

The barmaid's tawny gaze narrowed at Kora, and then dipped to the shining silver coins under her fingers.

"I don't know," she replied coolly. "A capital ship arrived late today and delayed all the shipments to town. Funny how that happens."

Her scrutinising stare slid over Aryn and Samuel, bruised and dishevelled, the former blandly observing the conversation, and the latter still attempting to dazzle the barmaid with his smile.

"How inconvenient, I was hoping to speak to him." Kora sipped from her replenished ale stein.

"I'm not sure when he'll be back. He always disappears. Now I'm managing this place on my own. Surrounded by incompetence."

"Any troubles, I'll sort them out." Samuel winked at her, and Aryn ran a hand over his face as he shuffled further into the corner of the booth.

The barmaid appreciatively nodded and returned to the bar, her hips swishing in the thin dress. Samuel sighed after her, and Kora's fingers brushed against the stained, wooden table, her metal bits absent.

"I'm going to marry that woman." Samuel beamed at her from across the room.

Kora suppressed roiling nausea. *Calypso spare her.* "You want to marry every barmaid."

"I have a lot of love to give." He waggled his blonde brows as she gulped her ale, wishing she could melt into the hazy, amber liquid. Aryn muttered a curse, rolling his eyes at his comrade.

Hours passed, and her steeled gaze on the entrance to the

tavern was unwavering as she waited for John to return. As Samuel ordered another round from the watchful barmaid, the door to The Abandoned Barnacle swung open, and Kora rushed to her feet, wide-eyed at the figure before her.

"I should've known that you'd be in an establishment such as this. How cliché."

Kora barked a laugh as the female glided towards her, encircling her long arms around Kora in a tight embrace.

"They have the best ale," Kora murmured into her friend's shoulder.

Bree Hydrafort towered over her, and her dark cloak swished around them as they pulled apart, smiling. Her smile dropped as she wrinkled her nose, followed by waving her hand through the air.

"You stink!" Bree clasped her nose dramatically.

A subtle stench of sweat, dirt, and salty ocean encased them. Kora's fingernails were cracked and filthy, her clothes rumpled with splattering's of dried blood hidden by her cloak. Her face was coated with grime, and her hair coiled around her ears, crusty from weeks of ocean spray. She supposed she *was* a little bit dirty.

"A few weeks at sea will do that," Kora said bashfully. A pointed cough sounded behind her, and she turned to an equally grimy Samuel staring at Bree in awe.

She was tall, and slender, her skin like deep, rich chocolate, and eyes as piercing blue as the sky. Individual gold loops wove throughout Bree's long, braided hair, matching the jewellery sweeping across her chest and wrists. She adorned an exquisite billowing purple dress, with subtle gold and black embellishments lining the folds of her skirt and sleeves.

"Lads, this is Bree Hydrafort. Bree, meet Samuel, my sailing master. Aryn, head of archers on *Hell's Serpent*."

Aryn stifled a choke on his ale. "*Hydrafort?*"

"Well . . . I'll be damned." Samuel stroked his braided beard. "Don't see many of you anymore."

Bree pursed her thick, plump lips. "My family have taken permanent residency in the Citadel. We no longer need to be in Aldara."

Kora gestured for Bree to settle into the booth, away from the eyes pinned on her voluptuous figure, and the riches that garnished it. Aryn warily marked her, and the scrutinous barmaid returned, placing another stein of ale down on the table. Her tawny eyes tried to capture Samuel's, whose grey gaze was now enamoured with the royal noble before him.

"A Hydrafort out in the wild." Samuel let out a low whistle, and Kora glared at him.

Bree shrugged and cringed at the stein of ale. "The lengths I go to see my best friend."

"*Best friend?*" Aryn squeaked, and he and Samuel gawked at Kora in astoundment.

"Bree's been my friend for a long time," Kora nudged her elbow as Bree sipped the ale, and grimaced. She'd always been more favourable of wine over any grog, since they'd first met ten years ago—shortly after Kora arrived in Aldara with Erick. After her *accident*.

They'd met at a gawdy noble's ball. Kora had been pulling and pinching at the gown Erick's servants had stuffed her into, scowling at strangers twirling around her on the dancefloor. Many eyes had been trained on her that evening, whispers circling the ballroom about the *lost girl* and her fresh, *ugly* scar.

Until Kora tripped on her skirts and fell during a dance, bringing down the daughter of the prestigious noble house with her onto the marble floor, and shattering Bree's elbow in front of the entire noble society. Bree had been grateful for the excuse to leave the ball and hide from society for weeks whilst she recovered, and Kora had visited her every week at Erick's behest to make amends with the Hydraforts.

They'd been best friends ever since. Bonded over their disdain for balls and uppity nobles.

"Don't make me sound old," Bree quipped.

"You mean to say you're friends—*best* friends—with the heiress of the House of *Hydrafort?*" Samuel leaned forward curiously.

"I wouldn't say the heiress . . ." Kora hummed, arching a brow at Bree.

"No, no," Bree waved her hands. "I'd say I'm governess of the house already."

They both chuckled at the silently stunned males, and Aryn's eyes darted between them, wide like saucers. The Hydrafort family were the closest relations to the royal family in Azaria. They'd been one of the first to venture with Admiral Darkon during the two-hundred-year war, resulting in becoming the wealthiest and most noble of all the houses.

In the eyes of citizens, Bree Hydrafort was a princess.

Who was sat, in a brawly sailor tavern in the port town of Stormkeep Fortress, drinking ale—almost.

"As much as I adore your company, why are you here?" Kora asked.

"I received news that you hadn't returned from Scarlet Bay. There were speculations that you'd shipwrecked in the Shaurock Sea when silence persisted." Bree's face was taut with the worry she'd experienced, and Kora placed her hand on her friend's. Aryn's stare narrowed on their clasped hands, his jaw ticking.

"I wouldn't believe it. Captain Kora Cadell shipwrecked?" She let out a single, sharp laugh.

"Aye, no one can best *Hell's Serpent!*" Samuel thumped the table.

Bree nodded. "I left the Citadel at the first mention you'd gone missing. I refused to accept that you, of all people, would be defeated by pirates. Or *worse*. Not with your amazing crew. I arrived a few hours ago and have been checking every tavern since."

"That's a long way to sail alone, Bree," Kora reprimanded gently as she squeezed her friend's hand.

"Yes, yes," Bree squeezed back. "I disguised myself on the ship and sent word to Erick of my arrival by hawk. His guards are outside the tavern as we speak."

"Please say you told your father you're here," Kora groaned.

She didn't need Otto Hydrafort, the governor of the house, condemning her. Not with her goals of advancement to admiral. Erick would be *furious*. Weeks of shamefully visiting their old manor in the upper district, bestowing gifts to Bree's family for ruining her debut in society, wasted. Bree had laughed it off, claiming she despised the restraints of nobility, but Kora knew, deep down, Bree thrived on it.

"Of course, I did," she gibed. "Wouldn't want you to get into trouble."

The two friends smiled warmly at each other, and Bree patted Kora's arm, her bright sky-blue gaze sparkling as she relaxed, knowing her friend was safe—and alive. Silence shrouded the group, and Bree attempted another sip of her ale.

"I can order you some wine, if you prefer," Kora offered.

"When in Aldara!" Bree raised her stein, shaking her head at Kora's offer, and took a hearty gulp.

Amber liquid spilled from the lip of the stein, trickling down her chin and splashing onto the table. Bree shyly wiped her mouth and grinned at Samuel and Aryn, who launched into a series of questions about her family, the Citadel, and her connections to the royal family.

Kora sat back, comfortably easing into the flow of conversation, whilst keeping her gaze fixed on the entrance to The Abandoned Barnacle.

No one else entered the tavern after that.

The room tipped and swayed as Kora sagged into her bed at Cadell Manor. Samuel, Aryn and Bree had convinced her to continue drinking at The Abandoned Barnacle, going as far as purchasing entire barrels of grog from the suspicious barmaid, named Circe Quinn.

What a funny name.

Kora's super smart and amazing plan to question John had been foiled, as the male never returned by the time Circe shooed them out with a cloth, swatting Samuel's wandering hands. Even Conan had disappeared—taking himself to bed so as not to be disturbed by their rowdiness.

What a moody mutt.

Kora placed a bare foot on the floor, using the cool, terracotta tiles to steady the dizzying torrents of her vision, and she blindly fumbled for the covers, hoisting them up to her chin. A chilling breeze wafted from the open window she'd dumbfoundedly climbed through to avoid the presumptuous eyes of servants, or risk awaking Erick.

What a spectacular idea. She was really, really, smart.

Dawn was in a matter of hours, and she groaned as her stomach threatened to heave up the contents of the evening. Kora reached out with her hand, seeking for a glass of water on her bedside table. Nothing but smooth, oak wood. Bile loomed in the back of her throat and she choked it down.

With one eye slitted open, she gauged the distance to her bathing chambers across the room. Nope. That was too far away. Nope, nope, nope. Not when her bed felt like a cloud, cushioning her sore limbs from falling through the window.

She giggled, but it croaked from her mouth, turning into a hacked cough.

Gods, she was thirsty.

She needed a drop of water, *anything*, to quench the burning within her chest. She'd jump into the fountain in the courtyard if she had to. The nausea churned and, as she nestled deeper into her plush white pillows, a droplet of cool liquid splashed onto her forehead.

Both eyes sprang open.

The room violently bucked and swayed once again, and Kora painfully peered at the white domed ceiling—where a small, rippling pool of water swirled. She flung back the covers with a shriek, and the circling water halted, then rained down. Straight onto her.

Oh. My. Gods.

She must be hallucinating. Had she been spiked at the tavern? She was *so* drunk that she was three sheets to the wind, imagining water floating in her chambers, soaring down onto her skin, coating her pores . . .

Actually . . . it felt *divine.*

Water filled her gaping mouth, drenched her hair, and soaked her clothes and bed in one mighty splash. Kora greedily swallowed, dampening the burning bile. The liquid was cool and crisp, with a hint of mint leaf. Her nausea settled and she fell back into the sodden covers, pushing her hair out of her eyes.

A chuckle caressed her ears, pebbling her skin. It coaxed down the edge of her jaw, to her chest, vibrating with laughter. Funny, she'd never heard the voice laugh before. Her toes curled, her legs entwining as an ember sizzled along her flesh.

The voice was so faint, so distant. The quietest, weakest of whispers, merely a breath fading in the air. The damp cocoon soothed her, and she gently hummed, as a faint caress of air brushed her hair until she fell asleep.

19

Kora gently thumbed the stinging edge of her sabre daggers as Erick set up the target practise dummies in the gardens. Murky water churned her memory, the scent of mint lingered in her nose, and the faintest trail of fingertips crossed her skin, making her thighs clench.

She'd never dreamt of her voice before. Or magic. Years of law ingrained to her that mages' powers crippled society, debasing humans to animalistic urges that'd caused Devania to topple. A shiver ran through her as sweat dripped from her neck, eerily like the droplets of water from her dream drenching her.

Erick had awoken her at dawn—after a measly few hours of sleep—and dragged her outside for a five-mile run. Who even runs at the crack of dawn? They'd followed the looping cobbled streets of the mid-district, near the residential outskirts behind the fortress. Every fibre of her muscles had screamed from her restraint on her stomach to quash the hangover from the pits of Umbra.

Vomiting in a neighbouring manor's gardens would be frowned upon, and she couldn't embarrass Erick. Yet, sweet relief would not grace her as she trembled in the gardens of Cadell Manor, desperate for him to quicken his haste preparing the dummies.

The sun loomed high in the sky as the summer heat scorched the land, and the dry grass had faded to wheat yellow, cracking beneath her boots. Cadell Manor nestled amongst the mid-wealthy district of homes, protected by the fortress. All were spaciously spread apart, containing their own extravagant gardens and courtyards for hosting, including stables.

Except for Cadell Manor, which contained a variety of assault weapons, target practices, and a training ring. How homely.

Behind them, towards the east, sat lush green rolling hills, dotted with far more wealthy, grand manors, fit for noble families in the upper district. Towards the west and south, the manor homes faded to the poorer, lower districts, containing tiny cabin houses and shacks. Built upon narrow cobbled streets that disintegrated into sandy paths the further away they were from the fortress.

Many families from those districts worked in the port town, or for the Blackstone family, or became travelling merchants, toiling in Scarlet Bay.

Kora was certain whichever family Blake hailed from still lived in those slums, his past tied to one of those tiny cabins. She dreaded to think which shack contained stains of his blood, drawn from his father's punches. How many times had he wandered the streets as a scrawny child, seeking herbs to patch himself up?

She'd tried countless times to encourage him to open up about his family, his past, but his eyes would always glaze over, turning to hard emerald before he distracted her with delightful, forbidden kisses. All she knew was he'd been the poorest of the poor, and used as a punching bag whilst his mother had been in a self-induced haze, oblivious to her own child's suffering.

No wonder he'd entered the trials. Now, he was a champion.

"Show me your knife throws," Erick commanded.

Shaking herself awake, Kora surveyed the four wooden-and-straw target dummies placed dozens of feet away, by the grey stone wall encircling their manor. Sheathing her precious daggers in her scabbard, she collected four small, yet sharp, throwing knives from the marble table by her side.

Wearily positioning before the first target, sweat poured from her brow, soaking her shirt from their run. She hissed at the blinding light of the sun, her head throbbing with pain as she raised her right hand and pivoted her feet, lunging into her throw.

And missed. *Shit.*

She nearly threw up there and then.

The blade bounced off the stone wall, and Kora winced as it sliced into the hardened, dried earth. Erick stood calmly, his arms crossed, not a flicker of emotion on his face. His warm, brown hair stuck to the sides of his face with trickling sweat, and he silently met her gaze and jerked his chin at the scattered knife.

Hanging her pounding head, she strolled to retrieve the weapon, each step threatening to split her in two, and returned to her starting position. Loosening a breath, she re-aimed her throw.

Missed. *Double shitting shit.*

After several more frustrating failed attempts, Erick peeled from his position, motioning to her to remain still as he retrieved the fallen knife. His silence was loud enough.

What was wrong with her? She'd won half her trails in the Darkoning intoxicated—it was the only way for her to survive her stubborn choice. To forget the souls she'd reaped, seeking a title that'd never been in their reach. Except for the males bred for it. She'd had no issues disposing of them.

But she'd left the trials a different person. Tainted by the blood of those who were buried deep underground. It was how she'd learnt to slip on a mask, to allow the red haze to consume her body, mindlessly flowing to the rhythmic music of slaughter.

Kora's speciality in her training had always been wielding daggers—even going as far as throwing an axe or two. But now, she could barely pitch a throwing knife with a little, inconsequential hangover.

Frustration and disappointment boiled within her as she furiously gripped a steel knife within her palm. She'd expertly struck Cannon down with an envelope knife of all things, had impaled Silas with the daggers strapped to her back, in the fury of grieving heartbreak.

Her stomach clenched, mind roiling at her failure.

As Erick knelt to reclaim the knife from the parched ground, Kora's grief swelled like a tide and her hands shook from the reverberating sound of Finlay's neck snapping, vibrating through her, down to the soles of her feet and into the earth.

"What's Marwood been teaching you on that ship?" Erick muttered. "Have you been practising at all like I—"

Two of the knives soared as he began to rise, Kora pouring her anger into the throw as they ferociously embedded into the misshapen head of the dummy. She instantly followed with the third to the heart, a mere inch away from Erick's head, slicing the top of his hair. He raised a brow.

The burning urge to fight, to expel the grief pummelling her organs, was overwhelming. Kora whirled, grabbing another two knives. They struck true in the head of the second dummy. She swung an axe, cleaving through the chest of the third.

A raven-steeled lance, propped against the marble table, beckoned her. She twisted, leaping forwards, using the force to propel the spear straight through the heart of the fourth target and into the sturdy, stone wall behind.

Erick quietly assessed her marks as she panted, hands on her knees, and retched on the grass. The contents of The Abandoned

Barnacle spewed all over the earth, followed by her breakfast porridge. Appearing by her side, he lightly stroked her back as she gasped for breath, tears pricking at the corners of her eyes.

Because she *had* been practising. But with Finlay, and not Blake.

"Tell me what happened," he quietly murmured. He'd always been so observant.

Kora straightened, shakily wiping her mouth with a grimace. "I had . . . a friend. He died. On the ship." Saying it out loud, on Aldarian soil, suddenly made it all too real. "Silas killed him." She met Erick's warm gaze. "And I killed Silas."

Her voice was so quiet, she wasn't even sure if she'd spoken out loud. In all her years of hunting pirates, she'd never once executed one through blind rage. She refused to stoop low to their level of mindless killing. She felt disgusting.

His jaw clenched. "Don't mistake me for a fool, Kora. I know it was Jack that we sent to Deadwater Prison."

"Then why make me decide? Jack had begged Silas to stop. We made a deal that he'd be fairly trialled in the courts. I wagered a lighter sentence for him."

"A pirate is a pirate. The council declared he'd be incarcerated to the prison. Does it matter which *one*?" Erick's questioning gaze returned. "He's where he belongs. If you wish to be admiral, these are the kinds of the decisions you'll have to make."

Kora then realised what else ate away at her. The *guilt* of committing Jack Flint to Deadwater Prison. He was doomed to live in the skin of his dead identical twin. All because of what she did. Even if she hadn't have hunted down pirates, lured by her secretive voice, she still could've saved Jack from his twin's noose.

And when she became admiral, she would change all of that.

"Why are the council enforcing sentences without proper trials?"

"Why are you sailing after pirates during a scouting mission?" he countered.

Ice crept into Erick's consistently calm stare, his jaw clenched so hard he could cut boulders on it. She bit her lip, refraining from admitting that a voice she'd heard for ten years told her to sail west. She'd end up in Deadwater Prison right alongside Jack. Mateys for life.

"There're things we need to discuss, but not here." He glanced to their right.

A grey stone wall intersected the gardens, separating the

training grounds from a courtyard adorned with lemon trees. An archway loomed in the centre, breaking up the simple brick work, with a lone figure lurking within.

Blake Marwood curiously glanced from Kora to Erick, to the pile of sick at her feet, to the destroyed target dummies. His eyes widened at the lance piercing through the fourth dummy, cracking the solid wall behind.

"Am I interrupting?" He audibly swallowed as Erick stepped forward, half blocking Kora—and her lump of vomit. Her muscles relaxed at Blake's presence, the individual fibres sighing with relief after clenching for so long, yet her gut still roiled.

A light sheen of sweat glistened underneath his swept-up groomed hair, from walking here from the barracks. He bore no sign of pain, and stood miraculously straight as his forest eyes scanned her, desperately seeking for an indication of her wellbeing.

She reciprocated the look, eyeing his wounded side, as if she could peer through the fabric of his grey linen shirt. Tucked into black trousers, and paired with laced boots, he was still striking, even if he'd been on the edge of Thanos' realm days ago.

"We're just finishing up," Erick gruffly replied, and addressed Kora. "Meet us in the parlour." He regarded her vomit-splattered state, and then her hair. "It's time for a haircut as well."

She was never sure why Erick always urged her to trim her hair short. Whenever she'd challenged it, he always had a different reason. To prevent her catching lice from other crew members, to give her a masculine presence when commanding a ship, or to show off her scar and make her appear threatening.

She gently curled a short strand by her temple around her finger. "I think I want to grow it out."

Erick paused. His gaze lingered on the reaching scar flicking over her cheekbone and traced the curve of her brow. Icy brown eyes blinked, the edges crinkling with age.

"We'll discuss it later."

An exhale of disappointment was all she managed as he marched to Blake, directing him into the sweeping glass doors of the manor.

Once they disappeared, Kora passed through the archway into the tiled courtyard, her step wavering. Standing by the flowing, three-tiered fountain, she splashed water onto her face and neck, washing away the sickening heat coiled around her. The water was cool, crisp, with a scent of . . . mint.

She stilled, cupping her hands under the flowing water, and

brought it to her lips, taking a deep gulp. Her knotted stomach finally eased, and she moaned as she devoured another cupped gulp. The depths of her mind tickled, and she observed the baying lemon trees, interspersed with large, vibrant green bushes. Prowling over to one, the minty scent overpowered her senses, burning her nose.

Her brows knitted as she peered back at the fountain. Dainty, green leaves floated on the surface. A warm breeze drifted through the green-and-white mosaic-tiled courtyard, ruffling her hair, and circling her body before wafting upwards.

Alright then, time to the follow the wind. Completely normal thing to do.

The current led her to the trellis attached to the corner tower of the manor overlooking the courtyard. Chunks of broken ivy and purple wisteria clustered on the ground by her feet. She craned her neck up to her bedroom window, the malachite-green shutters wide open.

"*Remember.*"

With a gasp, Kora's hand shot to her chest, gripping the talisman resting underneath her shirt. It warmed at her touch. The sound of flowing water in the fountain roared in her ears, and she yelped as the water sloshed, spilling over the lip of the stoned fountain's edge and spooling onto the mosaic tiles.

Something deep within her yawned, as if it were beginning to wake up.

Wake up from what? She had no idea.

F reshly bathed, Kora dressed in a simple, sage-green tunic and trousers, with silver stitching and buttons circling up the curve of her collarbone. Flying through the black-and-white hallways, she snagged crystalised ginger bites from the kitchen pantry, scoffing them to chase away the final dregs of the hangover. As she ran, she wolfed down a chocolate tart in three mouthfuls, licking her fingers, and rounded the corner into the grand parlour room.

The tension between Erick and Blake was palpable. She glanced to the glass windows, adorned with heavy black drapes and gold tassels, wishing for her familiar, comforting breeze to waft in.

Cadell Manor was one of the finer homes within the mid-district. Constructed from large, pale stone, with green shutters lining tall windows, and arched glass and iron doors. Most rooms were furnished with exquisite mahogany and oak furniture, and decorated with swathes of cream and black.

The ceilings rose high, and Kora lingered by the mahogany table, large enough to seat up to twenty, with Erick to her right, and Blake to her left. Coffee permeated the air, and her fingers trailed over the dainty cup and saucer on the table as she stifled a yawn. The run had been a stupid idea.

An aged map of the Azarian Islands covered the shining woodwork, candles in brass holders placed on the curling, frayed edges. Three islands were outlined in green: Aldara, and Talmon, with its smaller, sister island—Otrovia. In the centre of Shaurock Sea, was Peril Cove, stained black, and to the south-west, covered in grey and marked in red, was Galen. The enemy.

She tunnelled on the vast space between Aldara and Talmon. A thick black line scored across the map, separating Aldara from

Talmon and Otrovia.

The Black Abyss.

A deep, dark trench, miles away from Narrowfen Pass, that swallowed any vessel daring enough to cross its path. Rumours circled, entailing dangerous sea creatures that lurked deep within the Black Abyss, and some claimed it led to Davy Jones' Locker.

The only way to reach Talmon Island was to sail around Peril Cove, venturing close to Galen, and risking an ambush by pirates. Something Kora knew all too well. Bree had done just that when she'd heard Kora disappeared. Her heart panged. Her *royal* friend had sailed those dangerous waters to find her.

"You're looking better, Marwood."

Erick's scrutinising stare zeroed in on Blake's side, and Kora also cast her gaze over her first mate. He'd always been good at recovering from battles. Always the first to come out of the med bays healed and raring to fight again. Her red haze encroached the edges of her mind. No—she couldn't start thinking about that, about how his family would batter him senseless.

"Thank you. I am healing well." Blake dipped his head.

"Quite you are. An impressive feat."

"We discovered some things on our journey that we need to escalate immediately." Blake cleared his throat.

Erick glanced between the two of them, his face neutral. He'd found time to change, donning standard black trousers and a waistcoat, with his favoured burgundy shirt. It suited him well. His brown hair was ruffled, waving around his stern face. He gestured for them to continue.

"We came across a gathering of pirates by Peril Cove," the words rushed out of her. "They chased us, and we destroyed *Demon Sea Siren*."

Erick's eyes glinted at the mention of an empire ship. "What were you doing so far from Scarlet Bay?"

"Sightseeing," Kora replied sardonically, and before Erick could question her further, she barrelled on. She couldn't explain her reasoning for sailing to Peril Cove, other than lying about simple rumours of pirates gathering. But that wouldn't be enough to appease Erick. "There were five ships. But four were from *our* armada. And not just that . . . they were commanded by pirate lords."

"We defeated the pirate lord James Cannon, who'd stolen *Demon Sea Siren*." Blake's fingers pressed against the convex-edged lip of the table, turning deathly white, as if that small stability kept him upright.

Erick pinched the bridge of his nose.

"I should've known," he muttered. "During the first week of your voyage, our scouts informed us there'd been an attack on one of the ports in Talmon—near Ironwharf Outpost. Multiple ships stolen. Supplies, weaponry, the lot."

Blake frowned, his emerald eyes scanning the map. "That's right by the wenches' territory. They'd be fools to attempt to cross their borders."

Indeed, the witches called their scraggly sectioned-off land the 'Shannara Territory.' They were no more than curse-hexing, wild females, who dabbled in voodoo to scare off any wanderer who breached their preciously marked borders—or so she'd been told. That, and they were skilled hunters who would skin trespassers alive if they had the chance, eating the flesh.

"Latest reports say the guards at the outpost were all knocked unconscious," Erick continued.

Kora's mouth went dry. "Unconscious how?" She swiped a porcelain cup, draining the coffee in one bitter gulp.

"Some kind of smoke." Erick raised his brows at her paling face. "Why?"

"We had a similar incident on *Hell's Serpent*. All of our crew were unconscious from a sleep smoke in their quarters. We found out it was the Flint twins' handiwork."

Blake eased a step closer to her as she shuddered from the memory of that night. His fingers trailed along the convex edge, and she imagined her hand sliding down his bare arm, tracing the red scar from the battle with *Demon Sea Siren*, down to his hands, entwining her fingers with his.

She ached to touch him.

Erick's mouth thinned. "So . . . the twins could've been there when the ships were stolen."

"I interrogated Jack. He was insistent they joined *Demon Sea Siren* late, just days, or a week before they encountered us at Peril Cove."

"You'd believe the word of a pirate?"

Kora fumbled for a moment. She didn't want to admit—deep down—that she trusted what Jack had admitted to her after Silas' death. He'd been a broken male, with nowhere to go. He'd had nothing left to offer, other than his words at the time.

"It's true." Blake shuffled closer, his heat inches away.

"There's one other possibility," she murmured, and both males looked at her questioningly as she pointed to the scraggly section on the map. "They had help from someone else who'd have the knowledge to craft the smoke."

Blake cursed as his eyes landed on the Shannara Territory. "Of course! Those feral wenches can concoct anything."

Indeed, along with their hunting skills, the witches had mastered alchemy long before Admiral Darkon had united these lands. If the king could wipe them from the world he would, but the Shannara Accord Treaty between witches and Talmon forbade it, even if they *were* rumoured to practise magic.

Magic was *forbidden* under Azarian law. To speak of it was *heresy*. An immediate death sentence. The viceroys of the Citadel had declared that the witches only practised simple potion swindling, devised to trick the human mind. With the king's approval, they secured the treaty, allowing peace across Talmon Island.

"It'd explain the ruby chest you recovered. I've confirmed with a historian that the rubies are from Shannara. It's clear the pirates cut a path through their lands to the outpost. I can't imagine the witches allowing them in. They must have brokered a deal. The witches . . . working with the pirates," Erick rubbed his stubbled jaw. "This isn't good, but they haven't violated their treaty, so we cannot interfere."

"Not just that." Kora's pointed finger travelled down the map, stopping on the centre of Galen, and tapped once. "We have a strong belief the pirates are also allying with Galen."

Erick released a long exhale as Kora collected her satchel from beside her feet, placing it on top of the map. She revealed the stolen Galen trinkets inside, stomach churning at the sparkling gems. It was confusing to see something so beautiful come from somewhere so deadly and bloodthirsty.

"We found this in the ruby chest," Blake spoke in hushed tones. "On board *Demon Sea Siren*."

"We also saw three pirate ships retreating into the Mist," she added.

The pirates must have something valuable to secure alliances with two formidable forces. She nibbled another ginger bite stashed in her pocket as a hot flush overcame her. Perhaps her hangover wasn't finished with her yet.

Erick's face grew apprehensive. "The Mist?" he croaked, and his burning brown eyes lingered on her scar. He audibly swallowed. "Did you go into it?"

"Of course not," Blake scoffed.

Silence followed, as Erick peered at the gleaming wealth hidden in her satchel, and she contemplated telling him Jack's claim that the Mist was controlled. That it'd been created by a male, who had the ability to allow ships to pass through.

A side-eyed glance from Blake and she clamped her lips shut. To speak of *it*—to acknowledge *its* existence, was defection from the Talmon Empire.

Sun rays pierced through the tall windows, bouncing off the moonstones garnishing the trinkets, and casting a dazzling aural display around them. Kora's lips twitched, a lightness lifting her chest. Blake distastefully closed her satchel, his fingers flexing in revulsion.

"We may have instigated a war with the pirates after the death of Cannon." She drooped her head. Two wars fought for freedom and unity, and she'd potentially unravelled it all on an unseen voice's whim.

It all weighed on her shoulders, crushing her. She still wondered what Cannon knew—*how* he knew about her secrets. He'd said this wasn't meant to be her life. She internally laughed. Of course it wasn't, but pirates had derailed her off fate's course, wiping her future away.

But . . . Jack knew about her mysterious voice. She nibbled her lip. Did that mean Cannon also knew? Did the voice whisper to them too?

"Our war with pirates never ended. Not since the Galenite War. A death of one of their lords might work in our favour and weaken them finally." Erick's warmth settled her, as if he could see her worries splashed across her face.

"What did you want to tell us?" Kora asked, moving the subject along.

"The royal family of Azaria are sending a sentinel, to oversee the remaining expansion of the empire. You're to personally escort him across Aldara. Both of you." Erick's pointed gaze flickered between them. "I've had reports of exiles in the desert attacking camps near Scarlet Bay and the Southern Oasis. We can't risk anything happening to this sentinel. They will require protection at all costs. I cannot express the importance of this."

By the gods, this was intense.

"Expansion?" Her brows squished together.

"They intend to acquire the remaining islands," Blake spoke tensely, understanding fleeting across his face. "Our king is ready to become emperor."

Shock jolted through her bones. Ever since the Devanian Conquest ended over fifty years ago, it'd been the three islands banded together under the reign of the Citadel, acting as an extension of the royal Staghart family hidden away in Azaria, with Talmon as the lead, resulting in the Talmon Empire.

A select group of leaders, known as the viceroys, governed Talmon, Otrovia, and Aldara from Mossfell Castle, located in the heart of the Citadel. The governors of each noble house oversaw their protected lands and territories, and would report back to the viceroys of the comings and goings, and all that political nonsense Kora never understood.

She never paid that much attention to it all. But now . . . the king was making a gallant attempt at seizing the remaining unclaimed islands—Peril Cove, Calypso Islands, and Galen. To become Emperor Staghart of Azaria.

One united nation.

One empire.

"Indeed." Erick drew a breath. "The Aldara Council, and the Houses of Blackstone and Bellmoor have begun preparations for the final unification. We must protect the sentinel. And it's time to start decimating the pirates entirely."

"That's what I've been trying to do—"

Erick waved a sharp hand, cold ice leaking into the edges of his tone and eyes. "No, Kora. They've decreed that we now *kill* all pirates on sight. If any survive, they'll be executed—including any rebel who associates with them or assists them. No more trials. No more courts."

She blanched at his words. Jack had been lucky.

"They're walking dead men," Blake hissed at the mention of rebels.

"Or women," she added. Both males blinked at her. "What? A woman can't rebel and strive to topple a nation? How unkempt of her." She fluttered her neck drastically and Erick rolled his eyes, whilst Blake subtly hid a smirk, rubbing his mouth to prevent the curve surfacing.

It was no secret that not everyone agreed to the empire's rule on these islands. Resistance had increased over the past decade. The Azarian Islands had a tear down the middle of it, and Kora stood on the Talmon Empire's side, *against* the pirates. Intrepid unease unfurled in her core, as the threat of slaughter loomed on the horizon.

21

They had two days before they had to trek across Aldara to Whitestone Bay to meet the royal sentinel. The journey was five days by horseback, and five days back. Enough time before Kora could return to her cherished *Hell's Serpent*. Erick's sardonic tone had made her suspect her ship wasn't being repaired for two weeks, but he'd used it as a means to ground her to escort the sentinel. Otherwise, she'd have set sail this morning, fleeing to waters that greeted her with open arms, and soothed her scarred soul.

Blake pulled her into one of the shadowy alcoves of the many hallways of the manor. He shifted a metal plant stand that was overflowing with fern leaves, shielding them both from prying eyes. She tugged him into her embrace, their lips clashing, and a shudder vibrated through him beneath her touch.

Kora clung to his body, her hands sweeping across his shoulders and down his arms, entwining with his fingers. *Yes.* His thumb brushed along her knuckles, clasping her hands to his chest as he planted kisses along her jaw and down her neck.

She needed this. Needed *him*. After so much death and despair from their latest voyage, she needed that spark of life that sizzled between them. Needed his kisses to imbue her with his strength.

She needed to forget. Even just for a moment.

Heat sparked between her thighs and she jolted, knocking into him. "Sorry," she whispered, and he hissed, wincing as her fingers brushed his wounded side. Blake's gaze darkened and he pounced, the pain seemingly spurring his lust. He fisted her hair, craning her neck as his tongue caressed her mouth with desire. His moans echoed into her skull, and Kora's hands travelled below his waist, brushing the hard bulge growing.

"*Fuck*," he choked.

She smiled against his mouth, a giggle escaping her. Erick was still in the parlour down the hall, and the defiance caused the heat in her to blaze, wetness pooling beneath. She teased Blake's belt, and he jerked as she brazenly cupped his cock.

"*Asterya*," he growled. "Keep touching me like that and the servants will have to clean this floor."

"Maybe I want you to lose control." The words slipped from her mouth.

Blake's stare captured her, wreathing a chill skittering down her spine. He was always calm, always controlled, always collected. She wanted him as unravelled as her.

"Trust me, you don't want that." He unfurled from her body, checking the hallway for servants before straightening his shirt. "We need to be careful. If Erick saw us, he'd never let me within an inch of you again."

She nodded, uncomfortably wet between her legs, a passion unfulfilled cresting within. Blake peered at her, his gaze travelling downwards, darkening with desire. *Damn it, Erick.*

"Tonight. Meet me tonight. In the courtyard."

He reluctantly peeled away before she could answer, and quickly snuck through the winding hallways of the manor, returning to the barracks before Erick spotted him.

The scent of leather and petrichor lingered on her clothes as Kora stormed into her chambers, atop of the eastern tower. It was the only colourful room in the entire manor—Erick had succumbed to her every demand and whim for her sacred space.

What about green? It's more . . . fitting.

I hate green—no. This is what I want.

I just think that maybe it'd be better for you if—

I have amnesia Erick. Just let me have this.

A white domed ceiling connected to curved light-blue walls, meeting a terracotta tiled floor covered with sprawling blue rugs. A tunnelled passageway on the left led to the bathing chamber, and windows covered the curved wall to the right, her large bed nestled between them.

Trunks, full of history and fiction books—and weapons—were dotted about, along with an armoire, vanity table, and partitioned dressing area. Multitudes of candles burnt down to their wicks, wax spilling over the silver holders and melted onto the oak tops of her beside tables.

By the base of the nearest bedside, a cluster of wisteria and ivy leaves littered the floor. Opened green shutters lined the window above, and upon further inspection, the lock had been smashed open. She *had* climbed through the window last night. What a stupid idea that had been.

Kora followed the trail of leaves to her bed, and she gingerly touched the covers.

Dry.

She looked at the ceiling, where the curved arches of the dome met in the centre. A lone, eight-pointed, golden star hung from the centre, with golden rings banding the points together, a single jewel in its heart. No mysterious water floated up there.

Had it all been a dream?

And to think Erick tried enforcing the empire colours in here. She was sick of being surrounded by green and black. It felt too oppressive . . . too . . . she frowned, scratching her cheek. A shadow of a memory curled in her mind, shrivelling away before she could grasp its coils.

Keeping her gaze trained onto that very spot in the ceiling, she fell back onto the bed, a whiff of mint wafting up from her white covers. The talisman hummed against her flesh and she fished it from under her tunic. *Oh gods.* It was changing shape. It was still half gleaming teal, and half shimmering midnight, but the teardrop-shaped end had twisted, the spiral columns merging, taking on new, complex patterns. In the heart of the pendant, a subtle blue glow sparkled.

Kora tore the necklace over her head in a panic, hurtling it across the room, where it landed with a *thud* behind a trunk. Her heart fluttered as the blue hue died, fading into nothing. Alarming coolness crept through her bones, and she flexed her fingers as her joints oddly stiffened. The slumbering force within her slowly settled, blanketed with numbness, and she shakily ran her hands over her face.

She was insane. Utterly insane.

She *should* throw it away. Should smash it to pieces, and then bury those pieces so far away, in different locations so that they could never be recovered. Because, if she was caught with this charm, she would be hanged in an instant.

Magic was a threat to the kingdom. It couldn't be controlled. Magic was destructive. It was deadly. It was temptation. It was lust. It was greed. It was divine. It was beautiful. She needed to know more . . . *see* more.

Nibbling her lip, Kora hesitantly approached the wooden trunk, leaning over to glimpse the talisman. It had returned to its original form—a darkened-night shade of blue, and teardrop shaped. She picked it up, examining it. Had she imagined that, too? As her fingers gently traced the columns, a jolt of energy flew through her skin and, before her eyes, the talisman shone and moulded itself. Morphing.

Kora gasped as its dual colour returned, the end sharpening, twisting, *evolving.* Her core raged, as if it were reaching out to her. Hungrily. Her mind blanked, drowsiness sweeping over her eyes.

Instinctively, she placed the talisman back over her head, guided by an unknown force. The blue hue shone as she gracefully strolled to the window, her mind overwhelmingly empty. Except for a tiny scream, tearing from the depths of darkness of her broken mind. She couldn't feel her body, and her control evaporated as she watched through her own eyes with horror.

Wakeupwakeupwakeupwakeup.

Her arm raised, stretching, reaching to the sky with her palm flat out, and the waters of the fountain bubbled and rippled. She couldn't force her arms down. An invisible puppeteer was pulling the strings.

The ripple swelled, and the minty clear water trickled over the side, floating through the air. It trailed up the wisteria, twisting and turning, writhing with an unnerving aliveness before it latched onto Kora's palm, coiling around her arm like a vice.

It travelled and grew, until tendrils of water were snaking and circling all around her body, creating a shimmering clear armour as her uncontrolled body stared mindlessly out through the window. Dark spots dizzied her vision as she screamed from within her mental prison. *This can't be real. No.* She'd thought last night had been a dream but . . . *it was real?*

Was she a mage? *No.* It had to be this *thing* around her neck.

"*Remember,*" her mouth spoke, but it was not *her* voice. Kora cried from within, begging to be released from inky hands clasping at her soul.

"*Remember,*" it repeated with urgency. Suddenly, she fell, plummeting in an endless dark void. Her feet struck the sturdy terracotta tiles, the air of the open window graced her palm, and the coolness of the water circled her and rushed at her senses.

With a shuddering breath, as if she'd broken through deep water, her arm limply fell to her side and the water splashed to the floor, soaking into her rugs. Gaze transfixed on the fountain, she released a small, terrified sob as she placed one hand over her hammering chest. Over the dimming light of the talisman.

Utterly insane, indeed.

K ora stalked, her shoulders hunched and head bowed, winding through the narrow streets of the western side of the port town by Stormkeep Fortress. With a cloak covering her, she blended into the shadows of the leaning overhangs of crooked stores, mindfully skirting around any suspicious looking puddles.

After her spectacle with the fountain, she'd had to change again, this time opting for dark navy with golden stitching. Being seen in the empire's colours this close to the slums would guarantee a mobbing—or worse. Besides, her undergarments had been uncomfortably wet from her tryst with Blake.

A faint store bell rang several feet in front of her intended path, and she darted into a nearby alleyway. Peering around the corner, two males exited the Silvermaid's Emporium, chuckling to themselves as they held a peculiar glass bottle, filled with swirling, shimmering pink liquid.

"This'll do it," one spoke devilishly. "One sip of this, and I'll be married to Lady Tornton."

The other jostled him, swiping for the potion. "Hey! We paid half each—I'm using it, too."

"Oh really? On whom?" the first filthy beggar leered.

"I fancy Lady Tornton, too."

The two males halted by Kora's alleyway, and she sunk further into the shadows, grasping at the hood of her cloak to cover her glaring white hair.

"You can't steal my plan! I'm getting out of these shithole slums one way or another."

"You're just using Lady Tornton." The second beggar pushed him aside, plucking the potion from the former's grubby grasp. "I'm in *love.*"

The first male spat on the floor, croakily laughing. "In love with a lady? How?"

"I work in her manor. She just needs to . . . notice me . . . that's all. Then we'll be together, *ayterni.*" Hastened steps followed his voice along the cobbled stones. A potion that could cause someone to fall in love *forever?*

The first male cursed and lunged for the potion, igniting a sprawling fight, and the vial flew from their grasp, skittering across the waste-infested streets. Kora peeked from the shadows as they chased it between roving bodies walking up the path.

Dated stores lined the street, with market stalls popped up in front. Interspersing the buildings were aged, crumbling statues of the five Devani gods, their cracked hands turned out to accept prayers and offerings.

The western port town was all that remained of the old civilisation of Devania, before the conquest. Stormkeep Fortress had been erected in Azaria's image, made the new capital of Aldara, leaving the western town to fade into history where it turned squalid with poverty and disease.

Civilians yelled, kicking at the males, who shrieked as booted feet smashed the bottle, the shimmering liquid draining into the sewage systems. In response, the beggars leered, blaming each other for spending their final scrap of coins on the potion. Kora's lips pressed into a grim line. She wouldn't be surprised if they participated in the upcoming trials to compensate.

Kora slipped through the iron door of the Silvermaid's Emporium, and hung close to a darkened corner as she surveyed the store. It was one of the oldest buildings in the port town, achieving a grand three floors of varying trinkets, fabrics, and unique exotic jewellery from unknown lands—including spices that hailed from there, too. In addition to that was a secretive stash of weapons, available to those who were predisposed to appreciate the sharper things in life.

Shelves lined the walls, filled to the brim with the goods, broken apart by large glass cabinets displaying beautiful, shining geodes, impressively cut from the dangerous sea stacks of Narrowfen Pass.

Thick, wooden beams curved upwards from the paint peeling walls into the low ceiling, supporting the aging structure that Kora was sure was four—maybe five—hundred years older than her age. The Emporium had been here long before these lands had been united.

"Are you going to dither all day, or come greet me, child?"

The enticing items for sale weren't the only reason patrons frequented this store.

On the far side of the room, by a glass counter, stood Agatha Silvermaid. She was curvy, yet bony, with weathered and aging light-brown skin. Glimmering silver threads wove throughout her long, braided grey hair. Yet the striking thing about Agatha, were her all-white eyes.

"I may not be able to see, but I know you're there, Kora Cadell." Her voice was strong, and stern with a hoarseness Kora found comforting.

"Apologies, Agatha, I was ensuring we were alone." Kora stalked over to Agatha, placing a gentle hand on her thin arm. "*Sehwani,*" she spoke in Devanian.

"*Sehwani,*" Agatha replied secretively. Her white irises glinted mischievously with the use of the tongue of the gods. It was the first phrase Agatha had taught Kora, meaning one could see into another and observe their true self beneath their skin.

Kora's lips twitched in amusement. "I see you made those men a love potion."

Agatha waved a wrinkled hand, age spots blooming on her skin. Her knuckles were so swollen that her fingers had curved inwards, unable to straighten ever again.

"Gah, don't fret about that. I've ensured Lady Tornton's daily tonic has the ability of protection."

"Well, they broke the potion anyway."

Agatha smiled as she expertly navigated her way around, locking the store before leading Kora to a hidden room at the back through a small, narrow door by the spiral wooden stairs.

"You fiending thing," Kora chuckled as she sat down at a rounded table beside a slumbering fire.

It was a small, wooden box room, only big enough for a dark-stoned hearth, a small table with two chairs, that Agatha used for secret fortune readings, and a plush, red, velvet sofa, covered in knitted blankets. Drapes in dark hues of purple and red hung from the centre of the ceiling, cascading down before tying up in the four corners of the room.

"Business is business." Agatha brewed two cups of herbal tea on the hearth and placed them on the table, sliding into the chair opposite Kora. "Taxes are increasing every year. I need the coins. I'm an old, blind hag, you know."

Kora sat in silence, Agatha's blind stare weighing on her. For a blind female, she was highly perceptive, perhaps the most perceptive person Kora knew. Her skin itched beneath her golden embossed clothes. She would never experience the difficulty of making ends meet. She had the luxury of living with Erick, and being named the heir of the Cadell Manor and fortune, as well as the only female captain in the entire empire.

"For a blind old hag, you seem to be frequented a lot by patrons seeking . . . tonics."

"Gah," Agatha waved her off. "They pretend they don't understand what they're buying. That it's all just herbs and voodoo gibberish."

"Isn't it?"

Agatha's eyes sharpened, the whites intensely absorbing the space around Kora. She waved her hand again, brushing off Kora's remark. Agatha knew better than most what a person believed deep down, even when they wouldn't fully admit it. She just . . . *knew* things.

Kora's eyes snagged on the misshapen bony hands connected to Agatha's otherwise strong, yet aged body. Soon, they'd become so swollen, and too painful to move, and she wouldn't be able to continue with the Emporium.

Her heart skittered at the thought of someone else running the store. It was one of her safe havens on land to explore who she was; to read and learn about her passions for ancient and mythological history. Maybe she could offer Agatha a room at the manor? Perhaps she'd grow fond of the courtyard, surrounded by nature and herbs to use for her potion swindling.

"You smell different," Agatha quipped.

Kora startled at the comment. "Is that bad?" She sniffed her own pits, but was graced with sweet scents of jasmine and orange blossom.

Agatha let out a sigh. "Not your scent, you silly child. I can smell your posh soap from here." She wrinkled her nose. "Your essence is different."

"My . . . *essence?*"

Rolling her eyes, Agatha continued. "Everyone has an essence—a vitality of who they are, deep in their core. It is our very being. Some say it is where our souls are born." Agatha held out her knobbly palm on the table for Kora to place her hand on top. "Some people have special essences that house spectacular gifts—"

Once their flesh touched, Agatha stopped talking and sharply inhaled. Her white eyes met Kora's dead on, and she swallowed, fidgeting under that stare, and Kora could see the faint outline of where Agatha's pupils and irises should be.

"What is on your neck?" Agatha spoke slowly, thickly.

"What?" Tension seized Kora. She couldn't tell anyone what had recently happened. "Nothing? There's nothing."

"Do not lie to me," Agatha inhaled deeply, closing her eyes. "You carry something dark and powerful. Maybe dangerous."

Kora's hand flew to her chest, gripping the talisman as if she could shield it from Agatha's perception, whilst Agatha pressed into Kora's other hand, her long nails biting into her skin.

No, no, no.

What if Agatha revealed her to the empire? She needed the money. They would send Kora to Deadwater Prison for possession of a potentially powerful trinket—a magical charm. Or maybe worse. Mages were hunted and executed right in front of the king. Dragged across the islands and sea to the vast continent, knowing they were being hauled to their death during the weeks it took to make the journey.

All so the king could witness it.

"No . . . Agatha," Kora tried pulling her hand from her firm, knuckled grip. "Please! I-I don't know what it is." She stumbled for words, desperately seeking for where Agatha's allegiance sat. She may have taught her the history of Devania, but it didn't mean she wouldn't sell her out to survive the poverty rife in these streets.

Agatha yanked her forwards, the table painfully pressing into Kora's ribs. Hovering near Kora's head and neck, Agatha breathed in Kora's scent—her *essence*—and her eyes widened. She clicked her teeth and abruptly let go.

"Where did you find *that*?" Each word was clipped, and Kora sat back shakily.

Agatha had always been stern, sometimes scolding, but she'd never been aggressive towards Kora. She'd always displayed a fondness towards her, a sympathy for her unrecovered memories, and it was here in Agatha's Emporium that Kora had discovered her passion for reading and learning, especially about the ancient gods and the history of magic—or lack thereof.

The Devanian magic system had been broken into five factions. The first blessed from the gods in the form of the elements, and they bestowed it on the first humans that walked their lands as a welcome gift. Shortly after, witches evolved and emerged, honing their own special grasp on magic through the written hand, and chants echoed from their mouths, learning how to channel the magic without the blessings of the gods.

What interested Kora more were the fables. When the gods withered and faded, they breathed their final dregs of power into the land, and from it sprung three new divisions of power that blended with humans. She'd never discovered readings on what each faction contained, only that they were named the physical, illusion, and divine—along with elemental powers and witches. Creating the five forces.

But humans had grown greedy and lustful in their conquest for power. The gods' gift wasted upon their narrow-minded souls. They stopped praying, stopped granting offerings to the gods who'd blessed their ancestors, and magic died, withering like rotted roots in blighted lands. The Devanian scholars faded away along with the gods, and then the islands were united by Admiral Darkon during the longest war.

It was a mystery as to how many mages remained. Either their power had been leached through generations of ignorance to the divine, or executed by those who could never wield it. It was a historic tale Kora had delighted in frequently. And a pastime she'd kept secret from Erick, Blake, and Bree for the whole ten years of her carefully constructed new life.

"I found it on a pirate ship." She couldn't say too much without giving away valuable information.

Agatha's lips pulled back in a grimace. "That's a relic from the Silver Sisters clan, in the Shannara Territory."

Kora stilled. The most vicious, feral, and highly organised of the witch clans. Surely the witches wouldn't have gifted an ancient relic to Cannon? It must've been stolen.

"*What is it?*" Kora asked, not daring to look down at her chest in fear the talisman would come alive and swallow her whole. Her heart pounded.

"A vessel to contain formidable power. A way for mortals to harness gifts that couldn't be bestowed upon them by the ancient gods."

What was Cannon doing with a talisman like this? Did he have any idea of the power he beheld in a necklace casually discarded in a chest?

"Magic doesn't exist." *Anymore.*

But . . . maybe it did? She'd manipulated water. It had terrified her, and something otherworldly had guided her hand, but it'd still happened. This talisman had to be doing something to her, making her hallucinate or channel some kind of presence, like the voice.

As far as she knew, no one else still prayed to the mysterious beings that created these lands—but perhaps the witches did? The last she'd heard, they were potion swindlers like Agatha, but also practised ritualism, and conducted wild voodoo chanting to scare off trespassers.

Nothing more than filthy wenches, as Blake would say.

"Don't speak of that drivel *he* has been feeding into your mind," Agatha snapped, spitting the words. "You do not come to me, to my home, for all these years, and still insist that magic isn't real. That the history I have taught you is lies. Magical power never disappears, not completely. It is simply lost and reborn."

"I'm sorry," Kora bristled, her mask creeping in at the edges. "I must continue with this façade. You know citizens who believe in the gods are outlawed. Exiled to the Silent Tundra for heresy, or Deadwater Prison . . . or hanged."

Agatha huffed at the mention of heresy. To believe in the gods was to deny King Staghart—Emperor Staghart soon—the chance to be regarded as one. Kora huffed with her. There had been endless writings discovered on the Devani gods, and the language from their reigning era still lingered to this day. Secretly. Despite that, it *existed*. It was a history—true history—that the empire denied.

"I-I don't understand. This necklace is harnessing power from someone?"

A small smile bloomed on Agatha's lips. "No child, it is harnessing power from *you*."

The words she dreaded to hear.

"I don't have any powers! I'm not a mage," Kora denied, shaking her head, her ears ringing at the mere thought.

"You may not understand it yet, you may not see it yet, but it *is* there, deep within you. I can smell it." Agatha knowingly looked down, as if she could see right through Kora to her core.

Where *something* rumbled back, gleefully attentive.

She did know it. She'd *seen* it.

The water in the fountain. The water she'd choked on in the medical bay. The seas that ebbed and flowed, favouring her commands. The tide always on her side wherever she sailed. The splashing laps of water that flicked at her legs whenever she wandered along the bay. The thought of being contained to land, to forests, to dry deserts, made her stomach churn, and drove her to dive into the nearest lake and swim until she was surrounded with the expanse of blue.

"The empire may have tried their hardest to quash magic from this world, but it'll return. Power will be reborn," Agatha said.

Kora frowned. "Magic disappeared long before the empire spread through the islands. It was eons ago. Before the conquest."

Agatha paused, clasping her mangled hands together. "A lesson for another time. We need to figure out what to do with *it*." Her all-seeing blind eyes warily gazed on the talisman, as if it could hear them speaking.

"What does it all mean? What will this talisman do to me?" Kora's voice strained.

Agatha shrugged. "I don't know much, only that it will continue to absorb from you the longer you wear it. You have an affinity with a specific power, and it will leach whatever it can from you. You must keep it close. *Do not* let anyone see it. And try to not use your power too much."

"How can I get rid of it?" Kora pleaded. "How can I learn more?" The need, the drive, to discover more propelled her forward. A thirst for knowledge and truth that was constantly parched.

"You'll have to ask the Silver Sisters. For they created many of these vessels for mankind, and they guard them with their lives. I don't believe simply throwing it away will be wise. If your power is already leaking into it . . . you don't want it falling into the wrong hands," Agatha warned.

Travelling to the Shannara Territory was an ordeal. She had ten days to escort the royal sentinel across Aldara before she could return to *Hell's Serpent* and sail north for answers, and she was already building a list of questions for the sisters in her mind. To discover what they knew about the talismans, what it meant for her, and how she could safely dispose of it. Why she even had these powers.

"Why is this happening now? Surely mages manifest their powers at a younger age." Facts surfaced in Kora's mind from the many dusty tomes stashed away under Agatha's creaky floorboards.

Agatha's smile broadened wickedly. "Who's to say it hasn't?"

Kora traced her scar, following it from her temple to where it curled around her eye and cheek. A tingling sensation ran along the length of the scar, to the base of her skull and down her spine.

Had she been a mage before she lost her memory?

Were her family mages? Was that why they'd been

murdered?

Who am I?

"*Remember* . . ." the voice echoed in her mind. It was a fleeting whisper, so quiet Kora was unsure if she'd heard it. Agatha shifted in her stool, her knobbly knuckles grazing the ends of her braid.

Gods, she was getting a headache.

"I have to venture across the land soon, I'll be gone a couple weeks," Kora mumbled, sipping her tea now it had cooled, in hopes it would ease her swimming mind.

She reached into the hidden pocket lining the inside of the cloak, and dropped a small bag of silver bits onto the table. The sound perked Agatha up, and she fumbled for Kora, clasping at her forearm in gratitude.

"Thank you, my dear."

If Agatha could see, she'd realise the coins donned the symbol of *Demon Sea Siren*, stolen from Captain Cannon's personal stash of loot hidden within his desk. It was all Kora could offer her for now.

She would visit Agatha whenever she made port at Stormkeep Fortress and give her anything she could shave off the top of *Hell's Serpent's* plunders to help her get by. Agatha had granted Kora a haven, a place to explore and learn. She'd taught her the tales of Devani gods, the creation of the islands, and the beautiful language they spoke. Agatha had even let her assist in potion swindling, learning what herbs contained medicinal remedies, and which could cause a bout of sickness, paralysis, or even death.

Kora always presumed Agatha saw her as a daughter she never had—or may had lost once. Whenever she tried to pry into Agatha's past, she was met with a book flying across the room straight for her head, or the slam of the back door where Agatha would curl up and hide beneath her pile of blankets on her red velvet sofa and weep softly.

Kora knew better than to creep up on a crying, blind female with terrifyingly precise aim.

"I'll get you some books for research." Agatha rose from her chair, lifting her skirts and tapping on the floorboards with her heeled boot until a hollow sound followed. "Research is vital for learning. You may need all the help you can get before you reach the Silver Sisters."

Kora knelt, assisting Agatha in collecting two leather-bound tomes, the squared edges covered in rusted iron metal. One was dark blue, the other dark green, both embossed with flakes of pure gold into the lettering. It was hard not to let her eyes bulge from their sockets. The scripture was in Devanian, and she frowned, trying to understand the complexity of the words.

Agatha gently placed her hand on Kora's shoulder. "Don't worry, it'll come to you. I expect these returned here—in *pristine* condition."

Kora sheepishly smiled, remembering a time she'd accidentally set one of Agatha's 'spell' books on fire by dropping it in a puddle of spilt oil near the blacksmith's, followed by knocking over a lit lantern. Agatha had made her sweep and clean the floors of the entire Emporium for a month.

"I'll miss you," she admitted.

Agatha let out a single laugh and traced Kora's face, memorising the planes of her features. Her crooked fingers hovered over her cheekbones, lightly touching each one, before planting a kiss above each of her fluttering eyes.

"So will I, my child. Please be careful." Agatha placed a curled hand on Kora's chest, resting gently on the talisman, and sharply inhaled before retreating, wistfully wishing her a well voyage.

As Kora slipped into the darkening streets of the decrepit town, she couldn't shake the feeling of unease growing and seeping into the rest of her body.

23

Night had fallen, the stars shone brightly, and the moon beamed a pale, glistening light across the tiled courtyard of Cadell Manor. Kora lingered beneath a large lemon tree, her cloak blending her into the darkness as she stood watch, fixated on the climbing wisteria of the eastern tower.

Lit lanterns, attached to the exterior walls of the manor, created soft amber circles, intermittently illuminating the grounds. Kora peered at the dark night sky and her eyes strained, seeking out the familiar twinkle of the stars.

Thanos, please let him be there, please be happy and resting, she prayed, closing her eyes. When they opened, she clasped her hand over her mouth, holding in a scream as a tall dark figure smiled down at her, the whites of his teeth visible in the night.

"Having a nap?" Blake teased.

Kora swatted his arm. "You scared me half to death!"

"Well . . . we certainly wouldn't want that," his voice lowered, and a shiver ran through her as he stepped underneath the lush canopy of the lemon tree. He was so close their breath mingled in the chilled air, creating a gentle puff of smoke.

Blake cupped her cheek as he lowered his face to rest his forehead against hers. He inhaled deeply and released a sigh, steadying himself against her as she wrapped her fingers around his wrist, savouring his warmth. They stood for a while, holding each other, their breathing falling into synchronicity with their eyes shut.

"A lot is happening," he broke the silence. "I'm worried I . . . I won't be able to keep you safe much longer, *asterya*."

"I can look after myself," Kora retorted.

"Things are changing, Kora." Blake's emerald eyes turned as sharp as his tone. "If the king is trying to finally become emperor, it could cause *a lot* of unease around here. On top of that, lower societies are rife with mutiny. Wenches and pirates are allying . . . Galen is returning to the world."

She bristled at his words. She'd blocked the council's decree of slaughter from her mind for most of the day, but the hallow orders flooded back. They were *her* orders. She would have to stoop low, as far as mindless execution, killing pirates, and rebels, and anyone associated with them.

That would make them no better than Galen. She favoured witnessing enemies suffer in the courts and trials, followed by serving their penance in prison. Death was only admirable in warfare when her own life was on the line.

"Surely the continent uniting us *all* is a good thing?"

Blake's jaw twitched. "Maybe not. We've been commanded and lead by the viceroys since the conquest. The king and his ancestors haven't stepped foot on this land in *decades*. The viceroys have become comfortable here. The noble houses, too. Change may not be welcomed."

"Such old, stubborn bastards. How'd you know this?"

"I have connections. Being a champion of the Darkoning Trials has its perks." He winked, attempting to lighten the mood, but Kora turned surly at the memory of failing to become the champion of the trials, finishing second in Blake's shadow. He followed with a fluttering kiss to her cheek, and she waved him off with a small chuckle.

"You said there are mutinies?"

Blake nodded, his fingers trailing up her arms as he spoke. "Since we've returned to Aldara, I've heard reports in the barracks that there's been more resistance in the slums, Scarlet Bay, and the workhouses near Blackstone Reef. It stretches as far as the mining outposts in Talmon, as well. Pirates are liberating workers, and recruiting them to join their crew."

She gasped. Had she murdered civilians of the Azarian Islands on board *Demon Sea Siren*? They'd taken a chance of freedom from the workhouses . . . only to be obliterated by *her*. Blake's hands rested on her shoulders, squeezing lightly.

"If they join the crew, then they are pirates," he spoke firmly, reading the thoughts openly flitting across her face. Kora nodded once, painfully swallowing her guilt.

"Have you been to the lower district lately?"

"Why would I go there?" His hands tensed on her shoulders. "I have no reason to go."

"Blake, your family. They could be involved in the resistance movements. They could be hurt or—"

"They're not," he cut her off sharply. "Don't concern yourself with that."

Kora stumbled back at the coldness of his words, and she scanned his face, but it'd smoothed out into cold indifference. At her withdrawal, Blake sighed, looking at the dried grass and soil beneath their booted feet. He flexed his fingers, and they brushed the dainty leaves of the mint bushes surrounding them.

"I'm sorry . . . I don't like talking about it—about *them*."

His hands quivered, and he took a step towards her. A low-hanging lemon gently bounced against his head, and he reached for the yellow fruit, his hand enveloping it as he snapped it off the branch. Blake held it out to her and she took it tentatively. It was much larger in her hand, and she was surprised by the heavy weight of it as she clasped the peace offering between them.

"I'm sorry for pushing," Kora murmured. "I understand your past is difficult."

Their eyes met, and the electrifying connection passed between them. They both possessed secretive, troublesome pasts that pained them. They both yearned for escape from the shadows haunting them, finding solace within each other's arms.

A strong breeze drifted through the courtyard and the lemon trees groaned, thick green leaves falling from the gust and floating around Blake as his raven hair ruffled. She instinctively reached up, pushing his hair out of his dazzling eyes.

He leaned into her touch as the leaves caught in his hair and settled on his shoulders, making the green of his eyes blaze. He tugged her forward eagerly, and she dropped the large lemon, its fall cushioned by the grass. Her arms wrapped around his neck as his lips captured hers.

The leaves fell from his hair, tickling her, and she was enveloped in the swath of green nature. Blake deepened the kiss, backing Kora towards the trunk of the nearest tree, his hands reaching up to grasp the lowest branches, pinning her in the middle from all sides.

The trunk curved, moulding to her body. Its branches and shrouds of leaves closing in on her from everywhere, touching her skin. An earthy darkness scraped its talons down her back—or was she imagining it? Her muscles coiled as the threat of a wooden cage loomed.

Blake gripped the branches so tight his knuckles turned

white, and he inhaled deeply, seeming to consume the scent of lemon and mint, savouring the moment. Kora knew instinctively he felt more at ease on land, within nature.

Just as he would feel more at ease as commander of the armies, instead of her first mate. But those words between them always laid unspoken. His future always shrouded in darkness, always uncertain. Always dependent on *her*. He'd repeatedly assured her he was content by her side, but with the king's expansion . . . now she wasn't so sure.

A flurrying trail of kisses dragged her from her thoughts.

Kora's hands explored down the length of his chest, and brushed against his groin teasingly. Blake jerked at the sensation, causing another cascade of leaves around them and he smiled wickedly, a growl echoing from their rendezvous in the hallway. Her core ached, desperate for release, and heat rushed down to the apex of her thighs.

"I can't get enough of you," he moaned, his body flush against hers.

The smell of lemon and mint coursed through the air, and she nipped Blake's lip excitedly in the heat of passionate kissing. Gods, he was so handsome. She was so lucky to have found him, to be with him, through the horrors of losing her family, her memory . . . her life. She'd come out the other side, avenging her family one pirate at a time, with Blake supporting her the whole way.

She would be dead without him. Dead in the barren pits of the Darkoning Trials. Dead at the bottom of the ocean in Davy Jones' Locker after warfare with pirates. She wouldn't reside in the spirit realm of Umbra with her lost loved ones or Finlay. Not after everything she'd done. Not after killing innocents onboard *Demon Sea Siren*.

Jack was right—she was a murderer.

"Are you here with me?" Blake reared back, stroking his thumbs across her cheeks as her mind soared.

No better than a filthy pirate. No better than the killers of her family. She didn't deserve to be captain. Not really. She didn't deserve the friendship Finlay had offered. Didn't deserve the towering male before her who would follow her to the ends of the earth. Kora's heart clenched, her throat constricting with overwhelming emotion and a familiar throb in her head.

Water splashed in the distance and she froze.

"What is it? Is someone coming?" Blake scanned the courtyard.

She risked a sideways look towards the trickling fountain. Puddles of water soaked the tiled floor, stretching across and blending into an oblong shape, reaching in their direction. As if it had been crawling towards them.

"No—nothing. I thought I heard something."

Blake's eyes swept over the fountain and training grounds through the archway before he pulled away, and Kora's skin pimpled at the chilled air between their now separated bodies. He rotated his arm on his wounded side and winced.

"Are you still hurt?"

"I'm still healing. I'll be fine for the journey." He tapped his side lightly. It was remarkable how quickly he was healing, considering how badly he'd been sliced open by his own sword. Lucky bastard. "By the way, we were personally asked for this escort of the sentinel."

Her brows raised in surprise. "Who requested us?"

Her real question lingered beneath—who'd requested *her*, a female, to escort the royal sentinel? *The royal hound, more like.* Come to sniff about their business.

"A viceroy in the Citadel. It was all Erick would say."

"Our reputation precedes us," she mused. They had certainly made an impact at the trials as a combat duo, and now as leaders of *Hell's Serpent.* Despite her annoyance at being grounded upon land, she thrummed with the thrill of importance. If she nailed this escort, it would be another rung climbed on the ladder to admiral.

"It seems so." Blake's lips quirked with amusement, but quickly faded as a light flashed on in the lower levels of the manor. "I must go. They'll notice something amiss in the barracks if I'm gone too long."

Kora swallowed her disappointment. They would have ten days together soon, but then she would have to find a way to sail to Shannara without Erick knowing, and without Blake *at all.* He'd be gods-damned before he'd let her sail to the witches' territory. Guilt joined disappointment, and she loosened a breath before the emotions devoured her completely.

Blake mistook her sigh and placed his hand on the base of her neck, his thumb stroking up her throat. "I'll see you the day after tomorrow, my *asterya.* Then we'll have five days alone together." His eyes glinted as a sly smile stretched his face. "We can do whatever we want in the desert."

"Why not tomorrow?" Kora clamped down on her whiny tone. Five days alone with him was exciting, a real chance to explore who they were together. And a chance to finally unite intimately before she had to leave. But her ache burned so viciously she wasn't sure if she could wait till then.

"The captain of the barracks has requested I sit in to oversee training of the latest recruits before I disappear again." Blake feignedly smiled.

As the champion of the trials, and an excellent swordsman, he was regarded as a fine soldier and commander of armies. Yet he chose the naval military as his career, all so that he could be closer to her. It didn't prevent officers grabbing his attention whenever they made port, to participate in training cadets, and approving strategic plans for the empire's armies.

Kora offered a small smile. "The day after tomorrow then."

"At first light."

Darkness. Shadows. Fear.

She writhed in the bed. White silk sheets clung to her sweat-flushed skin. They wrapped around her like a coiled, slimy snake.

Out. She had to get out.

That thing lurked in the doorway to the chamber. Opulence of gold and moss covered every stone wall, every crevice.

She shouldn't be here.

Anywhere but here.

Her vision narrowed . . . tunnelled. Black encroaching on the corners of her sight. Her breathing caught in her throat as she screamed at the brush of hesitant, shaking fingers against her head.

Burning. Fire. Pain.

So much pain.

"She's dying!" a strong voice pierced through the veil of agony smothering her.

"The healers are on their way," the pillar of darkness spoke. A booming, yet chilling voice.

Wet. She was wet. Her long hair was plastered to her head and neck. Red. Why was it red?

"We can't lose her," the warm, strong voice echoed through her mind. Cold. She was so cold. His fingers pushed her hair back carefully and she moaned in pain. "She's fading quickly, she's leaving this realm."

The living statue of darkness spooled into the room, searching, reaching. It crawled up the bed, tentatively teasing around her body.

Get out.

Run.

"*Go away,*" *she rasped.*

Her lips were cracked and dry. Blood trickled from the corner of her mouth. Tired, so tired. The bright welcome of the gods lurked nearby. Maybe if she just closed her eyes and rested for a moment, she could gain the strength to fight back.

"*I'll see to it that she doesn't.*"

The darkness began enveloping her, wrapping around her head, sinking into the gaping wound by her temple, which was padded and stuffed with blood-soaked gauze. She endlessly screamed. A chilling, blood-curdling sound.

Out. Out. Out.

A pair of strong hands held her down, tying her hands to the corners of the wooden headboard whilst she convulsed from the invasion of her mind. Her soul. Her essence.

Get home. Run home.

*Her mind was sawn in half. Inky black tendrils snaked across her dazzling surface. A flare of agony—*snap.

Home. Get home to—who?

Remember—*what?*

Get out of my—*who was she?*

Searing pain lashed through the side of her head. Darkness swept over her . . . her mind went utterly blank.

Peace. Floating. Calm.

"*I'm sorry,*" *the warm voice whispered near her blood-streaked face.* "*I'm so sorry,*" *his voice cracked, broken with tears leaking from striking brown eyes.*

"*She won't be going anywhere now. Keep an eye on her.*" *The darkness slithered away from her and through the open golden doorway.*

Her eyes fluttered open for a moment.

"*Who are you . . . where am I?*" *she croaked with dryness.*

The male sobbed, telling her she was home. This was home. Home.

The tunnelling vision devoured her as healers frantically poured into the room, and she fell into a blank unconsciousness. No memories. No dreams. No past to relive.

24

Kora's scar throbbed all morning.

She relentlessly rubbed at her temples in circular motions, a salve of arnica she'd applied earlier coating her skin. Her headaches were getting worse, they hadn't been this bad since her recovery all those years ago.

A cup of herbal tea rested on the iron garden table before her, steam wafting into the air. Erick had allowed her to sleep in today, deciding the journey across the desert required a proper day's rest beforehand. *Thank the gods.*

It didn't stop Bree visiting and blabbering in her ears all day though.

"—and I said, I wouldn't be marrying any old beanstalk they found. Can you imagine? Me married to a noble lord who likes gardening?" Bree pursed her lips as she fluttered her lace white fan under the high sun. "Kora? Are you listening to me?"

"Marriage. Beanstalk," Kora murmured back, cupping her warm tea.

"Are you well?"

Bree continued to wave her fan against her exposed chest. She was a vision in white today. A simple milk-maid style gown, with a low, lacy sweeping neckline. Short puffy sleeves, with intricate strips of silver, laced around her arms, connecting to jewelled cuffs at her wrists. The dress flowed from her bodice, with dainty embellishments of silver woven throughout. Her braided hair was tied up, the gold hoops swapped for sleek silver tubes.

"Yes, I'm just . . . not sleeping well."

Kora glanced down at her usual tunic and trousers attire. She preferred her jerkins and breeches, but they were only for sailing.

Splatters of mud crusted the hem of her trousers, and she picked at some lint on her side. It wasn't that she was averse to dresses—if anything she'd love to try new styles, but it was enforced by Erick she should maintain this illusion of masculinity, of leadership and power, by dressing and styling her hair this way.

She did like how the leather jerkins fitted her body, strengthening her back, especially when her harness was attached with her blades. Her mind and body free, surrounded by peers who usually paid her no mind, except for the occasional glance at her chest or between her legs, but a glint of her blade would avert their gazes.

But when on land? She was restricted to stiff fabric, her limbs unable to manoeuvre as freely, whilst judgement poured from society that her two legs were visible, and not shrouded beneath layers of skirts.

Bree eloquently drank from her tea, her movements poised, her hands graceful. Kora placed her cup down, the porcelain rattling from the movement. She was so heavy-handed and rough. Even their hands in comparison made her pause. Bree's nails were pristine and perfectly edged, with supple, smooth skin that males would die to feel wrapped around their girths.

Kora curled a loop of hair around her finger, using it to cover a thick scar running down the length of skin. Maybe she should start wearing gloves? Salvage whatever unmarred skin she had left? Her hair was beginning to grow past her ears, and wisps hung across her forehead, which she'd attempted to shape in a flattering way.

Bree's bright, sky-blue eyes tracked the movement. "Has Erick finally given up on making you look like a boy?"

Kora spluttered on her tea. "I don't look like a boy!" She had the curves to prove it, even if he'd insisted she wear a chest binder during her first year sailing. She had promptly burnt it in the training garden, furious at the suppression. But he always claimed it was for her own protection.

"I can loan you some dresses if you like." Bree raked her stare over Kora. "I'll have them tailored, of course." They would be trailing on the floor if Kora wore them. Bree's tall, slender legs ensured she matched most males in height, but a flicker of daring hope bloomed. She'd like to see herself in Bree's attire. A chance to feel beautiful, and feminine, instead of just *one of the lads.*

"Besides, you'll have to wear whichever dress I choose when I get married."

Kora's eyes flickered up questioningly. "So, you *are* getting married?"

Bree waved a jewel-adorned hand. "Maybe. Probably. My parents keep pushing the idea. They've received news of the king's advancement on the remaining islands, and want me to marry into another nobility to create a *fortified front*."

"And their current choice?"

"That green-thumbed son of the House of Bellmoor. Cedar, I think," Bree muttered, her fan flicking sharply in her hand. "He's a beanstalk. A weed. I want a *man*. I want someone who's strong. Powerful."

"Careful what you wish for. Are there no other contenders?"

The noble Bellmoor family resided near the Ebonmoor Mountains. Favouring nature and the green pastures, they were the leading house in farming. Their territory expanded from the sacred mountains down to Whitestone Bay, representing the connecting bridge between Aldara and continent of Azaria. As one of the oldest houses within the noble circles, they rarely frequented any kind of public appearances, always choosing to send messages via hawk instead.

Kora could get on board with their introverted nature.

"There's the House of Barron, but my father wants me to marry into somewhere further ashore. He has a wayward son, apparently."

The Barrons were leaders in the naval military. The governor of the house—Admiral Barron—was the current leader of the Talmon Empire's armadas, and whom Erick directly reported to. The members of the Barron family also lived in the Citadel, along with the Hydraforts, who were the overseers of finance and business.

"What about the Ironguards?" Kora propped her feet up on the chair beside her as she basked in the hot summer sun.

The grass was more luscious and greener in this garden on the western side of the manor, as it was particularly used for hosting guests—which was not a regular occurrence for the Cadells.

Thick green hedges, and bushes full of bountiful flowers, including hydrangeas of all colours, covered all four stoned walls, along with small, herbal patches by the arched entryway leading to the courtyard in the northern stretch.

"*Please*, they have no brains between their ears. I'd bare feral children who'd beat people with iron sticks," Bree chided as she sipped her tea.

Servants lingered by the double glass doorway leading from

the parlour room, watching Bree's every movement. The thick black drapes flapped in a gentle breeze, and Kora made a small noise of amusement at Bree's retort.

The House of Ironguard ran the mines and the outposts across all the empire's islands. They were experts in crafting weaponry, as well as raising soldiers bred to enter the Darkoning Trials and survive it as champions. The epitome of brute strength, they sought glory in death on battlefields. They favoured the territory above Shannara, using their brutality and lethal weaponry as a force to prevent the witches from invading them, but they also stationed themselves at outposts across the lands.

"Is it too much to ask for?" Bree audibly sighed, her bosom heaving. "I want someone who makes my heart flutter. I want to be swooned. To feel that rush of heat from when he enters the room. I want to know what it feels like to be ready to *die* for someone, and to know he would do the same. To have every aching, *crushing*, thought to be wholly consumed by him."

Kora stared back at Bree wide-eyed. Since when had Bree become so . . . *romantic*? For the past few years, Bree had displayed a knack for business, assisting her father in elevating their family's outreach—and their coffers.

Since Bree became of age, she'd channelled all her efforts into proving to her father that one day she could become governess of the household—and their fortune. Kora frequently revelled in how they were both mastering the world as females.

But now? She was dead set on a marriage. Kora inwardly cringed.

"You've given this some thought." She winked at her friend. "Painful thoughts, at that."

Bree snapped her fan shut. "Perhaps. What about you? Any men courting you yet?"

Blake Marwood. Champion. Leader. Amazing kisser.

Kora spilled hot tea down her tunic as visions of Blake kissing her in the hallways of the manor invaded her mind. She cursed, shakily placing the cup back on its saucer. Far too dainty and fragile for her to handle. She needed a stein of ale. She dismissed the hovering servants, telling them she didn't need their help as they began peeling from their waiting stations.

A devilish smile curved Bree's luscious lips. "I knew it! I knew all those weeks sailing weren't just boring long days staring at the sea."

Looking at the sea was anything but boring for Kora.

"No. No . . . there's no one. I've told you before, they forbid against forming relationships in the armada."

"Rules are meant to be broken."

Bree giggled on her seat. Her intrigue and enthusiasm made Kora's breathing hitch as thoughts of Blake continued washing over her, followed by a wave of discomfort. Her headache speared through her mind, the pain increasing. Her chest ached, and she rubbed the spot above where the talisman rested.

"Tell me." Bree leaned forward. "Who has captured your heart?" She clasped Kora's free hand, her nails biting her skin. Bree's face had smoothed out, her smile vanishing as her grasp tightened with each passing second. "Tell me!" she demanded.

Kora paused, hesitation sweeping over her, and she was surprised by her own reluctance to divulge her best friend with all the details of her and Blake. It was *forbidden*, so the more secret it was, the better off they'd be. Even the heiress of the House of Hydrafort wouldn't be able to keep this a secret, friendship aside. Nobles were gossips through and through. Anything to throw their peers to the jaws of judgement and advance into the spotlight of desire.

She couldn't risk her relationship with Blake, or her chance at becoming admiral. Bree may be her best friend, but she was a noble. A different class. They were an entirely different species to the remaining island dwellers.

Yet something else . . . something unfamiliar niggled at Kora, and a lance of pain flashed from her throbbing temple. She hissed, tearing her hand from Bree's crippling grip, and grasped the side of her head as she bowed over. The pain relentlessly washed over her, and a small crack in her mind split open.

"*Remember, remember, remember, remember.*"

The voice chanted repeatedly. A familiar, deep, sweeping tone, growing louder and louder until the fountain in the courtyard to their left spluttered before turning off with eerie silence. Water cascaded over the stoned edges, spilling out onto the mosaic tiles and flooding the courtyard, spearing straight towards the western garden. The scent of rain clouds and steel stuffed up her senses, and Kora hacked a cough, rubbing at her nose from the invading smell.

A small droplet of blood stained her hand, and she quickly wiped it away on her trousers.

"What on earth . . ." Bree placed a comforting hand on Kora's back. "Kora, can you get up? Something's wrong with your fountain."

Bree's faint voice cried for help from the servants, who rapidly filed out into the courtyard, inspecting the fountain, and mopping the water in unified formation. Something within Kora lurched with a sudden urge to reach out and touch the water. To cover herself with it—to stop them from wiping it away.

"My head . . ." Kora moaned.

The mental crack slowly sealed up as she fought to wrestle control, one hand clasping at the talisman under her tunic.

This is my body. My mind. Get out.

"I'll call for a healer!" Bree's hands fluttered near her friend's face, her eyes full of concern.

"No, I'll be fine." Kora gritted her teeth and straightened. "It's starting to ease already."

"You don't look fine," Bree snapped.

"Stop." With the pain ebbing away, she twirled in front of Bree. "See? As I said, I've not been sleeping well."

Bree's bright, insightful eyes took a grand sweep of Kora, briefly hovering at her pink curling scar. "I've decided what your remedy is."

Kora raised a brow in curiosity.

With a sweet smile, Bree said, "A glass of ale."

Kora laughed, already feeling the crunching pain fade. She held out her arm. "If my lady would walk with me? I know just the place."

"I shall, kind sir." Bree curtseyed, fluttering her fan exaggeratively.

Kora pinched at the *sir*. She would never admit her lack of femininity was a sore spot, especially in Bree's overflowingly feminine presence. Several servant's eyes bulged at Bree bowing before Kora, and she rolled her eyes at the remark.

But the sting taunted her in the back of her mind, seeding doubt. Was her masculinity the issue barricading the intimacy between her and Blake? Why didn't he want to lose control? Was she not enough for him?

Together they walked arm in arm, down the lush hill from the mid-district manors and towards the edge of the port town, with Bree's guards silently in tow. Beams of sunlight glinted off the glittering turquoise ocean sprawling behind the town, and Kora drank the sight in, ambling along.

Wood and stone buildings painted varying shades of green, blue, purple, and red breathed vibrancy into the town. To their right, the pale stone of the towering fortress reflected the light of the sun before greeting sloping hills leading to the lower district on their left.

A tall thick wall of stone separated the paths to the districts and fortress from the port town—a third line of defence. Soldiers guarding the wall gate dipped their heads, their eyes widening at Bree Hydrafort gliding through the tall, iron-enforced archway in her floating white dress. Their gazes glazed over Kora before acknowledging the guards trailing them, grunting to each other about the heat.

She keenly navigated through the narrowing, cobbled streets of the port town until they ended up outside a tavern.

"Here?" Bree squinted at the fragmented sign hanging above the bay windows. "That barmaid didn't like us."

"Sure she did," Kora glanced sideways at her. "She took enough of my coins."

Kora tugged Bree inside The Abandoned Barnacle, who in turn nodded to the guards to remain stationed outside. She quickly waded through the throng of males, who kept a wide berth around Bree, their eyes raking over the jewellery adorning her body, and sat them down at a table right in the centre of the tavern.

"Isn't this a bit . . . exposing?" Bree glanced around, pulling her thin lavender cloak tighter around her. It was clasped together below her neck with a golden broach in the shape of the empire insignia—the four-pointed elongated star with a circle connecting the points.

"I thought we had fun last time." Kora forced a smile as a scowling Circe approached them. She was dressed in the same grey and burgundy combination, yet her bountiful hair was unbound, cascading around her face in gossamer honey brown waves. Her tawny eyes fixated on Kora.

"You didn't bring that lech with you?"

"Samuel sends his regards," Kora purred, as she slipped Circe two silver bits and a drinks order. When she returned with a stein of ale, and a glass of wine for Bree, Kora grasped her wrist, making Circe startle.

"Has John been here today?" A silver made its way onto the table.

Circe didn't miss a beat as she stealthily picked it up in one swift movement. "No, he's not working today. He's been absent the past couple days."

"Has he said where he's gone to?"

Circe shook her head. "He's sent me a kid to help fill in with cleaning up, can you believe it? I've practically got the run of the place now—without the pay."

She shimmied off, back behind the bar, and Kora glimpsed a two-pronged tail wagging from behind the edge of the counter. At least Conan was still here. He was a good pooch, even if he had an early bedtime like a grumpy old male.

"Care to fill me in?" Bree peered over her glass of dark red wine.

"Just curious about the barkeep, that's all."

"Is he the man you're courting?" Her blue eyes lit up. "Although, I had higher expectations for you."

Kora snickered as she took a deep gulp from her stein. "God—goodness, no. Nothing like that." She bit her lip. Nearly revealing her gods-damned faith, to a noble heir. She was slipping. All that chat with Agatha yesterday and she'd relaxed her guard. "Although, I wouldn't say no to a man with unlimited access to grog."

Bree let out a musical laugh, capturing the attention of several sailors, who courageously made their way over to speak to Bree. She sat back with amusement, sipping her wine, and Kora's ears settled into the pandemonium of sound around her.

She absentmindedly drank her ale, pitifully observing the sailors' attempts to speak to the heiress—or princess—until a conversation behind her sparked her attention.

"He's vanished. No one's seen or heard from him for a few days now."

"He's in hiding. Don't worry. Someone's just spooked him . . . said he's back next week to resume the search."

The voices were harsh and fervent. They echoed from the darkened corner of booths, and Kora resisted the urge to turn around to glimpse the male's faces.

"We've been searching for nearly a decade now. How'd we know she's still alive?"

"She must be. There's no alternative. What about Finlay? His latest report said he found a possible lead."

Kora's heart stopped dead as her world tilted on its axis. The males continued conversing.

"He boarded that ship—*Hell's Flipper*, or whatever. The captain's a mean son of a bitch. Did you know he hunts pirates? What a sick mind. Hunting humans for sport."

Her breathing hitched. *Hell's Serpent.* She clenched her fist, her short nails scraping her skin. Erick's plan had worked, they thought she was a male. Perhaps her reputation wasn't as renowned as she believed. And gods-damn wasn't that a knife to the heart.

Besides, pirates *deserved* to be hunted. Did these males not know the atrocities they committed? Did they not see past the bottom of their steins?

"Digs," the second male hissed. "Keep it down! And that ship docked days ago. You haven't seen him?"

"Shit, no. Maybe he's in hiding, too?"

"Best to presume the worst. We can't have this information leaking. Don't try to contact Finlay. We can't have his family getting wind of this. They can't know about John, either."

The flames of Finlay's burning body filled her ears like a roaring current.

"Do we assume the same about John? Do you think he's searching for Finlay? What if he doesn't return?"

A pause, followed by the shuffle of feet, and Kora clasped her hands under the table to hide the shake possessing them.

"Yes . . . it'd make sense. They'd never leave each other, but meet back here in . . ." the voices suddenly faded out.

Kora scrambled to look behind her. Two pairs of legs disappeared up the stairs, their voices floating away with them as

Circe carefully eyed the rowdy crowd, her gaze settling on Kora once again. A chill skittered down her spine as she attempted to casually sit back in her chair, grasping her stein to force the trembling to stop.

Her mind clouded with jarring thoughts, and her guts twisted as her heart ached with the loss of her friend . . . but her mind screamed at the *lies*.

Their friendship had been built on a *truth for truth*—had his truth even been real? Kora sucked in a breath, her eyes sliding to the shadowy staircase. Through the tangled mess of thoughts, only one stuck out.

Finlay Blackstone was a liar.

Had his family truly forced him to join her crew, or was it a cover up? He'd joined her ship for a reason, supposedly searching for someone. A female.

But she was the only female on *Hell's Serpent*. In fact, in the entire gods-damned armada. But apparently that *wasn't* common knowledge. Something screamed within her to find out, and she didn't need the voice prompting her this time, as alarm bells rang in Kora's ears, mind, and soul.

26

W atch her like a hawk." Kora leaned across the bar, using two fingers to signal said intense eye-watching at Circe. "Bree cannot be left alone. If anything bad happens to her, that's a black mark against your tavern. I have . . . women's needs to attend to in the latrine."

Circe's striking eyes bulged at the sailors swarming around Bree. One had ordered a bottle of wine to the table and topped up her glass, leaning over the heiress with hunger in his gaze.

"I won't let anyone touch her." Circe's face hardened, her orange eyes ablaze as she stormed over to the mass of leering males, snapping at them. With Circe's absence, Kora ducked behind the bar, edging to the stairs wreathed in darkness. But a snuffle at her booted feet cut her off, followed by a constant drumbeat against the tiled floor.

"Hello, Conan." She ruffled the hound's neck, carefully evading his drooling maw. "Will you let me pass?"

Conan snorted, pushing her back with his muzzle. He whined as he huffed at her scent and her fingers caught on a wooden tag clasped to the thin chain collared around his neck.

IF FOUND, RETURN TO FINLAY BLACK—

The rest of his surname had been scored by a knife. Kora's mouth dried as Conan kept nudging her, his snout snuffling every inch of her hands, arms, and chest. This was Finlay's dog. John was looking after him for Finlay . . . expecting him to return home. Her heart panged, and she petted the pooch's soft head.

"I'm sorry, boy," she whispered. "He's not coming back."

Droopy red eyes blinked. At least Finlay told the truth about being a Blackstone. John had said they thought Conan was a runt. Presumably, Finlay's family would have put him down for inadequacy. Nobility was deranged at times. She was glad Conan was here, safe and sound.

"You're a good boy." Kora tickled his neck as Conan sat down, his huge paws pushed together in refined poise. She rooted through the shelves of the bar until she located a cooler of meats, remembering John's path from feeding Conan the other day. His drooling increased as she dangled a raw steak, before throwing it into the heart of the tavern.

"Go get it!"

Conan barked as he flew after the steak into the crowd, sliding against the tiled floor as his jaws yapped in the air chasing his treat. She pivoted, nimbly sprinting up the stairs two steps at a time, ascending into darkness as the tavern erupted into chaos.

Kora wasn't sure what she'd been expecting . . . but it certainly hadn't been *this*.

The stairs led to a windowless hallway lined with four bolted doors. Each one had an unfamiliar symbol carved into the woodwork. Cold silence emitted from all but one, and she hurried to the end door, which was covered in whirling symbols that reminded her of clouds. Laughter rang behind it and she paused.

Should she knock? It couldn't be that easy, could it? There was no lock beneath the iron doorknob, and she held her breath. It warmed to her touch as she grasped it, heating her skin before opening on silent hinges.

Apparently, it *was* that easy.

A large square room covered the span of the tavern below, the windows draped in red swaths of sheer fabric, casting a sultry aura. Decadent thick rugs with vertical swirls lined the floors, masking the sounds of footsteps, and giant plush cushions in all shapes and sizes were dotted around in clusters for people to lounge on. Endless cream-and-black candles, precariously placed on low, dark-metal tables with glass tops, burned until the wax melted and shrouded the shining surfaces.

A female in scantily dressed clothing approached Kora. She wore puffed lavender silk trousers, along with a plunging lavender top that exposed her slender, tanned midriff. A sheer piece of silk hung across her face, connected to a silver chain looping around her nest of black hair.

Kora pulled her dark cloak around her, damning the internal green silk lining highlighting her imperial status. At least her cloak clasp wasn't the empire insignia. It was a winding leaf made of silver, gifted to her from Blake when they'd survived the trials.

At least fifteen, maybe twenty, people *relaxed* in the room, their faces shrouded by various coloured sheets of silk, or intricately embossed masks covering their eyes. Clustered in small groups, their heads were close as they spoke in whispered, soothing tones. A glass-and-silver bar, with a select amount of grog, dominated the corner closest to the stairs. Another hostess, dressed in pale-yellow clothing, flitted from the bar to the collective strangers, refilling their crystal glasses. *Crystal.*

Glass. Crystal. Masks. What was this place?

Kora swallowed at the wealth woven throughout the room. If the citizens outside—or even in the tavern below—knew what affluence lay hidden up here, it would be raided within a heartbeat.

"I don't recognise you," the lavender hostess murmured. Her voice had a strange accent Kora couldn't place, and she considered bolting downstairs. Her palm stung and she shook her wrist, rubbing the oddly warm skin.

"Oh, first time?" The hostess cocked her head.

"How did you know?"

She gestured to Kora's hand. "It becomes less unpleasant each time. First time I used the door, I thought my palm was going to melt off!" The hostess lowered her voice, "You must be a powerful mage to enter without a burn the first time."

Mage.

Words evaded Kora as her throat closed. She couldn't bring herself to admit it. That she was . . . *powerful.* It was an absurd concept, and she scoured the room, her pulse racing. If she were caught, she would be dead in an instant.

"Don't worry, we are all the same here." The hostess' eyes crinkled beneath her veil.

"Everyone here is a mage?" Kora croaked the words.

"Mage, or ally to mages. The door can read you from your touch, and keeps our enemies out. Pretty handy spell. Say, how did you find us?"

Kora wracked her brains. Her ability to think failing at the overwhelming discovery of a room full of mages and allies to the old ways, hidden behind an enchanted door. A name welled up from the entanglement of thoughts. The reason she'd come up here.

"Digs sent me," Kora lowered her voice, altering her tone to be more husky. "I'm afraid I don't have a covering."

She motioned to the lavender silk hiding half of the female's face, leaving her dark, kohl-lined eyes exposed. A shimmer of sparkling gold brushed down the curves of her face, and her skin sparkled with the powder on her shoulders, arms, and stomach.

"Oh!" The hostess raised her brows as she scanned the room. "I always have a spare. Here." She fished out a black silk mask, connected to a simple gold chain, and Kora quickly turned away to cover her face beneath her cloak.

"Thank you."

"You're welcome, sister." She bobbed in a small curtsey. "*Sehwani.*"

Kora stopped dead in her tracks at the old language. Seconds passed, and the female's dark stare grew concerned, the corners pinching in suspicion as Kora remained in stunned silence.

"*Sehwani,*" she replied.

The hostess visibly relaxed, and gestured for Kora to enter the mysterious room. Entangled thoughts sprouted in her mind. Had Finlay been aware of this place? He knew John, and this was John's tavern. It wasn't far-fetched to believe Finlay had been involved with this, too. And who spelled the door? Enchantments were part of witches' talent, not a mage-bestowed gift from a god.

She quietly walked through, catching snippets of Devanian spoken, and her stomach knotted as she sunk into an empty area of purple and black cushions. She keenly listened, understanding odd sentences in the ancient language.

Business trades.

Family feuds.

Their latest *exploits* at brothels.

The search for John and Finlay—*there.*

Kora shuffled closer to the two males a few cushion-circles away. She couldn't see their faces, as they sat with their broad backs to most of the room. She was also aware that she didn't have long before Bree would stride into the latrine to reprimand her for abandonment.

"—it's growing, is what our spies have heard. The Mist will take over the oceans if we don't hurry soon," Digs spoke quietly.

"Agreed. Time is running out. We need to find John," the other male followed.

"What if he doesn't return like he said? What if he's dead? *And* Finlay?"

The sound of bones snapping painfully echoed in Kora's mind. Silence, followed by a deep sigh. Even her breathing stopped. "We must suspect Finlay is gone. He wouldn't leave John this long. We will be amiss without them, but if both of our leaders are missing, then you and I are the next to step up."

Leaders. Kora squirmed.

Finlay was a leader of . . . *what*? An organisation? Kora's entire being turned cold. Had Finlay lied about the ultimatum from his family, as a cover for this secret life? Had she cremated an heir of a noble house without just cause?

Finlay Blackstone was a fucking spy.

She should've listened to Koji and returned his body, but she wasn't sure what to believe anymore. She should've listened to her instincts the first time about Finlay. Fiercely clenching her fists, her mind churned and spat out vitriol.

"Better get Circe to double up on the grog. It's not a Skytor Heiring without it," Digs spoke fondly at the mention of Circe.

What in the gods was a Skytor Heiring? She hadn't come across the term in any of Agatha's readings.

"You know she wants nothing to do with us. This is strictly John and Finlay's clan."

Clan? How archaic.

"Still, she could at least help us find *her*. We have a single description to go on, and it could be *anyone*." Tension roiled in Digs' voice.

"It's been so long, I'm starting to lose hope. I—"

"Well, hello there," a deep, sensual voice drawled by Kora's side, and she startled in surprise. So lost in confusion and betrayal, she hadn't noticed the male that had sidled up next to her. Way too close for her liking. Dressed head to toe in black, his dark face covered by a black mask, he laid on his side with a knee propped up. Unmistakable purple rings circled his dark irises from iridweed consumption. So, the drug had made it to the Skytors. He flashed a white, devilish smile.

"I've not seen you here before," he spoke in Devanian, and she swallowed her cresting nerves.

Digs and his comrade made their way over to the red glass bar, helping themselves to grog. No . . . the bar wasn't red. That was the reflection of the room. The bar was exquisite. Clear cut glass, banded by silver frames that snaked across the front like vines. The males warily glanced back over to Kora and motioned the lavender hostess over.

Shit.

"I'm just visiting," she replied in Devanian. Once the male saw her beginning to get to her feet, he gripped her arm with force. "Don't go. We could have some fun. I've never seen someone like you in here before."

He trailed a finger up and down her arm and wetted his lips. Nausea flitted through her as something dark slithered around her . . . something poking at the edges of her mind, looking for an invitation in.

Kora pushed back against the magic, imagining a strong watery current washing away the talons raking over her. The dark presence faded, along with her strength, and they both blinked with astoundment. She was sure this male had never been rejected *magically* before. Gods, she really *was* a mage. They truly existed.

Agatha was right, power would never be lost. It had been reborn. And here it was, in the dark upper floor of a rank tavern, on the main street of her beloved port town.

"I'd rather jump out of the window than touch you."

The male faltered at her magic block, and Kora took the opportunity to quickly skim around the hushed groups. She caught fleeting moments of strangers groping each other, their hands searching beneath veiled clothing, followed by poorly suppressed moans.

So, this room was also that *kind* of business, as she'd suspected. She supposed being a mage ally required *some* kind of stress release.

"Hey—you!" Digs called out from the side as Kora neared the door. "I don't know you."

"I'm new." Thankfully her voice was muffled by the silk covering.

"Nobody is ever new here," his voice darkened.

He was tall and broad like Samuel, but clean-shaven, with shaggy, dirt-brown hair falling to his shoulders. A pale ivory mask, with swirling silver marks resembling the currents of the wind, cut across his squared, unamused face.

"Tell me who you are." His large hands clenched into fists as he scanned her dark cloak.

"*Jump,*" the voice spiralled through Kora's mind, and she welcomed the comforting guidance that had been disappearing lately. Her stare slid to the right—to a small, square shaped window. Through the iron-bolted door at her back, the sounds of chaos smacked against the barrier, vibrating through the air.

Digs frowned, nearing her and the door.

Damn the gods.

"Me? I'm leaving." Kora ran and leapt, curling her body inward as she smashed through the window with flying force, using the sheer red drapes to protect her from shards of shattered glass.

The lavender hostess shrieked as Kora flung the red sheet, spiralling through the air before landing in a crouch in the dark alleyway beside The Abandoned Barnacle. Pain cracked up her legs, and she gritted her teeth from the impact. Being a mage would explain why she could leap from two floors high and not break a single bone. Her cheeks heated. As if she'd thought she'd inherited *good bone density*.

"Hey!" Digs leaned out of the window, his mask removed, and shock plastering his squared face. *Double shit.* He'd seen her survive the jump. She was a confirmed mage to the Skytors. No one could know that she, a captain, was a mage. Thank the gods her cloak still covered her white hair.

Glass rained around her, and she pushed into a running sprint down the filthy alley, darting around crates and yellow-tinted puddles to the main winding street that snaked through the heart of the port town.

As she rounded the corner at high speed, she smacked straight into a slab of muscle dressed in silver armour. Kora hastily removed the black silk from her face as the guard turned and stared down at her with unfeeling eyes.

"I found Miss Cadell," he spoke with a gruff voice. She exhaled with irritated relief.

Captain Cadell, you bilge-sucking—no. She wouldn't finish that thought. Her body crackled with energy, her veins alight with powerful thrumming. Was this her magic?

"Kora!" Bree squeaked from behind the line of guards. "What are you doing there? We thought you were still inside with the brawling!"

The guards parted like a shimmering silver wave, and Bree stood gracefully, smiling down at Kora as she motioned towards The Abandoned Barnacle with a sparkling hand.

Kora peered through the bay window at the figures scuffling and fighting, with Circe sprinting in between, flailing her arms. Conan excitedly leapt up at the crowds, his dual tails wagging, and sailors collapsed from the sheer weight and size of the hound.

"I took the back exit," Kora's voice strained as a tall figure with shaggy hair ran into the rupture of brawling males. "We should head back. Now."

"We suggest not taking our lady somewhere so . . . raucous next time," a guard spoke sternly.

Bree rolled her eyes, tugging Kora closer as they strolled through the streets towards the mid-district. There were no market stalls here, no crooked structures. The wooden and brick buildings were fresh, built within the last fifty years, in an array of colours. Tall and slender like Bree, with iron-glass panes, and not a single

Devani god statue. Instead, banners and flags of the insignia lined the streets, with silver-armoured guards stationed at every corner to ensure peace.

Bree launched into a monologue of the sailor-filled attention she'd received, followed by the fantastical *unruly* fight that broke out after a sailor had knocked someone's stein over—presumably because of Conan. Shame warmed Kora's cheeks.

Yet, her mind kept drifting back to Finlay.

He'd been a gods-damned spy. Who were the Skytors? Why was the Mist growing?

Who were they looking for?

"They're looking for you." She blocked the voice. No. No way. On Thanos' cloth she was not their target. Yet . . . Digs and the mysterious male had claimed they were searching for a female, and Finlay's lead had brought him to *Hell's Serpent* . . .

Why would they be after her? She was nothing. Just a captain in the armada. Being a mage didn't make her special. Not after discovering an obscene amount of them in a dingey room upstairs in an unsuspecting tavern. Clearly, mages have learned to hide in plain sight. A shiver skittered down her spine. Now she'd need to do the same. She couldn't grapple with her new reality, and deep-set lines marred her face as she failed to suppress her worry, questions swimming around in her mind until she felt dizzy.

"Kora?"

Her head whipped up as they neared the grand stone wall separating them from the residential districts. Blake stood at the end of a dark street connected to the main road, holding a leather-bound tan folio.

She stiffened as he approached, his eyes skimming over the guards, assessing the group of strangers she was with, and then they suddenly stopped at Bree as she stepped forward. He cleared his throat. "Captain Cadell." Followed by a nod. Kora inclined her head in return, ignoring the huff emitted from one of the guards at the mention of her title.

"Mr Marwood." The words twisted her tongue.

Bree nudged her elbow as her attentive stare raked over Blake. Observing, gauging—*devouring*. His raven hair glistened under the high sun, and his usual black attire fitted his strong frame; the golden empire insignia embossed over his chest.

"May I introduce Bree Hydrafort." Kora's voice choked at Bree's blue eyes lighting up.

Blake bowed respectfully as Bree held out her diamond-adorned hand. Wrapping his hand around hers, he lightly placed his lips upon it in a kiss. Kora sucked in a sharp breath as his lips lingered a second—just a second.

What the fuck.

"It's always an honour to meet a Hydrafort." He spoke with reverence, his voice taking on that democratic tone he used in meetings. Kora fought the urge to roll her eyes. *Such a show off.*

"Pleasure," Bree purred, and Kora's stomach twisted as Bree fluttered her fan. "Blake Marwood. Champion of the trials. I know *all* about you."

Since when had Bree been so aware of Blake? Kora gritted her teeth as he chuckled in return. His dark, *teasing* chuckle. The one he used only with her when they were together in private. It shuddered through her skeleton, conjuring flashes of heat in the shadowy alcove of Cadell Manor. Only yesterday, his lips were upon hers, so close to losing control his trousers were practically ripping at the seams.

Now those lips graced Bree's hand.

"You flatter me." He *winked.*

Her veins turned to ice.

"Your reputation is well-known in Talmon. In fact, from all I've heard, I feel as though I already know you."

Kora's mind raced as Blake and Bree conversed, her friend's twinkling laugh joining his deep, sultry tones, and Kora clenched her fists, directing her frustration down into the sensation of her nails biting her palms.

Their relationship wasn't a façade.

They couldn't tell the world they were together.

They had to flirt with others to maintain the illusion.

She repeated the mantras over and over in her head.

But—*Bree?*

"Kora, it is a *crime* that we've not been introduced sooner." Bree plastered one of her dazzling smiles on, resting her palm on Blake's bicep, her thumb sweeping over the curve of muscle. Kora's vision tunnelled onto it.

It was a *crime* that she was fucking touching her first mate. That thrumming in her body pulsated into a thunderous beat, filling her ears. Her red haze was unchecked, dampening her rational thought.

"Months and years out at sea makes it hard to go around introducing *friends*. It's not an easy job." Her sharp tone caused them both to glare at her.

Blake's face sent a warning look of, *watch your tone, don't give anything away.* Whilst Bree's forced smile spoke volumes: *don't mess this up for me.*

"We spent a lot of time apart ourselves, working in different fleets. But now, Captain Cadell is stuck with me as an unfortunate first mate." Another wink. Why was he winking so much? Did a piece of nobility get stuck in his eye? Despite the joking nature, the words struck a chord with Kora. A stinging chord.

"Oh!" Bree exclaimed, fanning her fan exaggeratively.

Kora hid her scowl as Blake's green eyes were drawn to the movement of the fan, perfectly positioned in front of her bosom. Bree's pale shimmering dress accented her rich dark skin, and Kora glanced down at herself.

She was tanned, but short in stature. With curves, yet muscled from years of hard labour in fleets. Her short hair was nothing in comparison to Bree's exotic braids, and Bree didn't have a single scar on her body or face.

The seeded doubts surfaced once again.

"You must tell me of your adventures! Kora never tells me any gossip."

A subtle glance from Blake and their unspoken connection passed through them again, electrifying Kora to her fingertips. Nope. That desire was still there. A Hydrafort does not—*could not*—know about their exploits with pirates, and skimming the profits off the top.

"I can assure you, it's not as adventurous as it may seem." Blake's lips twitched upwards into a smirk. "It's a lot of scouting, checking coasts, and carrying precious cargo."

"How disappointing. I'd certainly like to know more, especially about when you went missing in the Shaurock Sea." A pause, and Blake tensed enough for Kora to catch a glimmer of worry pass across his face. Why was he worried? "Perhaps over dinner?" Bree's tone dropped to a sensual depth.

"Oh, well I'm sure the captain and I—"

"No, no," Bree shook her head. "Just you."

Kora blurted out the next thing she could think of before she screamed. "I thought you were working in the barracks today?"

Her sudden question made them both halt, and Blake dragged his admiration from Bree to glare at Kora. In a blink, his face smoothed out into neutrality, the epitome of an officer's poise.

"*I am.* I had to liaise with officers stationed in the western town about some activity." His reply was blunt and indifferent, but something lingered beneath his tone, and she cast a wary glance towards the western town where the lower districts were. Where the Silvermaid's Emporium was.

Kora could read the thoughts as clear as day in his eyes. They were two sides of a mirror from their years together honing their compatibility as fighters. Always deeply attuned to the other. He'd been called away to dampen the rebellious fires lighting within people's hearts. She was sure enough that the folio in his hands was a list of names to be executed. Her breath caught in her dry, constricting throat, and she nodded meekly. She hoped Agatha was safe in her shop. Her gut knotted, before plummeting. She'd had a rebel spy on her ship for weeks.

One of the soldiers grunted, "We'd like to escort our lady back home."

"Of course, mustn't keep a lady waiting." Blake bowed, a grin pasted on his face, and Bree laughed in return, swishing her sparkling skirts.

"Feel free to call on me in the upper district," she swooned as he straightened, her hands *accidentally* brushing over his chest.

If the god of death could strike Kora now, that would be great.

"I'll see you tomorrow," Kora murmured, not meeting Blake's stare as the soldiers pushed them on, towards the gate in the looming grey wall.

"I hope to see you again!" Bree called after a few steps, and Kora bit the inside of her cheek as she carried on walking, not daring to look back to see the expression on his face.

Bree brimmed with elation. "Now *that* is a man."

"Blake? He's okay, I guess."

"Okay? A champion of the trials!" Bree fanned herself as she spoke. "Your first mate, a liaison of the army. He's strong, powerful, respectable."

"What are you saying?" Kora stopped walking and the guards halted, their armour clinking at the movement.

"He could be it." Bree smiled, casting a look back to the port town, as if she could look right through the thick protection wall and see Blake. "He could be the one. No—he *is* the one."

Kora's temper simmered and she spoke through clenched teeth, "But you have to marry into nobility."

"I'm sure my father can make an exception for someone like him. I mean, a champion! He could be a commander someday. He should be one already. I could help him. Odd that he's not tried to advance into the army yet. You wouldn't know why that is, would you?"

Bree continued walking at Kora's silence, towing her along, oblivious to her stiff reluctance. She wouldn't be able to stop a marriage like that, and Bree was right. Blake may have come from low, humble roots, but he'd more than proved himself with his achievements, and with the support of Bree's family, he could easily become the next commander . . . or even a viceroy.

A viceroy would never be with a captain.

It'd be years before Kora could achieve admiral status. She'd have to replace Erick first as commodore, and he was taking every step to drag that goal further away from her. It was too much time, and marriages happened quick in Azaria, especially for nobility.

But Blake *could* deny Bree.

She clung to the thought. He could reject her family's proposal. Maybe Kora could elope with him—*no*. The thought of leaving Erick, leaving Agatha, made her heart plummet.

Besides, if they eloped, they would be hunted down as traitors to the crown, and to the armada. Obtaining a ship to escape to the seas would be a guaranteed death sentence, and they'd become the very thing they despised. *Pirates.*

She was already a killer. A thief. Kora felt as though she were taking the steps to becoming a bona fide pirate. She'd already infiltrated a rebel's nest, blending in as if she belonged. Something she couldn't report without revealing her own magic. *Gods,* she was a walking criminal. The power coursing through her veins was a threat to the kingdom. All she'd have to do was start torturing innocents, and blindly murdering everyone that stepped in her path, and she'd easily fit in with Galen, as well.

Exhaustion swept in as the pulsing beat of power evaporated from her limbs, leaving a cold unseen residue, hollowing her core.

"Put in a good word for me, would you?" Bree spoke excitedly, her eyes sparkling as she envisioned her future. "I can tell you have a good friendship with him. Imagine—your two closest friends getting married?"

Kora didn't want to imagine it at all.

W hat's this?" Erick sat across from Kora at the large mahogany parlour room table, scrutinising the lemon placed beside her bowl of berried porridge.

"A lemon?" Kora replied between mouthfuls, shovelling her oats down before they commenced their journey to Whitestone Bay within the hour. Plates piled high with cured meats, spiced eggs, and freshly baked pastries covered the space between them. Black drapes fluttered behind her from the tall glass windows, letting in the scorching heat. Erick picked up the lemon with both hands and his frown deepened.

Kora paused as faint lines crinkled at the edges of his eyes, the lines in his forehead becoming prominent. Even the flecked greys in the sides of his hair seemed glaringly bright. When had Erick aged so much? His youth faded away from him faster and faster every time she returned home.

"Is this from our trees?" He turned the lemon over in his hands, inspecting it.

"Yes, why? It's just a lemon." *What was the big deal?*

Kora piled meats and eggs onto her plate next, washing her porridge down with crisp water. Praise the empire for inventing drinking taps. Their voices echoed within the grand room, and she always wondered why he insisted they ate in here when there was a smaller table within the kitchens. A much cosier space, compared to this black-and-white hollow room. Even the diamond-shaped black-tiled floor was cold. The cream wallpapered walls were bland, no flicker or indication of a life lived.

She wondered if Erick ate here alone when she was on her long voyages.

"It's massive," he observed, placing the lemon back down on

the table between them, the weight of it causing the silverware to rattle. "Unnaturally so."

Kora shrugged as she continued fuelling up her body for the day. She'd slept terribly. Tossing and turning, dreaming about Blake and Bree's wedding, and the idea that she would be left alone in the impending darkness. Unable to escape, unable to breathe, trapped in a coffin shrinking by the second.

Maybe she belonged in one.

Which was swiftly followed by dreams of Finlay rising from the dead, as an ash-covered empty shell. Hunting her down, his eyes and voice void of life, crying out that his death was her fault. That she had failed him. Her hand clenched around her spoon as she fought to swallow her food, trying to push Finlay—and his secret Skytor group—from her mind.

He'd been a spy. A rebel. She couldn't mourn him any longer.

"I thought Chef might like to have it . . . to cook with."

"Cook with? He'll be using it for *weeks*." Erick ruffled his papers, and his eyes continued to pour over his latest reports from scouts.

"Anything interesting?"

His jaw twitched. "I hope not, we have enough trouble as it is. You need to be careful on this journey to the south, Kora. The exiles are getting more daring in their attacks and are trying to take over the oasis as a camp for themselves."

"We'll be fine. Blake and I have handled worse."

"That's at sea. You're more skilled when it comes to naval warfare, with the safety and protection of *Hell's Serpent*."

Kora paused in her shovelling of food at the worried tone in his voice. It was so rare that he expressed his parental concerns. Their relationship thus far had been turbulent, but Erick had always been patient and nurturing, to an extent. Her first few years had been erratic, and his kindness had led her through the darkness of waking up to an unknown world, with an unknown name, and a voice rattling her mind.

But acting as her commodore took priority, and she desperately sought a family to anchor her. Their lifestyle couldn't grant the solid foundation. One of them was always at sea, which she didn't mind. It was better than this cold pile of stone. This manor had been declined life. It'd been created for a vast family, but was rendered with two lost souls who favoured being on the job than at home.

Erick's fiery brown eyes bore into her, and she had the sense she wasn't going to like what he said next.

"I've made the decision to request additional guards for the escort."

"What?"

Kora dropped her cutlery, and it clattered onto the table as she glared at Erick furiously. He knew what this would mean to her. It would suggest her incapabilities to carry through the mission. That she was weak. That, because she was a *female*, she wouldn't be as efficient. She wanted to prove everyone wrong.

"Kora, please." Erick pinched the bridge of his nose in exasperation. "It's not about *that*. I trained you myself, I know you're more than capable. But this is the desert. You're a naval captain, not a soldier. Marwood's leading this mission. He has the skillset for land combat, and the experience should it come to it."

"So . . . I'm being babysat, whilst Blake leads us all into his patriarchal glory?"

"Don't get petty. You've always been averse to the army, and this sits firmly in my division's repertoire. But *you* were requested to be the escort, so I've taken some extra precautions." His jaw ground with annoyance.

"I get it." She pushed back her plate, her appetite evaporating. "I wasn't *your* first choice for the contract."

Commodore Erick Cadell straddled the two worlds of the empire's defences. He was a leader of the fleets of the armada—just below Admiral Barron—yet he favoured the armies and being a soldier. A leader of the land, he preferred donning his dark tarnished armour and assisting in training the new waves of recruits whenever possible.

He'd been voyaging out to sea less and less lately, and Kora always wondered why he never hung up his sea-faring title and committed fully to being a commander or a general. Erick formally wasn't considered one, but he was respected and treated as one. As soon as he sacrificed that title, it'd be her chance to advance in the ranks. But, for some reason, he still held onto it, still believing she had more to learn. More training to do, more reading, more sailing.

Erick startled at her spat, and he faltered for his next words. His fiery gaze softened, and he placed a hand on the table, gently reaching out to her. Kora's throat closed at the offer of a father's comfort.

But he wasn't her father—not really. Legally, yes. And he'd tried his gods-damned hardest to raise a defiant teenager with a broken mind. But something in her still held on to her past. *Hope*.

A pitiful kernel of hope buried so deep. Hope that her *real* family had somehow survived.

Kora sucked in a retort as she tried so desperately hard in that moment to remember her past, her family, her life. Miserable blank darkness swept up to greet her, along with a dull ache in the side of her head, and she slowly placed her hand in Erick's, offering him a false smile. False because she knew she loved this male, but admitting it would cut her old life off. A chapter permanently ended.

She wasn't quite ready to let go of something she couldn't remember.

"Captain!" a familiar voice boomed from the grand entrance of the parlour room and Kora jolted, swiping her hand from Erick's.

Samuel barrelled in, his stoic face beaming as he eyed up the feast on the table. "You should've told me there's breakfast. I'd have come sooner, Commodore." He thudded down next to Kora, piling his plate high as she stared at him stunned.

"Mr Rommier." Erick's lips twitched in amusement. "My apologies."

"Wha-what are you doing here?" Kora spluttered.

"I'm coming with you."

Samuel smiled down at her as he tucked into his plate of meats and grains. He donned black leathers containing a rare fabric which would protect his body from all sorts of threats—including the scorching heat of the sun. His long wavy hair was tied up out of his face, and his short beard was braided, with silver thread coiled around it.

"I figured a navigational expert would be useful." Erick nodded at Samuel in a respectable greeting.

"He's a sailing master, not a cartographer," Kora muttered.

"What I do for you in my free time." Samuel nudged her with his beefy elbow and it nearly toppled her out of her chair. "Maps are maps. I know what I'm doing."

"Captain," an old voice sounded from the doorway again, and she startled at Aryn's silent presence lurking by the doors. "I see I'm not the only one." His eyes pinned on Samuel, who smiled with a mouth full of food, waving in return.

Aryn silently prowled over to the table, taking a seat beside Erick as they stiffly greeted each other, not meeting the other's gaze. His quiver and longbow were slung across his shoulders, and he was dressed in tan clothing, with a scarf wrapped round his neck and brown leather braces on his forearms. Kora eyed the thin tattoo across his cheek, her own scar tingling.

"Having a second breakfast, Sam?" Aryn's hazel eyes pointedly looked down at Samuel's mountainous plate. He'd trimmed his hair since they'd docked, and it was now shorter around the sides and back, whilst still thicker and longer on top. Dark brown strands of hair tousled like waves across his scalp, and his face was clean-shaven.

"Who's to say it's only my second?"

Kora rolled her eyes at her sailing master. "So, Aryn's here because?"

"My skills are valuable in the desert. Archery will be the one of the best defences we have, as well as hunting for food, if we run out. Something I have assured Erick about." His youthful face didn't match his wise tone, and it unnerved her.

She nearly choked on her food at the informal address. Bold. Very bold move from Aryn. This archer was becoming quite the interesting character in her crew.

"I promise, that's it. I'm confident in the four of you." Erick's strained smile didn't reach his eyes.

Kora eagerly gazed towards the entrance to the room in hopes of seeing a tall, dark familiar shadow, but was met with the consistent absence of whom she longed for. He'd said they'd meet at first light, but that'd been nearly two hours ago. Erick followed her gaze and shook his head disapprovingly.

Of course, he wouldn't allow Blake here unless it was vital. He always sought to keep them separated as much as possible when they were in Aldara, and it added to Kora's continuous simmering temper. She glared at Erick, followed by a jerk of the chin to her crew at the table.

Protection, my arse. You invited them on purpose. He wasn't worried about exiles in the desert, he was concerned about Blake getting in her trousers. Their plan for the desert had been sliced to pieces by Erick's sword. They wouldn't get a moment of peace together, especially with Samuel as part of the envoy. And Aryn was too insightful for his own good.

"There'll be more of you travelling back, but travel light, and travel fast. You'll be a bigger target as a larger group. The rebels will want your resources, maybe even the sentinel for ransom." Erick averted his stare from Kora, addressing the males.

"I hope this sentinel isn't completely useless," she moaned quietly.

Royal sentinels were uppity advisors to the royal family. They lived and breathed by the laws created by the monarchy, and sought to ensure the citizens of their lands abided by them. They frequently travelled across the continent in disguise, returning their findings to the king to advise on how best to enforce the law on heretics and criminals.

In this case, the sentinel was coming to snoop on the islands, the noble houses, and viceroys. Plugging the gap in advance for the king, on the island's weaknesses and strengths, and to commence establishing new laws for the unification of the islands and continent.

"Aye, I've mapped the route already," Samuel mumbled through food. "We'll avoid the desert until we reach the border, but we'll have no choice the closer we get to the south."

"Just keep away from the Southern Oasis. My scouts say the exiles are getting closer to claiming it." Erick cast a glance at Aryn, who disinterestedly observed Samuel fitting as many eggs as he could in his mouth.

As the males discussed strategies, Kora attempted to finish the remainder of her food. They had to take the bare minimum with them, to not overload the horses. It was the peak of the summer months, and the desert would be deathly hot, with the Southern Oasis being their only salvation if they ran out of water.

Erick's hot-and-cold eyes kept flickering back to her, but she moved her fork from her plate to her mouth as if she were a mindless phantom, her mind lost in thought. His observant gaze lingered on her hair, and she was glad to not be having *that* conversation any time soon.

"Wow . . . that lemon is *huge!*" Samuel exclaimed.

W ill you stop that racket? My ears are bleeding!" Aryn snapped from the rear of their convoy, a scarf covering his head and lower face from the heat of the desert sun.

Blake led their small entourage, perched tall on Erebus, the horse a striking obsidian with a midnight blue shimmer that glistened in the sun. He consistently scanned the endless, yellow horizon, pausing at the top of every dune to scout for exiles or rebels before motioning for the others to proceed to join.

Samuel and Kora had settled in the middle, joking, teasing, and jostling with each other. Their horses were twins, according to the stable boy. Both a sandy palomino colour, blending in with the grains of the desert, with darkened hooves and pale-wheat manes.

Leaving Aryn at the rear, always several feet behind, as their lookout. His horse had a fierce temperament, and had tried to buck him off a few times already, resulting in hushed curses that'd make a pirate blush. The horse was a fascinating chestnut red, like the shores of Scarlet Bay, with a strikingly pale mane, and it didn't take kindly to being too close to the others.

"I can try a different song?" Samuel grinned over his shoulder at Aryn.

They'd ventured south from the mid-districts of Stormkeep Fortress, following the border of the Bellmoor family's farming territory for as long as they could before they'd entered the Silent Tundra.

And how silent it was.

Even when the wind picked up, creating a biting whipping slash of sands barrelling against their faces, it was still silent. Once they'd crossed into the desert this morning, Samuel had sung shanties non-stop, and Kora was thankful for the slightly off-pitch, tone-deaf voice.

"Please don't," Aryn moaned.

"Well, I'm grateful for your singing, Sam," she smirked.

"That makes one of us," Blake muttered from the front. "I'm with Aryn on this one."

Blake had increasingly become withdrawn during their journey. The further they travelled south, the more his dark, brooding nature consumed him. He'd barely spoken more than a few words at a time as they'd trekked through the farming fields and dry desert. And he hadn't neared Kora either. Not as her first mate—nor her lover. Maybe he was also angry at Erick's order for additional guards?

She quashed the feelings of upset down. He was maintaining the illusion they were nothing more than co-workers. Yet, since that unfavourable encounter between him and Bree, Kora was unable to shake a sensation gnawing at her sides.

Not to mention the gentle hum of the talisman on her chest, constantly reminding her to seek out the Silver Sisters. She had to get rid of this charm as soon as possible, before someone noticed she was channelling a new, unknown power to it—or before it sucked her dry.

The thought of potentially losing her new magical discovery flowing through her veins made her heart droop, and she twirled her fingers through her horses' mane—Cadence—as she considered the possibilities of mastering the magic. Wielding it. Making it yield to her.

She could tame the seas, become an unstoppable force within the armada for the empire.

Or for yourself.

Kora had been gifted with the rarest of the magical factions. She had *elemental* magic. To possess it even now—centuries after the gods had faded—was near impossible. Elemental magic could only be bestowed as a gift from a god . . . or through their descendants.

What had she done to earn Calypso's gift? Why was it manifesting now? The talisman hummed, as if attuned to her thoughts. This all started happening when Blake gifted the charm. Clearly it possessed some kind of property to draw magic out of mages.

Did her family possess the same power? Had they descended from Calypso? It was an ultimate secret, and one that laid on her as heavy as the ocean's depths. No one could know, not even Blake, and the crack of shame and guilt split open a little bit more within her, pushing against the mask of neutrality smoothing her face.

It was a known law. Mages, and practising witches outside of their territory, were either enslaved or executed—more likely the latter now. King-soon-to-be-Emperor Staghart and his predecessors, through the decades, had decreed magic was a myth, and the one true power was the royal family who governed these lands. *Their family* was the closest to divinity the world would encounter. Anyone who still remembered magic, or believed it to exist, had long passed since the decree.

To be graced with their presence was a holy blessing, and many citizens refused to wash after meeting the king and his family, fearing to cleanse away the godliness they'd experienced.

Absolute hogwash, Agatha always said. And there was a room full of mages in a tavern to disprove it.

A minority of people in the lands believed King Staghart was not their true leader, and still wanted to invoke the *old ways* of Devania. Not the magic, but their customs and beliefs. But to speak of such things landed them a one-way ticket to Deadwater Prison—or here, in the desert.

It was the tear in the Azarian Islands. Those who believed in the king, and those who didn't.

"You're practically screaming to the exiles where we are." Aryn galloped closer, his horse bucking her head in protest.

"If Sam's singing is *so* bad, maybe they'll stay away." Kora smiled at Samuel who feigned being hurt, a large hand clutching at his chest. "They'll probably think we're murdering someone out here."

"Oi!"

Samuel swiped for her reins to knock her off course, but she tugged Cadence away. The horse exuded a sweet nature that warmed something within Kora. She regularly swished her tail in a cheery manner, and Kora told her stories during nightfall of her adventures at sea.

Samuel often ridiculed her for talking to Cadence, stating the horse wouldn't understand what she was saying. But whenever Kora looked into Cadence's dark eyes, a level of understanding stared back at her. She was a creature with a conscience, with thought.

Samuel reached out and lightly smacked Cadence's hind, and the horse suddenly bolted forward with a neigh. "Aye, she's off!" Cadence galloped ahead, picking up speed as they raced towards

Blake, who reeled in surprise.

"Kora!" he snapped as she charged past.

She should have tugged on the reins, halted the horse, or turned back, but they were still so close to Bellmoor's borders, and hadn't seen a single exile in two full days.

So, Kora galloped, and she cried out happily as Cadence's powerful legs pounded against the desert sand, propelling them up the oncoming sand dune.

"Stop!" Blake's voice was a faint whisper, carried away by a gentle breeze.

"*Run.*"

Kora's heart leapt inside of her chest as her guiding, invisible voice urged her on. Her watchful spirit, her floating protector. Cadence's speed picked up, and Kora wondered if she also heard the faithful spirit voice. Exhilaration flowed through her, and a laugh bubbled up to her lips as the winds of freedom toyed with her hair.

The sound of hooves chased them as Blake advanced on his midnight stallion. A thundering black speck against the vastness of the desert, with a matching darkened face. Maybe this will get his mood to dissipate; some friendly competition. Maybe he'll catch her and devour her on top of the dune.

Kora flicked her reins, enjoying the race, and Cadence pushed up the final hurdle of the dune with a fierce neigh that rattled through Kora's bones. She felt the might of the horses' muscle, the strength of her legs, the depths of her lungs.

A black shadow darted past them, and Blake pulled Erebus around to cut them off at the top of the dune. Cadence reared up, and the bags attached to the saddle swung backwards. Kora clenched her legs, holding on before she toppled off. She ran a hand down Cadence's mane, attempting to soothe her as the front of her body crashed down, causing Erebus to step back warily. Sweet but challenging-natured Cadence. She liked this mare.

"What are you thinking?" Icy words flew from Blake's lips. "You don't know what's past these dunes—there could be exiles lurking, waiting to attack any second!"

Good, time to start their game. "There's not been anyone for two days—"

"That's beside the point, Kora! You're not thinking. You could've gotten yourself killed . . . or us!"

"Cadence wanted to stretch her legs," she replied sulkily. "It's nice to hear you speaking to me for the first time in *days*." Her tone had taken on her unmissable striking edge. This was it. He'd laugh, and they'd race across the desert, enjoying the thrill of heightened tension.

Blake stilled. His face unreadable, and a chill crept over her despite the baking hot sun burning high above them. Oh. Wait—was he actually angry? At her?

Despite her protective clothing, consisting of a mix of leathers and shirts, her skin iced at the hardened, emotionless stare emitting from him. She tugged on the light, tan bandana wrapped around her head, and nervously wiped the glass of her goggles that protected her eyes from sand blasts.

"Don't do this. Don't start acting out because you're not in charge here."

The chill turned into a permafrost. *He said what?*

"What?"

"You're a captain, Kora. Of the mighty *Hell's Serpent*," sarcasm oozed from his mouth. "You need to start acting like it. But out here—out here *I'm in charge.*"

"We were both asked to escort the sentinel. It's a joint effort," she bit back.

"Not here. You will do as *I* say—that's final." Blake's glacial green eyes bore into her unflinchingly. The male was serious. This wasn't an act for their relationship. He'd been distancing himself purposefully—all for the sake of authority. For leadership. *For a title.*

"What's this patriarchal male bullshit?"

"Kora!" he hissed, motioning to lower her voice. "Erick put me in charge of this mission, and I'm seeing it through. Now get in line. Before someone gets hurt—or killed."

The words settled in her mind, and she became as quiet as the surrounding tundra. Had his desperation to impress Erick trampled all over their relationship? Was she no longer important to him?

Kora scanned his face, searching for the male who always supported her, who had vowed to serve and be with her to the end. Not even a hint of a smirk, or lust in his gaze. She was greeted with a cold, harsh face. A stranger's eyes that were not the warm emerald she had grown to love.

"Do not undermine me," his voice lowered as Samuel and Aryn trotted up the sloping edge of the dune. "You're here as an escort. I'm here as a leader."

The words were knives cutting into her skin, into her heart.

"Well then," she simmered as hot as the Sulfire Sea of the

north. "Don't let me stop you . . . *leader*." And as she trotted forwards, edging around Blake's horse, she leaned over and whispered, "I see all I'm good for is escorting to your *needs*."

Rage bubbled to his cool surface as Kora disobeyed him by taking the forefront of the convoy. Cadence brazenly swished her tail, her hair flicking into Erebus' face, and Kora hummed to combat the silent loneliness as they trudged on through the desert.

Samuel didn't sing another sea shanty after that.

They had ridden through two more, awkwardly silent, blisteringly hot days.

Two nights of sitting around their small fire, silently eating their small-portioned dry food and sipping at their emptying waterskins. Rationing whatever they had till they arrived at Whitestone Bay was becoming a challenge.

Blake had kept his distance so far from Kora his tent may as well have been in Galen. When he was present, he barely acknowledged her presence, but his jaw constantly clenched, his fingers repeatedly curling into fists.

Oh, she'd love to punch him. Get a few strikes at his legs, too. Maybe his groin.

She wasn't getting much use of it anyway. Their five-day trek across the desert, romancing each other under the stars, curling up in a tent together. Obliterated. Gone.

Their new routine consisted of retiring to their single, popped-up tents, shivering through the ice-biting darkness. Cadence slept by the entrance of Kora's tent, which she found comforting and endearing, and she'd sacrificed one of her blankets to cover Cadence's rippling, muscled body during the brisk, dark chills of nightfall.

Then they'd rise before dawn, packing their camp away in uniformed motion, working in a rhythm they'd now perfected, followed by covering their bodies with light clothing to protect them from the extreme heat and sun.

And then the authoritative pissing competition would begin.

At first, Blake hung back, perhaps in guilt, allowing Kora to lead the convoy on the day of their fight. Her chin had been high, proudly guiding their group through the dunes, liaising with Samuel for directions and ensuring they didn't wander too close to the Southern Oasis. After a few hours, he'd galloped to the front, forcing Cadence to retreat from the might of Erebus, the shadow.

Since then, it'd been consistent, unspoken overtakings. One leaping in front of the other, steering the convoy in a ridiculous zig zag path down the centre of Aldara. At least the exiles would struggle to track their footprints from the patterns. Hopefully. Perhaps Blake *did* have a point about compromising their position, but it was clear the exiles were nowhere near. Should she apologise? Her gut screamed, stubbornness sinking its claws. *No.* He'd called her an escort. He didn't deserve one.

"We'll be at Whitestone Bay early," Samuel called as they stopped to water and feed their horses under the shade of a rare cluster of palm trees. He flicked his ancient map in his hands, thick bands of rings sparkling on his fingers, unfurling the fraying edges as he peered at various lines intersecting the land.

"How soon?" Blake asked.

"At this pace, we should be there tonight. That's a record, for sure."

"Good, let's go now. The sooner we get there, the better." Blake studied the map briefly before nodding.

Blake hoisted onto Erebus, and motioned them all to follow him onwards. With a scowl, Kora mounted Cadence, and gently stroked her mane before squeezing her thighs, signalling to trot. Samuel sidled up to her side, with his twin horse—Rayne—gently nuzzling Cadence.

"What's going on with you two?" Samuel whispered.

"Nothing."

"Are you fighting?"

"No."

"Well, something's wrong between you."

"There's nothing between us." Kora's heart splintered.

Samuel arched a blonde brow as he glanced from Kora to Blake's stiff straight back. "I never said there was."

Kora bit her tongue. Damned the gods, her tongue was loosening of late. Her mask slipping. She needed to tread carefully, especially with this metal noose around her neck. A huff sounded to her left, and Aryn joined them, precariously eyeing his horse. She was stunning up close, and Kora was mesmerised by her colouring.

"I think she's slowly warming up to the others," Aryn spoke evenly, as if the slightest change in tone would set the horse off. Kora snickered as Cadence moved a couple inches closer to Rayne.

"She's lovely."

"Her name is Fajra," Aryn hesitantly stroked the horses' back with two fingers. "The stable boy said it means fiery, and he's certainly not wrong about that." Fajra flicked her tail in response.

"Maybe she should've been my horse," Samuel teased. "I like a fiery woman."

"Absolutely not. Not after all the effort I've gone to get her to warm to me." Aryn tightened on the reins. Fajra snorted, and Cadence flicked her head.

"Aye, that's how it is. Put in all the effort for scraps in return," Samuel laughed, patting Rayne's back. Kora's stare snagged on Blake. He was dressed in all black as usual, never wavering from the empire's uniform, with a wrap protecting his dark head.

"Rayne's a good boy, aren't you, bucko?" Samuel's large patting hand eased, teasing the horses' mane. Rayne arched his neck, guiding Samuel's fingers to a spot and he scratched it, the horse visibly enjoying it. Who knew they were such conscientious creatures?

"I thought you said I was *ridiculous* for talking to Cadence?" Kora elbowed him.

"Aye, because you speak of such trivial shite. No horse wants to listen to the top five manoeuvres with daggers, or the rankings of the crew. I tell Rayne *real* stories."

"Like stories about how you bed a barmaid at every port?" Aryn added. "Let me guess, Circe was your latest conquest tale to Rayne."

"You're just jealous," Samuel flexed his bicep. "Get some meat on you, lad. Then the lassies will swoon all over you." He smiled, but it wasn't his usual dazzling charm. "But if you must know, no. Circe is playing hard to get."

Kora patted his thigh. His quest for love was overshadowed by his sheer, devastating handsomeness. One would think females would flock to Samuel, eager to secure him as a husband, but it had the opposite effect. He could pick any female, but none of them truly picked him. A blush burned Aryn's cheeks, his dual tattoo dark against the reddened skin. She eyed the archer, his body tensing, the blush deepening as his golden-flecked eyes met hers.

"Is there a woman waiting for you back home?" she asked. Where even was his home? The accent in his voice was not of Aldara.

"Oh, no. I'm not into that sort of . . . thing."

"Liar. I know love when I see it," Samuel pushed.

Aryn's blush was borderline worrying, his colouring matching Fajra's, and he cleared his throat. "There may have been someone, once. But I don't know if I'll ever see them again. It's been years, and I find it easier to not create romantic attachments. Less pain, that way. They're better off without me, anyway."

Kora paused. Who had Aryn left behind to join her crew? Were they in the north, safe behind the Citadel? She bit her lip. "Well, whoever they are, I'm sure they'd wait for you. You're alright, Aryn Di Largo."

He impishly smiled. Maybe she should follow his philosophy of romance. Because her *attachment* was currently acting like the bilge grease on the underside of a pirate's boot.

"Well, this chipper conversation makes me crave some grog," Samuel muttered.

"I think you need a detox," Kora joked. But gods-damned, was her throat parched.

She hadn't considered how far away they were from any water source and her fingers itched. Blake had been at the forefront of her mind for the past two days, and she'd been bitterly obsessing over his comments calling her an *escort*.

Alongside her masculinity, her doubts skyrocketed. A year . . . and they'd never been fully intimate together. The desert had been her solution, to break the final barrier between them. But now . . . that barrier had grown, towering so high and thick she couldn't reach across.

Escort. Murderer. Thief.

The insults branded her mind. Did she deserve to be captain? To lead others when she'd committed atrocities that'd cause an executioner to re-evaluate their decisions.

"Everyone knows grog solves all of life's problems," Samuel's smile beamed, the initial sadness fading as he discussed his second love—alcohol.

"To be fair, I'd have a drop in this heat—"

"Aryn!" Blake snapped, interrupting him. "Return to your post."

Aryn bristled, his hands turning white as he fisted his reins. Kora inspected him with surprise—and curiosity—by his physical response. His jaw clenched, and his eyes narrowed at Blake through his thick lashes. Kora was glad to know she wasn't the only one annoyed by Blake's swaggering arrogance.

The bilge-sucking, mega scurvy—she couldn't finish the thought. Not when her insults were reserved for pirates and rebels.

"As you wish." He pulled up his scarf to cover his face, and guided Fajra to guard the rear of the convoy.

Blake's gaze snapped to Kora and she maintained his glare. Harsh against her vision, the sun beamed behind him like he was some kind of saviour. She scoffed, but her pulse doubled as she squinted. Darkness writhed around his frame, coalescing with Erebus until a huge form stared at her with ethereal, green eyes.

In one blink, it vanished, and his glare transformed into a frown. She shook her head as they continued their parade across the desert, downing the remainder of her waterskin in hopes of warding off the hallucinations.

T he entourage had arrived at Whitestone Bay a few hours ago. The coral and red-toned sunset dazzled against the peculiar, pale-coloured pebbles of the shoreline, nearly blinding them as they set up camp for the evening in perfected silence.

Once again, Blake pitched his tent as far away as possible from Kora's, and once they'd created a small fire and eaten their pitiful rations, she trudged up the stony coastline, keeping her back towards his stormy presence.

Lost in her thoughts, and brooding over her potentially ended relationship, her foot snagged on a rocky outcropping and she sprawled into a blissful pool of water. Large, jagged boulders surrounded the rockpool, creating a miniature cave with no ceiling, exposing it to the magnificent sky. The rocks were slick with ocean spray, and covered in algae, seaweed, and barnacles. She supposed they were better company than Blake's mood.

Kora gently rested her back against it, her eyes closing against the muted darkness of the early night sky. The only light available was of the waning crescent moon, twinkling stars, and the dim, orange embers from the campfire.

Hidden within the shadows of the cluster of large rocks, she rested in silence. Rolling up her trousers and removing her laced boots, her bare feet wallowed in the shallow rockpool, and she wriggled her toes as the cold water lapped against the skin of her ankles and shins. Good gods, it felt divine to soak her feet after five days of scorching heat—and no baths.

The ocean waves rolling onto the hard shore soothed her rattled mind, and the tension in her body unwound as the coolness of the rockpool eased the pains of riding Cadence for days.

The chilled liquid travelled past Kora's ankles, coiling around her shins to her knees and she jolted at the thin stream of water winding itself around her legs like a snake. Alarm filled her, and she motioned her hand to wipe it away . . . and paused.

It wasn't like a snake. It wasn't constricting her, nor circling her like it would with prey. The water *caressed* her skin, shimmering against the faint moonlight. The pain in her legs dulled to a tender soreness, and the water reached out to her outstretched hand, seemingly sensing her. Figuring out who she was.

"Hi," Kora whispered, awe blooming on her tanned face.

She flexed her fingers and the stream rounded its end to form a finger-shape symmetrical to her own. Was the water alive? Or was this her power?

Upon contact, she gasped as a bolt of energy shot through her, straight to her core, lighting that sleeping power buried deep within her. The water sparkled iridescently, taking on a bioluminescent glow and cascading into the rockpool.

The wet, slick rocks glistened a unique indigo, and the barnacles pried open from the animated water. It rushed forward, enveloping Kora's hand like a coil. She jolted, her body scraping the jagged harshness of the rocks as the water circled her, flowing up her legs and arms, and soaking into her light clothing.

Kora's heart raced, her breath shuddering, and the talisman shone beneath her tan shirt. The water writhed excitedly, racing around her body like a hyper ferret. She flailed her arms, attempting to shake the water off but it didn't budge, clinging to her like a lost child.

"Stop it!" she hissed, baring her teeth.

The water calmed, quietly looping around her in intricate swirling circles. She stilled and pushed away from the rocks, her back stinging with pain. As she winced, the water animated again, and she opened her mouth to order it to stop when she was suddenly overcome with a relieving coolness across her back.

It was healing her. Water had healing magic.

The discovery overwhelmed her, and her mind crested like an ocean wave, threatening to submerge her. Kora wracked her brain thinking through the individual factions of magic. It'd never been mentioned in any of Agatha's tomes, or her teachings, that there was such thing as healing magic. None of the descriptions of the gods included healing abilities, either.

There were *healers*, but they used traditional herbal remedies and medicines. If only she could've brought those tomes Agatha gave to her to research. *Damn it.*

She swallowed her escalating fear and drew a steadying breath, her hand fluttering across her chest, tracing the thundering pulse of her heart. Upon her exhale, she tensed her legs, willing strength to imbue them to keep her upright against the crescendo of energy washing over her in rolling waves.

"Alright . . ." she took another breath. "Now, you listen to me—whatever you are." The water paused, awaiting her next words, listening intently. "It's nice to meet you and all, but I'd appreciate it if you get off me now," she paused. "I don't have a . . . change of clothes." Her words stumbled. She was talking to mystical water, for god's sake.

Kora wasn't sure what she was expecting. Perhaps some kind of slithering motion back into the rockpool, but the moment she finished talking, the water simply *fell* from her body. It created a loud *splash* and she grimaced, waiting to hear—or see—if anyone approached her from the camp. The talisman still shone beneath her shirt, and she glanced around the darkness before revealing it.

"No, no, no!" she moaned.

The sparkling blue glow within its heart had evolved into the shape of a crystalised diamond, and the ascending teal had absorbed more of the midnight blue shimmer. The teardrop shape was developing into an intricate pattern of winding vines, creating a complex swirl with pointed edges that Kora's eyes couldn't trace without feeling dizzy. Only the top third remained the original design, exposing the light blooming within.

How much time did she have left? What would happen when it was filled with her power? Would she shrivel into a husk?

Nibbling her bottom lip, Kora studied the talisman, twirling it around in her hands, figuring out if there was some way to slow it down—or even stop it, by adjusting the woven swirls. She thumbed the pointed edges, her wet skin sliding over the smooth metal. As she turned the talisman over in her hand to inspect the other side, it sliced the inside of her palm.

With a pained hiss, Kora plunged her hand into the glowing water upon instinct. It rippled around her, and thin tendrils of her blood floated from her palm, mixing with the iridescent blue. Confused at her own actions, she removed her hand from the crisp, chill water, and her blood ran just as cold.

The slice had fully healed. Not even a faint pink scar remained. Her blood washed away clean, and her skin was supple and smooth . . . even her callouses had disappeared.

The talisman hummed, eating up her power.

She observed the dark expanse of the ocean. There was nothing out there for hundreds of miles. If someone were to sail from Whitestone Bay and keep going, they'd arrive at the continent of Azaria after weeks of sailing.

It was so eerily dark out there, as if a shadow had overcome the night—even the stars' twinkle seemed dimmer. Her gaze slid to the talisman in her smooth hand, and back to the blackened ocean.

No one would know.

Problem solved, right?

Out of sight, out of mind. No one would be able to find it, or steal her power—

Crunch.

K ora whipped her head to the direction of the sound. Heart hammering once again—she'd need to visit Koji at this rate—she placed the talisman under her shirt, the glow faded—thank the gods—and she scrambled from the rockpool to peer around the arching rocks.

Her sight strained into the darkness, and she held a bated breath as she listened intently for signs of someone watching her. In the distance, she could make out the campfire, the tents, and the horses. But where were her crew? Had one of them seen her and reported it to the others?

Her fingers fumbled over the laces of her boots, and she cursed as she tightened them in haste, severing her blood supply to her feet. Sprinting back to the camp, her heart lodged in her throat. Mouth turned dry. Her stomach knotted and writhed within her.

Please be there, please be there.

She'd rather face an attack from the rebels than discover one of her crew had seen her using magic. *That she was a mage.* A mage with a power that'd never been recorded in history. Agatha would simply *die* with glee when she found out.

As Kora neared the camp, she sighed with relief when she spotted Aryn propped up against Rayne's broad pale back, tending to his longbow. The fire blazed, warming both archer and horse, and he tested the taut bowstring, his gaze full of targeted precision.

Samuel emerged from his tent, situated behind Rayne, rubbing his belly and belching deeply. His face twisted as he belched again, pounding on his chest. He paused at Kora puffing from her sprint and smiled sheepishly.

"Apologies, Captain." He patted his stomach. "Something's not agreeing with me."

She casually waved her hand like she wasn't petrified she'd been discovered and was about to be hanged from one of the palm trees. "Not to worry, Sam. Nothing I've not seen before."

Indeed, she'd witnessed her crew go through all manner of illnesses on months-long voyages—where they'd even had queues for the latrine after a bout of dysentery. Many ended up jumping into the sea just to clean the filth from their bodies.

She'd take that over facing a death sentence, though. Kora surveyed the small camp and her voice wavered, "Where's Blake?"

"Sulking." Samuel pointed towards the sea to their right.

Against the blackness of the ocean, an equally dark figure sat alone on the shore staring out at the fathomless expanse.

"Did you see anything over there?" She motioned behind her towards the rockpool.

Aryn followed her pointed hand and his eyes narrowed. The dancing flames of the fire ignited the golden flecks in his irises and it intimidated Kora. "No . . . why?"

"Did something happen?" Samuel tensed, his hand clasping the sword at his hip.

"I-I don't think so . . . I think the darkness is playing tricks on me."

"It does that," Aryn's voice lowered as well as his eyes, hidden beneath his thick lashes. She glanced at him curiously. "Why are you wet?" he asked without looking at her.

"I went for a swim," she replied dryly. Both males paused and glanced at each other with a certain *look*. "You both could do with one," her captain's tone surfaced.

Rayne huffed in response, and Aryn raised a brow, whilst Samuel glanced down at himself as if he could visually see the stench and dirt before grinning.

"You just want to see me with all my clothes off," he chuckled.

There was no denying they all absolutely reeked from the sweaty, hot journey. Before they could ask another question, Kora rolled her eyes and muttered about speaking to Blake, which shut them up, and she stomped over to his brooding pit by the sea.

With his back hunched over, Blake's arms rested on his bent knees. A small lantern shone by his feet, casting shadows on his bowed head, hair covering his face. He sat just enough out of range of the sea water reaching him and the lantern.

Fine, she was happy to avoid the sea for a little bit, too. Calypso had given her enough jump scares already. She sat beside

Blake, mere inches apart, and copied his exact position, letting her head fall forward, necking craning. After a few minutes of stony silence, her neck and back ached, the pebbles bit her bum, and she couldn't stand being this near to him without being able to touch him. Even if he vexed her.

"How on earth do you sit like that?" Kora groaned as she flexed her legs, rolling her neck with a wince.

"Helps me think." His words were short and flat.

"Don't hurt yourself thinking too much," she replied overly cheery. "Don't want that pretty head of yours breaking."

Blake scoffed and lifted his head to stare at the night sky. The stars dazzling in his green eyes made Kora hitch a breath. It was like seeing a sparkling earth captured in those irises.

"Don't try to be nice to me," he spoke gravelly. "What I said . . . I," he paused and looked at her. "I should *never* have said that to you."

Kora snorted in response.

With a sigh, Blake stretched his legs beside hers. "What I'm trying to say is, I'm sorry. I acted like a bilge rat to you. You're *my* captain, Kora. More importantly, you're my partner, and I know how hard you've worked. The stress of everything is starting to get to me. Too many things are at stake—*you're at stake*. Perilous times are ahead. Too perilous for a—"

"A woman?"

Shame flitted across his face. "I can't lose you. Or let anything happen to you. I don't know what would happen to me if I did. If I'd even live . . ."

Her heart swelled. She couldn't imagine living without him either, not that she'd admit that. Instead, she smacked him across the arm, and he startled.

"You deserve that," she muttered.

"I suppose I do."

"But maybe you can grovel some more."

"Oh?" A smile sparkled. "Do you want me on my knees?"

Heat flashed, and she nodded. "Apology accepted."

Kora nudged her foot towards his, and Blake returned the movement till their booted feet touched, followed by their shins and knees. A shiver rippled through her, and she glanced at her first mate, nibbling her lower lip.

She considered telling Blake everything in that moment— about the forged letter upon *Hell's Serpent*, the Skytor clan searching for a female, and Finlay's involvement . . . and that the

Mist was growing. She swallowed, one hand hovering over the talisman and opened her mouth—

"How was the rockpool?" Blake asked.

Oh no, had he seen her? If he had, he wouldn't have apologised. Her corpse would be buried in the desert instead. Her hand fell from her chest to the pebbled shore.

"Fine," she murmured. "Felt good after the desert."

Their eyes met and he shamefully glanced away, Kora mirroring his motion. He audibly swallowed as their romantic desert getaway drifted out into the dark ocean.

"I know something else that'd feel good," Blake's voice lowered an octave, his familiar drawl returning, and Kora's toes curled in her boots.

"Promises, promises," she smiled.

Perhaps they could still try to capture a moment of their original plan? But no way could they get away with sharing one of the tiny single-person tents—let alone trying to keep quiet. Following her trail of thought, he glanced to the camp, his eyes wandering over the tents. His mouth thinned. *Gods-damn it, Erick.*

"Then again . . ." He exhaled as Samuel's laughter floated towards them, clearing his throat, and capturing her gaze again. "I want you to know that I'm honoured to have served on *Hell's Serpent.*"

Hidden words lingered beneath. He wasn't destined for the naval life. He was only there because *she'd* requested him, and Blake would follow her wherever she would go. Even if he was better suited to the armies. Except following her to the Silver Sister's clan, which was why she'd have to leave him in Aldara.

Kora wasn't even sure if she would return from Shannara— at least not in one piece, and guilt panged through her at the thought. At the secrets she was burying. So many secrets she felt like she was drowning in the waters lapping near her feet.

Her life was becoming a dangerous mix of mysteries and secrets.

One of her fingers brushed his as their hands rested near each other. A tentative, daring touch, and he softened at the gesture.

"Blake. I-I want to tell you that . . ." She struggled to form the words on her lips, her tongue twisting.

"I know, my *asterya.* Someday, we'll have the chance—the time—to unpack . . ." he gestured between them, "everything."

Everything?

Everything.

She loosened a breath at Blake's misunderstanding, their vow repeating in her ears. She still had time. Time to figure out Finlay's past, and what the Skytor clan were up to. Time to master her power, and dispose of this talisman before it devoured her and her secrets. Time before the magical Mist consumed the world.

Time to figure out the voice on the wind guiding her.

Gods . . . it was *a lot.*

All in the month leading up to her twenty-fifth birthday.

"Kora . . ." he withdrew as his next words washed over her like cold ice, "with everything changing, I don't know if I'll be on *Hell's Serpent* anymore."

Just like that, the cracks in her carefully constructed world spread, splitting open.

"What do you mean?" her voice was but a whisper.

Blake glanced away. "I know that I promised you, but with the next round of Darkoning Trials approaching, it's time for me to establish myself whilst I still can. There's an opportunity in the army for me to become a commander. And I . . ." he exhaled, "I think I need to do this. Everything's going to change soon. I need to make sure I'm in a good position before the chance passes by."

Kora tried to swallow the hard lump in her throat. She couldn't imagine *Hell's Serpent* without Blake. It meant they'd spend days, weeks, *months* apart—maybe even a year.

"I'll always be here waiting for you to return." The light in his eyes faded, and she continued nibbling her lower lip, the skin breaking beneath her teeth. "I'm doing this for *us.* So that we'll have a chance together. If I'm not your first mate anymore, we might be able to be together . . . *properly.* As commander, I'll be able to protect you." Blake's voice strained with the words, fighting to get them out. "I need you in my life, *asterya.* But the islands will be changing, the gravity of the final unification is greater than we understand. I must do this."

Kora saddened, her soul deflating. She shoved her selfishness aside, her screaming thoughts that she was going to be alone—*all alone*—in the vast seas. No one to be her mirror self. No one who'd understand her deepest, darkest fears and pains deeply seeded from the trials.

With a pinch of her leg, she forced a smile. "Whatever you need to do, I'll support you." She nearly gagged on the words.

Blake offered a small smile in return, relief oozing from him.

"Come," she pushed to her feet, Blake tracking her every movement with focused intensity. He gracefully stood, his dark presence towering over her, and a different kind of heat coursed through her. After a moment of silent smiles, they returned to the camp, where Aryn and Samuel regarded them curiously.

The small fire had been erected near the edge of the desert before the ground blended into the precarious pebbled shores. They'd discovered large palm tree logs, discarded from previous woodjacks passing through the area, to use as a seating area by the fire.

Palm trees decorated the edge of the desert as far as they could see towards the east, and to the west was the rising cliff face, with exposing dark, shimmering rocks overlooking the rockpool.

"Is the tantrum over?" Samuel asked, seated on a log by the fire. Blake tossed him a glare.

"You're getting a bit too mouthy for my liking," Kora remarked, as her and Blake sat down by the fire, keeping a foot of distance between them.

"Aye, you like my mouth just as it is," Samuel replied with a grey-eyed wink. Aryn shot him an incredulous look, whilst Blake tensed at the flirtation.

"What would Circe think to hear you say such things?"

Samuel's flirting was harmless, it was his nature. He was the only male she'd tolerate it from, besides Blake.

"Why?" Samuel's eyes glistened. "Has she asked about me?"

Aryn rolled his eyes as he sorted through his quiver.

"Who's Circe?" Blake asked, dark confusion clouding his face.

"A barmaid Samuel wants to marry."

And a potential rebel sympathiser, and abetter of a secret organisation called the Skytors.

"Hands off, Marwood." Samuel saccharinely smiled.

Blake held up his hands innocently. "She's all yours." His gaze slid to Kora, and she tried not to squirm under the beckoning lust hidden in his eyes.

They settled against the logs surrounding the fire, and she stared at the black expanse of the ocean. The rolling waves and the salt-water air soothed her once again, helping her ride out the raging torrent of anxiety that'd been sinking its claws into her since Finlay's death.

Aryn placed his longbow and quiver down, his attentive eyes scanning the area. "What do you think the sentinel will be like?"

She shrugged. *Another uppity, noble prick.*

"I'm expecting a total lubber," Samuel sighed. "He'll just be some appointed know-it-all that'll cower at the first sign of conflict. We'll probably need to hold his hand back through the desert."

"Royal sentinels are normally of the . . . academic sort," Blake mused.

"So . . . someone untrained in combat," Kora confirmed. "We'll have to be extra careful trekking back. I'm surprised no one's noticed us. We were out there for five days."

Five days of dry, uneventful tension.

"Especially with Sam's singing," Aryn muttered quietly.

"Who's to say they didn't? They could be watching us now." Blake inclined his head to the looming darkness of the desert. She followed his gaze, glancing between the baying palm trees, searching for pairs of rebel eyes glowing in the dark. "If I were them, I'd attack at our weakest."

"Which'll be when we have an extra person to protect," Aryn commented. "We'll be tired, hungry, *and* weaker on the journey back."

"Whose idea was this?" Samuel moaned.

Kora's mouth curved. "If that's the case, then I'm going to retire now. I suggest you all try to rest as much as possible. Set up a rotation schedule, stay alert lads."

"I'm taking first watch," Aryn announced, and he laid a hand on his longbow as if to say he'd shoot anyone who dared to come near. With his world-renowned precise aim, she wouldn't be surprised if he could shoot in the pitch black and not miss.

"Wake me when it's time to change," Blake replied sternly.

"We'll take turns," she added. "Samuel after Blake, and I'll take early morning."

They all nodded in agreement and retired to their individual tents—except Aryn, who nestled against Rayne. Fajra slept by his tent, with two blankets piled on top of her. Erebus slept beside her, their snouts pressed together, their black and white manes blending into each other.

Gods, even the horses were getting more romance than her.

Kora placed a thin threaded blanket over Cadence, gently stroking her silken mane before dipping into her tent. Blake had ducked into his own without so much as a goodnight—a painful reminder of their impending separation—and Samuel audibly belched from inside his own.

She curled up on the pitiful, thin sleeper mattress, grateful not to be able to feel the pebbles of Whitestone Bay digging into her skin. Her scar throbbed once again, and she regretted not packing a salve. Sleep crept on her swiftly, and she fell into a slumber as deep as the ocean before her, where no light could pierce her mind.

As if her dreams had been stolen from her.

32

"Are you okay?"

"What? Who is that?"

"Can you hear me?"

"Who are you? Where am I?"

Kora's voice echoed around her—wherever she was. She was neither here nor there. Up nor down. There was no light, nor darkness. She just simply was. A being. An entity. An existence floating on the—on the what?

"What's going on?" Her voice was so loud it bounced around, vibrating into the absence of existence. Did she even have any lips? A mouth? How was she speaking?

"You need to keep moving."

"I don't think I even can," she scoffed. She had no body. She was part of the cosmos. The very breath, life, spark of the universe. Past, present, and future converged, flowing through this folded vacuum. This void. Her inner beast yawned, recognising the growing mystical power unfurling around her.

"Keep running . . . they'll catch you soon."

She tried her best to imitate a frown. "Who's chasing me? The rebels?"

"Your enemy is closer than you know . . ." *the voice began fading.*

The rebels were close by—close by where? She was here, and nowhere else.

"No—wait!" *She couldn't be left alone here. In this emptiness. Kora surged, delving deep into herself, beckoning that slumbering beast in a panic. "Don't leave me!" she begged.*

"I'm always here with you . . ."

The voice had a hint of sadness. It sounded so familiar, and its melancholy tone caused sorrow, guilt . . . shame to rise within her. Why did she feel so sad?

She tugged on the faint, lingering thread of the voice. Pushing herself to follow it through the ether. She visualised it as a burning, bright, white unbreakable string, and the harder she tugged, the more her water beast growled, scratching at the walls to be released.

The brightest blue light shone from her, taking the form of a rippling, water humanoid. The voice gasped in response, and she blinked as the thread shone brighter, almost blinding her.

"Remember."

"I don't remember," Kora's voice cracked. "I can't remember you!"

She halted at her own words. Who was this voice? How did she even know that, at the end of the voice, there was a person to remember? Someone from her past, that was potentially alive? Or was the void playing tricks on her, haunting her with a ghost of her broken memory?

Why was it trying to force her to remember? Her past was forgotten. Gone. Inconsequential. She would never retain her memories. She needed to focus on her life of—wait. What was her life? Where was she? How did she get here?

"Who are you? Please tell me." Her liquid form bubbled from the overwhelming emotions roiling within her. "Where am I?"

"Remember, and you'll be set free . . ."

A force swept towards her, propelling her away from the white, burning lifeline she desperately clung to. Her water form dissolved, and she was once again a floating existence in the plain of the void. There was no sound, no air, no light. Nothing but inky, black darkness, as thick as tar.

And the enveloping scent of rain after a storm . . . and the sleek metal of weapons.

"Kora!"

She knew that voice.

"Kora, *wake up*!"

Her body violently shook as large hands bit into her flesh, and with a groan, her eyes fluttered open to Blake knelt over her, shaking her shoulders, his face panicked.

"*Wake up!*" he snapped again. His emerald eyes blazed.

"I'm awake!" Her voice came out raspy as she shoved him off.

Her face stung, and her body was stiff . . . and damp. She squinted against the blaring sun filtering through the flap of her tent. The air was already warm, and her short hair was plastered to her scalp with sweat.

"It's the morning? Why did no one wake me for my watch?"

She stepped out of the tent. The camp had been packed away, the fire doused, and a large ship, with grand purple sails listed on the glittering, cold-blue ocean in the distance.

"What the fuck is that?" Lethality dripped from her.

"The royal ship already arrived," Blake huffed as he began breaking down her tent with quick precision. "We couldn't wake you up. You slept through the whole night. I thought maybe you needed rest," he paused. "But then you slept through breakfast, and through our early morning scouts. It wasn't until I saw the sails that I came in to wake you." A sharp exhale followed. "I even slapped you. Nothing was waking you up!"

Kora pivoted to regard him. The right side of her face burned, laced with a stinging sensation, and she fingered her cheek.

"I guess I needed some rest . . ." Shock vibrated through her from her smarting cheek down to her feet. Blake had *slapped* her.

"You guess?" His face was stricken. "I thought you were dead at one point!"

She was taken aback by the quiver in his voice. Concern bared down on his shoulders, and his muscles tensed through his clothes. She reached for him, but quickly reared back as heavy footsteps approached. Samuel strode down from the palm trees lining the desert, with a bronze and brass spyglass in one hand, his face hardened like a boulder.

"I'm fine," she replied, gesturing to herself. Blake ran his sharp gaze over her with a frank assessment. It was so eerily similar to Erick's observant eyes it made her shudder.

"They'll be here soon," Samuel spoke as he stopped by her side. "They're not docking the ship. A boat with three men is rowing to shore, not the dock. I'd say thirty minutes tops."

To the east sat multiple docking piers, where ships normally docked for travellers and shipments. It'd grown quiet over the past decade and was left unmanned. To the west, past the cliff faces, was King's Guard Cove. An infamous port with a towering keep, used for transportation of prisoners to Deadwater Prison.

Samuel paused, raking his gaze over Kora's dishevelled state. His humorous sparkle had diminished now they were to be joined by constituents of the royal family. "Alright, Captain?"

"Just going to freshen up."

She shot Blake a glare and snatched her leathers, running to the hidden rockpool. Her shirt already reeked with sweat, and she knelt by the pool of water, splashing it against her flushed, sticky skin before pulling her leathered layers on with a grimace.

Her hair curled around the nape of her neck and she soaked it with water, pushing the growing lengths back. Kora savoured the brief relief of coolness before seeing to her needs and trudging back to camp.

Aryn hovered by the horses, lining them up, and checking their saddles and bags were attached correctly. She noticed Cadence had been strapped with more saddle bags than the others.

"Who's riding with who?" Kora asked as the rowboat neared. There must be a reason Cadence was carrying the most load.

"I'll take the sentinel," Blake replied quickly. "They can take the two guards," he nodded at Aryn and Samuel. "Eat this—*now.*" He handed Kora a small rationing of bread, dried meat, and fruit. "We all need our strength."

She gobbled it down fast enough to not even taste it, and her stomach twinged in protest. The sun baked the dazzling, reflective stones of the shore as the dark wooden rowboat came to a stop. The wood scraping against the pebbles set her teeth on edge, and sweat dripped down her back from the mid-morning heat.

Three large, muscular males disembarked from the rowboat. They donned black and grey clothing, with fine silver vambraces, and thin, yet impenetrable, silver armour covered their shoulders, abdomens, and thighs. Impressive Azarian steel. Highly coveted, and highly sought.

Gods' sake they're walking targets.

An exquisite purple stag, with a four-pointed star between its antlers was emblazoned across their torsos and backs. The symbol for the royal Staghart family of Azaria. The Talmon Empire had a demurer version of the four-pointed star, signifying it as an extension and subsidiary of Azaria.

"I thought you said sentinels were academic," she hissed to Blake as the three males approached.

One had a large sword strapped to his back, whilst another carried an elegant black recurve bow. Aryn eyed him intensely. The third had two hatchet axes sheathed on either side of his thick hips.

Blake audibly swallowed in response as the males effortlessly strode across the pebbles. Kora was certain their muscular thighs were wider than her head, and a tremble overcame her at the sheer threat of them.

To the left, the archer's long black hair flowed behind him, framing his pale skin. His facial features were sharp, long, and cold, with matching black eyes, and he bore the slenderest frame of the three.

To the right, the swordsman was the tallest of the three—even taller than Samuel. Dark pink disfigured skin snaked up his jaw, ending by his lips and ears, the colour stark against his light brown tone. His dark, thick hair was cut short, with matching stubble coating his wide chin. Despite his vibrancy, his hooded eyes were lifeless, the colour of dirt after death. He wore black, leather gloves. *Gods, he must be sweating.*

Blake stiffened, sizing up the swordsman, his own hand twitching over his golden cutlass sword. Which left the final one in the middle—who now stood directly in front of Kora.

The axe-wielder.

She craned her neck back at the towering mass of muscle. His skin was of the darkest chocolate, deep and rich, as were his eyes. His features were round and smooth, and his head was shaved. His hands, which rested on his dual silver axes, were covered in scars, with barely a centimetre of unharmed flesh visible.

"Which one of you is Captain Cadell?" His voice was deep, and boomed with an authority that made Kora's knees quake. His dark eyes swept over Blake, Samuel, and Aryn—not even acknowledging her presence.

She deflated at the question. They'd requested her—without knowing she was a female. Not only did the islanders think the captain of *Hell's Serpent* was male, but so did Azaria. Erick's mission to force her to blend in had worked better than he'd probably imagined. She bit the inside of her cheek at the disrespect and summoned her voice to her lips.

"I am." She sagged with relief at the strength in her voice. "We're here to escort you to Stormkeep Fortress." Kora gestured to her crew.

The three males finally looked at her and blinked with surprise. A blush crept onto Kora's face at the weight of their stare, and she felt small as she returned it. Their eyes lingered on the scar covering the side of her face, and she resisted the urge to stick her tongue out at them.

"An escort," the swordsman snickered as his eyes greedily roamed over her chest. "I can see why they let women join the navy here. Must be quite boring without some . . . entertainment." His voice had a slight lisp to it.

"Watch it," Blake threatened, but he winced at the word *escort*.

Kora could only imagine what kind of entertainment he meant, and she was certain it was the *forceful* kind. The axe-wielder raised a scarred hand, silencing his fellow swordsman.

"Excuse Callan. We don't let him out much, he's not used to seeing a woman fully clothed." He smirked, earning a glare from Callan. "My name is Theron, and this is Ivar."

Theron gestured to the archer to his right. Ivar tightly nodded, his mouth a thin, pale line, his arms crossed in front of him. Kora swallowed her irritation at Callan, and thanked Theron for the introductions, her palm sweaty as they shook hands.

"This is Blake Marwood, my first mate." Blake greeted Theron, ignoring Callan's slimy grin. "And Samuel Rommier, my sailing master. Aryn Di Largo—head of archers upon my ship." Ivar's pit-dark eyes widened at the mention of Aryn.

"How long till we reach the fortress?" Theron spoke frankly.

"Five days," Samuel replied. "We stop every night to recover from the heat, and we'll need to be on watch for exiles and rebels in the desert." He glanced at their weapons. "Which shouldn't be a problem."

Indeed, they were all thinking the same thing. Big, scary guards from the continent.

"Your islands are so tiny," Callan sneered. "Five days is nothing."

"We may have to stop more frequently with the added riders," Kora chimed in, ignoring him.

They weren't expecting three *overly sized* males to join them. Cadence would have to carry more supplies on her back to compensate. She glumly checked their faithful steeds, who all waited patiently under the shade of the waning palm trees.

When she turned back, Callan watched her with greedy intensity, his eyes unabashedly exploring her chest, down to her curved hips. His lips pulled back into another smarmy grin, and he winked at her. *Ew.* Her stomach churned, and she straightened her spine in response, holding her head high as Theron continued discussing the venture back to Stormkeep Fortress with Samuel.

"We were expecting a royal sentinel." Blake glanced behind the males to the empty rowboat.

Kora also cast her gaze towards the ship in the distance, expecting a second rowboat to deploy. These males must be the bodyguards, scouting the land for safety before the sentinel joined them.

"Oh," Theron smiled, his dark eyes sparkling. "I *am* the royal sentinel."

C allan's incessant drivel to ride with Kora in the beginning of their journey had Blake snapping at him to ride with Samuel, who was more than happy to keep a leash on the male. Kora was just glad to have his wandering, grimy hands away from her, but it didn't stop his leering empty stares. *Fucking creep.*

The archers perched on top of Fajra in bizarre silence, towards the rear of the convoy. Occasionally, she'd glance back to find Ivar tensely sitting back-to-back with Aryn, his longbow resting on his lap as his dark eyes scanned the barren, sandy horizon through a makeshift wrap protecting his face from the sand blasts.

They'd been riding like that for nearly three days, and had not spoken to each other once.

Theron rode with Blake, even going as far as offering to walk or jog beside Erebus to allow the stallion a reprieve from the weight. Intense, whispered conversations floated across the tundra from them, their heads close together as they spoke. They'd been practically joined at the hip since they set off from Whitestone Bay, and Kora only ever caught the odd word regarding the empire, the state, and the upcoming plans of the king-soon-to-be-emperor.

What it meant for the Azarian Islands. What it meant for *home.*

She supposed she *should* be more interested about the future of her homeland. Yet, all Kora could focus on was the thrumming trinket nestled against her chest. The growing magic flowing in her veins. She'd been mulling her revised plan over and over in her mind, chewing on the potential risks as they trotted through the blistering heat.

Escorting Theron back to the fortress was the top priority.

After that, she could flee to Shannara and dispose of the talisman, absolving her treacherous status to the empire. She was certain that, once the talisman was gone, her powers would diminish. She'd still be a mage, just a *normal* mage. After that . . . she wasn't sure. Perhaps the witches would use her for their voodoo practices and eat her flesh.

Nightmare tales, spoken in hushed tones through the winding streets of the port town, bounced through her mind. Rumours the witches hunted trespassers, killing them in slow, excruciating ways, and harvesting the flesh and organs for rituals . . . and for consumption.

The sun set against the distant dunes, and the bounding sandy slopes curved across the simmering glow of the ball of light. Ember orange tones blended into the yellow grains of sand, creating a decadent summer hue of warmth. Kora pushed her goggles onto her head, basking in the final remnants of warm light before they were plunged into the cold evening darkness.

Blake barked an order for them to set up camp for the night, and Cadence's tail flicked gently swatting Kora's back. *Time for rest.*

By Samuel's calculations, they had passed the Southern Oasis this morning, and should be well in shot of exiting the exiles' territory tomorrow, before crossing the Bellmoor border. The tension in her shoulders eased knowing Theron and his cabal would be off their hands soon.

Luckily, the royal posse had brought water, and enough rations to feed a small army, and the itch crawling around Kora's skin from the dry desert had eased more and more each day after she'd downed two waterskins.

As they set up camp that evening, they filled their bellies with fresh fruit, bread, and sea biscuits, as they'd done the past few nights—Cadence included. Kora even went as far as splashing cold water on her face, cleaning her pits and feet every night, and letting Cadence drink her fill to endure through the last leg of the journey home.

"Tell us Theron . . . what's Azaria like?" Kora asked as they lounged around the dim campfire.

It wouldn't be long until Blake doused it, paranoid of exiles and rebels locating them by the smoke. Theron and Ivar sat across the fire, the latter peering into the surrounding darkness blanketing the sky, the former sipping from his waterskin. Firelight danced in his deep eyes, and he let out a short, elated sigh, laced with acidity, at her question.

"Not too dissimilar from this." Theron gestured to the sandy dunes surrounding them.

Samuel, sat to her right, raised a blonde brow as he peered at the dunes enveloping their camp. "Sounds . . . charming," he spoke flatly.

A small chuckle escaped Theron. "Azaria is a harsh land. It is mostly hot, arid desert, with no chances of vegetation or crops growing. Our city is nestled in the north, where we have the coolest climate. Well . . . as cool as it *can* be."

Ivar grunted in response. His long black hair was tied and plaited at the nape of his neck, and a sheen of sweat glistened on his skin against the flickering light of the fire. Not a fan of the heat, then.

"Surely, there are more habitable areas?" Kora asked.

Blake collapsed to her left, equally distanced between herself and Theron. He brought his knees up, crossing his ankles before resting his arms on top. Aryn had wandered off to the tents and horses stationed far from the fire, scouting the edges of the rising dunes for potential intruding enemies.

She wasn't sure where Callan was, but hopefully he wasn't returning anytime soon.

"Yes, the south of the continent is rife with jungles. Trees bigger than you could imagine." Theron raised his hands in the air, stretching his arms wide to imitate the size, and Kora's eyes widened at the span of them—he was truly a walking giant. "It would take a small unit of men weeks . . . maybe even a month, to attempt to navigate it. The intensity of the jungle foliage makes it difficult to farm, so we import the majority of our goods."

"From us," she observed. "You need the islands."

Theron paused and then slowly nodded, his gaze lingering on the fire. "Our relationship with the islands is vital, and one we cherish deeply. We hope to continue to grow our bonds together through my time visiting."

Kora nearly vomited from the grovelling, courtly tone. So different from his original commanding voice when they'd first met. Almost as if it had been scripted for him to say. *Typical sentinels.*

"Isn't there a war waging between the two halves of your continent?" Samuel asked, sitting back on his large hands.

Theron's eyes flashed at Samuel's tone, and his face tightened at the subtle lack of fealty to Azaria being *their* continent as well. It wasn't uncommon for some islanders to separate themselves from the continent—albeit there were not many who would proudly declare so. The silent tear down the middle of the islands was ever-present. No one knew which side the people around them stood on.

One side believed the Azarian Islands were a nation in their own right, led by the viceroys. The other side were fanatics of the royal family, and all things Azaria. The former kept their opinions entirely silent compared to the latter. The continent dwellers even considered the islanders as rebels at times, if they didn't swear fealty.

And then there were the rebels, devout to the old ways. *That* was a whole can of worms Kora didn't want to touch. Not when she'd physically been in their nest. Perhaps the tear in the islands had a few cracks slithering through it.

That was all about to change soon.

Theron cleared his throat, setting his waterskin aside. "I can assure you . . . all is well in Azaria."

"But there *is* a war?" Samuel pressed.

"There have been some disputes with natives of the jungle. But there are no wars," Theron's tone sharpened.

From what she could remember of Erick's history lessons, the continent was barren. Worse than the tundra. Wars had raged between the jungle natives—the Loukash—and the Stagharts, until the ground had split, a cavern gaping open across the width of the land, as if the hardened earth had developed jaws.

It'd miraculously split the two peoples, forcing them to remain to their halves of the continent. But Erick had reported Azarians still attempted to build bridges to this day, sending scouts to scale the caverns and spy on the Loukash. Whilst the natives chose to guard their side, silencing any trespasser they discovered.

"I've heard that the king wants to expand to take control of the islands. To gain more troops and supplies for these . . . *disputes*," Samuel's words were slow and forceful, his stare not faltering as Theron's face darkened.

"*Samuel*," Kora hissed.

"Those are just rumours, Sam," Blake murmured, hedging around Theron's tensity.

"Rumours are impactful," Theron replied. "They can tear a nation apart, topple kingdoms and thrones."

"Good thing it's just a rumour then." Kora glared at Samuel, but his boulder-hardened face didn't waver.

"If you pull our troops and resources, you'll kill these

islands," Samuel replied gravelly.

"You should rein in your dogs." Callan's legs brushed against her spine, and she shot to her feet to create distance from him, cringing at the fabric of his trousers touching her. He peered down at her once again, with that disgusting, annoying grin. Definitely a creep.

"Watch your mouth," Kora spat.

"Oh . . . I intend to do much *more* than that," Callan's voice lowered along with his eyes as he hungrily surveyed her body. "Those leathers must be suffocating in this heat . . . why don't you take them off?" he purred.

"You will respect the captain." Blake stood, seething, his fists clenched at his sides in restraint.

Callan huffed a laugh. "Women are good for one thing only— and it's certainly not being a *captain.*" He leaned in, and her eyes watered at the reek of him. "Come on, give us a show." She tried not to gag at the smell of his breath. *Oh, she'll give him a show. A pointy one with daggers.*

"You heard her," Samuel's broad presence appeared next. "Watch your mouth, you lily-livered scourge." He smacked his spyglass against his hand, his intentions clear if Callan tried to touch her.

"*Callan!*" Theron snapped. "We are guests here."

"And as guests—royal ones at that—we should be treated as such." Callan's smarmy lisp made her shudder, but she stood her ground. Her fingers itched to reach for one of her razor-sharp daggers. "So . . . come, lassie. Sit on my lap and show me a good time, like the good little escort you are."

"Stand down!" Theron's commandeering voice boomed.

Callan merely snickered, reaching for her waist to pull her towards him. Kora recoiled, time seemingly slowing down. She was distantly aware of Blake slowly moving, and Samuel raising his spyglass, as she reached behind for one of her sabre daggers.

She would cut his fingers off if she had to. They'd been ordered to escort Theron safely across Aldara—no one would care if his lackeys were injured—or killed—in the process. Callan's gloved fingers were inches away from her body and she tensed, her fingers brushing her daggers.

An arrow shot through the air, stopping Callan short, and landing in the sand by his feet with a resounding *thud.*

Everyone froze. Theron and Ivar emerged beside Samuel, their weapons raised in a heartbeat. Kora looked to her right. And there was Aryn, chest heaving, his magnificent longbow aimed at Callan. The golden flecks in his almond-shaped eyes glowed with rage, and his grown-out hair stuck to his forehead with sweat.

"You will *not* touch my captain," Aryn spoke each word slowly, with a voice that sounded ancient. Kora's heart warmed at her protective crew.

"You missed," Callan sneered glancing down to the arrow in the sand.

"He never misses," Kora replied smugly.

Callan's face paled at the warning shot. Aryn stood frozen in time, nocking another arrow, aimed for Callan's head, no doubt.

Theron tentatively stepped forward, hands raised, his axes sheathed at his waist. "Now . . . let's all calm down. I apologise for my quartermaster. He *won't* approach you again." Theron glared at Callan. "You are dismissed, Callan. We'll talk later."

With a scowl, Callan stomped back to the tent he was sharing with Ivar, head down and muttering curses at Kora and her crew. Theron exhaled, and Ivar hovered silently next to him, his own dark recurve bow trained on Aryn.

"You can stop with the standoff." She pinched the bridge of her nose, feeling another headache coming on. "You're not going to kill each other."

After a few moments of tense silence, both archers ever-so-slowly lowered their weapons, making sure they placed their arrows back in their quivers at the same time.

All in their consistent silence. Utterly baffling.

Surely, they would want to be friends; swapping little notes on their archery activities. How to best shoot, who had the best bow, and so on? The bigger the bow, the bigger they were endowed? Whatever lethally trained archers discussed.

"I must apologise." Theron placed a hand on his chest. "He is a troubled . . . difficult man."

"Why are they here?" Kora placed her hands on his hips. "We were only advised of *one* sentinel to escort, yet there are three of you." Weighing down poor Cadence.

"My guards follow me wherever I go. I do not have a say in the matter."

"Guards?" Blake frowned. "You said he was your quartermaster."

"Same thing." Theron's voice grew quiet and distant. "I am also a captain, Kora Cadell, *and* a royal sentinel. Callan and Ivar are my royally appointed guards, meaning they must be with me *at all times*—including when I sail afar."

Weariness tinged his voice, fatigue edging the sculpted planes of his face. "You know as well as I do that guests do not fare well on long voyages. I appointed them roles to keep them busy. So that they *contribute* on ships, and do not waste any of our time or resources."

This was a male with no freedom. A male always watched, bound by the rules of his land. Kora met his gaze, and understanding channelled between them. She nodded in response, lost for words, and Theron bowed his thanks—captain to captain. Blake muttered some political nonsense as Theron retired to his own tent, Ivar silently in tow.

Even his steps were silent in the sand, barely sinking a centimetre. A walking predator.

"Aryn," she observed the flush-faced boy. His longbow was strung over his shoulder, its curved brown wood gleaming against the crackling fire. A looping pattern cascaded around the smooth shape. "Thank you. That . . . that meant a lot. To me."

Aryn's quick eyes darted to Blake, who'd begun dousing the fire. "Just doing my job, Captain."

As Aryn turned, briskly heading for his own tent, his head bowed and shoulders tense, Kora frowned at an invading disappointment carving itself into her chest at his response. At the sudden desire for friendship that devoured her.

34

H ands stroked up and down her legs.

Kora moaned softly as they travelled up, gripping her waist, lifting her shirt to expose her stomach. It was still dark, and the cool air swept in to brush against her bare skin. Those hands quickly followed, tracing her curves, and the strong wall of her core, before cupping her breasts. They were rough, and she wriggled at the twinge of pain.

Blake was *here*.

He was touching her, caressing her. *Finally*. They'd get their moment in the desert. It was daring, and her defiance sizzled at the risk of exposure.

His hands became earnest, tugging at her clothes, and she winced as they pressed hard enough to bruise. He placed his knees down the middle, pushing her legs open with a grunt, and fisted her waistband, fumbling with the ties.

Blake leaned forward, his tongue flicking up her neck, inhaling deeply. She turned her head to capture his mouth with her own, eager to breathe in the scent of him. The scent of—

Kora's eyes flew open as she grimaced at the stench of sweat . . . along with a familiar foul odour. Callan grinned, his hands pulling at her waistband as he rushed to remove her clothes. He'd discarded his gloves, revealing mangled, twisted flesh in a burning shade of red. His fingers ended in rounded, calloused stumps, his nails burned clean off.

"*You!*" she seethed. "Get the fuck off me!"

She pushed up, but there was barely enough room for them both in her tiny one-person tent, and his head bobbed against the roof as he perched between her spread legs. She shoved against his chest, and he laughed in response at the feeble attempt.

"You were enjoying it," he crooned, his teeth flashing in the dark. "Just lie down, dear. I'll take you on the ride of your life." *The audacious prick.*

"Get. Off. Me. *Now.*"

Kora shoved against him again, only to knock him a few inches. Callan was a solid wall of muscle. As a royal guard, he had to be the strongest, the fittest, the *fastest* to defeat their enemies. She had no doubt he would easily overpower her, and his grin suggested he knew the same.

In the confines of the tent, she didn't have enough room to move her legs to close them, or even drag herself away from him. Her knees touched the sides of the bolted-down tent, and her heart raced as a sickening heat crept over her body.

"Aye, I plan to."

Callan raised a hand, and his backhanded slap across her face was like a bolt of lightning. She fell back, her vision dazed, cheek smarting with pain as he shoved her shirt up to her neck and greedily lapped his tongue all over her skin. The very touch of him repulsed her, and panic bubbled, seeping in at the edges, taking over her body.

"*No!*" she cried. "Stop—"

A large, grimy hand clasped her mouth, muffling her cries, as his other disfigured hand trailed down to between her thighs. Tears sprung in her eyes as he gripped at the apex of her thighs, clenching, and rolling his palm painfully, a hiss snaring from his clenched teeth.

Kora manically writhed under his grip, her nails scraping his thick arm, trying to pry his hand from her mouth. She dragged it lower down and clamped her teeth down *hard*.

"You bitch!"

Callan slapped her again, knocking her head into the ground as his blood leaked from her mouth. Stars danced in her vision from the impact, the world tilting, and she distinctly heard him rip her trousers, then rapidly pulling down his own. She only had the saving grace of his twisted hands struggling with the ties.

"*Help!*" she screamed. "Someone—"

Please, Blake, please hear me!

He forced her shirt into her mouth as a gag after pinning her arms beneath her own weight. Kora cried against the fabric, and his gaze dropped to the talisman. With a smile, he gripped the chain in his fist, yanking it to the side and into the ground, choking her.

She gasped. Coughing at the crushing chain straining against her windpipe, cutting into her flesh. Her legs flailed either side of Callan as he smeared his blood over her stomach.

"I bet you're a virgin." He leaned down, inhaling at her neck. The sheer strength of him was unimaginable. He was nearly as strong as the Flint twins. Her nimble, swift nature wouldn't get her out this. "Damn . . . I hope you are."

He licked up the side of her face, following the curve of her scar. His tongue left a lingering trail of burning pain, as if her flesh couldn't bear the touch of him.

"I'm going to mark you like whoever did this to you. Ruin you for other men. No one will want to touch you once I'm through with you."

He reared back, chuckling as he removed the last of his trousers, his hard length springing up. Her mouth dried at the sight, her heart and soul emptying out.

It was happening.

No one was coming to save her, no one heard her cries—or they did and didn't care. It wasn't their job to stop abuse. To stop *rape*. She was a female; chattel for males to do with as they please. It was a male's world after all.

Kora pleaded with the gods, with Calypso, Thanos, *any of them*, in that moment. She hadn't prayed to them in so long, in such a desperate way, and she begged with her heart, her soul, her life. She beseeched her faithful voice, who watched over her, who guided her. Despite her inability to respond to it, she implored with everything she had in the hope it could hear her now.

All was silent.

Callan pumped his length, the tip wet as he tightened his grip on her talisman. Tears flowed down her cheeks. She couldn't breathe. She was going to die. Her fingers flexed beneath her back, but there was no water to summon, no liquid nearby to manipulate. Her water beast was hidden deep within her, too afraid of the monster before her.

Please.

I need you.

She wasn't sure who she was begging now. Who she desperately sought help from. Her mind cried viciously as Callan exposed the last of her body, her own trousers discarded, and a shiver shuddered through her.

Her body shut down, her mind escaping into a dark corner, away from the impending violation. She hadn't experienced this since the Darkoning Trials, where she learned to remove herself from the present . . . from the pain she couldn't control as she'd been beaten within an inch of her life.

Nobody was coming.

His finger ran up her slit, and she barely felt the sensation as she burrowed deeper into herself.

No one would save her, and she couldn't even save herself. What good were her powers, her water beast, if they couldn't prevent atrocities like this? The chain painfully cut into her neck as Callan flushed his body against hers, murmuring everything he was going to do to her.

Halting, his face contorted into a frown. His body quaked, his muscles rippling, and he released the chain. Kora sucked in a deep breath, panting, gulping down air, as Callan fell back, his hands clutching at his body.

"What is this?" He glared as he tore at his flesh, rubbing it, scratching until his caramel skin turned a similar shade of pink to his scarred neck.

Kora covered her body with the scraps of her shirt, now able to move . . . to be *present*. Callan trembled, his hands roving frantically over his body.

"What are you *doing* to me?" he snarled.

A blue hue encapsulated the tent, basking his face in a deathly glow, and his eyes widened in horror as she smiled devilishly, raising her shining hands, letting the light bloom. It was a minute amount of power, but it was enough.

She would save herself.

"You're a *mage!*" he hissed, and her smile broadened as his skin visibly rippled, his veins writhing beneath the surface. "Stop it!" His lisp thickened as that familiar pulse returned, racing across her bones, coalescing in her core before bolts of energy surged out, elevating her until she felt untethered from the world.

With his limp cock hanging out in the open, Callan dragged his churning body out of the tent. She delighted in the veins bubbling along it, coated in coarse sand. He whimpered as she followed him, one hand clutching the fragmented remains of her trousers.

"You'll . . . be hanged . . . for this," Callan spoke between panting breaths. He stopped and rolled onto his back, glowering in pain. "I'll tell them all."

"Dead men tell no tales."

Her throat burned and her voice was hoarse as she twisted her hand, imagining his blood churning in his body until he vomited, clenching his stomach. He moaned and begged, and she placed her booted foot on his neck, cutting off his speech—his air. Raging red bloomed as he choked, coughing, desperately trying to flood his lungs with air.

"Not so fucking nice, is it?" She glanced down at his limp dick and flicked a finger towards it, urging the blood to redirect itself. Callan shrieked as it shrivelled.

"Captain!"

The blue hue died from Kora's hands as Blake sprinted to them, a familiar palomino mare by his side. Moonlight bounced from his sword, his alert green eyes glaring in the darkness.

"I was on watch and heard a scream. Cadence was running towards—"

He halted to a stop, staring at Callan convulsing in the sand, her foot still on his windpipe. His eyes scanned the details— Callan's bleeding hand, his exposed length, her torn clothes, and tearful eyes. A dark shadow swept over his face.

"Tell me he's getting what he deserves." Blake's tone could have frozen the whole desert. Even Callan shivered.

"It's all her fault!" Callan rasped. "What'd you expect me to do? She practically invited me into her tent." Kora almost laughed at the blatant lie.

"I very much doubt that," Blake snapped.

He placed a comforting hand on her shoulder, and she nuzzled her cheek against his warmth. Callan's eyes widened in response. He'd not only attempted to rape a captain . . . but an *involved* captain.

"You two . . ." Callan wheezed, choking down air. "Insubordinate behaviour . . ." he spluttered beneath Kora's weight.

"Let him talk, *asterya.*" Blake smiled wickedly. Oh, it was time for a game. She stepped back and Callan rasped, greedily breathing in air.

"You're *together!*" Callan's shock was so satisfying.

"Yes, so don't try to pull any more I-asked-for-it crap. He knows better." Her strained voice caught Blake's attention. She could've sworn thunder danced in his eyes as he noticed the chain-like bruise forming around her neck.

"You were fair game," Callan seethed. "I'll tell them all. You won't be able to stand on two legs after. Captains can't be involved with their crew, and you're a—"

"That's enough."

Kora pressed down on his throat, and Blake withdrew his

cutlass sword, the tip hovering near Callan's limp one. Callan snivelled, and Blake chuckled darkly as he twirled the sword in his hand.

"What do you think we should do?" he asked, his tone playful.

"Hmm . . . hunting?" she mused.

"I don't like my prey sandy," Blake joked, wrinkling his nose at Callan. "We could castrate him?"

Callan started crying.

"That'd certainly solve a lot of his . . . issues. And protect all women."

"Shame they brought all that food. We could take a page out of the wenches' book and, you know . . ." Blake chomped his jaw, imitating eating. It was a dark move, even for him, but they were dealing with a monster on epic levels.

Kora bared her teeth at Callan, and she knew it was her deathly smile. The smile she used in the Darkoning Trials to deter her opponents. In fact, her and Blake had done this verbal torture game before on their captured enemies, dragging out their sentence, making them expect the worst before delivering them to the empire.

"It's not my fault," he spluttered. "She's lying to you! Tell him who you—"

"What's going on here?" Theron's voice cut through the hazy fog blanketing her mind, and Kora blinked as he approached, a smouldering presence against the black night.

"Why do you have Callan . . ." Theron halted at Kora.

He flinched at the splatter of blood peeking through her ripped shirt, and his gaze travelled down to Callan, who began pleading with Theron, his voice now a hoarse whisper.

"Your subordinate tried to rape *my* captain," Blake snapped. His barely contained temper was palpable, and Theron cautiously stepped back.

"Theron . . . please, she's a—" Theron cut off Callan's words with a sharp wave of his hand.

"I do not want to hear it! I am sick to *death* of you, Callan!" His voice was like the boom of a cannon, echoing through the darkness of the desert night. Callan's face slackened, shock permeating his pores.

Kora retreated to Blake, their bodies mere centimetres apart as Callan scrambled towards Theron. He stepped out of reach of Callan's bloodied, twisted hands.

"This is the last straw. You are done. I want you out of my

sight, out of my crew, my guard. Gone."

"Where will I go? I'm your royal guard, you can't dismiss me! Only the king can do that."

"*I do not care!*" Theron's jaw grounded. "Go into the desert, with the other exiles. You are exiled from Azaria. You are exiled from Aldara. *You are no more!*"

Callan sat back on his heels in disbelief, peering at the black expanse of the desert. "But . . . it's dark. And cold. I'll die!"

"*Be gone!*" Theron's voice whipped through the air and Kora winced. He unsheathed an axe, his expression pained as he raised it, aiming at Callan. "Don't make me do this."

The creep scrambled, pulling his trousers on, and shooting a deadly glare at Blake and Kora before darting into the night. His shadowed figure hurtled up the dunes, pausing to look back at them before disappearing down the other side.

She hoped to never see him again.

Theron sighed, sliding the sharp edge of his axe across his vambrace before re-sheathing it.

"I have no words," he swallowed his dismay. "I cannot apologise enough to you. I am deeply sorry. I hope this doesn't tarnish our relationship."

Cadence snorted beside them.

Kora leaned into Blake, her hands clutching at her torn clothes, holding the frayed edges together. He let her weight press against him, and his hand went to the small of her back to steady her.

"My captain needs to recover from this," he spoke sternly. "Callan's actions aren't your fault, nor responsibility." Rare fragility radiated from him, and a small kernel of pride flashed from her.

Theron nodded deeply, and that was enough to send her over the edge. To receive any form of a bow from a member of the royal court was of the greatest respect. Kora bobbed her head in return. Good gods.

"Will the king punish you for banishing Callan?" she asked in a near-whisper.

Theron peered at Callan's fading footsteps in the sand. "Do not worry about me. I'll be just fine."

His gaze followed the smattering of blood on her body before dropping to the ground in shame. Blake guided her to his own tent, fishing out a spare shirt and trousers from his pack, whilst Theron mumbled about taking the next watch rotation to ensure Callan didn't return.

"We shouldn't be sharing a tent," she hesitated as Blake handed her his clothes.

He shrugged in response. "I'll sleep outside if you want me to."

"I . . . thought it was you. I thought you'd finally decided to . . ." she couldn't finish the words.

Pain, followed by anger, flashed across his face before softening into pity, and her gut roiled. She didn't want pity. She'd been defiled, but beneath that violation, was hurt. She was upset it hadn't been Blake, and a slither of disbelief joined her torrent of emotions.

Her belief in their relationship cracked.

But she nodded anyway. She needed to know that he was near, that she wasn't alone. Before she ducked into the tent, Blake gently gripped her hand. The skin-on-skin contact overwhelmed her, and she recoiled at the touch, backing towards Cadence who followed her every movement like a second shadow.

"I'm sorry I . . . I wasn't there sooner. I should've been there like you wanted. Are you okay?"

Like she wanted? What did that mean? Did *he* not want her anymore?

His face creased with worry, but Kora shook her head, avoiding his expression as she turned away. After a quick rinse, desperately scrubbing her skin raw to wash away Callan's blood, she curled up on Blake's sleeper mattress and covered her curled body with a blanket.

A clop of hooves kicked against sand, followed by the familiar *thud* of Cadence taking up her residing spot outside. Such an intelligent creature, and more attuned to Kora's feelings than her supposed partner.

Her body was violated.

She tightened up, closing in until her knees touched her chest. Closing her body off to the world. Her heart ached, and she wasn't sure why. Her mind was numb . . . hushed. Silent tears threatened to spill, and she cried into the folds of the blanket as footsteps approached.

"What happened?" Aryn's voice drifted over. Without seeing him, she would've thought he was thrice his age just from his voice.

"Callan attacked the captain . . . the situation has been diffused." Blake's voice had a sharp edge. She didn't appreciate the tone directed at Aryn.

Situation.

Was that all it was to him? Just a situation?

"Why weren't we alerted?" Aryn snapped back. Heavy footsteps followed.

"Aye," Samuel conferred. "Who was on watch?"

"I was." Blake's blunt words somehow pierced her numb being. "I was far out, a couple dunes over. I came running as soon as I heard the screams. Where were you two?"

"I was tracking Ivar," Aryn replied quickly.

"I'm a heavy sleeper," Samuel mumbled. "Takes a storm to wake me."

"Tracking Ivar?" Blake's interrogative tone surfaced, and Kora's tears slowed as she frowned, her ears straining to catch their voices.

"I don't trust him," Aryn continued. "He snuck out . . . so I followed him."

"And?"

"Nothing to report."

Blake's sigh was audible.

"Where's Callan?" Samuel asked, the sound of metal against leather broke through the night, and she knew he'd unsheathed his sword. "I'll give that scourge a piece of my mind."

"And where's Kora?" Aryn pressed.

"Gone. Theron exiled him. The *captain* is . . ." silence followed, then footsteps thudded in the sand, nearing the tent. "Don't go in there," Blake commanded.

"I want to check on her," Aryn bit back.

"Why?"

She held a bated breath.

"I have some medical field training, in case she has any injuries." Despite their friendship blossoming recently, Aryn had always been the first to offer medical assistance in the past, even before Koji.

"You can check on her tomorrow—" Blake's voice cut out as she shuffled on the mat, her knees protesting at being curled up so tightly. She froze at the sudden quiet that slowly became deafening.

"I want someone on watch with Theron . . ." Blake's voice faded, along with the sound of muffled steps in the sand as the trio walked away from the tent.

Kora squeezed her eyes shut, her hand clasping the talisman sprawled on the sleeper mattress and, as she slowly opened her eyes, her fingertips shone blue once again. The tears streaming down her face lifted from her skin, the individual beads of water pooling together to form one, floating, iridescent ball. No bigger than the size of a pea.

Her body didn't crackle with energy, her core didn't alight with pounding bolts. It was as if her power subconsciously was trying to soothe her, displaying parlour tricks of beads of water, swirling around each other.

"*Run*," the voice returned to her mind and she growled at it. The voice could get fucked as well.

She pictured a mental wall building around her mind, block after block after block of sheer blue ice, until she was secure in her shimmering glacial dome. She wasn't sure whether it would be effective or not, but the voice didn't return for the rest of the night. Neither did Blake to sleep outside the tent. At least she had Cadence.

No one would save her in this world. She would have to save herself.

And that would start with mastering her power.

35

The rolling, lush green lands of Bellmoor's territory were in their sights, and the terror and tension eased from Kora's traumatised body as they neared the border.

She was sick of the desert. Sick of the sun. Sick of males.

Aryn had barely given her a glance over with his *medical field training* expertise. Mumbling to himself about gods-knew-what before mounting Fajra with Ivar after a very quiet, very awkward breakfast. All the males seemed to be taking a wide berth around her, so she stuck close to Cadence, repetitively running her hands through the mare's mane for comfort.

Blake and Theron had taken charge of the convoy, leading them across the final dunes. Aryn and Ivar scouted the rear, leaving Kora in her familiar position of riding next to Samuel.

His face had remained pensive for most of the journey, his usual jovial personality muted. Even his eyes seemed duller. Whenever she tried to capture his gaze, his grey stare would dart away, shame riddling his face. Why was he ashamed? He hadn't been the one to violate her last night. She shuddered. She hoped he didn't see her differently after Callan proved how easy it was to infiltrate her . . . *tent.*

Thank gods that was all he'd achieved.

She felt how Samuel looked. Kora had awoken with a hollowness within her, and her mind was lonely, confined to her new mental dome. She cast her eyes over Samuel. He'd tied his blonde hair up, knotted at the base of his head, with a selection of braids weaved throughout. She needed to know their friendship hadn't changed. That he didn't perceive her as weak. A question poised on her lips; she opened her mouth—

"CAAAWWWWWWWWW!"

Her head whipped towards the sound.

"Halt!" Blake yelled from in front.

They came to a stop atop of the final dune. Before them laid the remainder of the sparse tundra, blending into a canopy of palm trees and lush foliage lining the House of Bellmoor's border. Pushing her goggles up, Kora scanned the horizon, squinting against the early afternoon sun. In the far distance, she could just make out the pale, towering turrets of Stormkeep Fortress. The tension eased a fraction more. She'd never been so glad to see those ivory stones.

"CAAAWWWWWWWWW!"

The cry sounded again, from the west, near the edge of the green land cutting through the desert leading to the House of Blackstone territory. Six heads angled towards it.

"What the fuck is it? A bird?" Samuel looked at the clear skies. Kora's scalp prickled, and her body thrummed.

"I've got a bad feeling . . ." She swallowed the knot forming in her throat. A perfect bruise of the chain circled her throat, and she tentatively brushed her fingers over it. A painful reminder.

"CAAAWWWWWWWWWWOOOOOOOOO!"

Another bird-like cry followed, from the east, and she peered at the dense greenery trailing to the bountiful farming lands.

"It's a signal," Theron hissed. "We need to get to cover. *Now!*" He pointed towards the palm trees edging the Bellmoor family's territory directly in front.

"Flat out, it'll take us thirty minutes to cover that distance," Samuel replied, his large hands tightening on the reins.

"Then we better get moving." Kora glanced at Aryn and Ivar. "Can you cover us from the rear?"

Both archers nodded solemnly. A solid inch of space rested between their bodies, their muscles tight, holding their frames apart. What had Aryn seen when he'd tracked Ivar last night? Something was going on with them.

"Drop any excess baggage," Blake ordered her.

Out of them all, Cadence carried the most saddle bags. With a curt nod, Kora cut the ties to several bags with one of her daggers. Some of the others followed suit, dropping excess rations, even a tent and clothes. Anything but water and weapons.

"Don't look back," Blake commanded. "Don't veer off course. The horses will pick up speed as we converge onto harder ground. Have your weapons ready. And don't stop for each other, your goal is the border."

The cries continued, growing louder, turning into a low chant, and Kora's skin prickled in response, her breathing quickening. She couldn't spot anyone—anything—around them, and the chanting echoed *everywhere* with no source. A bolting shiver skittered down her spine. *This was bad.*

"Now!"

She flicked her reins, her knees tightening as Cadence leapt forwards. The horse's strong legs pounded the sandy earth, and they flew down the curving slope of the final dune of the Silent Tundra. Kora exhaled as the desert faded away.

She raised up off the saddle, keeping her head low as Cadence gained speed, her beautiful pale mane flying in the wind. A dark, thundering shadow galloped to her left, and Erebus approached with Blake and Theron atop, the latter wielding his axes, his deep, chocolate eyes scanning around them, high on alert.

"*Cadell!*" Theron's voice cut through the blasting winds.

On instinct, Kora veered Cadence to the right, just as a wooden, iron-tipped lance speared through the air, plummeting into the sandy ground a foot to her left. *Shit.* That'd been close. She reached behind, grasping one of her curved, sabre daggers, palming the malachite hilt. Its presence strengthened her nerves, and she urged Cadence to keep galloping.

A group of exiles converged from the western edge of the palm trees, armed with bows, lances, and crossbows. Giant boars, with thick tusks erupting from their dark, hairy jowls, interspersed the diaspora. Her gut hollowed as they advanced.

They bore weapons of the empire.

The ground flew fast beneath them, hardening as sand faded into grass. The horses' speed increased, shortening the distance between them and the exiles.

The exiles charged, raising their lances and bows. Samuel yelled from Kora's right and she spared a glance—a second group poured from the cluster of trees, equally armed to the teeth. Bearing the shining, silver armour of the empire.

Kora's mind roiled. First, their finest ships in the armada, and now their weapons and armour were stolen, as well. A puzzle piece clicked in her mind, the grand picture that was shrouded in fog brightening. *The attacks on the outposts.*

"Keep going!" Blake's voice commanded over the sound of the wind, the beating of the hooves, and the squawking hollers of exiles.

Kora's heart pounded as the enemy neared and her chest

tightened, her body breaking out in a sweat. They were seriously outnumbered.

Ivar began firing arrows as he expertly perched on Fajra, his legs wrapped around Aryn's slim waist to hold him steady, their bodies flush. Each body he shot crumpled—their fellow deserters stumbling over the bleeding corpses to continue their hunt of the royal convoy. The edge of the border neared, but it was blocked on both sides as their enemies closed in.

Kora paled as Theron revealed a small selection of throwing daggers from a hidden compartment in his leathers by his legs. No harm could come to him—*at any cost*. They needed to get him out of here. Erick's stern face flashed in her mind. She could not fail.

Blake whipped his reins, urging Erebus forward. The exiles' wild cries and stomping feet became a shrill noise in her ears. All she had were her two daggers to defend herself, to defend her crew . . . she had her powers . . . but she couldn't use those. Even if it *could* save them all.

Up ahead, she spied a small break in the swath of baying palm trees, leading to a narrow path within the foliage. They were roughly a mile out as she gauged the distance. It seemed wide enough for the horses to fit through, and an easy way to escape.

She squeezed Cadence with her knees, her voice tearing from her throat, challenging the horse to run, and to run *fast*.

Lances and arrows rained down upon them, and the cabal dispersed, evading the threatening might of weapons spearing their way. Kora sucked in a breath, momentarily thanking the gods as they weaved around the deadly metal rain.

Their luck was surely about to end soon.

Ivar fired more arrows, rowing down another ten exiles, yet they kept converging—pressing in until they circled the sides. She cried out to Aryn as a crossbow wielder took aim, standing atop of a cluster of boulders, steadying himself in the wind. Ivar reached around Aryn to take control of the fiery Fajra as Aryn nocked an arrow in his longbow, pulling the bowstring taut.

For a moment, his eyes blazed, the golden flecks burning as bright as the sun, before fading. Kora blinked, wiping the lens of her goggles.

He inhaled once and released, the arrow zinging through the air and plummeting into one of the crossbow wielder's eyes. He toppled off the boulder, his scream a whisper on his lips, blood spurting from his head.

But it wasn't enough.

Another male approached the fallen body, collecting the weapon to fire at them again. *Gods, how many people had been banished as exiles?*

They were so close she could distinguish their features. Their deeply tanned, rough skin. Their thinning hair, the loose, dirtied clothing, and makeshift leathers from hides of wild animals—and the brand marked on the centre of their foreheads from a hot poker. In the shape of the empire's insignia. Marred for life, by the kingdom that cast them out.

The sound of Aryn's longbow firing continued, a constant *whoosh* of air, and the eastern exiles fell in quick succession one after the other. A trail of bleeding dead, staining the sand. The exiles to the west faltered for a moment and Kora seized her opportunity.

"Ahead!" she yelled, pointing to the narrow clearing. They could make it. They just had to listen and follow her.

"We're out!" Aryn shouted, slinging his longbow over his shoulder.

"Stop!" A sudden commotion from Erebus had her twisting towards Blake. Theron argued with him before he vaulted from the rear of the horse, landing on the ground in a crouch, speckles of sand billowing around his huge form. Before Kora could comprehend what was happening, Ivar silently followed suit, dismounting Fajra with a feline's grace that unnerved her.

"What are you doing?" Samuel pulled Rayne up short, the horse rearing in protest. Aryn deftly pivoted Fajra, heading for Ivar, yelling at him to get back on the horse.

No . . . they had to get to the border.

"We will hold them off!" Theron armed himself as he sprinted towards the exiles. He threw his throwing daggers with an impressive precision that Kora couldn't help briefly admiring. As she slowed Cadence down to a precarious trot, Blake signalled her to gallop towards the border, his face urging her to get to safety.

The exiles spotted Theron and Ivar, and with a unified bellow, barrelled towards them, swords and daggers raised; a couple boars chuffing hot air.

As soon as Blake dismounted Erebus, giving the horse a light slap on the rear to escape to the trees, Kora yanked on Cadence's reins, causing the horse to whinny as they stopped. Blake squaring off with the incoming slaughter of exiles, armed with only his golden cutlass sword, made her gut drop entirely.

He shouted at Aryn and Samuel to take Theron and Ivar away—that *he* would fight the exiles alone, and Kora's heart knotted and folded over in response. Her bowels twisting, mind screaming, ears roaring.

The Darkoning Trials snared her mind as she relived the final contest . . . Blake fighting through wave after wave of soldiers to become the champion. She could still smell the blood, and the dirt-packed arena. The scent of burnished metal . . . and leather and petrichor.

That champion stood before her once again now, his green eyes blazing with fury. But this time, he wouldn't survive.

The red haze blanketed not only her mind, but her entire body. Her vision blurred, her features smoothing as the mask suppressed her fear, and allowed rage to grab hold.

Before she could convince herself to run to safety, Kora led Cadence to the edge of the palm trees, promising the horse she would return. Clasping her daggers in her sweaty palms, she ran towards the mass of raging exiles.

They didn't see her coming.

Like a phantom, Kora weaved through the mass of charging bodies, her mind emptied as she sliced through throat after throat, her daggers sharp and swift. She mowed down ten males before they realised there was a viper in the nest.

Each droplet of blood incensed the haze, a beast drinking on the mindless slaughter, fuelling her ire.

"That's right, condemn them. Send them to Umbra."

She nodded; unsure what voice occupied her thoughts. It sounded like her, but ancient. Bodies converged on Blake, and a growl ripped from her throat. She needed to save him, by any means.

Males and females diverted from attacking her crew, who defended Theron and Ivar, and speared towards her. The blood of her enemies dripped from Kora as she crouched into a defensive stance, raising her malachite sabre daggers. *Come and fucking get me.*

Several males sneered—their eyes catching her empire-branded weapons—with giant, thick cutlasses and broadswords gripped in their fists. The females hung back, warily eyeing her, lances shakily clasped to their chests towering above them. She urged them with her eyes to *run*. They didn't need to see this.

Their faces were gaunt, their eyes haunted. They didn't belong here. They didn't deserve to die. *What are you doing?* Something squeaked, breaking through the bloodied barrier wrapped around her mind. Yet, the males thrived on the violence and extremities of the Silent Tundra. Kora smiled at the small circle of enemies trapping her, inching closer as she settled back into the symphony of death.

"We've been looking for ye," one spoke. Most of their teeth

were missing.

"Isn't this a nice welcoming party." Kora wiped the blood from her face and flicked it off her hands. A snarl rippled through the circle.

The cries of battle and the clashes of metal drowned out as the toothless male lunged, reaching to grab her by the neck. She pivoted, twisting away, her arms twirling like a dancer. A female screamed as his body collapsed to the ground, his neck and torso sliced so deeply his blood gushed and bubbled onto her shin-high boots. She grimaced down at her feet, shaking her leg and causing the blood to splatter across her fighting ring.

"Ye are dead!" a towering, thick male growled.

A thick, jagged scar slashed across his left eye, his iris and pupil no longer visible, churning into a milky colour from poor healing. His stare narrowed onto her.

It unnerved Kora, looking into eyes—*eye*—that was so like Agatha's. She instinctively rubbed the left side of her temple, her fingers tracing her own scar, before beckoning him to attack with a sinister smile.

With a charging yell, the male thrust his sword, meeting her blow for blow as he forced her to the edge of the makeshift ring. She gritted her teeth at the unexpected sharpness of a sword poking into her back, his fellow exiles snickering. *Shit,* they had her.

Kora dropped and spun, bringing her daggers up to block the blow from behind she expected, but the exiles merely laughed at her, their swords loose at their sides. With a frown, she rolled backwards as the eyeless male swung his cutlass sword down with a roaring bellow mere inches from slicing her.

Too close. Get it together!

"Stop!" a high-pitched, wavering voice rang. "She has to stay alive!"

Kora panted as she rushed to her feet, her boots struggling against the blood-mixed-with-sand terrain. The eyeless male approached. Beyond the fighting ring, her crew defended the sentinel and his guard against the barrage of exiles. There were too many. She'd have to perform a gods-damned miracle to reach them.

In a raging fit, the male swung his sword with brutality—and she evaded every strike, her daggers parrying until she sliced his hand, causing him to drop the sword with a pained hiss. She brought her knee up, winding him, and forcing him to his knees as she pummelled the hilt of a dagger into the base of his neck. As he collapsed to the ground, her daggers pressed to either side of his throat.

"What does she mean . . . *keep me alive?*" Kora snarled in his ear.

"We're under orders not to touch ye!" he spat.

She scanned the crowd circling her. This wasn't a fighting ring—it was a diversion. They'd separated her from her crew, and she'd been too blind to see it. *Gods damn it.* The barrage against her crew teemed with bodies, all intent with the purpose to kill.

"From whom?" Kora tightened the gap between her blades until she nicked the surface of his skin.

"We don't know their names," a light voice spoke, and she glanced at a scrawny, too-thin female standing on the edge of the ring. Her cheeks were hollow, her scraggly hair tied up, with thin wispy strands framing her long face. A kindness radiated from the deep lines etched into her face, and the mask gripping Kora's essence relaxed, sensing a calm presence.

"It was more than one person," Kora confirmed, and the stranger nodded, her head bobbing on her pole-like neck.

First, Captain James Cannon. Then the Skytors, and now the exiles were after her. Her mind spun with overwhelming possibilities. Why would they want *her?* She was no one but a lost girl.

"Yes! They said not to harm you. But we didn't kn-know that it'd be like this." She gestured to the bodies surrounding them, the blood coating Kora like a second skin. "That you'd be . . ." Her brown eyes glanced away, unable to bear to look at Kora a moment longer.

Shame and horror flitted through her, and she tried to separate herself from the tangle of her emotions; the war between her two selves cresting. This was a trap. *They* were the enemy, *they* were exiles. *They* had come to kill them—kill, kill, kill.

"*Kora!*" Blake's voice pierced through her mind, and she spun. Piles of bodies surrounded her crew.

Another exile sneaked towards her, his lance raised, face twisted with violence. Blake ran, his face panicked, with Samuel, Aryn, and Ivar in tow. *Where was Theron?* Had they lost him? Worst yet, had the exiles killed him?

She kicked the eyeless male back to twist out of the attacker's way. His lance sliced her arm, and she cried out in pain as she darted to the side to get away from him. Sand blew up in her face, and she choked—choking once again—and flashbacks of Callan surged. Her breathing turned ragged, her arm sluicing with pain. She had to get away.

Gripping her bleeding arm, Kora faced the lancer and the sneering, eyeless male. He could see the terror rising from deep within her, her mask falling away. *Oh gods.* How many people had she killed?

The remaining circle of exiles disbanded, charging towards Blake and the crew, and they clashed head on, weapons cutting the air. Metal clanging, voices yelling. The boars scarpered across the dunes, fleeing the chaos. Through it all, Blake's gaze was trained on her, never leaving her face. His eyes wild with rage.

Kora stood with the eyeless male, his lancer counterpart, and the mysterious thin female. *Almighty Thanos, forgive my actions.* She was a murderer, like Jack had said.

"Tell me who gave you orders." She levelled the daggers in her palms.

"We're not telling you shit," the lancer spat back.

Kora snagged the haunted gaze of the female. "Tell me now!" The female's thin body trembled. Kora had one shot to guess, but her instincts roared with certainty. "Was it the Skytors?"

They all faltered for a moment—just a moment, but it was enough to know.

"Don't tell her anything," the eyeless male stepped forward. "They said to bring ye in alive . . . but they never said in one piece." He flashed an ugly smile.

Kora transitioned into another fighting stance, her arm bleating with pain, and she winced. The curve of her daggers gleamed like the brilliant red sands of Scarlet Bay, and she exhaled, her muscles falling into the memory of her fighting techniques.

"If you won't tell me . . . there're other ways to make you talk."

"She knows," the female pressed. "Just tell her!"

"*No*, Mags," the lancer snapped. "Kill her. She's not important anymore."

"Jason, if she knows the Skytors, then maybe she's not what we think!" Mags barked.

The eyeless male waved a hand. "We don't know *what* she is. And stop revealing your names!"

"*She* has a name, too," Kora interjected, twirling a dagger.

"We don't care!" Jason seethed. "Let's use her as leverage instead and—"

A throwing knife plunged into Jason's neck and Mags screamed, her shaking hands flying to her mouth.

"What the—" the eyeless male hissed as Jason sagged to the ground—Theron stood behind him, his silver armour flashing in the sun. *Oh, thank the gods!*

"I'd get back on the ground if I were you." Theron's voice was so low and dark, a portentous feeling overcame her, as if she were in the presence of something—or someone great. The two exiles eyed Theron's embellished stag symbol on his silver chest and collapsed to their knees.

"Are you alright?" he asked as he approached, after unarming the eyeless male.

Kora nodded curtly, squishing the anxiety down. Too stunned to speak. Guilt shone in his shadowed eyes. She hadn't brought herself to ask how he was faring after last night; the effect that banishing Callan had on him; whether he was worried about the repercussions from the king.

"We-we didn't know," Mags stammered, her hands shaking as she clasped them together in a prayer. "Please . . . we beg forgiveness."

Kora lifted a brow at Theron. Wearing the uniform certainly had its perks. The eyeless male scoffed at his counterpart, but Mags' eyes brimmed with tears as she repeatedly begged for mercy.

Blake, Ivar, and her crew shortly joined, panting as they sheathed their weapons. Blood, dirt, and sand coated every inch of their clothing and faces.

"They've all been taken care of," Blake murmured quietly to her and Theron, jerking his chin to the massacre. Theron inclined his head once in response. "You're hurt," Blake stated simply as he glimpsed Kora's arm. He reached out to inspect the wound.

"I'll be fine," she replied, edging away. The movement didn't go unnoticed. "Just a scratch."

"A scratch my arse," he parroted her words, but she couldn't smile. Not when she was drenched in blood. Not when she'd killed blindly on an epic scale for the first time since the trials. But the trials had been survival, a means to live.

This had been . . . murder. Bile crept up her throat, threatening to upheave her stomach.

With a tense exhale, Blake turned to their two captives, and she observed warily as he began his interrogation. "What are you doing this close to the border?"

"We don't know what ye mean," the male feigned ignorance.

Samuel grunted at that. "Everyone knows where the grass begins is where the desert ends." The navigational master clenched his fists, his grey eyes boring into the eyeless exile.

"Fine," the exile snapped. "We go where we please. We don't abide ye petty rules."

"The rules of the king *will* be obeyed," Theron's whipping voice cracked. "The territories are marked for unity. For prosperity of the land."

The exiles' branded foreheads glared back, and Mags placed a shaking hand on the eyeless male's arm. "Don't anger them, Doran."

"Doran," Theron repeated, and Doran glared at Mags with his one good, hazel eye. His thinning hair slicked across his shining dark head and he rubbed his crooked nose, wiping dirt across his squared cheeks.

"How'd you manage to track us?" Blake pressed.

Doran sighed, lowering his head as Mags' slender fingers tightened on his thick arm. Kora tracked the movement—the slight curl of her fingers, the intense stare of her brown eyes as she fixated on Doran's scarred face.

"We . . . couldn't track ye," he admitted slowly. "We knew there was a convoy passing through, but whatever route ye took across the dunes . . . it was impossible to find."

Kora and Blake glanced at each other, and she suppressed the small smirk threatening to bubble to the surface. Samuel's lips curled as he caressed the rolled map parchment peeking from his knapsack.

"Then *how* did you find us this close to the border? Your *kind* never venture this close." Blake's lips pulled back in disgust.

Doran's jaw clenched as he worked hard to hold the truth in. After a moment of silence, Theron revealed a hatchet axe, levelling it with Doran's head. He unwaveringly stared up the length of Theron's arm, his eye pinning on the stag and four-pointed star on his chest, and his face filled with hatred as he lifted his head to meet Theron's gaze.

Mags whimpered, her hands tightly curling around his arm, as Doran readied for an execution. She whispered erratically into his ear but Doran did not move, did not speak, did not even blink. Mags sobbed, begging Theron for mercy once again between wrenching, wet breaths.

"So be it." Theron's cold words echoed around them as he raised his axe.

"It was Callan!" Mags squeaked, and they all froze as she trembled, tears flowing down her cheeks. Pure shock bloomed on

Theron's face as he halted the axe mid-swing. "He told us where your camp was . . . where you were heading . . . how to best intercept you."

"No fucking way," Samuel seethed.

Mags' head bobbed on her thin neck. "He told us to challenge the border. That you'd least expect us then—" Doran nudged her, ordering her to be quiet.

Something within Kora violently twisted and knotted at the mention of Callan, scratching at the walls to either escape or attack, she couldn't tell. She tried to shut out the memories of the previous evening. But his blood he'd smeared over her, and the blood coating her now, became suffocating. She felt disgusting, she had to flee. To run until her lungs burned, to find the ocean, and wash away all the filth.

"How . . . did he find you?" Kora choked on the words.

With the cold darkness of the nightfall in the desert, she assumed Callan would have frozen to death, or been attacked by wild animals, potentially even die of thirst in the scorching day if he survived the night. But instead, banishing Callan had led the exiles right to her.

Doran's eye flashed at Kora, as if remembering she was there. That *she* was their prize. The Skytors' prize.

"We found him crying in the desert like a babe. Apparently . . . someone played a little *trick* on him." Doran bared his teeth.

Her mind and heart raced. *He knew.* He knew what she was and would tell her secret. She'd end up an exile like them, or a prisoner of the convoy, dragged to her death. There would be no imprisonment, not for a mage masquerading with a royal sentinel, especially with the new decree.

"He got what he deserved," she snarled, stepping forward, finding her voice.

"Where. Is. He." Theron's jaw worked with each word.

"He's not here," Doran muttered. "Said he couldn't bear the fight."

"Coward," Ivar's cool voice floated from behind, and Kora nearly jumped to hear him speak.

"There's no need to shout," Samuel whispered under his breath with a wry smile.

"He could be near," Blake commented. "Watching to see if we die."

"No," Theron shook his head. "This is a retaliation to last night. He's always been petty. He is banished, and he will be long gone by now, seeking a new life. It's his style to cut his losses and run."

"Why'd you attack us?" Blake diverted the conversation. "Are you after the sentinel?"

He glanced at Theron, who grew more agitated by the second, his hands fisted around the leather-and-silver wrapped handles of his hatchet axes. Even his eyes darkened with shadows wreathed around them.

Doran's single eye widened, his body rigid. "No. We're not fools. We all know the continent has no control here." Theron's tensity increased at the insult. "There's a bigger prize among ye."

In that instant, Doran hurtled forward, and Kora crashed against Samuel as he gripped under her arms, dragging her away from the attack, her wound gushing blood onto his hands.

Blake and Theron lunged for Doran, their weapons drawn and cutting the air. Doran evaded their weapons with unnerving speed, his body a blur against the sand. With a growl she'd never heard before, Blake leapt, his gleaming golden cutlass sword thrusted before him.

In a blink of an eye, Mags leapt in front of Doran, crying for them to stop.

It all happened too quickly.

"*No!*" Doran roared.

Blake's sword sliced.

Mags' gut split open; her bowels exposed, tumbling like ribbons. It was . . . she was . . .

"Mags!" Doran caught her limp body as she collapsed to the ground. "Mags! No, no, no." He began to weep.

Blake paled as Mags bled onto Doran. Her thin, ripped dress sprawled around them, and Doran's hands shook, hovering over her body as her lifeless eyes stared at the clear sky.

"My Mags . . ." he sobbed, bowing his head, pressing his scarred face against her thin strands of hair. He placed a kiss on her branded forehead and Kora's stomach soured. "Ye *killed* my Magdalena."

"As an exile . . ." Chills skittered down her spine at how frozen and detached Theron's voice had become. She had no doubt that thoughts of Callan fuelled his ire. "Her death is warranted."

"Warranted?" Doran rumbled. "Ye all murderers! Look at ye!"

Kora refused to meet the eyes of her fellow cabals. To lift and witness the bodies scattered around them. *They* were the ones covered in blood. Their weapons—and hands—dirty.

"You attacked us unprovoked. We defended ourselves," Blake retorted. Not an ounce of remorse. Should she be concerned? She felt positively sick, and she was sure that, if she moved too fast, she'd vomit over Mags' body.

"I heard about *ye*," Doran's voice dropped so low, so faint, as he glared at Blake, who stilled as Doran continued. "I know who ye are."

"Aye, everyone knows the champion of the Darkoning Trials," Samuel summarised. "It's hardly priceless knowledge."

Doran's smile was so sickening as his single-eyed gaze shifted to Kora, and across the remaining standing bodies of the convoy.

"There are many secrets among ye. What would the empire pay to know them all?" He cocked his head, and her heart leapt into her throat, threatening to cut off her air supply. Or maybe it had dropped, her body ready to expel anything and everything. Either way, she was going to combust.

"Enough!" Blake snapped. "We don't need to listen to this, Theron."

Theron's jaw twitched as he stared at Doran. He surveyed their surroundings, his dark eyes soaking in the litter of bodies in the scant desert. His dark skin glistened with sweat in the sunlight, and she felt small in his all-seeing gaze. Finally, he hung his axes back at his hips.

"Cuff him. He's going to Deadwater Prison."

Doran sucked in a breath. "I'd rather die."

"That can be arranged," Blake replied darkly.

They hauled Doran to his feet and he kicked out, resisting Samuel and Blake as Aryn approached with a pair of iron cuffs.

"No, stop. Please!" He caught Kora's stiff gaze. "Please, let me bury her. Let me bury Mags. She doesn't belong out here."

"Take him," Theron replied, as he stomped back to the horses by the border, Ivar glued to his side. The archer's black recurve bow hugged his spine, and his empty quiver bashed against his hip as he prowled.

Blake and Samuel dragged Doran across the sand as he cried out to Mags' limp, lifeless body, and Kora's gut churned as she peered at the thin, hollow shell of the female. Her cheeks were still wet with tears. Kora knelt, brushing her fingers over her eyes, and placed Mags' bony-thin hands over the gaping, bleeding wound of her stomach, obscuring her organs.

"We can bury her if you wish," Aryn spoke quietly.

"It's not the way," she replied with equal quietness. "We'll be seen as exile sympathisers."

A brief gust of wind circled them, ruffling Aryn's hair and he shuddered. "Maybe there should be a new way."

She turned to him. His golden-flecked hazel eyes resembled living gold as they burned against the simple desert. His face hardened, his jawline unmistakeably sharp from how hard he clenched his jaw. Even his hand tensely gripped the bowstring across his lean chest, and she placed a hand on his arm in comfort.

The tundra wind gusted around them, and she squinted as the sand lifted with the blast, circling, twining around their bodies like a cyclone, causing him to step closer. This near, a lingering scent of cypress and amber brushed against her senses. It was so familiar, and her mind sparked. Aryn's almond-shaped eyes searched her face, waiting . . . watching. The thin, dual-lined tattoo on his cheek filled her vision, and she gently touched her own face in confusion.

You're not going to follow me around all day, are you?

I wouldn't be a very good skildaj *if I didn't.*

Kora's hands rushed to his face and Aryn flinched at the contact. She remembered . . . he was . . . they were . . .

The memory faded, pouring through her fingers like grains of sand, and tendrils snapped in her mind, burning the sound of his voice away. Cold darkness spread through her, dousing her reflexes, and for a moment, his name toyed on the edge of her memory . . .

This male's eyes were stunning, and they traced every line of her face. He was a pretty male. Young, but pretty. A longbow arched around his back. Oh, an archer. She could do with a skilled archer on her ship to whip her archery squadron into shape. Perhaps Samuel could take him under his wing?

"Who . . . I . . . you . . . ." she fumbled for the words. "Are you . . . ." She frowned.

Wait.

The probing darkness hissed as she conjured a white thread, anchoring her essence. As it retreated, her mind clearing, she gasped—

Aryn.

She had forgotten him, *again*. Why was she grasping his face? She reared back, her cheeks heating. How embarrassing. She couldn't go around clutching her crew's faces. She was a captain for gods' sake.

He stared at her in astoundment. "Do you—"

Aryn's eyes flared in fright and he dragged her towards him, wrapping an arm around her as they collided. Retrieving a dagger from her back, he pivoted, blocking her as the sand blast settled, revealing Doran charging and screaming, Blake's cutlass sword in his chained hands as he attacked.

"Get away from her!" Doran shouted.

Aryn met Doran blow for blow, and Kora stumbled. Samuel yelled, his enormous form hurtling towards them, leaving Blake crumpled on the ground, his nose streaming with blood. Theron and Ivar were already by the horses, mounting them to race back to the commotion.

"Kora, run!" Aryn's voice strained as he fought Doran. The exile was so agile, so swift and *fast* that she watched dazedly. He was faster than Aryn. An impressive yet frightening feat.

"*Run.*"

She faltered as Doran forced Aryn to his knees, his slender frame weakening against the bulk of the other male. Her heart clenched.

"Aryn!" Kora threw her second dagger, aiming at Doran's heaving chest. Before it hit, Aryn caught it by the hilt, using the momentum to propel against Doran's weight. Why wasn't he killing him? Why was he continuing the fight? Aryn expertly ducked and parried, and *somehow*, she innately knew what movement he would do next.

Duck. Parry. Swipe.

"I know what ye are!" Doran seethed as he tried to pivot around Aryn towards her, and her blood ran cold.

"Run!" Aryn yelled once again, forcing Doran to crumple as he became a fury of strikes.

"*Run.*"

Kora's mind whirled as she bolted.

"*Run.*"

Her mental ice block crumbled.

"*Run.*"

One word screamed in her mind. A smooth, deep voice, pouring over her like silk, wrapping around her limbs, strengthening her fortitude.

"*RUN!*"

Towards Aryn.

Samuel mimicked her, and they converged on the fighting duo. Samuel's sword gleamed in the sun, and she barrelled into Aryn with the full force of her weight, knocking him into the sand as Samuel drove his sword into Doran's back, its end tearing through his stomach.

With a bubbled, wet gasp, Doran collapsed to his knees, clutching his stomach, the wound gushing and gaping. With a final breath, he fell, landing beside Mags, their bodies a bloodied, intertwined mess.

K ora soaked in the bath for hours. Sweet, blessed relief.
Upon arriving at Cadell Manor, she'd beelined to
her bathing chamber and set the hot water running, with
jasmine and orange blossom scents permeating the air.
Erick had been absent—out on *official commodore business*—when
they'd returned.

Blake had directed Theron and Ivar to the barracks, where
they would receive private quarters for their stay, before being
ushered into the limelight to oversee the final unification. Many
civilians had cast wary glances at their shining uniforms, the symbol
of the stag lifting eyebrows and shocked faces.

The final two days of their journey had been quiet, memories
of scattered bodies shuddering through them like a repetitive wave.
It haunted Kora still. She had killed in a blinded, raging fit. No better
than a filthy pirate. No better than Silas fucking Flint.

Mags' disembowelment flashed and seared into the back of
her eyelids. Doran's weeping scraped her eardrums. As she lay in
the bath, her hands shook, flinging warm droplets of water, but all
she could see was blood. She was covered head to toe in blood. For
the first time in a long while, Kora sobbed.

Gut wrenching, throat clenching sobs. She cried her despair
into her hands, wiping beautifully scented water over salty tears.
Her nose streamed, her chest pinched, and her heart cracked, riddled
with shame, and crushing *guilt.*

She had to be better. She had to do better. So many souls
needlessly condemned and lost to wander Thanos' weaving threads
of Umbra. All because she was desperate to heed Erick's orders to
keep Theron safe, and because Blake's life had been threatened.
Had it been worth it in the name of the Talmon Empire?

She hadn't realised how many exiles lived in the tundra. How many people the empire had cast out. How many of them were there because they simply favoured the old ways? How many were thieves? How many were raiders?

Kora sank beneath the warm water, letting it wash away her tears. Coated in an arnica salve, she kept her injured arm above the water, resting on the stoned edge of the bath. It'd been built sunken into the floor, with steps at the end for her to ascend. White drapes caressed the rectangular room, with large candelabras descended from the curved ceiling.

Blue light basked beneath the surface of the water and she shot up, running her hands through her wet hair with an exasperated gasp.

And there was *that* problem.

Callan knew she was a mage, and he was loose in the world. What was to stop him from telling people what he saw? What she did? The only option was to flee to Shannara, not only to dispose of the talisman but, if she were discovered, Shannara might be the only safe place left.

And, to top it off, the exiles possessed empire-grade weapons and armour, and pirates sailed prized ships that were now hidden in the Mist. Erick had said there'd been raids upon outposts during the first week of *Hell's Serpent's* scouting mission. Somehow, the stolen goods had ended up in the exiles' grimy hands.

The cogs clicked together, with the Skytors as the central piece. Why would they enlist the exiles to locate her? They knew who she was, and where she would be, especially with Callan's tip. She trailed her fingers through the water, her mind churning out scenarios.

What was Finlay's connection? Had he planned to lure her to The Abandoned Barnacle when they returned from their scouting mission? She flexed her fingers and the water rippled, forming into little beads of comfort swirling in the air, dancing around her.

The three groups formed a triangle in her mind, pirates, Skytors and exiles, all somehow connected to her. But . . . *why*? She wasn't special. If they were after her power, there was a room brimming with mages in the tavern.

Kora's mind whirled and swam with the what ifs, whys, and hows, until she focused her attention on something else. Grabbing a bar of soap, she attacked her skin, scrubbing it raw as dried flakes of blood, dirt, and sweat drifted into the water, churning into a muddied colour. There was no way she would use this water to heal her arm.

Besides, it would be too suspicious if she had a miraculously healed arm after nearly becoming a chicken skewer. Not everyone could heal as fast as Blake. Lucky, gifted bastard.

After feeling thoroughly cleansed, her arm re-bandaged, she emerged from her bathing chamber in a silk robe to find Erick perched on the edge of her unmade bed.

Donning a simple yet elegant dark-green tunic with black trousers, the golden insignia embellished over his left chest blazed, and she swallowed looming bile as Mags' and Doran's branded foreheads filled her mind's eye. She focused her attention on the small medals of honour lining his shoulders, highlighting his accomplishments in the navy.

"I'm surprised you've not shrivelled up," he joked. "Odelina fetched me, worrying you'd drowned."

She waved her hand at the mention of their head servant, Odelina. A fussy, no-nonsense mannered female who tended to dote over Kora. However, she had a strict 'no servants entering her quarters' rule. She liked being able to do things for herself, and having her own privacy and space away from the swarming hustle of the world.

"She frets too much."

"She only frets over you."

"Jealous?" She smirked as she sat at her vanity table, raking her hands through her white locks in the mirror. They curled past her ears, and she grinned, finger-rolling them into gentle waves that cascaded around her heart-shaped face. A pair of lapis-lazuli eyes stared back at her, and she whipped her gaze to Erick's brown, fatigued eyes. He looked tired, and his wavy, grey-flecked hair was tousled, as if he'd been pulling on it.

"Not of this room." He observed the piles of books and oddly placed trunks, the clothes casually draped over the partition. His eyes narrowed as they landed on the candle-wax covered bedsides, staining the wood, and the assorted weapons dotted round the room. "You could let the servants clean in here once in a while."

"No, thank you."

"When did you last clean—"

"There are more important things than *cleaning*," Kora bared her teeth in a grimace at the word. Besides, everything had been perfectly placed, her own little world of organised chaos. She faced him, cocking her head to the side. "Or am I no better than the manor housewives that grace the mid and upper districts?"

"Point taken."

He awkwardly averted his gaze as she slipped behind her partition to begin dressing, and she winced as she pushed Agatha's green and blue tomes behind the partition with her feet. She'd have to hide these someplace better lest Agatha smote her like a god.

"Can I . . . ask you something?"

"Of course, my child."

The endearment from Erick warmed the cockles of her heart. He had no other children—gods, she didn't even know what his life was truly like before her. He scarcely spoke about it. Whenever she probed, she was met with his icy side, and a stiff indifference causing him to disappear into the basement of the manor, returning with bloodied knuckles after a few rounds with their training dummies.

"Do you know if anyone from my past ever came looking for me after . . . you know? Was there anyone who asked for me?"

Silence. She ducked her head around the partition. Erick sat on the bed, his face pale, his hands clenched on his lap.

"No . . . no one came," he spoke quietly.

But Captain James Cannon had come. Finlay had come. The Skytors had come. Gods, they'd sent an unfathomable entourage of exiles after her. She was certain of this triangle of allies. That stone of fortitude beaming in her gut. Perhaps this was part of her essence? An innate, instinctive truth?

"How do you know? What if they couldn't find me? You said yourself you pulled me from a shipwreck caused by the pirates. Maybe my family survived—"

"Your family are gone, Kora. I searched the seas. But no one survived, only you."

The words slapped her across the face.

Erick's warm tone dropped a few degrees. Kora paused as she finished buttoning her tunic. She wore similar tones to his, to highlight her captain status, with silvery buttons curving across her chest and ending at her side.

"What about this?" She emerged from the partition, her fingers brushing the side of her head.

His jaw clenched and he looked away. "As I've said before, it happened during the wreckage."

"Was there anything odd about the wreckage? About me?" her voice wobbled. "You said I nearly lost an eye. It must have been brutal. And the voices I heard after . . ."

It was dangerous to ask these questions, but she wanted to

know more. She *needed* to know she hadn't subjugated herself to the same level of the murderers that had robbed her life and ripped away her family's souls, condemning them to Umbra early. She would've been dead along with her family if Erick hadn't intercepted.

That single token of gratitude had fuelled her desire to follow in his footsteps. To hunt pirates and wipe them from Calypso's seas. To prevent more children, more innocents, ending up with their lives torn apart like a ship cleaved in two.

"Other than you nearly dying, if that's what you mean. As I said, your mind was still readjusting to the attack. But you're fine now." It was like talking to a stone wall. The same response year after year.

"But what if—"

"Why are you asking?" He stood abruptly, his face taut. "It's been years, Kora. I thought you'd realise by now you *have* a family."

She stilled. Erick's commanding presence dominated the room, and she bowed her head with guilt. She wasn't sure why she was asking these questions; suddenly compelled to dig up history. All the while, this male was standing before her as her father. He'd *volunteered* for the position, for gods' sake. He was always here, waiting for her to return from her adventures, always worrying over her safety.

And he'd trained her into the most lethal weapon a female could be in this world.

"I'm sorry," she mumbled. Her drying hair flicked into her eyes as she kept her head bowed to him in respect.

With an exhale, he stepped forward, lifting her chin, and brushed her growing hair from her eyes. It flopped over the side of her head. His assessing gaze raked over her face, before landing on her neck.

"What's this?"

Kora's hand rushed to her neck, panicking that the talisman was visible, but instead, her fingers brushed over lightly bruised skin.

"Did something happen?" Erick's tone turned glacial as he inspected her neck. "Who did this to you? Was it Marwood?"

She was taken aback at the insinuation that Blake could ever be capable of such violent treatment. Little did Erick know about the depth of their bond . . . and Blake's gentle caresses that caused hot flames to lick at her skin.

"Theron's right-hand man," she strained as she fought to keep the memory at bay. "He didn't believe my vagina justified me being a captain."

Erick's face twisted as his fist clenched near her neck. "I'll kill him. Is he here?"

"Theron banished him into the desert." She flinched at his curled fist so near to her face. "Callan's gone . . . he won't be coming back."

"Cal-lan," he sounded out the name slowly, "is a dead man if he crosses any of the borders."

Kora loosened a breath as Erick stepped back, his gaze observing all of her for any further injuries. She resisted the urge to touch her bandaged arm beneath her tunic. Maybe Callan crossing the borders would work in her favour. It would be one way to permanently silence him about her powers . . . or spark a conversation leading to her magical discovery. Her heart fluttered.

"What else happened out there? Anything I should know?" He raised a brow and tapped his foot.

"The journey was quiet out. We arrived early and met Theron and his two lackeys. There was a minor incident," or *situation*, as Blake had called it, "which resulted in Callan's banishment."

"That doesn't look minor to me. Anything else?"

"Nope," she forced a smile. "Smooth sailing."

Blake had ordered them all to keep the exile attack under wraps, with Theron in keen agreement. It'd look poor for all of them, slaughtering that many exiles. If the empire wanted them dead, they would've been hanged in the first place.

She'd been surprised at the sentinel's eagerness about the decision. Wouldn't he want to report it? Or was he filing it away for later, ready to spring it on them in his report to the king? Targeting Aldara as a 'problem' island.

After an excruciating pause, Erick finally spoke. "We have a meeting soon." He strode for the door. "Meet us in my study when you're ready."

Kora nodded, words eluding her as she battled her inner screaming demon at the mention of Callan, and the potential hunt for her being orchestrated.

"And Kora?" He looked back as he opened the door. "I like the hair."

I'm the sailing master, and I say this is the best route." Samuel exasperatedly pointed at the large map stretched across Erick's mahogany desk.

"No, that's too long. Why not go straight across towards the Sulfire Sea?" Blake traced a line across the map.

"No, no, no!" Samuel moaned, pulling on his beard.

The bickering sounds faded out as Kora hung back, leaning by the entrance to Erick's office. It was made entirely of wood—a similar chestnut tone to his hair and eyes—and decorated with floor-to-ceiling wainscoting. Deep-green velvet drapes hung from the large, black-arched windows on the left side of the room.

"Neither route will work," Theron's voice cut through the grown males quibbling.

A small lit fireplace donned the rear of the room, and bookcases with glass cabinets lined the right-hand wall, filled with an impressive suite of literature and endless reports. Right in the centre of the room, beneath a brass candle chandelier, laid the large mahogany desk.

Her attention snapped back to the group. Samuel stood near the fire, his large hands pressed on the aged, faded map of the Azarian Islands. Blake stood to his left, Theron to his right, and Erick next to him. Ivar hung in the shadows pocketing the corners of the room, his dark clothing and hair blending in.

"What did I miss?" Aryn strolled through the doorway, taking position against the wall next to her.

"Just . . . this." She waved a hand to the males arguing over the map, pointing at which route to sail to Talmon Island. *Gods spare her.*

Erick had called a meeting for a debrief of their ten-day

escort. After seeing the bruises on her neck, he knew all didn't go well. Blake had given a shortened, yet tense, explanation of the voyage, expertly skimming over what happened with the exiles— not letting Erick know how many there had been . . . and what a bloodbath it'd become.

If the truth came to light, they'd be stripped of their ranks for gross misconduct. The exiles may be banished from society, but they weren't fully-fledged criminals.

And their blood stained their hands.

It wouldn't matter now. Their bodies would've become food for the wild animals lurking in the desert, perhaps the boars. Or any surviving exiles who were starved enough to taste one of their own, but there weren't many of them left. Just like the pirates, she'd trimmed the exiles down to a scant amount. Still, the Skytors must be powerful to organise a large number like that. What kind of power had Finlay possessed in his trembling hands?

Theron had barged into the manor mid-meeting, walking with a royal's pride as he declared he required passage to the Citadel *immediately*—and he was invoking their contract as his escorts. Most probably to ensure they didn't blab about what happened in the desert. Whether it was the exile massacre, or Callan, she wasn't sure. Either one would stain his royal reputation.

The relief had washed over Kora like a thunderous wave. It meant Blake had to remain employed to *Hell's Serpent* just a bit longer as Theron's escort. They hadn't had the chance to speak of his future yet. She feared she would become utterly undone once they did. That a line would be drawn in the sand that neither of them would be able to cross again.

"The Black Abyss has grown more treacherous," Theron gestured to the black spot staining the map between Aldara and Talmon. "If we attempt to cross it, we will not survive."

"You know this *how*?" Suspicion creased Samuel's brow.

"I wouldn't be a very good sentinel if I didn't know these things."

She bristled at his words. Something about them was so . . . strange. Odd. Familiar? She rubbed the dull ache in her temple. Aryn glanced at her, raising a brow, the tattoo on his face stretching from the movement.

Indeed, Theron was an especially intuitive sentinel. Kora narrowed her stare, raking in his rippling muscles, untarnished armour, and secret compartments woven throughout, containing his throwing knives. The way his eyes seemed to be all-seeing, ever observing his surroundings as if he could see through to someone's core.

She'd met a sentinel once before. They'd been a weedy, snivelling thing, turning their nose up at anything they deemed *less than*—which included Kora herself. She had flashed her teeth and daggers at them and sent them scarpering back to their dry kingdom.

No—Theron was certainly not the *usual* kind of sentinel.

"Can we sail around it?" Blake traced a slim gap between the Black Abyss and Peril Cove on the map.

Kora stepped forward to the desk, slipping between Erick and Blake, Aryn silently hovering near her as he too scanned the map. "We'll be too close to Peril Cove," she murmured, "and last time we did that . . ." She trailed off as she met Blake's emerald gaze.

She'd miss that gaze. Those secret looks they would shoot each other, their unspoken connection coursing between them. She averted her stare before the cracks in her world shattered.

"What about the other side?" Theron pointed towards where the Sulfire Sea engulfed the coast of Otrovia, famous for its marshlands and swamps.

Samuel shook his head. "The Sulfire Sea is also *treacherous*. It's like sailing through boiling water. It'll break the ship apart before we even reach the shore."

"And it's acidic," Aryn added.

"The king wants to control these islands. Fat lot of luck it'll do him," Samuel muttered to himself, rolling his grey eyes. "Draining us dry of—"

Theron and Erick combined threw Samuel a glare, and Kora kept her eyes glued to the map, unable to handle another confrontation as Blake hissed at Samuel about holding his tongue.

"I just don't understand why we're sailing again. We've just completed a contract," Samuel retaliated. He'd been exceptionally quiet during the journey after the exile attack, his soul wearier than most. Samuel *loved* sailing. But now he didn't want to?

"My reasons for reaching the Citadel are none of your concern," Theron snapped. "Appreciate that I want to continue lining your pockets with silver, *sailor*."

Kora blocked out the bickering as the Black Abyss captured her attention. Legend said it started as a trench, formed when the islands were cleaved apart by the gods, each island becoming a home to a strong, elemental force. The Devanian scholars never confirmed which island belonged to which deity, but Kora liked to think Aldara was Calypso's.

Over the years, the trench had expanded deeper and wider until it eventually became the yawning jaws of death within the ocean. Any who dared to cross it would meet their demise. Sucked into it, never to see daylight again. It resulted in the unfortunate black splash of ink on every sailor's map of the islands. The darkest part of the seas. So deep and black that sailors couldn't see their fingers in front of them if they succumbed to its depths.

"We have to go around." She traced a line with her finger. "Around Peril Cove, past the Calypso Islands." Her finger moved westward, towards the Mist, before shooting northwards past the small littering of tiny islands and looping back round to the east above the Black Abyss.

"You'll be risking yourselves between Peril Cove and the Mist," Erick observed.

She chewed the inside of her cheek. It was a risk sailing towards Galen—towards the growing Mist. But there was no other way when observing the map . . . and something about the shrouded, red-marked island tugged at her. Beckoning her to sail to it.

"It's the only way," she pressed. "It's either that, or risk the Black Abyss."

"Those pirates may still be there," Erick pushed back. "Last time you sailed there, you nearly didn't make it back."

Blake cut her a warning glance and she suppressed a glare. She didn't need prompting about holding her tongue, too.

"We'll follow the standard shipping routes," Blake proposed. "We can sail under a fake flag, try to blend in with the exports."

Theron nodded. "It's a good idea. Sail under the guise of one of the noble houses' goods shipments."

"What's to stop the pirates attacking us anyway?" Kora replied bitterly. "Besides, they'll recognise *my* ship."

"Unless we sailed with another captain?" Theron's question was brazen. "You're welcome to join, as a crew member."

Deathly quiet settled as Kora peered through her lashes at the dark male. His vambraces glinted in the sun where his arms folded across his chest. If he offered the contract to another captain, it would free Blake, and push him towards the army. Her heart seized. She'd have to settle for impersonating goods shipments.

"We're taking my ship."

"Captain . . . maybe we should—"

"We're taking my ship!" she snapped at Samuel.

She wouldn't have her plan to reach the Shannara Territory jeopardised. By sailing with her own ship, she could control the navigation—and Blake's employment. It'd worked out perfectly so far, with Theron's urgency to reach the Citadel.

As his escorts, they would be invited onto Talmon Island, and into the renowned Citadel. Where she could sneak off and trek across the island to Shannara, leaving Blake in charge of *Hell's Serpent* and the crew. He wouldn't be able to join the army if his captain had abandoned her post. It was a risk she was willing to take. For him.

And it'd keep her at a distance from the Skytors. She'd bet her entire coffers they'd avoid Talmon if they could, seeing as it was the empire's headquarters.

Yes, it was all coming together nicely.

Even if it meant she may never become admiral. May never fulfil her vow of eradicating pirates. But she couldn't do any of those things anyway with this death sentence hanging around her neck every second of every day.

"Taking your ship where?"

Kora blinked at the figure lurking in the doorway. "Bree?"

Bree stepped forward, holding her chin high as her rounded blue eyes grazed over the tense individuals in the room. Her royal-blue skirts swished around her, so eerily similar to the colour of *Demon Sea Siren*. The finest gold jewellery adorned her, dazzling against her deep, rich skin, and her braided hair was swept up, the golden-infused braids floating around her neck with each step.

"Miss Hydrafort," Erick bowed. "We're just in a meeting—"

"I can see."

Only an individual of noble status would dare cut off the commodore. Bree's inquisitive stare flicked over Kora before landing on Blake, and Kora's gut knotted. *No, not now, please.*

"Where are you taking your ship, Kora?" Bree approached, placing a hand on her friend's shoulder, her fingers curling until they bit into her tunic. "Are you leaving me again?"

Kora forced a smile. "I can't stay, unfortunately. We're heading to the Citadel."

"Oh!" Bree clapped her hands. "Amazing news! I also require travel to home."

"You're going home?"

"Yes, my father has summoned me," Bree glanced sideways at the map. "Can I travel with you? It'd be *so* good to spend some more time together." Bree smiled sweetly at Blake, and nausea churned within Kora. *Calypso spare her.*

"We have no time to escort civilians," Theron's brooding

voice cut through like a cold splash.

A small snort sounded from Samuel as Bree twirled on her foot to face Theron. Their similarities were uncanny as they both regarded each other, casting the same, judgmental royal stare over each other. She hovered at his muscled frame, breath hitching.

"I can assure you I'm no mere civilian," Bree paused, her full lips pursing. "But . . . *who* are you?"

"Theron," he replied bluntly. "Royal sentinel to the Staghart family."

Bree's slow blink was her only indication of surprise, followed by a toss of her braids over her shoulder. She stepped closer to Theron. "Well, Theron *with no last name*. My family owns the Citadel, and I will be coming on this voyage. I'm sure, as two people cut from the same expensive cloth, you would understand the necessity of a summons."

Kora raised a brow at Bree's boldness and cut a look towards Theron. Indeed, he'd never shared his last name, or Callan's and Ivar's. A shroud of mystery surrounded this male, as dark as his own shadow. Theron stilled as Bree invaded his proximity, her bosom fluttering with each breath.

"Perhaps we can spend the voyage getting to know each other," she purred. "I'd like to get an insight to what my cousins are up to across the seas." She placed a jewelled hand on his armour and Blake tensed. Bree was outrageously brave. No, *stupidly* brave.

Theron looked down his nose at Bree. Disgust, or something similar, fleeted across his face before it tightened, and he adverted his gaze from Bree to Kora.

"Be ready to set sail at dawn, Cadell." He strode out.

Ivar melted from his shadowy corner, silently prowling across the wooden floor. He paused next to Bree and dipped his head, his dark eyes devouring her, before following Theron out of the manor. Aryn's inquisitive stare never left Ivar's movements until he was out of sight.

"Well," Bree flicked her fan open and fanned her chest, drawing the eyes of all males in the room, except Erick. "Isn't this exciting?"

"It certainly is," Blake responded tensely, his jaw clenched.

Kora was sure excitement wasn't the word for what she was experiencing.

The glowing white figure had been drifting around the dome for a while now.

Kora sat, her legs crossed inside the protective glacial blue bubble she had built brick by traumatised brick.

Her sanctuary.

For the past few nights, since the exile attack, she'd been materialising here. Waking up in the in-between of reality and dreams. Past and present. Life and death.

Tap. Tap. Tap.

The white thread, slithering like a snake, had taken the form of a tall figure. Its glowing hand created a constant tapping noise as it searched for a way in. A way to break through. A way to break her.

"Go away," she moaned, rubbing her face. Would she ever get any peace?

Since she'd built the mental dome, it had waited patiently outside, as if it were watching her. Never leaving, never moving . . . that is until now. It circled the curved structure, tapping every clear, blue-tinted brick. Its glow had dimmed, but it lit the void lingering outside.

Tap. Tap. Tap.

"Go away!"

She fell back, summoning a plump cushion to soften her back and head. She wasn't sure why it *still lingered. Why the connection was still hanging on by a literal thread. Why she could hear a voice no one else could.*

Was she insane? Probably.

The incessant tapping continued, steadily growing faster and louder until it became a ringing in her ears. She marched to the edge of the dome, glaring at this simple, white, annoying, mystical thread pretending to be a person.

To be someone she knew.

"What do you want?"

It responded with a single tap.

"I don't need you anymore," she growled. Her rippling, water humanoid form was all she could manifest in this place, and her growl bubbled in her liquid throat.

The white thread spasmed, the figure shuddering, almost as if . . . as if it were laughing at her.

"What?" she snapped. *Her temper flared and her skin steamed. "I needed you. And you weren't there. You've been in my head, yapping and nudging for as long as I can remember, and when I* needed *you—where were you?"*

The glow dimmed further.

"That's what I thought," she muttered.

She sat down by the edge of her shimmering, protective dome, and rested her head against the mystical bricks. She could almost feel the cool surface. Pity it wasn't real, it was a nice reprieve for her headaches.

"Let me in."

Kora shot forward as the thread spread its fibres against the brick by her head. Its hand stretching and unfurling into a webbed structure.

"No." She shuffled back. "Never. Never again."

PART THREE

THE CITADEL

T he Mist was thick, dark, and roiling.

Hell's Serpent crashed along the surface of the Shaurock Sea. Kora scowled at the cream shipment sails that'd replaced her fine black ones, billowing in the strong gusts of winds terrorising the ocean. The bow dipped and swayed, and ocean water sprayed onto the foredeck causing sailors to slide across the slick wood as the ship rocked.

"This is an omen," Theron spoke darkly as she retained her grip on the helm, muscles barking in protest.

"I didn't take you as superstitious." She steadied her legs, breathing into her core as *Hell's Serpent* continued to lurch in the violent waters.

"You are telling me that this storm—and *that*," he pointed at the cold, growing Mist, "isn't a sign?"

"We're captains," she exhaled a sharp, cool breath as she angled the ship towards Peril Cove. "It's a common hazard of the job."

The Skytors hadn't been lying. The Mist had grown—*a lot.* Tendrils of it seeped out from the main mass shrouding Galen, floating across the water like a weaved web waiting to catch its prey, all the way to Peril Cove. She'd prayed the whole voyage there in hopes of an easy journey.

The gods had ignored her prayers and sent a storm instead. *Typical.*

Shadows lurking in the Mist writhed, as if it were teeming with dark, unknown creatures. She shivered, and churning nausea rose in her gut. It left a bitter, bad taste in her mouth.

"We should've gone *my* way," Samuel muttered from behind. He stood with his brass spyglass glued to his eye as he surveyed the expanding mists.

"The Black Abyss would have been worse . . . trust me," Theron replied.

Samuel remained silent at Theron's words and directed Kora as he scanned the Mist. Up ahead, Aryn perched at the top of the main mast, his arrow nocked for potential attacks, his archery squad strategically placed all around the ship. Blake was stationed in the brig, ensuring cannons and weapons were kept dry and accessible. She was sure Ivar had melted into the darkness of the ship itself. Always watching Theron like a hidden shadow.

Bree had taken residency in Kora's quarters, deeming it suitable for her *needs*, so Kora had been slumming it in the crew's quarters the past week, which had turned out to be jolly good fun. Who knew drinking and gambling every night would lift weary souls?

Her sailors had their hands on deck, pushing their lithe bodies to the limits as the relentless ocean crashed over *Hell's Serpent* wave after wave after wave.

"Watch it!" Theron grabbed the wheel, his strong dark hands spinning the spokes. She gasped as the ship lurched starboard side, circling around a reaching tendril of Mist she hadn't realised she was drifting towards. "We don't know what happens if we touch it."

His dark brown eyes scanned the Mist. Shadows rimmed his lids, bleeding into his skin like spiked veins and she gazed at him curiously—had his eyes always been that dark?

"It's just mist," Samuel released a sigh of annoyance. "Nothing bad will happen if we sail through those little tendrils."

"I am not sure it is."

She suppressed her shock as Theron stepped away, wrapping a hand around a green shroud, and he gazed out towards the Mist as if he could see *something*. Her neck strained as she craned her pale head to peer around his mass of muscle and glistening wet armour.

"Are we sure about this guy?" Samuel whispered as he offered to take over the steering of the ship. His long blonde hair was soaked, and had been tied up on top of his head with a black bandana to keep it out of his eyes. "If we have to avoid every scrap of mist, we'll sail directly into Peril Cove."

"He's the royal sentinel," she quipped. "As far as we're concerned, he's basically the king. And *yes*, avoid the Mist. I'm sure there's a gap up ahead."

Samuel rolled his eyes, his face hardening as his thick arms steadied the ship against the rolling waves. His navigational tattoos were stark against the gloom of the sky, matching the grey of his eyes.

As the storm surged, the Mist thickened, and Kora squinted against the dense air settling on the ship. The gap she'd spied north east vanished, overcome by the expanding tendrils. *Why was it moving so much?* She swallowed her unease as the thick mass over Galen roiled, churning out smoke that drifted across the sea.

Kora retrieved an old compass from her pocket. It was a simple black square, with golden painted edges and handles. In the heart of the compass was the empire's four-pointed star. Her thumb brushed the worn edges. It had been on her when Erick had rescued her from the wreckage. The northern stretch of the star acted as the indicator of true north, and her eyes widened as it spun circles, never settling.

Shit.

A familiar burning tingle warmed her chest, and the thrum of power hummed from the talisman as the Mist stretched and pulsated. Tendrils snapped, writhing along the ocean's surface.

"Sam . . ." her voice faded away as sailors yelled, leaping away from the greyed Mist slithering over the deck.

"What the *fuck*!" Samuel exclaimed, as the Mist swallowed *Hell's Serpent* whole.

Kora's senses were blinded. The muted light of the stormy sky vanished, and the density of the Mist was so thick she couldn't see her own hands. Just endless, dark grey. Devoid of life or light.

"Kora!" Samuel bellowed, his voice seemingly everywhere. It was odd to hear her name on his lips.

"I'm here!" She reached out to touch the helm but her hand met nothingness. *Fuck, where was she?*

"Kora!" Blake's voice echoed.

"Kora!" It blended into Aryn's.

"*Kora!*" Now it was neither male, nor Samuel, but something *other.*

"Blake? Sam?" She stumbled blindly, following her instincts of the ship. She took two steps forward, and a spoke rammed into her ribs. *Thank gods.*

"Sam! I'm at the wheel! Where are you? Theron?"

Silence.

Her breathing quickened as she focused her hearing. It was as quiet as the Silent Tundra, in fact more so. There were no blasts of wind here. Even the ocean waters had stopped raging. The ship was eerily still.

"Sam . . ." she wavered. "Theron . . .?"

Tentatively gripping the wheel of the helm, Kora's fingers brushed over the familiar grooves in the ebony wood. She continued moving her hands until she reached the malachite stone embedded in the heart of the wheel. Using it to centre herself, she spun the wheel with a deep exhale.

"*Let me out . . .*" she willed the Mist, praying she could break through.

". . . *let* me *in*," the voice replied.

A shudder rocked through the ship, the wood groaning. It fought to escape the invisible grip of the Mist as it listed, turning to what she hoped was north east. The talisman shone beneath her longcoat, and she jolted as a brush of wind caressed her face, a shock shooting from her scar to her dozing water beast.

"*Let me in . . .*" The voice was male. It sounded so human, so real. "*Now . . . you need . . .*"

"What . . . *who* are you?" her voice broke, tears threatening to surface, confusion clouding her as she strained against the grey cloak enveloping her ship. Even with the talisman's glow, she couldn't see further than a foot ahead.

"Let us out!" she begged.

"*Do not . . . trust . . . him.*" The voice faded, along with the gentle brush of wind.

Kora's ears rang with the deafening silence surrounding her, and she swallowed as she raised both hands and summoned the ocean waters. Her veins thrummed, energy pulsating from her core and cascading along her limbs. Her water beast purred, delighting in the chaos as the ocean crested.

The strain to break free from the Mist's hold crushed her, as though heavy, iron anchors weighed down on her arms, forcing her to sink through the deck and into the ocean. Her neck arched, her jaw clenched as her legs trembled, her arms shaking from the force of wielding the seas against magical Mist.

"I am Captain Kora Cadell," she whispered. "I will not be conquered."

The ship lurched forward at her command, and the symphony of the storm restored. As the Mist waned, the sounds of her crew simultaneously returned all at once, and her talisman's glow winked out.

"Captain!"

"Kora!"

"I can't see!"

"Help me! Where is everyone!"

"Cadell."

Theron's voice cut through the wave of noise. Within a blink, *Hell's Serpent* raced through the final dregs of the Mist, and Peril Cove came into focus. The storm had worsened, the skies cracking open with a downpour of relentless rain.

"Please tell me you saw that!" She was rooted to the spot, her hands gripping the wheel so tight the wood splintered.

He nodded, his own face stricken. Samuel lumbered up the stairs to the quarterdeck with Aryn and Ivar in tow, both panting and pale.

"What . . . the fuck . . . was *that*?" Samuel sputtered.

"The Mist," Theron summarised.

Samuel shot Theron a glare, his hand reaching out to the railing to steady himself against the storm. *Do not trust him.* Her gaze raked over the four males surrounding her.

"Where's Blake!" she shouted over a gust of wind. It was so strong and cold, and it whipped across her body leaving a trailing wet sting on her skin. The smell of salt water coated her and she licked her lips. The sea was unforgiving . . . but divine.

"He's checking on Bree!" Aryn winced as the winds continued to circle and thrash against the ship. Disappointment filled her, and she shoved the thought of them together—alone—to the back of her mind as she sailed *Hell's Serpent* through the increasingly violent storm.

Samuel appeared beside her, placing his hands on the wheel with a nod. Together they navigated the crashing waves and howling winds, working in tandem to keep the ship afloat. To keep the crew alive. Aryn watched from starboard side, whilst Theron kept his near-black eyes trained on the Mist.

As they cleared the last archipelago of Peril Cove, Theron leapt back from the railing. "Cadell . . . we have a problem."

Kora propelled across the slick wooden deck and grabbed hold of the nearest shroud, hooking her feet into the ropes as she climbed a few feet. Across the unending tempest, ships emerged from the Mist. Her blood ran as cold as the rain pouring down her face.

Red, yellow, and grey sails.

Before them, an impressive vessel surged, leading with gleaming white sails that were dazzling against the gloom and grey. Lined with silver embellishments, an infamous, silver Pegasus figurehead glistened with moonstones.

Dread coiled within her gut.

Galen.

Galen had returned.

40

"Which one of you is Captain?"

Kora held her breath as she crouched behind the door to her quarters. The pirate lords and mercenaries from Galen had boarded *Hell's Serpent*, cornering her crew on deck. As much as she'd liked to cannon fire them all to Umbra, a Galen warship altered the game. Their artillery had been formidable in the Galenite War, and she couldn't risk Theron. *Not a chance.*

But instead of allowing her to withstand the boarding, Blake had shoved her into her quarters, demanding she hide. She didn't have time to drag Theron in here with her before the thundering of boots stomped across the gangplanks.

"What's happening?" Bree's whisper floated from beneath the four-poster bed. She had squished her tall frame, with a knife clasped to her chest for protection, behind the cream covers draping over the side of the bed.

"I am," Blake's voice echoed through the wood. *Gods*, he'd make a fine captain.

"Who is it?" Bree whispered again.

"Round them up!" a voice barked. "I want them in a line!"

Kora bit her lip as her crew yelled, and her heart hammered violently as she tried to push away the mental images of them blood-eagled on the dead misty shores of Galen. This was all her fault. She should've been careful sailing the Mist, or they should've taken a different route.

"*Kora!*" Bree hissed, poking her head through the covers.

"Shh!" Kora waved her back under the bed.

"Tell me what's happening! Is Blake okay?"

Kora rolled her eyes as she pressed her ear to the door. She should be out there, defending her crew. Killing the Galenite scum. Not here, babysitting Bree.

"*Stay hidden.*" Blake's order drifted through her mind. "*If we are captured, you need to get a message out to the empire. One of us needs to survive.*"

The Galen warship had shaken them all to their core. Never, did anyone think Galen would return—*could* return. Typical it had to be when they were escorting Theron to Talmon.

"Look-y what we have here," a female voice drawled. "Royal scum."

Kora closed her eyes for moment, praying for Theron's safety.

"Leave this ship, now," Theron's commanding presence vibrated through the door. "Take me and spare the others." A growl followed, presumably from Ivar.

The yells and cries of Kora's crew crested, and she instinctively reached for her sabre daggers. She'd go down swinging to save them, and Theron.

"We only want the captain," she replied, followed by the sound of metal on leather. The sound of an incoming execution.

"Touch him and you die," Theron threatened.

The female laughed, and it unleashed something within Kora. Her water beast awoke at the sound, and her body sizzled with energy, as though she were soaring. Within a beat, she crashed through the door onto the glistening wet deck, the stormy wind and rain whipping her black longcoat.

She unhooked her throwing knives from her belt and, with razor precision, flung them at the first armoured mercenaries she saw. They collapsed to the ebony deck, blood spilling from their throats, mixing with the rain and ocean spray. The crushing guilt from the exile attack raged, roaring at what she'd just done. But they were Galenites, and this time, it was warranted.

Blake was hunched over on his knees, hands shackled behind his back. His black hair was plastered to his head, and his green eyes flared with dread as Kora charged across the deck. A female with long, braided silver hair towered over his knelt body, an estoc sword poised above his heart. Panic consumed his face.

"No," he mouthed repeatedly over, his voice lost to the storm.

The Galenite female's dark, deer-like eyes widened in shock, her jaw slack at Kora's presence and she commanded her mercenaries in Devanian to attack. Kora echoed the order to her crew, and they descended upon the Galenites, led by Samuel, Aryn and Ivar. She approached the mystery female, her daggers gripped in both hands.

"Don't lay a filthy finger on him," Kora snapped.

"You . . ." the female gaped and stumbled back. "How . . ." She looked towards Blake, who returned her stare with raging silence.

"What are ye waitin' for?" a male to her right seethed. He wore a striped brown and red longcoat. "Kill him, Skylar!"

The female—Skylar—shook her head, strands of silver hair falling from her braid and lining her light-brown-skinned slender face. The presence of her unnerved Kora, and she flicked her wet hair out of her eyes. Skylar's gaze snared on her scar, and she paled. Blake tensed as two of the pirate lords converged, enclosing around them. *Well, shit.*

"I'll do it meself," the captain of *Fallen Angel*—judging by his red attire—hissed, as he raised his falchion sword. Deep heavyset wrinkles lined his weather-beaten skin.

Kora instinctively responded, twirling her daggers.

"Come and get him then." She bared her teeth.

The pirate lord lunged with a battle cry.

"No! Wait Hector—" Skylar shouted, pulling away from Blake.

This close to her, Kora's whole body screamed, her head pounding with relentless pain. As she battled Hector, the ocean undulated, each wave growing bigger until *Hell's Serpent* violently roiled on the surface.

Calypso spare her. Her power couldn't manifest *now.* But something about Skylar triggered it, Kora's water beast scratching at the walls, begging to be released.

Before Kora could spear Hector through his hollow chest, a horn blared through the howling tempest and she whipped her head. Several Talmon Empire warships approached, and at the front was *The Burning Dragon.*

Erick's ship.

"Retreat!" the pirate lords commanded their sailors.

With ropes attached to masts, the crew of *The Burning Dragon* swung through the stormy rain, landing onto *Hell's Serpent* with menace and causing shudders through Kora.

"No! Hold them off!" Skylar glowered at Erick landing onto the deck.

Fiery rage blasted from him as he fought his way to Kora, his dark armour winking out pale silver Galenite mercenaries like stars fading into the night.

"Cassidy, get her!" Skylar ordered in Devanian, pointing at Kora.

Cassidy?

The use of the old language shook Kora to her bones, and she stumbled before *Golden Harpy*'s pirate lord, wreathed in patchwork yellow clothing, and long, brown boots laced up to *her* thighs. She beamed at Kora, exposing sharp teeth lined with red lips. Coils of brown ringlets were bound by a dark bandana, hidden beneath a tricorne hat.

Kora froze. A *female* pirate lord.

Hector, and the mysterious grey pirate lord, fled the ship, their eyes bulging in fear at Erick's presence.

"Kora!" Blake cried out as a rope snared around her. She slipped on the ocean water coating the deck, falling to the floor as the thick rope tightened around her chest, pinning her arms to the side. Her head smacked against the wood, salted water washing over her face and body, and her vision blurred as pain sang down her neck into her back.

Throngs of red and grey pirates swung and leapt from *Hell's Serpent*, abandoning the Galenite mercenaries. They held their ground, fighting the oncoming wave of empire sailors, but Kora's crew had been forced to the forecastle, fighting off lingering *Golden Harpy* pirates.

Cassidy pulled on her lasso rope, dragging Kora across the deck to the edge of her ship, kicking and screaming. *No, no, no!*

"Hurry!" Skylar snapped, her doe-like eyes warily watching Erick battle through the remaining mass of mercenaries. "We need to get her away from him!" *Who?* She was surrounded by males.

Iridescent clothing—the colour of labradorite—hugged Skylar's tall athletic frame. She leapt from the edge of *Hell's Serpent* like a bird, extending her arms to reveal a hidden fabric connecting them to her body. She soared across the ocean expanse, floating on the tempest winds, before landing onto *Golden Harpy*.

Kora's skin burned against the wet wood as the thick rope crushed her chest. Cassidy raced across a gangplank, hauling Kora to the very edge of her ship. Her fingers clawed at the wood, nails breaking and bleeding, her precious daggers discarded by Blake's knees. He wrestled on the deck, trying to break free of his shackles.

"Kora!" Erick plunged his sword into the gut of a mercenary.

"I'm coming!" A series of mercenaries fell as he sprinted for her.

"Captain!" Samuel's voice followed. He leapt from the forecastle, tumbling over the balustrade. Ivar and Theron remained, each working in tandem with a group of sailors, forcing pirates back over the gangplanks.

Kora screamed in pain as her back bashed against the railing of her ship. *Golden Harpy* flanked *Hell's Serpent*, and Cassidy and Skylar stood on the yellow-sailed ship, pulling the lasso until Kora couldn't breathe anymore. Gangplanks fell as the remaining pirates rushed onto their ship, and mercenaries jumped overboard as empire sailors barraged across the deck.

Erick, Samuel, and the sailors were all running for her. But they wouldn't make it.

Her legs pushed against the railing, hopelessly trying to hold on to her home in time for her family, her friends, to reach her. Several mercenaries grabbed hold of the lasso, heaving with their might, and the rope bit into her skin, cutting through her jerkin as she resisted with a wrenching scream.

An arrow ricocheted through the air, spearing into the dark brown wood of *Golden Harpy*. Aryn sped down the length of *Hell's Serpent*—his longbow raised. Every arrow fired embedded into *Golden Harpy's* railing—narrowly missing Skylar's fingers as she gripped the edge, desperately trying to haul Kora onboard.

Why was he missing?

Her vision tunnelled as half her body hung over the side of *Hell's Serpent*. She could barely see for shit. Maybe he hadn't missed? Stormy seas crashed against the ship, seemingly reaching for her. *Hello, sweet ocean.*

At the sight of Aryn, Skylar faltered, losing her grip on the lasso, and it curled and trailed down the side of the ship like a snake.

"What are you doing!" Cassidy screamed into the storm. "You're letting her go!"

Kora collapsed backwards, and Erick caught her before she hit the deck.

41

Kora wrinkled her nose at the smell of the disinfectant salve as Koji Sanatorre lightly brushed his fingers over the burn marks across her chest and arms, smothering her skin in the cooling gel. Behind him, Blake paced around the med bay, running his hands through his damp, raven hair.

"I can't believe it . . ." he exasperated. "Galen are *back*."

Koji gently hummed as he inspected her head. A small smattering of blood stained her white hair, and she winced as his bony fingers probed the wound with the eye-watering herbal salve. *Gods that stuff reeked.* "Their return has been foretold for some time," he murmured quietly, his golden slanted eyes growing distant, the lines in his aged face creasing into deep thought.

Blake paused in his pacing and eyed the ancient healer. For a moment, his emerald eyes burned with green fire, and Kora bit her lip. He was growing more irate the closer they sailed to the Citadel, and she didn't have the capacity to ease his mood swings.

Koji inspected her bandaged arm, tutting at her poor job of patching it up. The rope had narrowly missed her wound from the exiles in the desert. Maybe she deserved all these battle wounds.

"That'll do," he continued, oblivious to Blake's increasing temper. "No more fighting," he scolded, and shuffled out of the med bay with his medical bag in tow, seeing to the remaining crew on deck. Kora's heart squeezed as the memory surfaced of Finlay following Koji around after their battle with *Demon Sea Siren*. That squeeze quickly frosted as she remembered his lies.

Whilst she'd been unconscious, they'd sailed after the Galenite warship and pirate lords. But they had *sailed faster than the wind*, according to her crew, escaping into the Mist. And no fucking way were they sailing back into *that*.

"We anticipated this would happen." Kora shrugged her shirt and jerkin on, her jaw clenching against the sting of the fabric on her rope burns. "This confirms they're allied with the pirates."

She hooked her talisman over her head, securing it beneath her uniform, and it flared in response for a moment, morphing into its evolved shape. The continuous, warm, gentle hum of power returned.

"They . . . they nearly took you from me," Blake choked, his eyes so wide they nearly bulged from his sockets.

Kora tentatively reached out to hold his calloused hand, and he shuddered as their skin touched, fiercely pulling her towards him and placing his forehead against hers as he cupped her face. She jolted at the contact, and her mind flashed to Callan groping her—violating her—with his disfigured hands.

"War is coming, *asterya*," Blake warned. "Galen attacked us. The pirates *are* allied with them. Rebellions in the lower districts. They want to see us fall."

She squeezed her eyes shut against his words. They were painful to hear—to acknowledge. "We'll be together throughout all of it," she murmured back. "We'll survive." Together, until they went their separate ways. She bit her tongue, holding back the words. A mountain of secrets clawed up her shoulders, hooking its claws into her mouth and stretching her pained smile.

For a moment they stood, breathing in each other's scents, using each other's strength to steady themselves. She breathed through waves of memories, reminding herself it was *Blake* touching her. His hand fell to her throat, his thumb brushing her thin skin, and her pulse fluttered beneath his touch, her nerves flayed.

Kora whispered in awe into the quiet of the med bay. "We went into the Mist."

He withdrew his head "So . . .?"

"Jack said the Mist was controlled by a man—"

"Don't believe a word from that *pirate*," Blake's gaze darkened. "Magic doesn't exist, Kora."

"What happened with the Mist was unnatural." She stepped back. "Almost as if it chased us."

"It's just the weather," he sighed. "It doesn't mean anything. Shaurock Sea always has bad storms, you should know this."

He glanced at the space between them, and she averted her gaze from his sharp stare. His jaw ticked in response as she clutched her body, shoulders hunching inwards. A chill swept through the room and she shivered. *So tired.* She was *so* gods-damned tired.

"What are you saying? Do you believe in magic now? Do you believe the word of pirates?" Blake spat the final words out and she flinched at his tone.

"Ahem." Erick filled the leaning doorway of the med bay, and Kora sagged with relief as he stepped into the room, his warm eyes narrowing on Blake's rigid stature.

"Commodore," Blake bowed, hiding his clenched fists behind his back. "We're just—"

"You're dismissed," Erick waved a hand, his eyes frosting. Kora turned her head away at Blake's incredulous stare.

"Apologies, Commodore . . ." Blake's throat bobbed. "If I have done anything—"

"Marwood, don't make me repeat myself." Erick's hand rested on his sword's hilt. "I'd like to be alone with my daughter."

Kora closed her eyes again, pressing her lips together to prevent them from trembling. She distantly heard the door shut, and her legs gave way as she sunk to the cot. Erick sat across from her, the adjacent cot creaking under the weight of his dark armour.

"I'm sorry . . ." her voice cracked.

"What are you sorry for?" Erick frowned. His sodden green cape sprawled across the rickety cot, and water dripped onto the wooden floor. The consistent *drip, drip, drip* soothed her enough to speak.

"I-I froze. I failed. I let them board my ship, I let them . . . they . . ." She hung her head in her hands as emotions bubbled to the surface. "Galen returns and I . . . I can't . . ." She gasped as tears sprung in her eyes, cascading down her freckled cheeks. Great, all she did now was cry. It was *exhausting*. "I don't understand!"

He placed a gentle hand on her knee and his warmth radiated through her clothes, all the way to her bones. His wavy hair hung limp, and the grey strands were stark against the darkness of the med bay.

"Theron is safe. Talk to me, Kora. What happened?"

"The Mist. I . . . we went into it." A shuddering breath wrecked through her. "Well, more like the Mist *took* us . . . swallowed us whole. It was so strange. It made me feel so . . . *sad*."

She hadn't been able to get the male human voice out of her mind since, where it repeatedly circled like water down a drain, the voice swirling around and around. Who was he? Did she know him? Why did his voice make her want to cry? Make her want to scream. Make her want to cleave the Mist in two.

"What did you see?" Each of Erick's words were clipped.

"Nothing . . ."

"Did you hear anything? Was anyone there?"

She frowned as he leaned forward, his hands gripping her forearms urgently, pulling her hands from her face. "Kora, did you *see* anything?"

"What? No—there was nothing."

"Are you sure?" He searched her face, his warm hands tightening, the sensation causing anxiety to flare deep within her. "You can tell me."

"Yes! Let go of me!"

Erick glanced at his own grip in surprise and released her. Exhaling a sigh, he pinched the bridge of his nose.

"Do you know something?" Kora clasped her trembling hands together. He'd always been wary of the Mist, always ordering her to stay away from it. *Forbidding* her to sail near it.

He shook his head in response. "No. Do *not* go near it again." He stood, his face taut, motioning for them to leave. "My ships will follow and protect you the rest of the way to the Citadel. We can't risk them sailing out of the Mist again."

"Thank you." She breathed in the comfort of Erick. "Why did you come? How did you know that we'd need . . . help." Each word was forced in reluctant admittance. *Gods help her.*

"I had a feeling."

"You were *so* brave."

Bree fluttered her lace fan, her golden jewellery sparkling in the late-afternoon sun peeking through parting grey clouds. Kora leaned against the edge of her ship, one hand gripping a shroud rope to keep her sanity intact.

"Well, it was a team effort." Blake grinned as he nodded at Kora. "I'd be dead if wasn't for my Captain." *You and me both.*

Bree cast a sideways glance at Kora, her forest-green skirts swishing across the drying obsidian deck as she *swished* closer to him. "But *you* sacrificed yourself for her. Such an honourable man." Bree pursed her lips. "A *real* captain stands up for their crew."

Kora's hand tightened so much she was sure she'd have to visit Koji again for more off his off-putting salve. *Almighty Thanos,* she wasn't sure how much longer she could keep this stupid façade up.

"Marwood, Cadell." Theron appeared with Ivar.

Bree excitedly fanned herself at their presence, yet Theron's dark gaze trained on Kora. When Ivar's slinking form hovered a step behind Theron, his near-black eyes lingered on Bree for a moment, his throat bobbing, before scanning the horizon.

"I need to discuss our arrival at the Citadel." Theron jerked his chin at her quarters. "Especially after recent *events*."

"Of course." Blake bowed farewell to Bree, taking her hand in his and placing a delicate kiss on the back.

Kora averted her gaze, swigging her waterskin to settle the rising nausea. Gods, she wished it was grog. She needed a vacation, preferably on an isolated island, with barrels and barrels of rum. And sea biscuits.

"Fill me in later," she exhaled, her eyes glued to the calm, glittering azure ocean.

Blake opened his mouth to argue but Theron replied, "Take whatever time you need, Captain. Rest is important."

The formal address warmed her chest, and she bowed to Theron, her white hair falling across her face, shielding her inner pain. At least Theron understood she needed just *five minutes* of quiet.

Bree snapped her fan shut and flicked her braids over her shoulder as the males disappeared into Kora's quarters, their steps heavy and their shoulders low. It'd been a rough journey.

"You think he's not good enough for me," Bree quipped as they inhaled the crisp, northern salted air. Oh, good. So, she wasn't getting her five minutes of silence, after all.

Kora raised a questioning brow.

"Blake. I've seen how you are when we're together. It's clear you don't approve."

Kora sighed. "Yes. I don't think he's good enough." *Because he's mine.*

"I hope I can convince you otherwise." Bree placed her smooth chocolate-toned hand on top of Kora's sun-kissed scarred one. "You're my best friend. I want you to be happy for us."

Kora swallowed her tears, her fear . . . her secrets. Her carefully constructed life was slipping through her fingers.

"We're nearly home!" Bree gleefully announced, pointing to the cluster of small islands in the distance.

"Aye!" Samuel yelled from the quarterdeck. "Calypso Islands port side!"

She peered at the smattering of palm trees, sandy beaches and caves creating the Calypso Islands. This far away, it looked like a brown and green rock drifting on the northern Shaurock Sea. The islands were the first sign ships neared Talmon Island.

"My father would tell me tales of Calypso." Bree's eyes sparkled at the islands.

"The *goddess* Calypso?" Kora was sure her ears were stuffed with seaweed. Why would a noble know the Devanian legends?

"She was beautiful, and desirable. Her hand maidens were mermaids she created from the bowels of the ocean, and then Kaiah—the earth god—gifted her the islands for her mermaids. He loved Calypso, so he made lands in her oceans so they could always find each other. Always be together, and not cleaved apart by their own elements." Yearning filled Bree's sigh.

"I'm surprised your father told you such stories," Kora spoke quietly.

She'd read the same tales in Agatha's tomes—about the creation of their world, and the four elemental gods that ruled unchecked. Moulding and shaping the waters and lands until it became Devania. The kingdom of the divine. And how divine it'd been for thousands of years. Until the gods disappeared, magic along with them, hundreds of years ago.

And *man* came to rule.

Now it was Azaria. Kingdom of humans, murderers, and pirates. All achieved through the two-hundred-year-long Devanian Conquest that ended over fifty years ago, just for the Galenite War to take its place.

"He believes it's important to know the history of our enemies. Of their fables of magic and gods. I just think it's so romantic."

"Sure," Kora mused. "A story of romance and mystical creatures." She wriggled her fingers in the air.

"You laugh now, but I've heard there's a *prophecy*. From the witches."

"How do you know what the witches are prophesising?"

"Just listen!" Bree smacked her arm. "The witches say the gods will choose someone who will bring forth prosperity to the land, and defeat the evil that lurks, restoring the gods' home to what it once was. They will have unimaginable power—power of the world itself."

"That's a lot of responsibility."

"I think it's fascinating," Bree's bright blue eyes devoured the ocean. "Imagine if it were true. Someone chosen to defeat the pirates and the rebels. It couldn't mean anything else."

"Well . . . it's just stories. Only the king has that kind of power," Kora swallowed her lies. That prophecy hadn't been in any of Agatha's readings or teachings, meaning it was *new*. And somehow, Bree knew it.

A horn sounded behind them and Kora whirled in alarm, her eyes frantically searching for those gleaming white sails that stole her breath away. *The Burning Dragon* sailed beside them. It was larger than her ship, with intricate flame detailing, luscious green sails, and a vicious dragon figurehead. Its maw was wide open, and lined with razor-sharp teeth made of malachite stone. At full capacity, the ship housed up to six hundred sailors—far more than her two hundred.

Erick stood at the edge and, with one leap, he swung from his ship to Kora's, landing with a grunt as he straightened his knees.

"Erick?" She hurried over, with Aryn materialising at her side. Bree hung back, her stare wide.

"Commodore," Aryn dipped his head and Erick carefully regarded him, the lines of his body tense beneath his armour. He turned and waved to his ship, and another horn blasted through the gentle breeze.

"I'm sending my ships ahead to scout the final part of the route." A messenger hawk circled the top of the main mast of *The Burning Dragon* as it angled away from *Hell's Serpent*. "I've just received a missive from the Citadel." His face was grave as he clutched the missive, its golden wax seal broken, staining the paper.

"What is it?"

"Galen has declared war." Erick's brown eyes were panicked, and Kora's heart pounded. He was never panicked. He was always the calm, observant one. "They're coming, Kora. Galen is going to attack the Citadel."

F loating wooden decks jutted out of towering rock. Thick ropes, as wide as Samuel's body, connected them to naturally formed caves, encasing one side of the rust-toned mountain. Strings of lanterns littered the mouths of the caves, with fires burning on the centre of each deck, and ivy snaked up the mountain, trailing under the decks, as if nature supported the structure.

South Wharf Station was a notorious stopping point for travelling sailors. Some decades ago, after the Talmon Empire had established themselves on Talmon Island, a lone architect had travelled out and chipped away at the mountainous, isolated island lingering off the cliffy coast of the Citadel.

Sailors from all walks of life bustled along the floating decks, in and out of the lantern-lit caves. Merchants had settled in various levels, providing taverns, inns, and stores to suffice every weary traveller's whim. Kora was certain there was a brothel on the top level.

The architect had created the ingenious invention of an internal pulley-system. Miner's shafts in the heart of the mountain that had been developed into wooden platforms, with various connecting ropes and handles.

Kora tentatively stepped onto one with her core crew—and Bree—lumbering onto it beside her. Samuel's grey eyes flew wide with wonder, and she realised he, too, had probably never ventured to Talmon, just like her.

Theron and Blake grabbed hold of the pulley system, and raised the platform until they reached the middle levels. A rounded smooth tunnel, with ivy intricately cascading throughout, led them to one of the caves with a tavern built into it, and Samuel let out a low whistle as they all stepped into Ignitus Rocks.

Rich, red-and-orange-toned rugs littered the floor, keeping the coldness of the rock at bay. Lanterns hung from the ceiling between stalactites, casting a warm glow. A bar made of the same rusted rock encased the left side of the cave, and on the floating deck low, burgundy velvet armchairs were circled around fires. Small, mahogany tables stood adjacent to each armchair, with candles burning down to their wicks encased in dark holders.

Multiple sets of eyes swivelled towards the group, and Kora could only imagine what they looked like together. The towering presence of Samuel, the dark royal sentinel, the shadowy predator that was Ivar, the formidable, fiery Commodore Cadell, the best archer in the world, the latest champion of the Darkoning Trials, and the near-enough princess of the Hydrafort family.

And then there was Kora.

The lost girl.

Whispers weaved throughout the cave, echoing off the smoothed stone, and she flushed at the attention they attracted.

"Well," Blake murmured, "let's get a drink."

"Best thing you've said all day." Samuel stormed towards the bar.

"Put it on my tab," Erick called, as Aryn, Blake—with Bree hot on his heels—and Ivar followed Samuel.

"I wouldn't have done that," Kora taunted. "He'll drain your coffers dry."

"They know me here," Erick replied dryly.

She lifted a surprised brow. Such a small insight into his life, but she held the information close to her heart. *How many times had he been to Ignitus Rocks?*

"Let's sit over there, we need to talk." Erick motioned for Theron to follow. "Why don't you join the others?" His pointed glance skewered her, and she froze mid-stride at the dismissal, feeling like a child being told she couldn't join the adult's conversation.

It wasn't often when Erick the commodore ordered her around, and she'd learned the hard way to listen to him—even if it went against every instinct she had. Because he always had her best interests at the forefront of his mind. *Or some nonsense like that.* He took this parenting thing too seriously sometimes.

"Oh . . . of course." She awkwardly stood for a moment as the two males slipped away, their voices hushed, their faces strained. Something wasn't right, and by the gods she would find out. She turned to her crew at the bar.

Bree clasped a goblet of wine, her bright eyes fluttering at Blake, who smiled lightly as they conversed. Samuel had three steins of ale, chugging them down whilst Aryn shook his head, sipping his single stein. His fingers kept brushing his bowstring, his golden-flecked hazel eyes darting towards Ivar, who leaned with his back to the bar, arms crossed, his black eyes trained on Theron and Erick across the cave.

Kora placed a hand on her chest. They were all precious to her—except Ivar—and she hoped, she *prayed* she wouldn't lose them—any of them, in the face of the oncoming war.

War.

She never thought she'd see the day she would be actively involved in a *war*. It changed everything. It made her dizzy. All her plans were foiled, there was no way she could slip off to Shannara now. No way she could prevent Blake from joining the army when they would need him most. At least she was out of the Skytors' grasp.

He glanced up, his green eyes scanning the cave until he found her, and the tensity within him visibly relaxed as he waved her over to join them. With a stiff smile, she trudged over to Blake and Bree, the latter turning surly as Kora ordered a large stein of ale.

Kora leaned against the floating deck's edge beside the sheer drop of the mountain below. She trained her gaze on the Citadel in the distance. Shining like a grand beacon against the black drop of the sky, the sea terrorised the jagged cliffs it sat upon.

Blake exhaled next to her as a crisp, cool breeze ruffled his raven hair. *Gods,* that level of handsomeness should be illegal. His entire body was tense and rigid, and when he looked at the Citadel, a glimmer of a green ember burned in his eyes, ringed by shadows.

Samuel and Aryn lounged inside the cave, the former nursing his many steins of ale, the latter constantly trying to stop him from invading the bar and bankrupting Erick. Theron, Ivar, and Erick had retired to an inn, ensuring they had rooms for the evening before they sailed to the Citadel tomorrow.

Several sailors had cornered Bree, asking her a multitude of questions about the noble houses, and the Citadel they were never allowed to visit. Only residents, or visitors with formal invitations were allowed in. Bree all-too-quickly welcomed the attention, and her musical laugh wafted on the gentle winds encasing them this high up. Her blue gaze repeatedly swivelled in their direction, her smile straining until her porcelain skin looked ready to crack.

Below the deck, Kora glimpsed her black-and-green crew, drinking and singing in various taverns. They deserved it—gods, they *all* deserved this one night off. She'd even partook in some dubious gambling with Samuel, granting some of the silvers he'd lost playing Cribbage weeks ago. It felt like a lifetime ago.

"Everything's going to change," she blurted out.

Blake startled and leaned forward, placing his arms on the wooden beams lining the deck. Only a strip of wood, carved to resemble the whirling pattern of clouds in the sky, prevented them from plummeting to their deaths.

"Hmm, agreed, my *asterya*." He shuffled closer.

"Blake . . . I'm scared," she whispered out loud. Admitting those words sent a palpable shiver through her. It was all too much, and it was all happening too fast.

His eyes softened, and he gently placed a hand on her shoulder. This time, she didn't feel the warming blaze whenever their bodies connected. She could only feel the tensity of Blake, the stiff indifference, as if he were a stranger bumping into her.

"I promise you, I won't leave your side. I'll be there at the end. *We* will be there at the end—together."

"Don't make promises you can't keep."

His gaze sharpened, his fingers tightening slightly, small enough that it'd be hard to notice. But Kora had memorised his touches and his caresses until they were imprinted in her mind.

"I . . ." he was at a loss for words.

He'd already broken one promise about remaining on *Hell's Serpent.* She wasn't sure whether she believed he could keep another. She was surrounded by lies and secrets—and it was becoming hard to tell which were real. He gripped her shoulder, his strong hands clenching around her arms, and she winced as his grip rubbed against her healing rope burns, but Blake didn't let go.

"We will be together till the end, Kora. I'm not letting go of you."

"Maybe . . . *I* should be letting go of *you*." She'd thought about it long and hard. He'd already decided to seek employment in the army, and that kind of distance wasn't feasible. Their time wasn't now. Not with a war approaching.

Perhaps the empire was right, relationships between officers were a bad idea. They'd only be distracted, unable to commit to what atrocities laid ahead. If they survived the war . . . then they had a chance.

Blake flinched, his face drooping in shock. "You don't mean that. You're pushing me away because of the war." His grip tightened so much that Kora hissed in pain, but he still didn't let go. "Don't do this *again.* I can't lose you Kora, I need you with me, beside me."

What are you doing?

Leaving.

No . . . Kora. Don't leave, please. We'll get through this together.

One of us must die Blake . . . this is for the best.

She gasped, shoving past the memory of the night before the final contest of the Darkoning Trials. It'd been one of her lowest and darkest moments. And she'd nearly thrown *everything* away.

"I'm not *doing* anything. I'm thinking of what's best for you!" She tried to break free from his grip, but Blake was as solid as the stone of the mountain. *By the gods.*

She'd been selfish their entire relationship, and she was done. She was ready to leap, and free fall into the abyss, releasing him from their vow.

"You're what's best for me! I have no future without you," he pleaded.

"I'm just in the way," Kora mumbled, tears threatening to surface. "You could achieve so much more without me. The empire needs you."

"You are *everything.* Everything I have worked for and more." His plead turned rough, and her neck cracked as he shook her. "I have done *everything* for you, to be here with you. You have no idea! We made a vow!"

"I-I know, Blake, stop it . . ." she fumbled at his hands. "You're hurting me!"

Just like that, a shadow cast over Blake's face as the moon dipped behind a cloud and he released her, staring at his own hands as if he didn't recognise them. *Almighty Thanos.* That conversation did not go as she'd planned.

"Kora!"

Bree staggered over, her goblet of wine sloshing over the wooden deck, staining her purple gown tangling around her feet.

"Bree? How many of those have you had?"

"That . . . is none of your concern," Bree's words slurred as she dazedly smiled at Blake, her blue eyes sparkling. Her perfect mouth parted as she exhaled, her full bosom rising in her tight corset.

Calypso spare her, this was the worst timing.

"Why don't you spend some time with a royal noble?" Bree's attempt at purring was nauseating, and she trailed one finger down Blake's chest, her fingers tracing the buttons and buckles of his black attire.

"Not now," Blake spoke gruffly, his stubbled jaw clenched.

Not now? Kora stared at him incredulously—what did that mean?

Bree's stare slanted to Kora.

"*You*," she hissed, and Kora blinked in shock at her friend. "You're always in the way. I saw you two together just now. *You* just don't want *me* to be with him. Well, I have news for you, Kora Cadell, the champion would never stoop so low to be with someone the likes of you."

Kora's mouth dropped open as Bree flattened her palm against Blake's chest in a feeble attempt to claim him in front of her.

"Bree! What . . . why . . . why would you . . ."

Blake didn't remove Bree's glistening hand, and stood there as statuesque as the towering station. Kora glared at them both, her simmering temper threatening to boil over. *Stay calm, stay calm.*

"Bree, this is just the grog talking." Her teeth clenched as she tried to suppress the haze. *She's drunk. She doesn't mean it. She doesn't* know *your secret.* "I get you have worries, but just because we spend a lot of time together it doesn't mean anything."

The lie rolled off her tongue too easily. Below, cries rang out as a wave of the ocean sprayed up against the lower decks of South Wharf Station. A familiar pulse speared her chest, and her fingers flexed as she warded off the tempting pool of power brimming.

"No, no, no," Bree shook her head violently. "I *see* it now. You want him. Well, he's *mine*. As the heiress of the House of Hydrafort, I can claim him. *Right now*."

The ocean lurched, and Blake's eyes widened as a rolling wave lashed up, nearly reaching their level. Bree squeaked as droplets of salted water sprayed onto the decking, but Kora didn't budge.

"Stop it Bree, you don't know what you're saying. You know you can't do anything official without the marriage rite in the Citadel. Think of what your father would say."

"Listen to her," Blake murmured in a sickening attempt to be gentle, still not removing Bree's hand from his chest. *Bastard.* "You've had a lot to drink. I'm flattered, but you're not thinking clearly."

Bree huffed a laugh, her musical twinkle fading and replaced with something . . . ugly.

"I bet he hasn't fully *committed* to you yet." Bree's sly grin made something snap in Kora as Blake's face paled.

What did she know? What had he told her? In fact, what had Blake and Bree been *doing* together in all those moments alone?

This time, the ocean wave cascaded up the side of the mountain, spilling onto multiple decks, drowning fires and flooding caves. Her mental glacial dome shattered as she loosened the leash on her power. The wind whipped into a gust, and it stroked down the length of her back like a yearning caress.

"*Use your power,*" the male voice flooded her mind, as if keeping it at bay had made it stronger, more relentless. "*Get away from them.*"

Kora's fingers twitched, and the ocean water spooled around Bree's and Blake's feet, reaching for their ankles. Bree cried out, leaping away. It felt like an extension of her body, as though her own fingers were snatching their ankles, ready to drag them to the depths. Bree's goblet of wine clattered to the ground, dark wine mixing with water as she slipped, falling with her arms flailing.

Kora flashed back to when they met, of Bree falling the first time, with no one to catch her as she shattered her bones on the marble ballroom floor. She instinctively reached out, swooping to catch Bree before she disgraced herself in front of the mass of sailors who'd grouped inside the mouth of the cave, hiding from the sudden ocean storm that raged. Bree breaking her bones again would be a headache none of them needed right now.

Well, that's what she told herself. Was it an attempt to reconcile the surviving dregs of their friendship? Maybe. But as she steadied Bree on her feet, she shoved Kora away.

"Don't!" Bree snapped. "I'm fine!"

She glowered at Kora, even if Bree wasn't aware of Calypso's gift that Kora possessed, as though everything that'd happened was her fault. The ever-present pit of shame and guilt tunnelled deeper into Kora's core.

"I'm going to retire," Bree smoothed out her gown. "Blake, would you assist me?"

Kora stilled as Blake nodded tentatively without hesitation.

Her attempt at saving their friendship—and avoiding the nightmare if they delivered a noble in a cast to the Citadel—and her vow with Blake, simultaneously thrown back at her face.

"I'm sorry," he spoke. "She's not herself. She needs help walking, let alone thinking."

As Blake aided the staggering Hydrafort heiress to the inn, Kora stood on the decking alone, her clothes soaked, and the wind roaring in her ears as her heart splintered.

"I'm here. You're not alone."

43

The inn Erick had chosen was decadent. Floors lined with emerald and gold runners, and rough cave walls covered in tapestries depicting the Talmon Empire's history, interspersed with wooden doors leading to rooms.

Kora followed the winding tunnel, her fingers brushing over the tendrils of ivy hanging from the ceiling. *Room four,* the innkeeper had said. It was like a maze, and she exhaled with relief when she located her door. A brass plate, entwined with leaves and the number four etched into it, shone in the flickering light, next to a tapestry depicting Admiral Darkon.

He stood atop a pile of bodies, Staghart flag in one hand, the flames of the land roaring behind him as he fought in the end of the conquest, before the empire existed. His black hair shrouded his equally dark eyes, hiding his face. Darkon had perished not long after uniting the islands, succumbing to infection and illness from the war.

Shame he didn't have Koji there to help him. His salve worked wonders. Despite its stench.

Key in hand, she moved to unlock the door, but stilled as the sound of a familiar voice floated through the cavernous tunnel.

"It's growing stronger every day. I've had reports of it escaping the trench."

Erick.

"We cannot kill it—we have to find some way of containing it."

Theron.

She glanced at the brass key hovering by the lock. After a moment's hesitation, she pocketed the key and followed the sound of their voices. Keeping her steps quiet on the runners, she clung to the shadowy walls, hiding from the light of dotted lanterns. She paused when she reached a door slightly ajar, a thin beam of warm light cutting through the tunnel.

"I know, I know." Erick's sigh was familiar. Kora was sure he'd be pinching his nose.

"I have connections with Shannara," Theron's voice was hushed. "I can request them to—"

"No, no," Erick cut him off. "We cannot get the witches involved, not with the war looming."

She bit the inside of her cheek. It wasn't uncommon for the empire to offer contracts and resources to the witches in return for their services. Surely, that's what they meant. She desperately hewed to the idea that their connection with the witches was purely contractual, and in respect of the Shannara Accord Treaty.

Even if witches were allying with pirates . . .

"There's someone else we can ask, but you may not like it."

A thick pause.

"Who?"

"The Skytors."

Almighty Thanos. Had she heard that right?

Kora's hands shook. Her mind roaring. Cold shock swept over her, and she leaned against the wall for support as her world tilted. *The gods damned Skytors.*

"Absolutely not," Erick snapped.

"They will be able to do it undetected."

"*No.* If they get caught, it'll be catastrophic. We cannot risk it. It'll jeopardise too much. If they discover my name, they will turn against us."

We? Us? Her vision swayed. Erick *and* Theron knew the Skytors—knew what they were, *who* they were. Had he known Finlay, or John? What was Erick doing, working with rebels? Was he aware of the mages they harboured? Or the exiles they'd enlisted to capture her in the desert? And how did Theron know them?

Just when she thought she'd escaped the Skytors, *they still followed her.*

She collapsed against the wall, her legs unable to offer support. She placed a hand over her mouth, muffling her ragged breathing.

"We have to do something," Theron's dark tone levelled, his words so sharp they could slice flesh. "The kraken is close to escaping. My king does not need a creature capsizing and killing every sailor in the seas. Not with a war at stake."

What?

A kraken was a myth . . . wasn't it?

"It won't do that," Erick murmured casually.

Apparently, they're real. She shuddered. *A fucking kraken.*

"What? It's a kraken. Of course, it will."

"Trust me," Erick exhaled, followed by the sound of a stein placed on a table. "It is under control."

"By who?"

"Davy Jones."

Theron scoffed. "That's just legend."

"The Black Abyss appeared ten years ago, Theron. It started as a normal trench, that'd been there for *thousands* of years, completely harmless. Then one day, it grew. The waters turning so black and so deep no creature could survive it. But one did—the kraken." Erick's voice turned solemn.

"Yes, and now it's trying to escape. I do not need the story, Cadell."

It unnerved Kora to learn Theron called them by the same name. That it rolled off Theron's tongue with such familiarity, as if Erick and him were . . . *friends.*

"There was a war between us and Galen at the same time," Erick continued, ignoring Theron's growing impatience. "A man involved in that war was Davy Jones. He fought for Galen, possessing impossible . . . abilities. He could do things I've never seen another person do."

"And how does Davy Jones control the kraken? His legend is that he's dead, and drags sailors' souls to the depths of the Locker. A tale to scare children."

"Some legends are real. He controls the kraken because the Black Abyss *is* Davy Jones' Locker."

Theron scoffed again in disbelief. "How do you know this? How is this even real? His legend has been around for decades, not ten years."

"Because . . . I sent Davy Jones to the depths of the abyss myself when—"

Crack.

Kora froze. Her hands had dug into the rocky ground without her realising, and water oozed from the terrain, latching onto her skin. *No, no, no.* The crack webbed, skittering up the rough wall, splintering the wooden doorframe, and the wood creaked, the frame shuddering.

"What's that?" Footsteps approached, the beam of light

darkening.

Kora lurched forward, descending into the pocketed shadows of the tunnel. She couldn't get caught, but she'd been unable to hear another word. Another *lie*. Surely it was all still legend. Blind trust in bedtime stories. Krakens weren't real. Davy Jones wasn't real.

But Erick's association with the Skytors was real.

Her world had been created and nurtured on a bed of lies. No one was truthful, not even herself. How could she be if she'd been born from lies? If everyone around her lied, surely she was destined to become a liar herself?

Kora stormed into her cave-like room, flinging onto the rickety wooden bed and delving underneath the thin, sage-green covers. Her talisman burned her skin, and she was sure it was evolving again after her spectacle outside.

She didn't care anymore.

Nothing mattered anymore.

It was hard to care when she wasn't sure what was real anymore.

T he Citadel was a golden fortress towering all around them. Kora craned her neck as her eyes drank up the vast size of the place. It was four times the size of Stormkeep Fortress, and in the heart of it was a domed castle made of stone, with gold crusting every edge of every line of square. Moss caked the structure like an external protective layer.

Large windows ascended two floors, with curling panes made of solid gold, and something about the overflowing opulence tickled the farthest regions of her mind.

Outside of the golden spiral and domed castle were the outer turrets and streets of the Citadel—all made of the same gold-flecked stone and moss. Beyond, was the city, consisting of bricked homes, green slatted roofs, and gleaming glass and cobblestoned roads lined with luscious bushes and trees.

The cabal stood inside Mossfell Castle, the very centre. The beating, thrumming core of the Talmon Empire, and opulence shone everywhere Kora looked. Gold and silver candelabras, golden embossed furniture, furnishings made of silk and velvet, white marbled floors with rivulets of gold. Heavy velvet drapes tied with golden sashes matched the shade of the looming forest hugging the rear of the Citadel.

She lingered by the grand windows, memorising the view of ocean waves between them and South Wharf Station. Her scar pounded viciously, and no amount of arnica salve was soothing it. *Gods damn this headache.*

"Welcome!" a male voice resonated across the large room, commanding the attention of Kora and her crew. Bree had departed once they'd arrived at the Citadel, barely glancing at her or Blake as she scurried away to her family's estate nearby.

It's fine. It's fine. It's fine.

Theron strode forward. He shook the hand of the male, his sheet of midnight hair glistened like oil. Several courtiers flanked his large form, and they dispersed, lounging on the chaises dotted around the room, luxuriating in front of the roaring marble stoned fires.

Erick followed Theron, and the male beamed, his thin lips revealing a sharp smile as he clapped Erick on the back with a rough laugh. He towered over Erick, and was broad shouldered; muscled to the point Kora knew he'd spent a fair amount of time fighting.

Eying him curiously, she slowly approached, with Aryn and Samuel flanking her.

"You've seen better days," the male chuckled at Erick who laughed back. The sound was foreign.

Blake silently thrusted his arm out for a handshake, and the male turned from Erick and greeted him coolly. As Kora neared, details came into focus. The male's skin was weathered, his face scarred, features all angular and sharp.

"Mr Marwood," the male's voice turned stern. "Keep up the good work."

Kora frowned. *Who in the gods was this person?*

His dark eyes caught hers, and she stopped dead in her tracks. Thunderstorms lurked behind his cold stare. Something about them made her freeze, her blood turning to ice as she regarded the male.

"You must be Erick's protegee," he murmured, advancing past Blake to Kora.

She reached out her hand on impulse under Erick's observant stare, and the male took her hand in his, the touch making her want to recoil. His skin was *so* cold, and every inch of his deeply tanned palm was calloused and rough.

"She's turned into a fine specimen, Erick." His voice was like raven's claws scraping over her skin, and she resisted the urge to snatch her hand from his. "You've done well."

She wasn't a puppet to be gawked at, and she glowered. Since last night, she'd refused to meet Erick's continuous stare, or Blake's. They were all strangers to her now—just like this male before her.

"Do you know who I am?" he asked, his lips tilting. She shook her head, too aware of his hand on hers, her fingertips numbing as his palm clenched.

"Admiral Bastion Barron, at your service." Barron feigned a bow, his smile sharp like a shark's as he winked at her.

Kora's eyes widened and she spluttered. Her idol. Her dream job. "It's an honour to meet you." Her cheeks heated, embarrassment steaming from her ears.

This was Admiral Barron?

She reined in her shock as Barron introduced himself to the remainder of the crew, the withdrawal of his grip a welcomed relief. This was the male she inspired to be—to someday *replace* as admiral. His portrait had never been painted, and she now understood why. The male made her skin crawl. Not like Callan did, but there was *something* off about him.

Meeting her idol was . . . anticlimactic.

"Welcome all, to Mossfell Castle," he commanded the room with ease. "I'm grateful to have you here, albeit under such strenuous circumstances. Tonight, we will have a feast! One last ball to celebrate the Talmon Empire—*our* empire—before we begin preparations to quash the threat of Galen." His stormy gaze fell upon her and she swallowed under its weight.

His lithe, muscled frame donned a dark green waistcoat with golden buttons, overlaying a billowing white shirt tucked into black trousers. No weapons adorned him—none—and she surveyed the vast reception room. All the courtiers were relaxed, no weapons nearby to grab, no scabbards lining their belts. It was a jarring sight to her.

"Thank you for your generosity," Erick replied quickly.

Blake nodded in turn, his emerald gaze trained on the marble floor, his face so pale she worried briefly—just briefly—about him.

"We have a lot to discuss," Theron urged, Ivar grunting in agreement. *Bet you do.*

"All of that will come," Barron waved a thick hand. "For now—rest, recover. I'll see you all tonight. Mr Marwood," Blake's head whipped up, his eyes wide. "Follow me."

Kora faltered as Blake followed Barron out of the door he'd entered, disappearing down a long windowless hallway. Where were they going? What were they talking about? Why would he want to talk to Blake?

"Are you alright?" Aryn appeared at her side, his brow creasing.

Kora nodded curtly.

"He gives me the creeps, too."

She glanced at her archer. His hazel eyes darted about, drinking in the same details she'd noticed.

"We don't have time for a feast," she muttered. She couldn't think of anything worse right now.

"Agreed," Aryn murmured, as Theron and Ivar bid farewell, their gazes lingering on her before heading to their assigned chambers. "I'm going to do a perimeter check."

Kora raised a brow.

"What? Just because we're in the Citadel doesn't mean we're safe."

Except it did . . . didn't it? The Citadel was impenetrable, with the station nearby to vet any travellers seeking entry. Surely, they were finally safe, and could let their guard down just a little bit?

Aryn tugged on Samuel's arm, who chatted up one of the female courtiers, her face burning crimson at his abrasive language and thick, tattooed arms. Samuel's demeanour was a rarity here.

"No, what . . . wait!" Samuel moaned as Aryn shoved him out of the grand room.

Leaving her alone with Erick.

His warm eyes tracked her every movement, never wavering, as if he were waiting for her to explode. "Kora?"

She stared back silently. She had no words for him right now. She needed to unpack what she'd heard last night—the legends, the lies, and she couldn't confront him, not without revealing secrets of her own.

So, Kora turned around and stalked out of the room without another word.

A gown of deep royal-blue caressed Kora's body. Its sweetheart neckline swept across her chest, exposing her shoulders as sheer fabric circled around her upper arms. Tendrils of sparkling silver coated the corset, dripping down into the flowing skirts. This gown had been designed for her; it fitted her body like a second skin. She stared at herself in the tall mirror, unable to recognise the person she'd become.

Her white hair was slicked back, and various silver charms adorned her rounded ears. A line of black kohl circled her eyes, making them burn a fiery blue, and glittered silver had been dusted across her lids and shoulders. The servants even added some to her scar, and she turned her head, gazing in wonder as it sparkled against the moonlight bleeding through the bay window.

She was . . . pretty.

A secret smile played with her lips as she cocked her head. She felt powerful. In a different kind of way. She removed her talisman—it was too risky to wear it—and stuffed it into one of the many throw pillows clustering the grand, four-poster bed in the chamber.

Since her little *spat* at South Wharf Station, its shaped had changed again, and she now realised it was evolving into an eight-pointed star, with a glowing, diamond heart encased in an intricate swirling cage.

She cased the room. Large armoires lined one wall, along with a dressing partition, and a doorway to private bathing chambers. Every wall was the same solid, large stone, lined with gold and moss. The furniture was various shades of green, and white rugs with golden tassels lined the stoned floor.

A white oak desk in the corner had pristine thick paper atop it, along with a quill and ink. Beside it were empire wax seals, identical to her own onboard *Hell's Serpent,* with lumps of gold wax. Her lips pursed as a calm coolness settled from the talisman's absence, dampening her temperamental water beast. Good, she needed calm right now.

"Well," Kora gulped. "I guess this is happening."

She hadn't worn a gown since the night she'd met Bree. As she left her room, navigating the winding hallways towards a large, sweeping marble staircase, she focused on staying upright in the ridiculous shoes the servants insisted she wore.

She decided she liked dresses. Heels, not so much.

As she descended the staircase, she faltered at her crew waiting at the bottom. Samuel turned first, his jaw gaping. His unruly blonde locks were swept back and tied at the back of his head. His suit was of the deepest violet, the lapels a shimmering black, with a violet cravat and black waistcoat.

"Captain," he whistled, and she smiled shyly.

Aryn flicked his head, his golden eyes widening as Kora descended the final steps. His floppy brown hair had been smoothed out and tucked gracefully behind his ears. His attire was like Samuel's, in shades of dark burgundy, with a golden sash snaking across his chest. His quiver and longbow were absent, no longer attached to him, and he grinned sheepishly, his dual tattoo crinkling.

"You . . . you're," Samuel stuttered as she joined them, "you're a *girl.*"

Aryn and Kora glanced at him, taken aback. Then slowly, she beamed at Samuel, a laugh escaping her lips.

"What did you think she was all this time? A dog?" Aryn shook his head.

"Well, no. But . . ." Samuel's eyes roved over her body. "Look at you."

"Easy there," she snapped her fingers at his wandering gaze. "I'm not another barmaid you can charm."

"No," he murmured. "You're certainly not."

"You look stunning."

She stiffened as Erick descended the staircase. Clad in attire fit for a king, the commodore unhurriedly approached, his stance tall in his forest-green velvet suit. Adorned with a golden waistcoat and a black cravat, he strode with a royal's grace, his fingers sweeping against the marble balustrade in a gentle caress.

As if he knew this castle intimately. As if he'd been here all his life. *Big, fat, liar.*

Kora narrowed her eyes as he cleared the final steps, and Aryn shifted away, tugging at his collar.

"Shall we?" Erick held out his arm, his voice tentative.

She could tell he knew something was wrong, and didn't want to test the waters between them just yet. Not in front of the admiral. But their awkwardness was affecting her crew. Samuel and Aryn's gazes averted, their hands wringing. So, she took Erick's arm, and the four of them strolled to the towering set of gilded marble doors leading to the ballroom.

The size of a capital vessel, it spanned for hundreds of yards in every direction. The ceiling was at least three floors high, and a skylight window dominated the centre, casting beams of moonlight into the marbled room.

Endless dancers graced the floor, twirling and spinning along to music played by a string orchestra at the rear. Large marble tables lined each side of the room, filled to the brim with exotic spiced meats, seafood, herbal rice, and boar stew. Lemons, oranges, and melons as large as her head were fanned on silver platters—enough to feed an entire kingdom. Crystal bowls were filled with enough grog to kill Samuel. Rum, ale, and wine, along with punch for little lads and lassies.

Golden-paned glass windows exposed the left side, and a large roaring fireplace, as big as her chambers back home, took up the right side. Her vision swirled along with the endless dancers in an array of colours.

"Erick," a raking voice appeared beside them.

"Barron," Erick replied, his grip tightening on Kora ever so slightly.

"Captain Cadell," Barron bowed gracefully in his black suit. It hugged his muscles and accented the darkness of his hair and eyes. She eyed him curiously, casting her stare over the black waistcoat, cravat, and shirt. It was unusual attire.

It reminded her of *Hell's Serpent.*

"Would you honour me with your first dance?" Barron smiled.

"I don't think that's wise. I was hoping for some time with Kora," Erick answered before she could, and she cut him a glare.

"I'm sure you have plenty of time to spend with your . . . daughter," Barron spoke smoothly. "I'd like to get to know your protegee. After all, she is the only female captain in my fleet."

At last, someone who could acknowledge and respect her.

Erick's mouth thinned as she untangled from his grip, placing her hand into Barron's icy one. He guided Kora towards the dancefloor and whispers followed, the crowd parting for them like a wave. She averted her gaze from watchful eyes surrounding them, as Barron placed a hand on her waist, the other taking her left hand. Every muscle within her tensed.

As the music swelled, he took off, and she concentrated on keeping up with his steps, stumbling in the awful footwear she'd been forced to wear. After a few beats, he slowed, a wry smile on his lips.

"Not a dancer then?"

"No," she replied breathlessly. Had she always been this unfit? "Dancing isn't a required skill when you're sailing a ship."

He laughed, the sound causing her muscles to tense so much she thought she'd snap in two. Why was she so nervous? A gentle puff of air circled her, and she tried to force herself to relax as Barron spun her across the dancefloor, their steps in time with the string notes.

"I understand you want to become admiral," Barron murmured, his mouth too close to her ear for her liking.

"I-er, yes. I do. Not that I aim to replace you, of course," Kora swallowed her anxiety. *Gods,* what was wrong with her?

A chuckle rippled from his broad chest. She felt so tiny in his arms.

"Don't let go of that ambition. You will progress, as long as you know where to remain loyal. It will serve you well. I made a good choice in who to escort the sentinel. Pity Theron hasn't shown his face tonight. I've been eager to make this next step with him."

Kora's brows flew so high they nearly faded into her hairline. *Barron* had requested them for the escort? He must've known of her and Blake's achievements via Erick, believing they'd be most appropriate for the job.

Good gods. It'd ended in a massacre. They had been the *worst* decision. It made sense to an extent. Her and Blake had achieved their careers through a deadly contest designed to create killing machines. And that's exactly what the empire received.

He leaned closer. "Besides, I have my heart set on a far greater goal now."

Before she could enquire, he spun her again, and pulled her back close enough she could hear his steady, slow heartbeat. His fingers splayed on the small of her back, and his thunderous gaze dipped down to her lips, tracing the sharpness of her jaw. The music swelled, the notes cresting and rising like a wave.

"Unfortunately, I've decided to focus my efforts on my position as viceroy for the Citadel," Barron rumbled into her ear. The proximity caused every hair to prickle across her skin, and her shimmering scar to *scream*. "Which means . . . you have a chance to step up."

Her eyes widened as reality slammed in. *Almighty Thanos.* She was dancing with a *viceroy*—with a leader of their lands. Her grip slackened as she craned her head, trying to create space between their bodies. She glimpsed Erick standing at the edge of the ballroom, his brown eyes transfixed on every single movement they made. His mouth was so thin, his lips had practically disappeared.

As they twirled again, she saw Blake standing on the opposite side by the windows, his face glowering with rage as he, too, watched them waltz across the sleek marble floor. Another twirl, and Bree came into focus, her face poised in restrained shock as she lingered at the entrance to the ballroom with the Hydrafort family. Kora glanced away, shame oozing from every pore.

"I-I didn't know," she stammered.

Dancing with a viceroy was a bold move—a dangerous one. It pulled her into the public eye. Not only that, but she knew all viceroys were married. All had established homes, families, or wives.

And here one was—the one who lived in the gods-damned castle, dancing with a single, lone female that wasn't his wife. The whispers surrounding them surged, and Kora's cheeks burned as her ears picked up on the accusations.

On the scandal.

"I wouldn't listen to them," Barron spoke quietly. "My wife is not well. She is in our chambers resting, tonight. I just *had* to experience you for myself. Erick has kept you hidden away for far too long."

What?

"I-I'm sorry," Kora withdrew from his grip, unable to bear the wave of rumours and gossip encircling them. Barron paused. "This isn't right. I will *earn* admiral, not cheat my way to it."

"Very well." His dark eyes scanned the ballroom and the whispering faded instantly. "I must say though . . . you *are* stunning, Kora Cadell." He glanced at her gown, and she clasped her arms around her body. "As stunning as the ocean. The gown was a good choice. I'm glad it fits."

His words were gentle, like a caress, but her heart hammered. *He* had chosen the dress. She no longer felt pretty, but like the puppet he'd made her feel when they'd met earlier. Dressed up and wheeled out for him to display to the courtiers.

Barron sauntered off into the throng of dancers, black hair glistening in the moonlight. Kora hurried to the edge of the crowd, sucking in deep breaths as she steadied herself against the marble feast table.

What was she doing? What were any of them doing? This whole thing was ridiculous. *War was coming.* Shifting uncomfortably in her gown, she shakily poured a goblet of what she hoped was strong wine.

46

That was some show." Bree poured a goblet of wine, nudging it across the table towards Kora's empty one.

"I didn't know he was a viceroy." She swiped the golden goblet, hoping it was a peace offering. She wasn't sure how much longer she could bear this broken friendship. She'd been ready to sacrifice Blake at the station, setting him free, before Bree had trampled all over her grand gesture.

Swigging the goblet, she coughed, sloshing the hazy, bitter liquid.

"*Please.* You were doing this for attention. You wanted to make Blake jealous."

Why would Blake be jealous of Barron? He was old and creepy. Kora spluttered on her wine, downing its soured remains. That wine was off, but she wouldn't waste a single enticing drop.

"You've got to be joking. I didn't even know he was Admiral Barron until today!"

Bree smirked. Her dress was a vision, its golden opulence dazzling, nearly blinding Kora. A small golden tiara, infused with emeralds, rested on her nest of braids, and Bree flicked them over her shoulder as she poured a second goblet of wine for herself.

"I suppose that's only something *important* people would know."

Kora smashed her goblet down on the table and it cracked around the foot, the marble splintering. She splayed her fingers, hoping to cover the cracks to the valuable table. She'd have to watch that newfound strength.

"Since when . . . did you become such a . . . bitch?" Her words slurred. Did she just call her friend a bitch? What was wrong with her?

Bree scoffed, her eyes piercing Kora. They flickered to her scar, and her face twisted. "No point covering up something so . . . ugly. Everyone here knows that you're nothing. You're a lost reject, taken under the wing of a notable commodore. You're a charity case, nothing more. A thorn in the empire's side. My family's side. They *pity* you, Kora. You don't belong here."

The familiar haze blanketed her mind, and Bree's words bounced off it, numbing Kora to her core. She mumbled incoherently, and Bree's musical laugh filled her ears as she glided away, her skirts trailing on the marble floor, walking like she owned the gods-damned place.

Oh, wait. She fucking did.

Whenever Erick approached, Kora evaded him at every corner, all the while continuously helping herself to goblet after goblet of wine. She twirled across the dancefloor, slipping in the heels, her ankles barking in protest.

Bracing against a marble pillar wreathed in white and green sheets to catch her breath, Blake's laughter swarmed her ears.

Peering round the pillar, her nerves escalated as the Hydrafort family lingered nearby, dominating the room like royalty. Their gowns and robes matched Blake's attire of black and green, with Bree centred in the group like a shining, golden nugget. Her parents—Otto and Rashi—beamed at Blake, whilst Bree's younger siblings, Theodore and Alodie, observed the feast.

She'd spent weeks with them all, visiting Bree when she'd broken her arm a near decade ago. A cold family towards outsiders, but they regarded each other on shiny, towering pedestals. They all still looked like they possessed lances up their arses.

The former sibling exuded disinterest, fidgeting in his suit, pimples marking his adolescent face, whilst Alodie's huge eyes sparkled, until they landed on Kora, recognition flashing. She tugged on Rashi's skirt, dainty finger pointing to the pillar, and Kora fled, tripping in her heels as she lunged into the heated dancefloor.

Bodies propelled her across the space, her mind lost in a hazy, bitter sea that left a bad taste in her mouth. She spun and spun, unable to tell which way was up or down, until a pair of thick hands landed on her shoulders.

"Cadell."

She met panicked, dark chocolate eyes. Black rimmed their edges, and Theron panted, dragging her from the crowd into a shadowed corner leading to the servant's exit, near the musicians.

"Therrrrrrron!" she cheered. "Wherehaavvee you b-been,

matey?"

"Kora?" Her name was weird on his lips, and she giggled. "You are three sheets to the wind drunk, snap out of it." A glass of water appeared, and he tipped it to her lips. "Have you seen Ivar?" He scanned the room as she stumbled in his arms, spilling water down his brown shirt. He wasn't dressed for a ball, donning simple trousers tucked into laced boots.

"Thisss is a b-ball. What areeeyouu wearrrring?"

"I have been looking for Ivar. Has he been here?"

Kora could feel his pulse beneath his shirt, and it was erratic. She shook her head, and attempted to joke about him needing to visit Koji, but she couldn't get the words to form on her lips. *Thanos, what's going on, pal?*

"Theron, what's happening?" Erick appeared, stricken as she swayed in Theron's embrace. "Kora?"

She rolled her eyes, wiping dribbling water from her mouth.

"What's happened to her?"

"She's drunk as a skunk. Have you seen Ivar? I cannot find him."

Erick cursed, shaking his head. "You need to get out of here . . . I'll help . . ." Their voices faded in and out, her hearing distorting. "She needs a . . . I'll find you . . ."

Theron nodded and slipped out the servant's exit.

Erick tentatively wrapped his arms around Kora, guiding her through the crowd. She glimpsed Samuel in the corner with a hoard of females circling him, blending into one, sparkling, poofy person. Aryn observed nearby, tensing when Erick nodded to him as he assisted her out of the ballroom.

Her pounding headache felt as though her mind was being cleaved in two. *Gods,* how much had she had to drink? Her vision tunnelled, swimming, and she grumbled at Erick as her stomach threatened to show the whole ballroom how much she'd exactly drunk.

He slipped off her silly shoes and they stumbled up the grand staircase. Tripping on her skirts, Kora fell through her bedroom door with a grunt. She tore at the forsaken gown, suffocating in swaths of shimmering fabric, and collapsed onto the bed. Erick sighed, lifting her feet under the covers before departing.

What felt like hours passed, the room spinning violently before she could fall into slumber. The last thing she saw was a lingering shadow behind her door, and the last thing she *felt* . . . was a creeping coolness dripping down the side of her face.

K ora? You need to open your eyes."
Kora groaned, nausea churning in her stomach.
"Wake up now, you silly child!"
Her eyes flew open. She knew that voice.
"Agatha?"

Her void-defying, glacial dome had not shattered like she thought, but thick, deep cracks lined the curve of the shimmering blue bricks. The light of her little protective world seeped through the glowing cracks into the nothing beyond.

And before her knelt Agatha. Kora stared in shock as Agatha leaned forward, her knobbly, aged hand taking Kora's rippling liquid one.

She was real. She could feel her. Agatha was really here. And not only that—her sight had returned.

"Your eyes . . ." she whispered.

Gone was the endless white, replaced with piercing black pupils and gleaming beryl irises. Every time Agatha blinked, a new colour appeared in her eyes, shifting from red, to blue, to yellow, and green, and so on. It was a stark contrast to the opalescent white and gold robes caressing her aged, withered body.

"Kora, you need to listen to me." Agatha's comforting hoarse voice brought tears to her eyes.

"How are you here?" she asked dazedly as she reached out to touch her grey braided hair, rubbing the course strands laced with silver thread.

"It's not important. I've come to warn you, child."

"Warn me?" The dome shuddered and she yawned, sleep clutching at her, trying to drag her back down to its slumbered depths.

Agatha's bony fingers clenched Kora's jaw, forcing her to look at her, and she jolted in surprise that she was able to command her water humanoid form.

"Listen to me," *Agatha pleaded.* "I don't have long."

"What . . . where are you?" *A distant feeling of panic stung the edges of Kora's blanketed numbness, laced with a stomach-clenching nausea threatening to submerge the dome in a torrent of unbearable spinning.*

"Do not trust them, do you hear me? You can only trust one person, and *he's right there.*"

Her ever-changing stare glanced behind Kora, and she turned to find her lingering thread, in the shape of a figure, lurking beyond her dome. Ever waiting.

"No . . . no. I can't, Agatha. I'm never letting him in again."

She blinked drowsily, her eyelids scraping like sandpaper. What was wrong with her? The edges of her vision blurred. A cold blanket had been thrown across her mind, dulling her senses.

"How . . . do you . . . know him?" *the words stumbled from her lips, and she groaned as her vision darkened.* "Agatha . . . I don't feel well."

The cracks in her dome splintered, expanding into a webbed structure, every brick creaking around them.

"Trust me, Kora," *Agatha whispered.* "Let him in, you need to do it—do it now."

Reluctantly, Kora waved a hand, and her precious dome came crashing down. Before the shards rained onto them, they simply evaporated into little beads of blue smoke. The thread struck, poised like a serpent, wrapping around her form, winding, and winding.

"I miss you . . ." *the words echoed over and over, from Kora's lips, as she descended into the darkness of the void.*

The talisman was missing.

It was fucking missing.

Kora had turned the room upside down, ripping pillows from their covers, tossing bed covers across the room searching for the wretched thing. After thirty minutes, she collapsed by the side of the bed, panting.

It was gone. *Fuck, fuck, fuck.* This was disastrous on epic proportions.

And with it, her water beast had died inside her. Even if she focused, she was met with cold absence. She attempted manipulating the water on the bedside—nothing. Agatha's warning drifted through her mind. *You don't want it falling into the wrong hands.*

Kora raked her hands through her short waves, her heart clanging against her ribs as she tried to recall the previous evening. It'd all become so hazy after her dance with Barron—what in the gods had happened? She didn't remember returning to her chambers. Shock and shame still haunted her, along with a hangover from the pits of Umbra. Her scar thrummed along in time with her heart, and she groaned.

How could she lose it? She'd taken it off for *one* night, and she'd lost it. It had to be in this room somewhere . . . maybe if she disassembled the bed itself? She'd expected relief when her wish of disposing it had been fulfilled, but instead, all-encompassing dread smothered her, squeezing her diaphragm until she bolted for the bathing chambers, spewing last night's wine.

After rinsing her mouth, she collapsed by the bed, shakily tracing the silvery beads of her ballgown discarded on the floor. Hiding beneath the dread, a sliver of grief wrapped in ice consumed her, devouring her organs until she was a husk.

It was lonely without her powers. She felt *weak.* She hadn't realised how comforting the beast had been, a second skin protecting her, nurturing her.

"Kora?"

A gentle knock rapped at her door, and Blake peered around the door curiously. His forest green eyes raked in the tossed covers, pillows, and throws, and Kora crumpled on the floor, her hands fisted in the shimmering ballgown. His stare lingered on her for a moment, assessing the same way Erick did, before melting into an unwelcomed softness.

"I see you've made yourself at home," his drawl returned.

She didn't respond, wouldn't even *look* at him. She couldn't handle this. Handle the lies. The deception.

"*Be strong* . . ." the voice had returned.

Steeling herself, she stood to face him. She'd dressed ready for battle today, in the hopes it would strengthen her. Covered head to toe in black leathers, buckled together, along with her favoured blades hidden in their scabbards on her back. As much as she adored her sailing jerkin, she desired full-body strength and protection.

Blake cleared his throat, noticing her defensive stance. His thumb brushed a dark satchel slung across his shoulder. *Odd.* He rarely used a satchel, preferring to keep everything hidden in compartments in his leathers.

"We've been requested for a meeting." His demeanour was so soft, so gentle. She looked away, focusing on a fascinating speckle of gold on the stone wall.

"Kora," he stepped forward, shutting the door behind him with a sigh, then leant against the desk beside it. "I know what you must be thinking, but *please* believe me."

"What am I thinking?"

A clenched fist ran through his raven hair.

"That there's something . . . that I . . ." He couldn't even voice the words, and for the first time, she looked at him with something close to disgust.

"That you're cheating on me with Bree?" The words had been spoken. All her worries and concerns voiced into the world. He visibly flinched at them.

"I promise you, it's not what you're thinking. She just needs someone—a friend."

"*I'm* her friend! Or . . . I was." Venom laced her words. Venom not only at him, but Bree as well.

Why was she suddenly acting like this? Had their friendship for the past ten years meant nothing to Bree all this time? Did Kora's vow with Blake mean nothing? Even if she'd been ready to give him up, she still planned to reconcile after the war, when they knew they had a true chance.

"I couldn't let an *heiress* stagger back to her chambers drunk." Blake's gaze sharpened, and she huffed in disbelief at his response. "She was vulnerable, those sailors would've made advancements. If not for her bed, then her riches."

She scowled. He *did* have a point, and Otto's stern face flashed in her mind. Him and Rashi would rain thunder down upon her crew if anything had happened to their precious eldest daughter.

"What about me?" she breathed, fisting her hands at her sides. "I was vulnerable on that deck."

He frowned. "We both know you can take care of yourself when it comes to—"

"That's not what I mean."

He stilled, raising his hand before letting it fall limp to his side, as if he'd changed his mind about touching her. Blake's fingers wrapped against the edge of the desk, his elbow knocking against the polished wax seals, and they wobbled on their heavy metal bases.

"I was giving you a choice," she spoke through clenched teeth. "I was doing the *honourable* thing and letting you go. We both know I've been holding you back. Just for Bree to ruin it."

The *lack of commitment* remark had stung so deep, it still reverberated in Kora's mind.

Blake winced and exhaled. "You were pushing me away, not letting me go. I'm sorry I broke my promise. With this war, I can't be in service to you anymore. And Bree doesn't know anything, I *can* promise that."

In service? Was that what they were, then? A business transaction?

"Excuse me?"

"No," he raised his hands. "Let me finish. I'm trying to tell you, that I could have left at any time, but I *didn't*. I followed you everywhere. I went along with every crazy scheme, every impulsive voyage. Even when it seemed insane, you somehow always knew where pirates would be. But I can't anymore. As you said, everything is changing."

"Changing so much you'd rather chase after a noble?" She laughed bitterly.

"Why are you fixating on her?" He threw his hands up. "You are my everything! I need to ensure we win this war, so we can be together! But I can't do that whilst in your crew. And Bree is just a cover up. I'm not cheating on you. I'm just using her to divert attention from us!"

His eyes flared as the truth spilled from his lips. For a moment, she felt sorry for Bree, but it quickly surpassed as heat bubbled, erupting into a small ember in her chest. And not the fun kind.

"We are *already* together! At least, I thought we were. Apparently, you never thought the same. I have always been *right here*. But you never saw me, not really."

He'd believed it was a service, their vow some kind of agreement, a means to an end. And parading with Bree was the final insult, both to Kora, and female-kind. Just because they were a façade, didn't mean he had to pretend to *be* with someone else . . . especially her *best friend*. There were plenty of single officers.

And to make it worse, Bree had fallen for it. So much so, she resented Kora. Their friendship broken. Kora had allowed a male—her blind devotion to a male—tear them apart.

His mouth gaped. "What are you saying?"

She side-stepped around Blake, opening her door. "When it comes down to it, it'll never be *me* that you help, only yourself. Because this," she gestured between them, "is never going to be real."

"Wait—"

She slammed the door in his face.

S omewhere on the way to the war council, Kora had gotten
lost.

In her stubborn fury, she hadn't asked Blake where
the meeting was held, or how to get there. And she was sure
as Umbra not returning to ask him. They needed some space, and
she needed some time to think.

The Citadel was a never-ending labyrinth, with hallways
leading to dead ends, and spiral staircases hidden in shadowy
corners that somehow took her back to where she started. Not one
servant had crossed her path, and there was no sign of any courtiers
from the feast.

Life had simply vanished. *Creepy.*

Ready to abandon all hope, her skin flushed with sweat from
running around, she spotted a large gold-paned glass door, hidden
behind heavy-set green drapes. With a sigh of relief, she hurried
through it, embracing rays of sun on her face, and fresh air
compared to the musty smell of stone and moss.

Blinking against the sun, she realised she was still in the
grounds of Mossfell Castle. Sprawling gardens laid before her,
interspersed with willow and wisteria trees, and statues cut from the
finest marble. Her feet moved before she could think, and she
followed the light-stoned path winding throughout, her eyes darting
back and forth, absorbing the lush scenery.

It was as if the gardens were breathing. They felt so . . . *alive.*

Endless flowers in all colours imaginable, and citrus trees
adorned with fruit so large it was impossible. Not only that, but
vegetation from all walks of the islands lined the pathway. Plants
and foliage she knew were native to Otrovia and Aldara, and yet,
here they were. A piece of every territory had been snipped and

planted here, a showcase of greenery growing under the Talmon Empire's domain.

She paused before one of the marble statues towering above her on a square platform, encased in neatly trimmed shrubbery. A single sheet of fabric draped the female's body, covering her most modest areas. Her long hair billowed, reaching the curve of her behind as one hand covered the left side of her face, poised to hide a secret. The other arm stretched out, signalling to the skies.

The longer Kora stared, the more she realised it wasn't fabric covering the female's lithe body—but a river of water, winding all the way up to her fingers. Kora quickly scanned the remaining statues dotted throughout the gardens.

Oh. My. Gods.

She stumbled back from Calypso, Goddess of Sea, pivoting to sprint to the nearest statue on the right, which was settled in its own squared-off viewing area overflowing with flowers and miniature bay trees. A dual-faced, muscled, male statue, standing on boulders stacked on top of each other, with vines of leaves wrapped around his body. His hands were cupped together, fresh yellow roses resting within them.

Kaiah, God of Earth. Also, Kaiah, *Goddess* of Earth, depending on who told the tales. Here, they clearly believed Kaiah was male. But nature was fickle like that. The deity of the earth had never been recorded as a set gender, because nature created all life, and therefore, was *all*. Some texts had even depicted them as a fawn, or a wildebeest.

Kora whirled again, her heart quickening as she navigated the stoned pathway to the next statue. Her breath was as hot as the sun beaming above, and the muscles in her legs strained. She still felt woozy from the feast, and hoped she wouldn't vomit again all over this beautiful garden.

Gods, what had been in that wine?

Stones flicked beneath her boots as she skidded to a halt, surveying a sun-baked, scorched statue. The marble was crusted in an odd, red-and-black-toned powder.

Igniso—God of Eternal Flame. Depicted kneeling, his head was thrown back in anguish as flames engulfed him. Tiny black rocks scattered around his bulky form, and his fingers were painted red and black as they curled around the flames. The grass had faded to wheat yellow, cracking beneath her boots from dehydration.

She ran to the next statue.

Thanos, God of Death. She recognised it immediately. Her

favoured god to complain to. A figure covered in a cloak, his face unrecognisable, hidden in the darkness of his hood. A simple, grey cloth covered his clasped hands, symbolising the veil between realms. A deep crack lined the middle, stretching from head to toe, as if someone had taken an axe to it. His square was barren, surrounded by plain stone. Even the nearest tree had withered, its roots curling, breaking the surface of the earth.

With a frown, she hurried along to the next one, nearing the end of the gardens, where she paused. This statue had been decimated. A pile of rubble, and old marble stone covered in dark soot, had been left to rot in the sun. She inspected the larger pieces, seeking a pattern of clouds, and her suspicions confirmed.

Haizea, Goddess of Wind.

A snapshot in time. Kora turned, surveying the greenery. The windowless walls of the castle surrounded her, enclosing the gardens from prying eyes. What were the empire doing with statues of Devani gods? And why were they *here*?

Footsteps approached, and she instinctively ducked behind the hedge lining the small, plain square Haizea's crumbled statue resided in. A figure breezed past, her flowing green-and-white robes floating behind her. Her long, gossamer-brown hair tumbled down her back in waves.

Kora silently followed, using the foliage and weeping willows as cover as the female drifted towards one of the statues. Peering around the thick trunk of the tree, Kora squinted, consuming hard-to-see details of the mystery female. Leaves tangled with her hair, and when she breathed in, her senses were overwhelmed with the scent of roses . . . and something bitter underneath.

A small black awning jutted from the stone wall, shielding an unfamiliar statue from the light. It was made of black marble, not white, and Kora could barely make out the statue's features, other than it stared down at the ground with eyes closed, hands turned out ready to accept an offering.

Giant shrubs and ferns enclosed the space, and the female knelt before the statue. She tossed her shimmering hair over her shoulder, exposing milky-white, smooth skin, and round, green eyes surrounded by thick dark lashes.

Her face was so stunning that Kora nearly stumbled from the tree. The female's looks rivalled Bree's—and that was an accomplishment in itself.

The stranger began murmuring quietly, whispering to the unknown statue, and rocking back and forth on her knees. Kora strained to capture her words, her mind full of shock to witness a member of Barron's court praying to one of the gods, even if she wasn't sure which *one*. There'd only ever been five. Maybe one had faded from the records along with the Devanian scholars?

She leaned forward, eager to hear the words flying from the female's red-painted lips as she arranged multiple black bowls in a crescent circle. She raised her arms, extending her palms as she tossed her head back. A wide smile spread across her lips, as one hand whipped to her own throat, clasping before trailing down to her breast.

She fondled herself, breathily moaning as she began untying her robes, spreading her knees apart. *What in the . . .* Kora needed to leave. Prayer to the gods was deeply personal. Yet she couldn't tear her gaze away.

The female flicked her robes open, exposing her supple body to the statue, and she resumed chanting, her voice a near-whisper. Kora shuffled forward—

Crack.

The female's head whipped around, and Kora dropped to the twig-laden ground. *Shit!*

"Who's there?" Her voice was not beautiful. It was deadly, like an asp. A voice that commanded a room, that made soldiers quiver, that sent enemies fleeing.

It was how Kora imagined the gods would sound.

Her blood ran cold, and she crawled, keenly aware that, if she were caught, it wouldn't end well.

Gods damn her curiosity.

To her relief, a set of glass doors were nearby Haizea's ruins, and Kora used the shadows of the trees, keeping to a low crouch, half-running, half-tripping, her stomach churning. Her heart hammered until she threw herself into the cool clutches of the castle's shadows.

The tension of the war council meeting hung heavy in the air. Kora arrived late, and her cheeks still burned from the number of eyes that had turned to her when she'd stumbled into the grand chamber. Many of those eyes had lingered on her scar, whispers rolling across the crowd.

She hadn't expected an audience. Apparently, Barron didn't do anything small.

The chamber was like an amphitheatre, with rows of circular stone seating jutting from stone walls. Moss had been sprinkled to create cushioned seating, and she wriggled awkwardly on it, feeling as though all the moisture had been drained from the atmosphere. Her leathers felt tight and constricting, and she licked her dry lips, wishing for a gust of ocean air or spray of water.

Even a trickle of rain would do.

At the bottom, in the centre of the great room, was one very large, *golden* diamond-shaped table. Barron sat at the head, flanked by the familiar brown and grey wave of Erick's hair, and Theron's gleaming dark head on either side. Sat with them, were the remaining seven viceroys, including Otto. His dreaded locks were swept to the top of his head, and he'd exchanged his shimmering, ballroom attire for a simple black suit.

Sunlight poured in from a gaping hole in the ceiling—no windows, just one, huge, perfectly round hole to the skies. Kora squinted. A whirling pattern had been carved into the rim of the hole, but she couldn't make it out.

Unfortunately, arriving late meant she was left with the empty seats right at the back of the chamber, so high up, and too far away from everything. She could do with Samuel's spyglass right now. She scanned the crowd, seeking a familiar head of blonde hair or longbow. Nothing.

But her gaze located Blake instantly. Like a gods-damned moth drawn to a flame. He was sat at the front and bottom, to Barron's right on the first row, and his entire demeanour was different. Gone was the drawling first mate, and instead he was as stiff as a gangplank, his eyes trained on the back of Barron's head.

And next to him . . . was Bree.

He's got to be fucking joking.

Kora looked away. She didn't want to know if she'd imagined Bree placing her hand on Blake's knee. The ember erupted in her chest, and she sucked in moss-tainted breaths to tame her anger— her *pain*.

Why was she putting their friendship before her feelings? Clearly Bree wasn't. And why was Blake sitting *there*? He had no business sitting on the first row of the council meeting. It was reserved for the closest advisors of the viceroys and their immediate family. Like Bree.

Unless he had sat there . . . *for* Bree.

Blake's words earlier had nearly ripped Kora's heart. She was sure whatever they had was now over.

There was no water beast to soothe her, and a hollow emptiness had carved out her essence. The longer it was absent, the more a rage simmered, alighting her skin. A rage at Finlay for lying to her, at Erick for withholding secrets from her. A rage for Blake tossing her aside and seeking out Bree's affections.

Her hands shook. Despite the fire raging within her, the skin of her chest felt unnaturally cold. She missed the talisman. In her blind devotion to securing Blake's employment, she'd disregarded the very thing strengthening her. Changing her. Evolving her.

Had she really wanted to hand it over to the Silver Sisters? Kora fidgeted on the moss dampening her leathers. Agatha never confirmed the talisman would truly suck her dry, turning her into a husk. If anything, it felt like it had stabilised her power, making it easier to channel.

But it didn't matter now. It was gone.

"*I'm here.*" A small, warm breeze tickled down the length of her neck and she breathed it in. It smelled and tasted of steel and something familiar. *He* smelled familiar.

But she had something new to focus on, to funnel all her rage and misery into. Her talisman was missing, along with her infinite sea of strength. And someone in this room was the thief.

And the Citadel had statues of Devani gods.

It was time to wipe the slate clean and start again.

What good was planning everything anyway? It'd only granted her disappointment and misery.

"Galen have announced their attack," Barron's voice was a clap of lightning, bolting across the amphitheatre, and she jolted from her seat, her back smacking against the stone wall. "They seek to scare us, but they have only fuelled our fire."

A murmur weaved through the crowd, but Barron waved his hand and it instantly ceased. She leaned forward. The male had power, and Kora could feel it rippling from him from where she sat.

It was how she imagined freezing to death felt like.

"I have invited you all here," Barron gestured to the grand room, "to show you that we will stand with our people, and we *will* protect you from those who threaten us. My subjects, you are all *so* important to me. Each and every one of you." Barron's gaze landed directly on her and she stopped breathing.

Indeed, she was confused as to why the majority of the citizens of the Citadel were at a *war* council meeting. She'd been expecting just Barron, his advisors, and her crew to be present. His eyes hovered on her for a moment, and he smiled before directing his attention to those at the table—the *important* people.

"What do you propose we do?" a weedy-looking viceroy asked.

Wharton Bellmoor then, judging by the beansprout frame and white hair. And sat beside him, was Jacinth Blackstone. Drowning in black lace, a mourning veil obscuring her face, her black-gloved hands were placed on the golden table, twiddling a quill as she took notes. Kora shrank into her seat.

Most of the viceroys were also members of the noble houses, with a couple of independent wealthy males placed among them. Except for Jacinth. She had advanced as a viceroy over her husband, not for compassion in aiding citizens, but for her cold cunning in politics.

And they all looked to Barron for direction. Kora shivered. Why was he leading the meeting? Viceroys were meant to be equal rulers.

"We will meet them head on," Barron declared. "We will take the war to them, away from our lands."

"But how?" a gruff voice asked—an Ironwharf. His name evaded Kora. There were only so many uppity nobles' names she could remember. "We don't know what their defences are, or their numbers. We can only battle them on water, which means we are limited to our armada."

The murmurs returned, voices panicking and worrying.

"My people," Barron's cracking voice silenced them. "Do not fear. Our—my armada is *strong*. I have no concerns about the capabilities of the fleets. But we are also prepared. I knew this day would come, and I possess a weapon. A weapon that has never been seen before, and we will use it to crush the parasites that plague our lands."

An applause echoed across the room, and dizziness swarmed her. A sickening twist of her guts. What kind of weapon could battle an entire armada *and* pirates? Were the Skytors aware of such a weapon? For the first time, Kora worried about the enemy. They wouldn't stand a chance.

"What's the weapon?" A viceroy leaned forward.

"I must keep it secret," Barron replied. "As much as I adore you all, my subjects, I cannot risk your safety if our advantages are revealed."

She surveyed the room. Did he suspect a rat? She knew the feeling all too well.

"We've had reports of pirates and rebels attacking our outposts. Witches in Shannara are leaving their territory and breaking the accord. Marshans are defying their noble leaders—the House of Draiglo in Otrovia."

The viceroys squirmed in their gilded seats, and Kora sat back, exhaling a shaky breath. It was more than Galen—it was *everyone* they were up against. The Marshans of Otrovia were considered outsiders in the islands. Normally, the Draiglo family weren't included in the suite of royal nobles, after a private disagreement between them and the Hydraforts years ago resulted in them being exiled from society. It was them versus the world.

A prickling sensation ran down Kora's neck. Something wasn't right.

"And when we defeat the scum, we'll finally claim Galen under the flag of the Talmon Empire."

Cheers and clapping roared, spectators beaming at their saviour for the islands. At the possibility of eliminating their decades-long enemy, Galen. Had none of them realised what Barron implied?

He was planning on killing them all. She knew it in her essence-empty guts. In place of her power, intuition screamed at her that something was very, very wrong.

Theron suddenly stood. "Under the Staghart flag, Admiral."

The tension grew so thick Kora could barely swallow, and the viceroys murmured amongst themselves as Barron and Theron stared each other down. Theron's usual dark shadow didn't linger. Maybe Ivar was sat in the upper levels?

"Sentinel," Barron's voice purred, dragging out every syllable. "You must understand, these are *my* lands."

"You are mistaken," Theron snapped back, his armour shining beneath the sunlight filtering through the hole in the arched ceiling. "You are an extension of the *Staghart* Empire. The Talmon Empire—the viceroys—are a hand on the body of the emperor. This final unification will elevate you to a recognised Staghart province."

Barron threw back his head and laughed. "Do you take me for a fool? I made this empire what it is today. The viceroys are the foundation of everything here. Without us, it'll all fall apart. Without us, pirates would have run these lands into the ground, impoverishing them. Without us, there are no Azarian Islands."

"As sentinel, it is my duty to remind you—"

"Enough!" Barron's voice made Theron *flinch*. Kora startled forwards. *Where was Ivar?* "I brought you here for a reason, Sentinel." Barron clicked his fingers, and a pair of doors in the far corner of the chamber opened. "Or should I say . . . Prince Eli Staghart."

What. The. Fuck.

Theron stumbled backwards in shock as the crowd gasped, and he shot a look towards Erick, who blanched. Barron's shark-like smile surfaced as a set of four soldiers marched through the doors. Kora rushed forward, her body moving without thought. The steps were three strides wide, and her short stature made it difficult to race down to Theron.

Where in the gods was Ivar?

"Barron! What are you doing?" Erick shot to his feet, his face stricken, sending his chair flying back.

The four soldiers advanced, covered head to toe in black armour, with malachite slithering throughout it like cracks. They were the size of Samuel and Theron put together, and an acrid, sour stench filled the room.

"Theron!" she warned, and he spun, unsheathing his axes as the soldiers advanced. Even their faces were covered with green-and-black helmets. A small eye slit was the only indication there was a living being hidden beneath the armour.

"Take the traitor away," Barron drawled in a bored tone.

"No!" Kora flew down the stairs, her mind frantic as Theron

wrestled against the guards. The closer she got, the more the cold permeated her skin, into her bones. Her head throbbed relentlessly. She *had* to do something.

"The king will take this as an act of war!" Theron yelled as they dragged him across the stone floor.

Barron spun to face Theron. "Good. I've been waiting to make my move on your father for a long, long time. Your defiance against our rule marks you as a traitorous spy for our oppressors—the Stagharts. You have ruled over us for far too long. Now, it's our time."

Kora landed into the ring with a grunt, and several courtiers cried out as she revealed her daggers. They scrambled back, fleeing into the ground floor tunnels connected to the council chamber. Screams and shouts echoed as the viceroys and their families remained on the front rows of seating.

Erick's face melted into horror as she advanced across the floor, a blanket of red hazing her mind. Bree squeaked across the ring and leaned closer into Blake, wrapping her golden hands around his bicep. His face was blank—not an ounce of emotion as his eyes bore straight into Kora.

She snapped.

"Kora, don't!" Erick's voice sounded so distant she barely heard it.

One of the guards released Theron, the remaining three wrestling to force him through the set of doors leading to complete, cold darkness. His hatchet axes swung, his face twisted with rage, eyes flaring as he fought for his life. The guard approached her, and her eyes watered from the odour—or was it just her rage? The ember in her chest ignited as she faced the mysterious guard.

"Stand down!" Erick's voice didn't register.

All she knew was rage. Disgust. Pain.

"*Stop!*" the voice begged her. She shut that out, too.

"Captain!" a familiar voice rumbled. Probably just a stranger.

Her world visibly crumbled, and she threw all her rage into attacking the guard blocking her path to Theron, the *prince* of the royal family, who was being dragged to the dungeons by his legs. It was outrageous.

Her dagger shattered as soon as it connected with the guard's black chest plate and Kora careened in shock, splintered pieces of silver clattering to the ground, leaving the malachite hilt clasped in her hand.

"What . . ."

A vice-like grip closed around her neck and Kora spluttered, her body lifting from the stone floor as the guard held her with one, impossibly strong arm. His thick grip tightened and she choked, images of Callan flashing across her eyes, merging with the faceless guard.

The sound of the doors closing behind Theron's screams clashed through her skull.

"Barron, let her go!" Erick beseeched.

Kora flailed within the guard's grip, her vision tunnelling, her hands scratching violently at the armour until her fingernails bled. Erick charged, his hand poised on his golden sword, his face a mask of such pure terror that she wept, drowning in her tears.

"Belay, soldier," Barron commanded.

Air flooded her lungs as she collapsed on the ground, Erick's arms sweeping to cradle her as she muffled her cries into his chest. She was never more grateful for his cape than in that instant, as he shielded her from the scarily silent crowd of noble spectators who were brave enough to remain.

Blake remained impassive. A walking phantom, and she frowned as Bree shook her head, shuffling so close to him she was practically in his lap, disgust dripping from her judgemental stare.

"Let that be a lesson to those who are not loyal to the *Talmon Empire*," Barron bellowed. "The time is now for us to defeat *all* of our enemies. It's time for a new world."

She shivered in Erick's arms as he rubbed her back. Her shattered dagger laid at her feet, and Barron approached, pausing before them. His boots prodded the jagged pieces of silvered steel.

"I hope your protegee understands what's at stake here, Cadell." Kora looked up at Barron, his eyes tracking the tears on her cheeks, and the corner of his mouth quirked. "She may be the turning tide in this war."

"They're gone."

Kora peered around Erick's cape. The indoor amphitheatre had emptied out of its viceroys and noble spectators, leaving them huddled on the stone floor. She'd been too ashamed—too terrified to move. Images of Callan still burned the back of her eyelids.

That, and the shock that Theron was a prince. She had been

escorting a *prince* across the desert. She'd been joking around and drinking with a prince.

A prince Erick knew.

She tore from his comforting, warm embrace.

"Kora," he sighed as he stood beside her. "What's going on? Talk to me."

She chewed the inside of her cheek, flesh turning sore as she collected the pieces of her dagger.

"We can get you a new one."

"I want this one." Her back felt strangely unbalanced with one dagger sheathed. A part of her was missing, an extension of herself had vanished, leaving her disorientated. Along with the talisman, the two had become a parallel force, keeping her upright. Power blooming from her front, and steel protecting her back. "Did you know?"

Her throat burned, and she was sure she'd sport a fresh bruise around her neck soon—a reminder Barron was all too happy to bestow on her. That *he* was king in these lands. She needed to stop landing at the mercy of males wrapped around her throat.

Erick stilled. "Know what?"

"About Theron—Eli."

He shook his head silently.

"What about Barron?"

"No. I'm surprised as much as you are. I knew he recently became a viceroy, but I didn't realise . . . the extent."

"Surprised?" She turned to face him, clutching the pieces of her broken dagger in her hands. Her blood dripped on the floor.

"Yes, surprised. I'm not privy to a viceroy's plans, Kora. Barron may be . . . an old friend, but he's still my leader. Are *you* not surprised?" Erick frowned at her hands.

"No," she trembled. "I am fucking *furious*."

"Kora," he inhaled sharply, reaching for her hands. "We have to—"

"*We* don't have to do anything. I'm so sick of this—of everything! The lies . . . the . . ." She couldn't talk about *that* with him just yet. That he had a friendship with the sentinel he'd ordered them to escort, and they both had connections to their supposed enemies.

"We came here to fight a war against bloodthirsty Galenites. But *now*, we're fighting a war against *everyone*." Witches. Skytors. Pirates. Marshans. "Lead by an egotistical male. If *we* are against *everyone*—then are we truly fighting for justice? For freedom for our empire?" Erick flinched. "And if we try to push back, it's clear he's ready to kill anyone who gets in his way." Kora threw her hands up, and the shards of her dagger rained around them. Erick winced as one caught his shoulder, but she didn't even blink, her chest heaving with fury.

"He's asking too much of us. This will kill us."

"Kora . . . if we don't do this, we may lose everything. Our home . . . our *family*," his voice cracked on the last word. "This is what war is about. Making the hard decisions. When you become admiral, you will have to do the same."

She scoffed at the word *family*, and his brown eyes saddened. For a moment they stood in the large, suffocating silence of the council chamber. Every second that passed, the more her fiery rage withered. Doubt filled her mind, and the only thing she knew in this moment was that this war was *wrong*.

She didn't want to be admiral if it meant sentencing everyone else to the Locker.

"I don't know who to trust anymore," she admitted.

"You can trust—" Erick stopped short, his stare narrowing behind her, and she turned to face a tall, dark figure approaching from a tunnel connected to the ground floor. Erick stepped closer as Blake emerged from the shadows, his face taut.

"Kora." His voice was distant, cold.

"Blake."

His eyes flickered to her bleeding hands, but the blank expression remained. "I need to talk to you. Outside."

"Marwood, not now. We're in the middle of something." Erick placed a hand on her arm.

She glanced between the two males, as they stared each other down. Forest green against the brown of tree bark during a sunset.

"I'm going with him." She peeled away from Erick, and something close to pain and worry flashed across his face.

Blake's mouth twitched as he gestured to the tunnelled darkness. Between Erick and Blake, Kora knew she'd rather face the despair of her broken relationship with Blake than face the lies and secrets between her and Erick.

Because if she ever lost Erick—her only family—or discovered he'd lied to her all this time, she wasn't sure if she would ever recover.

She had already lost one father. She couldn't lose another.

50

They strolled in silence all the way to the Emerald Forest surrounding the Citadel. As if some fresh air would somehow rectify everything between them. Kora had heard legends of the forest's mysterious nature. People would go missing here, and when their friends and families searched for them, they'd hear their screams echo from the trees instead.

As they walked, breathing in this supposedly required *fresh air*, the forest expanded, thickening from a mix of light greenery into dark pine trees and weeping willows. Shadows between trees darkened, and the bark became twisted, roots breaking through the ground like hands reaching for saviours.

She shuddered, carefully navigating the claw-shaped roots.

"Natives buried the dead here," Blake broke the silence. "This stretch of forest was barren land the Devanians used as a burial ground. After some time, trees grew from the buried bodies . . . creating life."

Kora peered at him curiously. He never cared for tales from the Devanian era, yet here he was, speaking so casually, as if he knew all about it.

"I can't tell if that's beautiful, or horrific," she murmured.

Keeping her bandaged hands clasped at her front, she jumped over a log, following his charging presence through the winding forest. Her palms stung from the shards of her dagger, and she wished they were out at sea, surrounded by the only environment she thrived in. If her magic still worked, she could heal herself with water. But they were so far from the ocean now, she couldn't hear the waves, or see the glistening, blue horizon.

"Sometimes, the most beautiful things are also the deadliest. Despite this land once being barren, used as a dumping ground for death, it took what it'd been given, and turned it into something . . . *more.*"

Her mind flickered to the Galen moonstone chest, full of beautiful yet deadly weapons. Those recovered chests were locked deep in Stormkeep Fortress' vaults. Never to be seen again.

Blake stopped by a tree. Its branches hung down, cascading around them like a clawed, green hand. He gently brushed a leaf, rubbing it between his thumb and forefinger. The tree groaned and she jerked beside him.

"It's just the wind." He almost chuckled.

"Are you sure it's not the dead?" She knew the sound of the wind, and that wasn't it.

Their eyes met. His smile dropped. "Do you think we can do the same?"

"Groan like trees? I don't have the lung capacity." She hoped the joke would ease the trepidation cresting within her, but looming shadows writhed in the corner of her eye and her pulse raced.

"We've been dealt a shitty hand, just like this land." He took a step forward and she retreated one. "Can we . . . can we salvage this? Turn it into something more, something great?"

She swallowed. Hard. "You tell me."

"You know what I want." His gaze darkened as her back brushed against the nearest tree.

A small clearing laid before them, circular with mounds of thick grass and scattered, moss-covered rocks. Thick, dark trees rimmed the edge, their roots clawing across the ground to the centre, where the smallest beam of sunlight pierced the canopy.

"Do I?" She arched into the tree as Blake halted, his body so close she could feel the tensity vibrating from him. "Apologies if I'm confused, but you're the one giving mixed signals. You were sat with Bree at the council meeting."

His jaw twitched and his fists clenched. *Not a good sign.*

"I couldn't find you, and she requested me to sit with her. I couldn't deny it in front of the admiral."

"You cannot deny her quite a lot, it seems."

He leaned forward, until his hot breath blew in her face. "I cannot deny *you.* I cannot live without *you.* I've told you many times, you are my *everything.* You are my reason for existing, my reason for *life.* Just like this forest, I would be barren and dead without you."

Oh, shit.

"I know I've made some bad decisions," his fingers brushed

the column of her throat, his stare narrowing on the bruised flesh. "I know I've made mistakes," his hands swept to clasp her shoulders. "I've broken promises," he placed a kiss on her neck, and her body unforgivingly shivered. "I've not listened to you," his kisses trailed up her neck, and across her jaw.

She trembled with resistance, her willpower slowly evaporating. If this male continued, she wasn't sure what she would do. Her heart felt broken, and her mind was a pool of chaos, but her body . . . gods, her body was ready to be a traitor and surrender to his touch.

"I've waited for you for too long. I need you before I lose you," he whispered against her ear before capturing her lips in a harsh kiss, and he instantly parted her mouth with his tongue, exploring her with urgency.

"Tell me we're real," he moaned. "Tell me this isn't over."

He cupped her face, pulling her towards his tall frame as he fisted her hair, tugging her head back to angle her mouth better. Well . . . she couldn't answer with his tongue in her mouth. But she didn't pull away. Her heart cried for him, for his touch, for his warmth.

"Kora . . ."

Hearing her name on his lips sent an untenable shudder through her. It somehow felt *more* intimate. He repeated her name like a prayer, his touches growing desperate with urgency as his hands explored down the lengths of her body.

"I need to know, my Kora," he whispered against her ear before nibbling at her lobe. "Are we real? Does this feel real?"

More kisses followed and she gasped, her body trembling with deep buried desire that'd been suppressed for so long. Months—*years*—of always being *just* out of reach to each other, at the precipice of *falling* for each other, but never quite taking the leap of faith.

"We never said those words," Blake's mouth parroted her thoughts and she quivered beneath his tightening grip on her waist, her hips—gods, it felt like his hands were *everywhere*. Leaving a trailing sensation of wicked hot flames.

"I—"

He cut her off, and she startled as she was sucked into him. The scent of petrichor mixed with the earthy forest made her dizzy, and her footing stumbled. She grabbed onto Blake's chest, making him groan.

"Blake, I—"

"It's okay, *asterya*. I'm sorry for how I've acted. It's all been . . . a lot."

For a moment—just a moment—she was back on *Hell's Serpent*, kissing her first mate, the sea breeze encasing them as they passionately embraced on the deck. The promise of forbidden love driving their desire towards each other. A simmer bloomed in the pit of her stomach.

Blake's moans cut through her sizzling heat. She wasn't on her ship, and this male was no longer her first mate. He was a stranger. Who Bree was clearly infatuated with. And Barron had just declared war. On everyone.

Kora pushed him back until he leaned against a branch. He lazily smiled as he attempted tugging her with him, but she fumbled out of his grasp, whipping her hand up to create a barrier. His face dropped, the glisten in his green eyes fading.

"We need to talk."

He groaned, running a hand through his hair. "That's never good. How about, less talking, and more kissing?" He reached for her, but she slapped his hand away.

"Stop distracting me with all . . . *this*." She gestured to his body.

"You just gestured to all of me." He cocked his head, his lips curling.

"You said you've not listened to me, I'm asking you to listen to me now." Her heart squeezed as he straightened. She wasn't sure where they stood, and what she said next may disrupt this new dynamic. "We need to stop Barron," she declared.

"What do you mean?"

"I'm going to appeal the war. We can't—*he* can't declare war on *everyone*."

"He's not?" Blake absentmindedly brushed the length of the branch with his hand. "He's being proactive. Taking the war to our enemies."

"And who are our enemies?"

"Galen, of course," he shrugged, and relief flooded through her. Perhaps she'd been wrong. Maybe it was only Galen that Barron considered a threat and—

"And Prince Eli," Blake said it so formally that Kora had to really look at him to make sure the words were coming from his mouth. "He's our enemy, too, and we need to protect ourselves from all threats."

It was an echo of Barron's speech, and a blow to her rising

emotions—that he considered Theron his enemy. They'd been chummy together a matter of days ago.

"What . . . you . . ." she exhaled, steadying herself. "How can you think that?"

Blake nodded, his obsidian hair falling across his eyes. "He infiltrated our islands under false pretences. He wants to continue the tyranny of the Stagharts. He's one of *them*. He's a clear spy, his skills in the desert prove that."

She gaped. *What in the gods was happening?*

"Now is *our* time," he continued. "We need to show the admiral what we can do. If we win this war . . . we could get *everything* we want. No more forbidden relationships. No more hiding in cabins and forests."

She hesitantly stepped away from the branches. "You want the war," she whispered.

"And you don't?" He followed her, his face downright petrifying. Pale and sharp, and his eyes ablaze against the dark green backdrop of the forest. "You said so yourself, you want to eradicate *all* pirates from our lands. This is how to do it."

Not a shred of his familiar persona remained, and the scorching heat that'd burned between them frosted. His tone was so . . . cold. So detached, and she struggled to comprehend the stranger before her, her heart and mind at war with each other. *What the fuck was going on?*

"I don't want a war against Azaria—against all the islands. We *will* lose. We can't fight a continent that large, not with Galen at our backs."

"You're thinking too small," he waved a hand, dismissing her fear. She glared at him. "Barron has his weapon, and with it, we can *do* anything. *Be* anything."

Kora took a step back for every advancement Blake made, until the sharpness of a boulder in the clearing scraped her leg. The groans of the trees echoed around them, and she closed her eyes blocking out how they sounded like the moans of the dead.

"Do you even know what this weapon is?"

"No. But I have full faith in our leader to restore the lands."

She was going to be sick. "This isn't right. A war won't win *me*." She edged around the boulder. "Do you even hear yourself?"

"You're wrong," he snarled, and Kora startled at his venom, tripping against the flat edge of the boulder. Blake grabbed her arm, dragging her to him until their bodies collided, his arm snaking around her waist. "I've worked so hard to get us to this point, Kora.

And I will not let you jeopardise it."

"What's that supposed to mean?"

The ground rumbled beneath her, and his grip moved to her shoulders to steady her as trees creaked, their leaves falling, coating the clearing in a suffocating wave of nature.

"You're impulsive. You can't control your emotions, and you let them get in the way. Today was a prime example, attacking the guards to rescue a traitor. We are *so* close to the end now, and I want you there beside me."

"The end of *what?*" she snapped, pushing against his hands. His body was immovable, rooted to the spot as she resisted his grip. "You're not making any sense! This war will destroy us!"

"There you go, with the emotions again." He leaned in so close that she stilled. "Listen, my *asterya*," he placed a kiss on her neck. This time, she didn't shiver. Hot flames didn't lick her skin. She was repulsed. "You will do as I say moving forward," his tongue followed. "We will rule these islands, and the scum will weep at our feet as we destroy them. Together."

Revulsion roiled through Kora. She was *not* a mindless killer. She refused. She may have committed a heinous act in the desert, her soul marked by their deaths. But she wouldn't destroy her home. Apparently, Blake had no issue doing that.

Her mind won the war within. Despite those dregs of *feelings* clutching onto his image, this was not the same male. And she wouldn't lose the home she'd so carefully curated, over Barron's stupid war.

"Get fucked. I want nothing to do with this, or you."

Rage consumed his face, and regret filled her as the ground *shook*. The Emerald Forest *screamed*, and she plummeted to her knees, covering her ears as the cries of the dead roared, ravaging her hearing.

Grass writhed around her knees, clutching her leathers. The forest was *alive*.

"*Run*," the voice pierced through the cries and groans. "*Run now, get away from him!*"

"I can't!" Kora cried as her body seized.

She collapsed on her side, her skin tightening, and when she looked down at her hands . . . her body was *withering*. Her fingers rapidly decayed until they were just skin on bone, and her throat burned, her insides turning dry and hollow. The pain was immeasurable.

The groans increased, and tree roots shot up from the ground, breaking the surface in human-like clawed grips. She was turning into a corpse. The forest was claiming her.

"*You need to get out now!*" the voice was panicked. "*Use your magic, you're going to die!*"

"I can't!" she repeated, whimpering, her voice hoarse and cracked. Her lips sagged around her mouth, bloodied teeth falling onto the ground. "Help me!" she begged the voice.

"*I can't . . .*" the mirrored words were so painful to hear. "*I can't do anything!*" It was full of despair.

Blake crouched, his brow furrowing as he swept her thinning hair away from her face. "Who are you talking to?" he asked curiously, studying her calmly, with no shock or surprise that she was *desiccating.*

"Did you . . ." Kora coughed out the words, her mouth like sandpaper. "Bring me here . . . on . . ."

"Purpose?" Blake cocked his head like a predator. "Yes."

Death was so near. She could feel its cold, numb embrace waiting for her. She commenced her prayers to Thanos in her mind, readying herself to be spirited to Umbra. *Sweet, dark relief.*

"My *asterya.* I would have followed you to the ends of the earth. I would have made you my queen. If you won't do as I say . . . perhaps the forest can change your mind to stay with me. All you have to do, is ask."

She whispered her final word. "Bree."

Fuck you. He'd tricked her. Those apologies and kisses had been double edged, laced in beautiful, deadly lies. He'd distracted her, just as he always had. And Bree wouldn't be in love with him, proposing *marriage* to him, for no reason. He would have done something to make her think she had a chance.

He sighed. "You need to let this obsession with Bree go. She's nothing compared to you. You're special, Kora. As I said, I want *you* by my side—not her. She's just a diversion until we win the war. Then there will be no obstacles between us. Just ask me. Ask me to stay. Ask me to be your everything again."

As Kora's last kernel of life held on, her body so dry and tight, a shell of what she once was, she released a puff of a scream as her skin sagged, entering the stages of decomposing. She'd rather die than submit herself to another second with him.

The earth beneath her cracked open.

Blake sprinted back with a surprised yell as a wide tunnel of water shot up from the ground, cracking the boulder and enveloping Kora. She gulped it down as it cocooned her, soaking into her crusted, withered pores. The small kernel in her chest exploded into a river of power as her water beast returned in full force. In the process, something *snapped* within her mind, and silence wrapped around her skull.

She emerged from the shooting vat of water, to discover Blake with a toxic smile and a knowing glint in his eyes. Her body was invigorated, her life restored, as well as all her injuries healed. She was distantly aware of her hair floating, as if she were submerged in water. Her hands glowed blue as she raised them.

"This war isn't happening. You lied to me about Bree, I know you did."

"You also lied," he gestured to her glowing form. "Don't forget that, *asterya.*" He paused, observing her power. "You don't recognise me."

"Don't call me that," she snapped. "I don't know you anymore. You're a stranger to me now."

Shooting a line of sharp water, it sliced his shoulder and he fell, blood gushing from the wound. Her heart lurched and she hurried towards him, her hands hovering over his shoulder. He was going to bleed out. *No, no, no.* She couldn't have done this again. She couldn't have another life on her hands.

Without thinking, Kora summoned her power, washing it over the deep gash. His blood mixed with water, pouring into the muddied ground as Blake hissed with pain. He gazed up at her in wonder as she healed him, her hands convulsing. Mud caked their clothes, and she slipped on the wet ground as she knelt over him.

"I'm sorry," she whispered.

"Emotions," he replied softly. "Don't let them get the better of you. Please remember that."

He reached up, tucking her hair behind her ear before running his thumb across her lower lip. A cold prickle followed, but her arms felt too weak to push him away. The stench of petrichor and bitter soil made her head spin.

"You're the best thing that ever happened to me. Tell me, Kora, were we real?"

"You sound like you're saying goodbye. We can . . . we can be friends." *What was she saying?* "Maybe not . . . now you know I'm . . . a mage."

She'd just signed, sealed, and delivered her death sentence.

Blake's jaw clenched as his wound stitched itself together. A slice of pain ripped down her side and she tumbled, gasping. Her vision shuddered as she crumpled beside him, and he leaned over her, frowning. He touched her shoulder, and she cried out in agony as his hand came away dripping with blood.

Exhaustion crept in as the blue glow evaporated from her hands, and the vat of water shooting from the cracked earth reduced to a dribble. Cold mud slicked her palms, coating her hair, and Kora shivered beneath his warmth.

"The most interesting mage I've ever met," he murmured.

Blake's dark smile was the last thing she saw as her magic ceased to a tiny wisp.

51

The sound of metal clicking tore Kora from her dreamless sleep, and she pried her eyes open, blinking against the summer's day light shining through the bay window of her chambers. As her vision settled, her eyes focused on a familiar, dark figure, holding her hands.

"Blake . . ." Her mouth was as dry as the Silent Tundra, and she reached for a glass of water, but was met with resistance. "Blake . . . let go of me."

He wouldn't look up. He kept his green stare trained on her hands, an audible swallow from his throat.

Click.

She jolted as cold metal snapped around her wrists, securing them in place. Pain seared down her shoulder, and she gasped as he sat back, revealing a three-pronged key to the shackles binding her wrists.

"What . . . what are you doing?"

He silently stood, expression set in hard stone, his black leathers still caked in mud that was dusting the ends of his hair. His shoulder was fully healed, and he leaned over, tightening the cloth wrapped around her, making her cry out from sudden, blinding pain.

She glanced at her side and paled. Her shoulder was gushing blood, with gauze and several cloths tied around it already soaked through.

"Blake . . . I'm bleeding out, you need to—"

He silenced her with a kiss. It was fervent, and she was trapped between his lips and the wooden headboard. Unable to pull away, he gripped her chin forcefully, placing bruising kisses against her lips. This male was *obsessed.*

The forest flashed, spearing her mind like a destructive arrow.

He'd seen her power. She'd nearly killed him. Her throat closed, her guts twisting until she felt like her body was sinking into the bed. Deep into the belly of Umbra. Where she belonged.

He wanted the war. He supported killing innocents so the empire could maintain their illusion of control. So, he could win *her*, by superseding laws, and advancing in the war to possess power.

"Blake, no. Stop!" She wrenched her head to the side, tears pricking at the agony of turning her head. But it didn't hurt as much as her heart. *That* had imploded into a million pieces.

"I'm sorry. One day . . . forgive me." She frowned as he placed his lips against her forehead, his thumb stroking her bruised throat. "She's ready!" he called, stepping back, his power-hungry eyes glancing to the door.

Several guards marched into her room, followed by Barron and the Ironwharf viceroy. He was clean-shaven, with not a single strand of hair to be seen on his head, including his eyebrows. Deep lines covered his permanently scowling face, and he sported the famous Ironwharf blue-steel armour, with a large longsword attached to his back.

His eyes looked simultaneously tired and kind, and she averted her gaze, granting Barron her attention. He wore similar royal attire to when they'd first arrived at Mossfell Castle, but every item was black. His tar-like hair was scraped back, tied at the nape of his neck, and she shivered under the intensity of his stare.

"It's a shame this has to happen under these circumstances. I do love a female tied up." Barron flashed a smile and she blanched. What was about to happen? *What was going on?* Blake twitched beside her. The hunger in eyes had drained, resulting in a vacant stare.

"There has to be a misunderstanding," Kora spoke thickly. "If this is because of what happened earlier with Theron—"

"Do not speak that traitor's name." Barron flicked his wrist, then inspected a piece of lint on his sleeve. Kora looked desperately at Blake. He was her only chance of survival right now.

And it sickened her.

"Blake," she tried reaching for him, wincing through the pain, but he evaded her. "What's happening?"

"Don't pretend," Barron crooned, approaching the edge of the four-poster bed. His stormy gaze roved over her body, pausing at her ruined shoulder, before continuing. "You have committed a great injustice, Kora Cadell. You've spat in the face of my empire—

after everything we have done for you."

"If . . . if this is about the *forest* . . ." she trod carefully. Had Blake told them about her power? If he had, she wouldn't be shackled, she would be *dead*. Her shattered heart pounded so viciously, the individual pieces vibrating, her body thrumming with fear.

Barron paused, his eyes flicking from her to Blake, whose body visibly tensed under the weight of Barron's stare. It shocked her to see Blake *shrink* away from someone. His confidence and drawl had evaporated completely.

Silence continued. It was unbearable as Barron surveyed them, his beady dark eyes assessing every square inch of Blake, and then Kora. Her lips trembled, threatening to explode with secrets just to alleviate the palpable quiet.

"No, this is about something *else* you've done."

Barron clenched a hand around the pillar of the bed, his knuckles turning white. He radiated power, and it filled the room to the point she felt she were being crushed by his presence.

"I haven't done anything," she whispered. Her pulse fluttered, and she glanced back to Blake. Was it about them? Had they found out about their relationship? Her emptied heart twisted. Their vow was as broken as her dagger.

They were broken.

Barron chuckled, rubbing his stubbled chin. "Stop looking at *him*. Look at me."

She whipped her watering gaze back to the dark figure before her. Was that a hint of jealousy in his voice? The Ironwharf viceroy cleared his throat, the kindness in his eyes replaced with irritation.

"It's come to our attention that you are not . . . satisfied with your position," Barron dragged out the words, and she clenched her legs shut. "You have decided it fit to *steal* from the empire. To take unsanctioned plunders and reap the profits for yourself."

"I . . . what?" The blood loss was making her lightheaded.

Barron clicked his fingers, and a guard handed him two leather-bound books. The colour drained from her face and dread coiled in her gut.

No.

"We found these stashed in your chambers today during a routine search." Barron opened one of her ledgers, reciting the contents of *Hell's Serpent*'s plunders over the years—and every amendment of the treasure they'd acquired. To protect her crew, she'd only listed the profits going to herself.

She was a stupid, *stupid* girl.

"By my estimate, you have stolen *thousands*," Barron whistled. "That's quite a debt to owe."

"What . . . how . . ." She cleared the dryness in her throat, her mind racing. "When did this *routine search* happen?"

She'd given those ledgers to Erick when they'd returned to Stormkeep Fortress with Jack Flint. How had they ended up in Barron's hands? Erick wouldn't betray her . . . *would he*? Shit, where was he?

"That's none of your concern," Barron dismissed her, but he inclined his head to Blake.

Blake's jaw twitched. He glanced down at her. His darkened eyes flashed, his fists clenching.

And he bowed his head to Barron . . . in submission.

"*You!*" Kora bolted forward, rage dulling the tearing agony as she staggered to her feet, thrusting her shackled hands at Blake. She'd depleted her magic from healing him—what a *stupid* mistake. He deflected her attack, spinning her around and wrapping his arms around her chest, pinning him against her.

"Don't do anything rash," he whispered in her ear like a lover. "If you want to stay alive . . . and Erick, then you best behave."

She glared at him, tears brimming in her eyes. How dare he. How dare he threaten Erick. She couldn't believe she'd ever loved this fucking bilge scum.

"Where's Erick?" she seethed.

"Stop entertaining her," the Ironwharf viceroy huffed. "Let's get this over with."

"Where is Erick?" she screamed. "*Erick!*"

"Just a moment, Garvan." Barron approached her, flipping through her ledgers. "This is rather impressive . . . such a shame." Barron invaded her proximity, a twinkle glistened in his eyes as he stared down at her. That twinkle made her stomach lurch, as he stroked the edge of the ledger across her jaw, to her lips. Blake stiffened, his grasp tightening across her chest. "You were going to be very *valuable* to me in this war."

"Fuck your war," she spat at him. With Barron this close, her head felt like it was going to explode.

Barron released a long exhale, wiping her spit from his face. Then he licked his fingers. She shoved against Blake in disgust as Barron smiled. "Do you not want to save the world, Kora Cadell?"

"Not if it means killing innocents for power."

She was so blind. The empire was as bad as Galen. Countless, futile wars, and for what? These islands deserved the gods' abandonment.

"People have killed for less. I will build these islands in a new image. Where only the most deserving thrive."

"When it's you versus the world, it usually means *you're* the bad guy. You can't kill everyone who disagrees with you."

Barron merely laughed, and gestured to Garvan. Kora's stomach plummeted, a cold sweat breaking out and puckering her flesh as he produced a second set of shackles.

"Kora Cadell," Garvan began as she fought against Blake, screaming as he clamped a thick metal collar around her throat. "You are hereby stripped of your title as captain," the lock clicked and she kicked her legs out, her throat burning from screaming. "You will be sentenced to the dungeons of the Citadel. Without trial," a chain looped from her throat to her wrists, "as a prisoner of the Talmon Empire. You are charged with forgery, embezzlement, and thievery."

Garvan knelt, and the guards pinned her flailing legs down as he secured a third set of thick, cold shackles around her ankles. The metal snapped together, allowing no give between her limbs. She couldn't even walk. Tears poured down her face as she screamed for Erick—for *anyone* to hear her.

"You hereby acknowledge your status as a prisoner of the Talmon Empire, thus, you are now *owned* by the Talmon Empire. To recover the profits and loss to the state, you will work under the direction of the viceroys until your debt has been paid back. If you are unable to repay your debt, the viceroys will determine a just punishment . . ."

Garvan's voice faded out as he continued reading her rights—which were none. Her life was over. Her dream no longer existed. Kora turned utterly numb as they guided her from the room, dragging her across carpet runners, down twisting gilded hallways of the Citadel. Tapestries lined the walls, depicting the empire's ascension. The final one before they exited the guest wing illustrated Barron in all his glory. Surrounded by gold, his arms raised as citizens praised him.

She spat at it as they whipped round the corner. *Fuck him.*

She was no longer a captain. Her whole world, completely shattered into tiny, irreparable pieces. She'd been content putting Blake before her dreams, risking fleeing to Shannara for that pathetic trinket.

How wrong she was. This was inconceivable.

"*What do I do* . . ." she reached out into the void, seeking the only companion she could think of.

Empty nothingness slammed against her mind.

The connection was severed, she could feel it. There was *nothing* on the other side of the void. Not even a flicker of *him*. Something was wrong. Her mind had never felt so silent . . . so alone. Ten years of comforting guidance had been ripped away.

And somehow, that hurt even more. Her muscles weakened as defeat consumed her. She had royally fucked up.

They descended the marble staircase leading to the ballroom, and the guards lifted her, allowing her the small reprieve of not bashing down step after gilded step. How thoughtful.

"Kora!"

Erick rushed towards them, his sword drawn, green cape billowing behind him.

"Barron! Stop this! What are you *doing*?"

Kora sobbed at the sight of Erick squaring up to his oldest friend, his face taut with fury. His rich brown eyes *burned* with rage.

"She has committed a crime, Cadell," Barron spoke calmly, signalling the guards to continue carrying her.

Erick snarled at Barron. "Let my daughter go. *Now.*"

Barron stilled, his dark gaze sliding to Erick. "You forget, *Erick.* I gave you everything, and I can just as easily take it away."

Erick faltered, his face slackened as devastation consumed him. He glanced to her. "You wouldn't . . ."

"Try me," Barron challenged. "Marwood, take him away. He doesn't need to see this."

"Tell me what happened," Erick pleaded. "Kora, talk to me!"

She opened her mouth but only a hoarse rasp escaped after her screaming.

"She stole from me," Barron answered. "Now she will be punished."

Blake advanced towards Erick, forcing him back with surprising strength. Erick cried out, grasping for Kora, his fingers barely brushing her steel chains as Blake held him at bay. They continued their march towards the dungeons, and panic seeped into the edges of her numbness.

Garvan pushed open the gilded, large double doors to the ballroom, and she grimaced as they strode in, her body hanging between the silvered guards like a wet blanket.

"Why . . ." she rasped, ". . . here?"

"I like to make a show," Barron replied. "Show everyone

what happens if they dare to cross me. Fear is what keeps people in line. Fear is how you control others."

Indeed, multiple courtiers lined the walls, and servants still cleaning up from the feast the previous evening. Their fearful eyes tracked her across the floor, and whispers floated across the grand room, echoing off the marble floors and stone walls.

"It's *her*."

"The adulterer."

"She's a whore."

"She's a *killer*."

"The royal slut."

"Filthy *pirate*."

Kora closed her eyes against the painful words. She'd been branded many things in her life, but losing her title as captain hurt the most. Tears tracked down her face, splashing onto the marble floor.

After the ballroom, they paraded her chained body through various rooms—offices, the throne room—which was divine—grand living chambers, the solar room and, eventually, an attached barracks overlooking the cliff. Her gauzes and cloths were so soaked through they trailed down her arms.

She hoped the blood loss would make her pass out soon. She couldn't bear this any longer.

Multiple guards pivoted as they entered a large space—an indoor training ring. The ground was packed with dirt, and weapons lined the walls beneath large square windows. Dummies interspersed the room, along with wooden benches that guards and soldiers lounged upon, drinking from kegs.

A domed ceiling curved across the space, decorated with detailed paintings of the Galenite war. Pictures of death, destruction, and blood. The ground was littered with red splotches—blood, she realised.

"Men!" Garvan yelled.

Everyone stood to attention, their eyes ogling Kora's chained, bleeding body.

"We have a traitor to the empire with us today." Garvan gestured, and she whimpered at the sea of male gazes trained on her. Most were disgusted, some were *angry,* and some were lustful—hungry. Those gazes made fear spike up her spine and her pulse race. "Make her feel welcome."

They flaunted her down the centre of the training ring, and the soldiers leered, shouted, and spat. Sweat dripped from their lethally honed bodies, humidifying the air. Some even jabbed her sliced open shoulder and she howled in pain, her consciousness teetering on the edge, only to have blood-dried dirt thrown at her.

Throughout it all, she prayed to Thanos. The only god she'd welcome right now.

As they made it to the other end, shame and terror smothering her until she couldn't breathe, her body screaming with agony, a slender figure leapt out, stopping the parade.

"Mr Di Largo," Barron bemused.

Her heart lurched as she met golden-flecked hazel eyes. Aryn aimed his longbow, his hair tousled, and his muscles flexed as he nocked an arrow.

"I wouldn't do that if I were you," Barron smiled, signalling the soldiers surrounding them.

"No one harms my captain."

"She's not a captain anymore," Garvan huffed.

"She is to me."

Endless tears welled as Aryn cut Kora a hopeless look. All at once, he was young and old, his ancient voice soothed her, and a familiar scent of amber and cypress washed over her. He always appeared when she needed him, he always *knew* when she was in trouble. As if . . . as if he were . . .

Kora's eyes widened, her scar flaring as Barron ordered him to stand down. Was Aryn her mystery voice? Had it been him all along? How could she have been so blind?

"Aryn!"

Samuel shouldered through the crowd like the boulder he was. He halted at Kora, chained and shackled, and smothered in dirt, her shoulder gushing blood. His mouth settled into a grim line, and he placed one fisted hand in the other, subduing his rage. Her legs shook in terror for her crew. Samuel's grey eyes slid from Barron to Aryn.

"Aryn . . . stand down."

"You can't be serious!" Aryn shook his head.

"Aye, listen to me." Samuel approached Aryn. "Look around." His eyes flashed, and she understood—there was nothing they could do. No one could help her. Not while they were in the heart of the enemy.

Gods, the Talmon Empire was now her *enemy*.

"She has betrayed the empire," Garvan scowled. "Learn quick and fast, lad, if you want to advance in our ranks."

"She hasn't done anything . . ." Aryn whispered, his face

going into shock. Samuel stepped beside him, placing a giant hand on his shoulder. His tattoos rippled in the light. "I've failed . . ."

She sobbed as he lowered his longbow, his astute gaze drinking in the mass of soldiers surrounding them in the barracks. He flicked his gaze back to her and something passed between them—a silent promise. The tiniest kernel of hope bloomed in the torrenting darkness raging within her. A small slither of blue light, glittering in a sea of despair.

"Well, this is all very moving." Barron clapped his hands. "We have a dungeon to get to."

As they carried Kora out of the barracks, she kept her gaze trained on Aryn until the doors slammed shut behind them.

PART FOUR

GALEN RETURNS

K
ora peered through the bars of her cell, inhaling the scent of death and ocean spray. Built inside the cliff, beneath the Citadel, the vertical dungeon tunnel consisted of rings of iron-barred cells leading to a death drop to the ocean.

Thick, curling tree roots and rotting vines drooped from hardened soil at the top of the prison spiral, and at the bottom was a wide mouth leading to the ocean, with clusters of sharp, jagged rocks. Her cell was right at the top, amongst the rancid earth. Vines coiled along the ceiling, reaching to ensnare her, and she squirmed.

"No! No, please!" a shriek rang several rings below.

"Aye, get this wench overboard now!" Garvan's voice followed.

Kora couldn't see the commotion. An iron-railed walkway spiralled downwards, allowing guards to assume watch, and separating the cells from the death drop. Several cells to her right was a gated section in the railing, leading to a wooden plank. She'd spied the very same plank upon every ring, allowing guards easy access to chuck prisoners overboard.

"*Please*! I don't want to die!" the other prisoner's pleas echoed off the bars.

"Time to walk the plank, lassie."

A screech of metal, followed by screams, and the wooden shudder of the walk plank. Those screams continued, down, down, down—

Splat.

"What have they done to you?"

Kora silently regarded the familiar healer working on her shoulder. A clump of red-stained gauze flew onto the cell floor, littered with dirt, debris, and gods-knew-what from previous occupants.

"Do you believe in the empire, Koji?" her voice was barely a whisper.

His aged, deft hands halted sewing her wound and she winced. Even with heavily applied arnica, she could still feel the prick of the needle. It was nothing in comparison to the pain consuming her entire essence and soul.

"I told you once before," Koji murmured quietly near her ear, his golden eyes glinting in the torch light. "I'm not the empire."

"Right," she coughed from her feeble attempt to chuckle. "You follow the coins."

"Unfortunately so."

She raised a curious brow at him as she gripped one of the bars of her cell. They perched on a wooden bed, connected to the blackened wall by rusted chains. Decomposing hay coated the bed, with a thin, torn woollen blanket as a pitiful excuse to keep the cold at bay.

"Before the trials, I'd never taken a life," she swallowed. "But then . . . killing became survival. I had to survive those trials. I wouldn't allow my stubborn decisions to become the reason I died." She winced at the needle sliding through her skin. "I vowed I'd never do it again but . . . I'm a reaper. I'm the empire's personal blade to their enemies."

"We live in a harsh world," Koji replied softly. "Survival to you may be a weapon, but survival for me is money. Survival to another is food. We all have our own demons."

"I don't know what to believe anymore," she admitted. She wasn't sure why she was splitting herself open to this healer. She had no one left. He reapplied a salve over her fresh stitches, grog-soaked lavender permeating the rotten air, before re-bandaging the wound with clean gauze.

"Then find something." Koji sat back as he tied up his leather portmanteau and frowned at the wall opposite them, his wrinkles deepening. "Sometimes, it can be as small as a symbol."

She followed his gaze to the opposite wall. It was near-black, like all the walls in her cell, eroding from the elements, and covered in ghastly, slimy *waste*. A giant four-pointed star had been carved into it, the symbol stretching from floor to ceiling, wall-to-wall, with the circle connecting the four points as thick as her arm.

"Not all symbols are worth believing in."

"Perhaps," he motioned to the guards to unlock her cell, "but you'd be surprised at what you're willing to believe when you have nothing left. A word of advice though . . ." he lowered his voice. "Be careful with who you trust to write your letters."

As Koji's steps shuffled away, casting Kora a final saddened glance, she opened her palm to find a single golden doubloon placed inside.

In dungeons built into a cliff, with the ocean raging at the bottom, and the wind whipping up like a contained cyclone, was the worst kind of sleep Kora had ever experienced. Even nights on the ship in sea storms were nothing compared to *this*. The woollen blanket did nothing to protect or shield her, and when her fingers turned blue with frostbite, she knew these dungeons were where they sent prisoners to die.

Propelled by basic survival, she snapped the chains of the wooden bed, which were so decayed they crumbled in her fingers. Fortifying the corner furthest away from the bars of the cell, and using the wooden bench as a shield from the bitterly cold winds, she packed the space with hay.

Collecting the pitiful woollen blanket, she draped it over as a final protective layer. And that's where she stayed, curled up with her limbs enclosed beneath her, her teeth chattering as the winds blasted through the cells.

In the morning, several bodies were thrown off the planks.

It soon became her routine, as days passed in the dungeon. No one visited to demand she start repaying her debts. Koji wasn't allowed to visit again, so she tended to her shoulder herself, keeping the wound clean and dry. Prisoners were given one meal a day—a repulsive, lumpy gruel that was tasteless, with one stale sea biscuit, but she lapped up the small cups of water like it was the gods' nectar.

Every day, she tested to see if her magic had replenished, and all she could muster was a tiny droplet of water in the air. Whenever she pushed further, her shoulder would explode with pain threatening to knock her unconscious, her breath escaping her lungs. Even with the ocean so nearby, she felt oddly disconnected from it.

It was an ocean of death. More and more bodies were hurtled over the railings every morning, and the splattering of their bodies against the rocks, followed by crashing waves, woke her up every night like a nightmarish melody.

And when she wasn't sleeping, she was fighting against the cold of the brutally harsh and unforgiving winds. The cyclones were so loud her hearing was torn in two, her mind roaring until even her thoughts were painful night after night. And if it wasn't *that*, then she was vomiting gruel into the chamber pot, unable to confront the pain and loss her broken heart was drowning in.

Kora sat back against the wall, twirling Koji's gold doubloon in her grimy hands as she stared at the symbol across the cell. It was a constant reminder. The Talmon Empire was vast and mighty, and they were all small little cockroaches to be destroyed. It was oppressive, and it made her *sick*.

It made her angry. She wanted to see them all burn.

"Lucky you, it looks like you got the executive suite."

That familiar drawl was like metal claws dragging down her spine, followed by the stench of petrichor. Blake hovered near the bars, his keen green gaze raking in her makeshift den in the corner. She quickly pocketed Koji's coin and stood to face him.

"Although . . . you've seen better days."

She growled, and he jolted back in surprise, and her stare scraped over him. He was dressed in fine attire, fit for a royal. The forest-green tunic was striking against his complexion, with black trousers and a belt. Gold accents crusted his collar and cuffs, and his cutlass sword gleamed at his side.

A glance downwards, and she was met with her black leathers, crusted with mud, blood, and dirt. Koji had torn the left side so he could access her shoulder. She ran a hand through her locks, but her fingers could barely brush through the matted, lank lengths. Her hands were *filthy,* and crusted with slime and blood, her wrists swollen with red welts from the shackles. They'd left the metal collar on her throat—a reminder she was property. That they *owned* her.

"What do you want." A demand.

Blake opened his mouth then shut it, watching her warily. "I've come to give you a second chance—a *final* chance." She huffed a laugh, withdrawing from the bars. "I can put a good word in with Barron," his voice wavered. "You're of no use to me here—"

"I'm not a prized pet you can wheel out!" Kora snapped. "What were you thinking? That I'll start doing magic tricks and win their favour?"

"It's not about that." His eyes flashed.

"No? Magic is *forbidden*, Blake. Just like you and I were. We were never meant to be, and look where we are."

"Kora . . ." he swallowed, learning towards the bars, "I want you. I *need* you."

She paused, lifting her gaze to his eyes. They were pleading and desperate, and she faltered for a moment, the scattered remains of her heart lifting with shameful hope.

"I know we've never been good at words," Blake's breathing turned ragged, and she tried to suppress the yearning cresting within her traitorous body. "But I love you."

Finally . . . after all this time. She'd waited for gods-knows how long for those words, for that admission of love. It was everything she relied upon to give her strength to become an admiral—to be able to have a world without pirates . . . and Blake at her side where they could finally express their love. And she'd nearly sacrificed her dream for it.

But now, she didn't feel an explosion of warmth in her chest. She was as bitterly cold as the cyclone winds, and her toes curled in her boots in the worst kind of way. Blake blinked at her silence.

"Without you, I . . . without you we cannot win. We need you," he urged.

"You've got to be fucking joking!" She slammed her hand against the bars. "The man who never believed in magic, who refused its existence, has come crawling to me so he can use me in this war. Using *love* as a tactic to push me into something I don't want."

"Your power is unique. With it we *will* win. We will get everything we ever wanted! Everything we talked about—together. I thought you still wanted that." Hurt pinched his face.

"I don't want *this*."

"Don't choose this path, *asterya*."

"Don't. Call. Me. That." She bared her teeth in a snarl.

Blake's face hardened, his desperation melting away like a façade. "Final chance, Kora. Join me, or you can die here."

The coldness of his words penetrated her chest, turning it into a barren frozen ruin. *Their façade had been a façade.* There never had been anything between them, it'd all been one continuous lie. She'd been a pawn in his game—a way for him to excel the ranks and gain favour with Barron. Her dreams were never the goal for them to be together. To think she'd been willing to risk it all for *love*. It'd just been another façade to mask his.

This entire bloody time.

"We were never real," she replied, the words spoken out loud, settling like a chilling confirmation.

Blake sighed against the thick slimy bars of her cell, a glimmer of regret rippling across his face before his features smoothed out into detached coolness.

"Are you going to tell him?"

Blake paused, frowning at her question.

"About me? My . . . gift."

"There's no need," he replied bluntly.

"Where's Theron? Is he here? And Ivar?" Kora inhaled sharply.

She'd wondered if the prince was contained in one of these cells . . . or if he'd been one of the many bodies tossed to the watery depths below. She'd called his name, and Ivar's, the first night, but had been treated with a smashing *visit* from the guards.

She learned her lesson quickly to keep her mouth shut.

"They're not here," she deflated at his words. "You won't see—"

"Captain!"

Her stomach leapt to her throat as she jumped towards the bars, hope blooming in her chest. Samuel and Aryn had come for her, they had—

An unrecognisable soldier hurried across the railed platform outside the cells—straight to Blake.

"Captain, we need you above. There's been a . . . disturbance," he addressed *Blake*, who glanced warily at her, and that burning rage consumed her all over again.

"*Captain?*" she seethed.

Blake shrugged disinterestedly. "A spot opened up."

"How *dare* you. How fucking dare you!"

And just there, sown in gold on the side of his healed shoulder, was the captain ranking. He'd taken her title, her position. *Her life.*

"You had to put me in a cage to get what you want!"

He arched a smooth brow. "You put yourself there. I told you the impulsive plunders were unsound."

"You gave Barron my ledgers," she snapped. "You betrayed me. You betrayed our crew."

He'd been stressed about losing his champion title. Claimed he was leaving *Hell's Serpent* and changing career to become a commander. Instead, he'd taken a shortcut . . . straight to her position. That power-hungry gleam twinkled in his sickening eyes.

"It was illegal. Barron wanted a full report of *Hell's Serpent*. Of you. I did what I must for the benefit of the empire."

"I don't stand by draining our workers dry. You should know better than most what it's like to live in the slums. Surviving on scraps whilst the nobles hoard wealth."

Blake stiffened, and a slow blink followed, a million emotions passing his face. His hand flew to the hilt of his sword, as if it steadied him. The stranger appeared once again, grappling to mould his expression into cool, frosted neutrality.

She knew that feeling. Except, this time, she'd tossed her mask so far away, allowing numbness to gracefully cocoon her.

"You used to be loyal," disdain dripped from his lips. "You've changed."

Oh, by the gods, she had. And she was glad.

"What of my ship? My crew?" Her voice cracked as she gripped at the bars, her palms sliding over black sludge.

Blake's mouth twitched. "You don't have a ship, or crew, anymore."

"Captain," the soldier pushed. "We must go."

"I doubt you'll see anything beyond these bars again."

And he sauntered away, dragging her stolen life behind him. Releasing a shattering scream that burned her lungs and throat, Kora's eyes brimmed with hot tears as she yanked viciously against the bars of the cell. She screamed and cried until her voice was a hoarse whisper, consumed by the approaching evening cyclone. As Kora curled up in her makeshift wind protector, her tears cleaning away the dirt on her face, she wished for the God of Death to visit her.

53

Bang.
Kora bolted from beneath her woollen blanket, tufts of hay clinging to her sticky leathers.
Bang. Bang.

She scanned her surroundings. She was still in her cage. The cyclone winds had settled. It was still night.

Shadows lingered everywhere in the spiral dungeon, interspersed with sombre, red light from wooden torches. Yet her cell remained in perpetual, cold darkness. Prisoners weren't allowed torches behind their bars, and after the first couple days in bleak lighting, her eyes had slowly adapted to the blanketed night.

Bang.

Creeping around her den, she cautiously approached the bars of her cell. The cyclone winds didn't normally sound like that. They sounded like a ferocious roar, followed by the rattling of chains, creaking of bars, and the cries of prisoners as they froze to death.

She rubbed her hands together, blowing hot breath into them, keeping her blanket wrapped around her shoulders as she crouched near the bars, peering into the doomed spiral.

"Over here!"

Two dark-armoured guards hurtled past, racing up the spiralled walkway, and she tracked their movements like a predator. Something was happening—something big. Her spine tingled. Had Galen arrived already? Had the war begun?

If the war was happening, she needed to escape immediately.

More guards ascended the spiral, lances and swords gripped in their hands as they yelled to each other. She was roughly ten cells from the top of the spiral, which connected to a stoned staircase leading to the barracks.

"*Attack!*"

Her heart pounded. Galen *must* be here. She quickly scoured the only area she could see—no sign of any guards. They had all abandoned their posts for the battle above. She reached through the bars, picturing the ocean of death in her mind's eye looming at the base.

Summoning the water, her teeth clenched as sweat trickled down the side of her face. Her shoulder stung, but she delved deeper, reaching for her water beast, coaxing it to the surface with the promise of revenge.

Prisoners below screamed, followed by the slosh of water against stone. Ocean waves roared through her ears, and she released one, long, excruciating yell as the pain in her shoulder shot down her arm. It wrapped around her fingers, trying to force her to stop, but she braced against it, her eyes brimming with pained tears as water trickled up the spiral.

It was mediocre compared to what she'd been able to conjure before—but it was enough. Even if it nearly broke her, she would save herself.

As water slithered up the bars of the cell, shaping into a key and reaching the sludge-crusted lock, a figure dropped in front of her cell, and Kora fell backwards with a violent shudder. She frantically scrambled through the waste away from whatever fresh hell she was about to experience.

"Kora! It's me!"

The door to her cell swung open, and Erick strode in, racing towards her.

"Erick . . .?" Shock consumed her.

"Come, we don't have much time." Aryn emerged behind him, his longbow gripped tightly in his hands. Blood splattered his youthful face, stark against the black tattoo on his cheek.

"I was just breaking myself out—before you interrupted."

Aryn wryly smiled. "I'm glad your humour's still intact."

Leaping to her feet, she swayed from malnourishment and, as Erick steadied her, he wrapped a black cloak around her shaking body. Verbal apologies swept over Kora as he clasped his arms around her tingling skin and her limbs weakened. He had defied the empire . . . for *her*.

"I'm sorry," he repeated. "I couldn't get here sooner. I tried everything. That *bastard* Barron!"

"Go now. Chat later." Aryn motioned to them, and he averted his gaze from Erick as Kora followed Aryn, his slender frame brimming with tensity.

"Where's Sam?" She exhaled shakily as she stepped onto the walkway.

Bang.

Aryn glanced up, soil and vines raining around them. "He's giving us some time."

It wasn't the war—it was her crew.

"Hurry!" Erick yanked her in his direction—*down* the spiral walkway.

"What? Where are we going? We need to get Sam!"

Neither male answered as they propelled down the walkway, Erick leading from the front, and Aryn covering the rear as always. The spiral was empty. Whatever Samuel was doing was causing enough commotion for the guards to abandon their posts.

Good gods.

"It's her!"

Prisoners in the cells clanked their metal cups against their bars. Their voices crying out in anguish as Kora barrelled past.

"It's the pirate-hunter!"

Her stomach twisted. It had never crossed her mind that some of the pirates and rebels she'd sentenced over the years would have ended up here, a place worse than Deadwater Prison—and *survived.*

"Oi! You!"

"You ruined me life!"

"Stop that wench!"

"You're a filthy rebel like the rest of us!"

The voices swirled around in her mind, merging with the courtier's slander when Barron had paraded her around the castle. Gods, that must've been over a week ago.

"Don't listen to them," Aryn hissed as they raced to the bottom.

The cyclone winds were strong down here, and their cloaks forcefully whipped around them. Kora's skin stung from the bitter harshness. If she'd been sentenced to one of these cells at the bottom, she'd have died that first night.

Erick led them to a small, stone platform connected to the base of the spiral walkway. It was so dark down here, and the torches sputtered out from the winds. She sucked in a tense breath as a single guard turned to face them on the platform.

Shit. They'd been caught. Every muscle recoiled on instinct, reaching to grip her sabre daggers—but her hands snagged on thin air.

One dagger had been shattered to pieces . . . the other had been stolen.

The guard was covered head to toe in sheep's wool, packed beneath his armour. Leathers covered every inch of flesh—in between the metal plates—on his wrists and joints, and wrapped around his head like a fuzzy blanket.

"You're late," the guard mumbled through his protective wrap.

"We were held up," Erick snapped, hiding Kora behind him.

"You know my fee."

Erick's hands flicked to his belt and froze. With a curse, he patted around his waist in a flurry before letting out a frustrated sigh.

"What's going on?" Aryn stepped forward.

"I lost it—the payment. We were ambushed on the way down here. They've sliced right through my belt."

"Ironic," Aryn muttered.

"Not now!" Erick barked.

What in Umbra was going on?

Kora peered through the darkness, to *really* look at Erick. Blood soaked his clothes and clung to his hair. His gold-and-malachite pommelled sword was gripped in one shaking hand, and his armour was *dented*. Only something incredibly strong could do that. His cloak was shredded, along with a thin cut along his neck that was crusted with blood.

"What happened?" she whispered. "Where's Sam?"

No one acknowledged her.

"No payment, no boat," the guard grunted.

"We made a deal," Aryn snarled, and she startled.

"I deal in money. I can easily lock you all up instead. You wouldn't survive the night."

"We can't go without Sam!" Kora shrieked. Panic bubbled inside, until it grabbed her in a chokehold. "We can't leave Sam, Theron, *or* Ivar!"

She didn't deserve this. Everything they were sacrificing to free her from the spiral dungeons. Her life wasn't worth *three* lives. Did they even *want* to defy the empire? It baffled her to be chosen over something they'd all devoted their lives to and bowed their loyalty to for years—or their entire lives, in Erick's case.

She was nothing. Nobody. A pity case.

"Kora . . . Sam made his choice." Aryn's hooded eyes saddened, and her heart clenched inside her throat. "We can't find the others. We need to leave now. Sam's giving us this one shot."

"No . . . I don't want him to do that! Don't let him do that. I'm . . . I'm *nothing*. I'm not worth it. They'll kill him!" The ocean sprayed up against the stone platform and Erick warily glanced at it.

"You're worth *everything*," Erick replied with confidence. "Samuel stayed behind to give us a chance."

Us.

"You're not going anywhere without payment." The guard raised a silver-tapped lance.

Erick raised his sword in return, and Aryn advanced with his longbow.

More death. More loss. It was too much.

"Wait!"

Kora stumbled forward, fishing out a token from her leathers. She offered her open palm to the guard, the small gold doubloon perched on top. The guard gingerly picked it up, turning it over in his gloved hand and inspecting it intently. His eyes widened as he pocketed the coin, and he glanced at her curiously.

"Where'd you get this? It's very old."

"I found it. Is it enough?"

"Aye." *Thank the gods.*

They all exhaled simultaneously as the guard led them to a secret passage tucked around the corner from the platform. Carved into the jagged cliff, the tunnel's walls were slick with ocean spray, and smelled like rusted stone. Vines snaked across the curve, delving and twisting into the cracks and dips of the stone, winding around stalactites on the ceiling.

After what felt like an eternity, they emerged out onto a hidden bank of boulders and moss, at the base of the leering cliff. Seaweed clung to the balustrades of domed platforms built into the side, all the way to the top. An outpost that'd been abandoned since the Galenite War. Kora craned her head back and looked up to the beacon of the Citadel at the top—and a raging fire.

"You set *fire* to the Citadel!"

There would be no coming back from this. They'd be hanged if they were caught.

Aryn followed her gaze. "It was Sam's idea. He set a timed explosion with the kegs in the barracks. Leading towards the castle, and away from the dungeons."

"Sam blew up grog?" she squeaked, bewildered. Pride flitted through her, but was quickly replaced with dread. An all-consuming dread of what the empire would do to Samuel.

The ocean was calmer here, waves lapping against the bank and the air was completely still. No cyclone winds, no biting cold roaring and slicing her skin. The quiet seemed *loud*.

"You never saw us," Erick muttered to the guard as they hurried to the small pinnace boat with a ripped sail.

"Aye. I best be off—"

BOOM.

Rocks rained around them, smashing into the mossy bank, and Erick sprinted, shielding Kora with his armour as shouts rang above. The guard pelted into the secret tunnel.

"THEY'RE ESCAPING!" he cried as he vanished.

Warm light blossomed from the varying outpost platforms, and the dread coiled in Kora's gut threatened to expand, snaking into her limbs, freezing her in place. They'd found her. They'd drag her kicking and screaming back to those slimy cells.

An ocean wave crested, tugging at her, beckoning her to leap into the sea.

"We need to go! Kora, move!" Erick pulled on her arm but she was rooted to the spot. Frozen in fear as the light burned brighter, bouncing off the slick wetness of the stalagmites.

"What are you doing!" Aryn grabbed her other arm, but she couldn't move.

And just like that, a blonde head of hair appeared.

"Sam . . ." she whispered.

Both males stilled, whipping their gazes in Samuel's direction, where he stood behind a balustrade halfway up the cliff.

"He's going to make it," Aryn breathed. "Sam! Jump!"

But Samuel wasn't moving. Blood smattered the side of his face and his clothes. He limped as he waved a thick arm, and a sob tore from her chest.

"Go!" Samuel bellowed, and darted back into the outpost, the flickering of torches and cries of guards following him.

"Now!" Aryn yanked on her arm, nearly dislocating her shoulder. "He's distracting them!"

"No!" she cried, as she collapsed onto the single deck. Aryn wrapped a second cloak around her from where it had been stashed in the boughs of the boat, as Erick began frantically rowing. She didn't realise she was shivering.

"I'm so sorry," she whispered to the winds, as they rowed away from Talmon Island. Away from her ship, her crew, and her missing talisman.

Fires engulfed the horizon, burning the fortress into cinders.

Somewhere, deep inside, Samuel, Theron, and Ivar were suffering. And she had abandoned them.

I n the distance, smoke billowed from Talmon Island like a black spot.

Erick had rowed all night, and Aryn took over in the morning. The males had barely spoken more than two words to each other, Samuel's sacrifice hanging over them. Their goal was to escape to Calypso Islands and devise a strategy from there. It'd take several days on a pinnace boat with a broken sail.

Thankfully, supplies and rations had been stashed below the small deck, and Kora sat cross-legged, gently nibbling on cured meat, her stomach roiling at the invasion of solid food. She could never eat sea biscuits again.

Erick watched her intently, his brown eyes assessing every detail on her until they settled on the collar on her throat. His expression morphed into a glacial rage so fierce, she squirmed on the bench.

"It doesn't bother me that much."

"Don't lie. It's a disgrace."

Her skin prickled at his words, and she set down her rations, glaring at him.

"Fine—let's talk about lies."

Erick raised a brow and Aryn halted his rowing, turning to face them curiously. The sail listed in the gentle breeze, and they bobbed along the azure surface of the sea.

"I *know*."

Erick and Aryn glanced at each other. The former worried, the latter . . . tense. She wasn't sure what was irking Aryn, but he was constantly on edge.

"What do you know?" Erick hedged.

She spluttered at the males. Two sets of eyes bored into her, like they were both trying to read her mind. "I *know* that you knew Theron—Eli—*whatever*. That you were . . . I don't know, friends?"

The tension in the two males dissipated and Aryn resumed his rowing.

"Friends?" Erick smiled, like it was a joke.

"Don't play dumb with me. I heard you both at South Wharf . . . talking about the Skytors and Davy Jones."

Aryn jolted and cursed as he dropped an oar into the ocean, and Erick hurtled forward, trying to grab the handle but it sank into the dark, watery depths. She could've easily beckoned the oar. The tingle of her power had returned now that she was back where she belonged . . . in the ocean.

"Shit." Erick pinched the bridge of his nose as he sat back sighing. "How do *you* know the Skytors?"

"They attacked us in the desert." She flashed back to Doran and Mags. The same vision danced behind Aryn's tired eyes as they shared a reproachful look.

"You never mentioned that before." His gaze pierced her.

Unspoken words crossed the space between them. They had never told Erick during the debrief after escorting Theron. Blake had made it clear not to divulge the information. In fact, Blake had made a lot of decisions for her. Her jaw clenched so hard at the realisation that her teeth nearly snapped.

"We handled it," Kora retorted. Handled was probably the wrong word—they had *obliterated* an entire populace, and their blood still stained her soul and haunted her dreams. "What are you doing working with the rebels? You've been hunting them for years! Or is that another lie, too?"

His mouth thinned. "Kora, there's a lot you don't know—" Aryn coughed, and Erick pinned him a glare. "We don't have time for this."

"Now is the only time."

Aryn regarded them, silently perched at the end of the boat. The sun had risen to the peak of midday, and they were still *too close* to Talmon Island. But she couldn't stop—she needed to know *now*.

"Yes, I hunted rebels. Like you, I was doing it for revenge." She stilled as a faraway look overcame Erick's face. "I . . . I had a wife once . . . Eleanore." Silence hung heavy in the boat. "I was away on a simple scouting mission as a captain, and when I returned home, she was . . . they had . . . they'd *butchered* her. The rebels targeted multiple attacks on officers in the empire, ransacking their homes, stealing intel, and murdering their loved ones in the process."

Horror roiled through Kora, and she clasped the edge of the wooden bench to steady herself.

"Eleanore was pregnant with our first child," he continued, and he looked at the sea, his eyes watering. "I lost everything in one day."

Aryn's shoulders hunched and he bowed his head.

"Erick . . ." she placed a hand over his. "You never told me. I'm so sorry."

"Barron took me in after that. I was young and naïve, and he turned me into the man I am today. He helped me turn my pain into ambition, and I went out and hunted down the rebels . . . and then I found you."

Silver lined her eyes and she squeezed his hand. She already knew the rest.

"I may have lost the love of my life . . . but I gained something so precious in you."

Aryn sank further into the boat behind Erick.

"So, no, it wasn't a lie, Kora." The sternness returned to Erick's voice, and shame rose to her cheeks. He had this entire *life*, an entire history of pain and survival before her, and now he was throwing it all away *for* her. "I vowed to protect you with everything I had. I cannot lose another child. So I kept the reports of the Skytors from you, afraid you would go after them in your own pursuit of revenge. History *must not* repeat itself."

"But you work with them. I heard you. You and Theron worked with the Skytors, and the witches." Doubt crept into her voice. Had she imagined it?

Erick shook his head. "The odd contract here and there to serve the empire. It was a way to keep tabs on them. We couldn't eliminate a whole group of people without just cause. It'd be suspicious, especially with the witches and their accord."

And that's exactly what Kora and her crew had done, but no one had raised suspicions . . . yet. Fortunately, the witches governed themselves, but any attempt to kill them would lead to catastrophic war. Ironically, that was happening regardless of the empire upholding the treaty.

Witches, rebels, Marshans . . . would all be killed in this war.

She frowned. "But—"

"As I said Kora, there's a lot you don't know."

Her voice died on her lips. She'd been sheltered by Erick

without realising it—and by Blake. Both working within the ranks and tiers of the empire, hoarding vital information that could have changed the course of events that landed her here, as a fugitive.

Kora thought she'd been important. As the only female captain, she'd thought she was special and valued in the armada. That she'd been seen by the empire as a rising star to become the next admiral. But she wasn't. A female pirate lord was out there—Cassidy. And Skylar, the Galenite mercenary, had wielded respect from her crew, despite their bloodthirsty intentions.

It was only the empire that oppressed females.

It dawned on her she was only favoured as the commodore's daughter—and that's all she ever was. She only had sway and status because of her surname—which wasn't even *hers*. She'd been used by Blake, springing him into the empire's clutches.

She was so stupid *and* blind. Maybe Bree was right.

"What now?" she mumbled, forcing the words out. "What do we do now? Are we rebels?" It sickened her.

Aryn picked up the single oar with a sigh. "We survive," he replied, and attached a sheet of metal used to patch the pinnace boat to his longbow with rope. His gaze hovered on Erick's haunted face as he relived his past. Aryn placed the oar and longbow into the ocean and rowed them across the shimmering liquid surface in silence.

Kora twisted the piece of ripped sail, pouring blood into the ocean, before dipping it into a fresh bowl of sea water. Talmon Island was still in their sight on the distant horizon, and it made her nervous.

"It's worse than it looks—" Erick's voice cut off with a hiss as she continued to wipe away the dried blood on his neck.

"Don't lie."

A ghost of a smile crossed his face at her parroted words. The cut was thin but deep, clearly from a sword. Luckily, it'd missed the artery running down his neck.

"Get yourself one of these," she tapped the metal collar wrapped around her throat. "Lifesaver."

"It's certainly a fashion statement. I'll consider it."

She sat back, inspecting the slash through his skin. It'd stopped bleeding, and all she could do was tend to it with sea water until it healed, to keep infection at bay. She was still unsure about revealing her power. Would Erick still love her? Would he cast her out? Would he use her, and turn her in to the Talmon Empire, gaining back their favour?

Sweat trickled down her face, causing an uncomfortable sensation beneath the metal enclosing on her windpipe. Her leathers reeked with mud, piss, and sludge from the dungeons. Erick had ripped the sleeves from the shoulders, allowing her a small reprieve from the heat.

Aryn had taken a break from rowing and was below deck, tending to his own wounds, and taking a much-needed rest. She'd splashed sea water onto her face, and partially healed her shoulder when neither male had been looking.

Despite the talisman's absence, the pool of her power was growing, her water beast slumbering, ready to be unleashed. It was a small comfort to know she hadn't lost this one token of strength. Maybe without her power, the talisman no longer worked. Its function obsolete without her source. Whoever stole it would be rendered with useless jewellery.

"You said you were ambushed?" she recalled.

"As soon as you'd been taken by Barron, we grouped in my chambers. I know what you've been doing on those ledgers Kora. I've always known." His pointed stare made her blush like a scolded child. "I admire your passion for your crew and their wellbeing, but there are rules and laws for a reason."

"They were starving," she whispered. "Even when we were the most successful in the armada, they still starved. Their children starved. I couldn't allow all it, or allow the empire to reap all the benefits from our plunders."

"I understand—"

"Do you? We live in a manor in the mid-district. We have *servants*. Those servants' husbands are in *my* crew, bringing home whatever they can to survive. The Citadel is made of literal gold! They have more than enough, yet they keep taking more."

Her gaze caught on the insignia branded on his armour. It meant unity. What a load of bullshit. What kingdom is united when it's forced into varying districts, favouring nobility over the impoverished. Erick's brown eyes flashed, followed by deep thought. His lank salt-and-pepper hair curled around his face, and she tunnelled on the wrinkles settling into the tanned planes of his skin.

"I'm sorry. I know that's not your fault."

"Your passion is outstanding Kora, it always has been." His lips curled into a small smile.

"The ambush . . .?" She sat back on the deck, hiding from the afternoon sun in the white sail's shadow.

He cleared his throat. "Samuel hatched his plan rather quickly, but it took us a while to map out the castle, figure out the best areas to target with the explosions, even with my knowledge of the layout. We had a few delays." Indeed, the Citadel was a labyrinth. "We learned the guard's rotation schedules, and then we had to find which ones we could bribe. Those not entirely loyal to Barron."

"How long was I down there?"

"Just over a week. It *killed* me that I couldn't get to you sooner." Erick spoke thickly. "Having to act normal around Barron, pretending I approved of his decision." He almost snarled. "Marwood strutted around like a damned peacock." Her gut twisted. "We were all set to go. But just as Samuel began the trigger of explosions, a group of soldiers in the barracks attacked him, led by Garvan's son—Egon. Apparently, he didn't appreciate Samuel's allegiance to you."

Kora flinched.

"Us and a couple of rogue guards intervened, giving Samuel time to get away and start the sequence." He gestured to his wounds and she nodded slowly, understanding sinking in.

"They're going to kill him," she whispered shakily. "All because of me."

"No, they won't." Aryn popped up from below deck. Shadows rimmed his eyes, and his floppy hair was slicked back with water. "They're going to use him."

"What? How?"

"If they wanted you dead, they would've killed you instantly." He stepped onto the deck. "They put you in that dungeon and left you alone for a whole week for a reason. They want you alive, and they will use him to get to you."

Blake's words echoed through her mind. *We need you. Your power is unique.*

The pinnace listed in the sea, and Aryn grabbed onto the broken sail, his eyes pinned on Kora—on her scar. The ocean water sprayed onto the deck, circling around her as her mind relived Blake's betrayal.

"I don't know why," she spat. "I assumed it's because I'm a Cadell."

Erick lifted both brows.

"No other reason?" Aryn pushed.

"I don't know? They said I owed the empire, and that they owned me."

Aryn scoffed. "No one could ever own you."

Something lingered beneath his words, and she glanced between Aryn and Erick. The former stared at her so hard his eyes bulged, and Erick curiously inspected the water on the deck, following it down to the ocean.

"What's going on? There's something you're not telling me."

"There's something *you're* not telling *us,*" Aryn replied.

His ancient voice unnerved her, and his golden stare sent hairs prickling down her arms. Was this male truly her mystery voice? They didn't sound the same, and right now Aryn frightened her. His youthful demeanour rippled, and beneath it, something old and deadly lurked.

"I don't know what you mean," she lied.

"Just admit it."

"Aryn," Erick warned. *What was that?* Why were they acting so weird?

Waves crested in the sea as she pushed to her feet on the rocking pinnace. The ocean breeze stirred into a gust, and she wiped her hair from her face so she could assault the males with her deathly glare.

"Admit what?"

"*Aryn.*"

"It's over, Erick," Aryn turned to him, his golden eyes burning as bright as the sun. "It's *all* over. Sam is a prisoner, and we're fugitives, exiled from the empire. The war is returning. It's happening all over *again.* She needs to know. She needs to remember. We need her back."

Kora's jaw dropped with astonishment.

"No, it's too soon. I can't." Erick's glacial presence surfaced, but beneath, panic lingered in the flare of his eyes.

"We've waited years. *I've* waited years! You knew you had to let go of her someday."

"What's going on!" Kora waved her arms. "I exist! I'm right here! Stop talking about me like I'm nothing! I deserve to know what's going on."

"Kora," Erick took one of her hands, his breathing unsteady, his warm, rough skin scraping over her palm. "It's about your past. We need to tell you—"

A foghorn cut off his words, blaring across the horizon, and Kora gasped, her body trembling at the sound. She *knew* that sound.

They all turned to the west as a second foghorn blasted through the skies.

White sails. Moonstone gems. A Pegasus figurehead.

"No, no, no . . ." She stumbled back into the sailing mast as an entire fleet of Galen warships rapidly sailed across the ocean, faster than any ship she'd seen—faster than her own *Hell's Serpent*. Erick blanched, and he curled over, vomiting. Aryn remained silent, assessing the formation of the warships, his lips curving.

Panic seized Kora, freezing her solid as the warships headed directly for them. They were *impossibly* fast.

No, no, no. Not now.

Another horn ruptured her ears, and she twisted her head to the north, in the direction of the sound.

"You've got to be kidding!" Aryn *laughed* out loud, and she was sure sailor's mania was settling in.

A massive fleet of majestic mahogany ships—with green sails branded with the golden four-pointed insignia—sailed in from the north. Every second that passed, the closer the two fleets converged.

And they were right in the middle.

E rick's head whipped back and forth between the two fleets as they advanced, and Kora peeled away from the small mast, her heart erratically thumping beneath her ribs. They had to move quickly, or risk being ripped apart by the hull of one of the warships that would easily tear through the pinnace.

They needed to choose the lesser of two evils.

"You both need to choose now! Which ship will we survive on?" She raised her hands.

"What?" Erick and Aryn echoed.

"Choose now—Galen or Talmon."

It was like asking which way they would like to die.

"Talmon!" Erick barked. She supposed their chances of survival were *slightly* better there—if not highly minimal. Better to face tyrants than blood-thirsty, mindless savages.

Aryn glared at him viciously, but his ire was quickly replaced with shock. Light bloomed from Kora's hands, trailing up her arms like coils, and she gritted her teeth as the ocean water pooled onto the pinnace, circling up their legs like a second skin. Resistance pushed back, and she trembled as she delved into her slumbering well of power, past an unknown barrier.

"Hold your breaths!" she yelled over the rising cries of battle, and the *boom* of cannons as warfare unfurled. Erick yelped as ocean water consumed them, dragging them beneath the surface—just as the pinnace was smashed in half by a Galen warship.

Joyous warmth spread through her as she commanded the sea. Her power felt unlimited, the barrier broken within her. It rejoiced with her as she speared their bodies with the current towards one of the empire's warships. Her body was alight with energy once again, her shoulder healing completely as the water cocooned her like a long-lost love. It snaked around her body, her veins thrumming with a fathomless strength. She nearly felt whole.

And she was *glowing*.

Once they neared the mahogany hull, Kora directed their bodies upwards, shooting them out of the sea like sirens leaping to ensnare sailors.

"Grab on!"

Their hands flung out, grappling onto the side rigging of the ship. Water dripped from their hair and clothes, and the males panted, their eyes wide with shock—and something else. She didn't spare a chance to look at them too closely, mostly in fear they would be repulsed . . . or afraid.

"Keep going!" She climbed the rigging and propelled over the thick railing.

It was chaos.

The ships had already collided, and the deck was fraught with both Galenite mercenaries, in their pale-stone armour, and Talmon soldiers in their opposing black. The sound of metal and shouting roared around her and she paled. She'd never experienced true war, and the sights, sounds, and *smells* were ghastly.

"Kora!"

Erick thudded beside her, his shredded wet cape slapping against the wood, followed by Aryn. They both stared at her wide eyed, heavily breathing, and Erick was . . . *shaking*.

"How long?" Erick pressed. "How long since your powers returned?"

"My . . . what?" Kora shrank back.

Erick glanced around. No one had noticed them yet.

"You knew," she whispered, her voice trembling. "You knew!"

The shame in Erick's face broke her completely. He had *lied*. He'd kept her past a secret.

Her yell attracted attention, and a swath of Galenite mercenaries approached them, breaking through the folds of Talmon soldiers. Erick unsheathed his sword and leapt in front of Kora, fighting them off. Aryn raced up to her, his eyes distracted by something in the distance, and grabbed her hand, hauling her to the quarterdeck.

"No! Erick!" she cried as Aryn dragged her away from her father. "Let me go!"

Surrounded by mercenaries, his green cape sliced and trickled to the deck around him as he fought with a ferocious might. Seeing

Erick in battle had always inspired her—he was a force to be reckoned with—but now it sickened her violently.

Aryn's grip was impenetrable, even with her regained powered strength, and she couldn't shake him. They raced up the steps to the quarterdeck and stumbled into a towering female dressed in a labradorite flight suit.

"Skylar!" Aryn skidded to a halt.

Skylar turned, her doe-like eyes raking over them as she withdrew her estoc sword from the gut of a soldier, wiping blood across his corpse. Her braided silver hair whipped in the wind, and a smile slowly spread across her lips.

"Isn't this a pleasant surprise." Her voice woke the water beast within Kora, and her hand whipped out instinctively, shooting a bolt of razor-sharp water at Skylar. The female leapt into the air, her flight suit expanding as she flipped graciously around Kora's attack before landing on her feet.

"So predictable," she crooned.

"Skylar, not now," Aryn snapped, his grip tightening on Kora. She tried to pull away, but Aryn tugged her back as if she weighed nothing.

"I'm just playing," Skylar shrugged.

"We need to get Kora somewhere safe. Now is our only chance."

Aryn *knew* Skylar—he *knew* the Galenites.

The pain in Kora's chest felt like the whole ocean was pressing down on her, and nausea churned in her gut as she assessed one of her closest friends.

Another liar.

Another secret.

Her life had never been real. All of her relationships were fake.

Aryn averted his gaze, his jaw working as he pleaded with Skylar.

Skylar's eyes flashed at the mention of Kora's name, and she surveyed the battle around them, her mouth thinning. Kora peeked a glance down to the deck and gasped at the horror. Bodies and blood littered the deck, and more mercenaries and soldiers were swinging onto the ship from flanking vessels, propelling into the clutches of death.

The booms of cannons ricocheted through the air as the naval battle undulated in the sea around them. Smoke billowed from ships, tainting the sky. Arrows and lances soared through the air, embedding into the chests and necks of their enemies. Waves of yelling, crying, and moaning rang in her ears, and her bowels turned watery.

This was what Barron wanted—and this was only the start.

Thinking his name somehow beckoned him, and a familiar, dark figure landed onto the foredeck, the sound vibrating through the wood of the ship. Darkness leaked all around him, and she felt his ripple of power all the way from the other end of the ship. Like a beacon, Barron's thunderous eyes found her immediately, and he smirked.

Apparently, he wasn't finished being an admiral. But how had he found her on this ship?

Her mind screamed, her scar burning with an intensity that made her cry out, clutching the side of her face. Skylar frowned at her, but then instinctively whirled, using her sword to block an attack.

"Get away from her," a familiar voice growled.

Kora's world tilted on its axis as Blake attacked Skylar. He was splattered with blood, his leathers torn, and his face twisted with savage rage. A thick, writhing shadow followed him, echoing every movement he made, causing Skylar to stumble, her efforts weakening.

"Get her out of here!" she shouted to Aryn.

Blake's gaze snapped to Aryn and Kora, and it fell to their clasped hands. With a roar, he pushed Skylar back with frightening force, her body flying back into the side of the ship with a *crack*. Aryn stepped in front of Kora, firing an arrow. It shot into Blake's shoulder and he cried out in anguish, reaching to snap the arrow from his body.

"Kora, you need to run—now!" Aryn fired two more arrows into each of Blake's legs, but it didn't stop him.

"I . . . I can't. I'm not leaving you like Sam!"

Aryn offered a half smile, his hawk-like gaze trained on Blake. "We need you to survive—*run*."

"I'm tired of running!"

Blake's attention whipped to Kora. At the sound of her voice, he ripped the arrows from his legs and charged forward. With one hand, he grasped Aryn by the throat, and she cried out as he tossed him over the side of the quarterdeck balustrade, into the teeming mass of swords below.

"You don't need to run, my *asterya*." Blake stooped over her. His presence was suffocating, and her power shrank within his proximity. He ran a finger down the side of her face, tracing her scar. It burned so mercilessly that stars danced in her vision.

"I'll take care of you . . ." he murmured as his finger trailed down to the collar at her neck. He smiled at it. "You look so beautiful in this."

"You're fucking deranged!"

Kora stepped back as Skylar bolted from the side, her sword swooping up between them. Kora dropped to the deck, sliding across the slick wood as Skylar fought Blake once again. She was limping, and her face winced whenever she raised her sword above her shoulder.

"You need to go!" she ordered Kora. "Find my siblings they're—"

Blake cut her off as he lunged for Kora, but Skylar effortlessly blocked him, twirling around before bringing the pommel of her sword up to his chin knocking him back. The move was eerily like one of Kora's. Skylar was . . . she was *protecting* her. Kora watched her with astoundment. Why was Skylar, a Galenite, protecting her? Surely, Kora was a threat to Galen. She could be used as a weapon—

She sucked in a breath.

A weapon.

I possess a weapon. A weapon that's never been seen before.

Barron had insisted on her joining their war effort. Did he know? If Erick knew, then what's to stop Barron knowing about her power?

Leaping to her feet, she descended the stairs to the main deck. Skylar was pushing Blake back to the edge of the quarterdeck, and Kora would rather take her chances in the throngs of battle than be left with her ex-lover and a brutal Galenite.

She ducked, dodged, and rolled away from attacks on the deck, and a gleaming piece of silver snagged her attention. She knelt, grabbing a light cutlass sword before she fought her way across the deck to Barron.

Boom.

A cannon fired through the air across the ship, narrowly missing the main mast. A ship to the right exploded, chunks of wood and debris cascading in the air and plummeting all around her. Severed, sharp pieces of a brig impaled a soldier through the neck. Several more soldiers were knocked unconscious—or she hoped they were. She didn't stop long enough to see whether more pieces of a ship's hull were protruding from their bodies.

There was only one way to end this war—and it was with Barron's head rolling across this deck.

She'd been used by everyone, and she'd be gods-damned before she let Barron do the same. She'd been kept in the dark, hidden away from society. She'd been lied to. She'd been betrayed. She'd been abused, locked up, and chained.

And Captain Kora Cadell had had *enough*.

Now it was time to break free.

She would not be conquered.

56

Both Galen and Talmon soldiers fell at Kora's blade.

Rage propelled her, and her water beast roared alongside her, drinking on her bloodlust as she cut a path across the deck. Barron never left the foredeck—in fact, he never moved. He was flanked by those disgusting guards in black-and-malachite armour, a single eye slit in their helmets. Their stench was palpable.

And no one approached him.

It incensed her drive. He thought he was untouchable, even where he stood—above the battle—was a mockery. An allusion to his status of *head* viceroy. A mere self-appointed title. She was all too happy to bring him down to their level and—

A group of Galenite mercenaries blocked her path.

She growled, the red haze numbing her thoughts as she raised her sword, ready to cut their throats for daring to obstruct her, when a lean figure stumbled in front of them, his hands exposed, his dark brown eyes wide. He had short, curly silver hair, and brown skin that glistened in the light. His eyes were round and deer-like, and a labradorite suit clung to his slender frame.

He looked a lot like Skylar.

"Woah, woah, woah." His voice was oddly familiar, and she tilted her head.

Her water beast growled once again, the sound vibrating in her throat. All she knew was *kill, kill, kill.* And this male was in the way. Kora twirled her sword, her hands glowing blue as water rippled up the blade. Something about this male irked her, and her power crested, desperate to be unleashed.

"Listen to me, *cildbah.*"

The use of Devanian made her pause. Why was he calling her

a kid?

"State your business," she replied in the native tongue. Her voice was otherworldly. It didn't even sound like her.

"Just trying to stop a friend from doing something stupid."

"A friend?"

The male nodded, approaching slowly with his hands still raised. A red leather strap circled around his forehead, keeping longer coils of his hair out of his face.

"You remember me, *cildbah*."

The word sparked something deep within her. "I'm not stupid—you are," she snapped.

The male smiled and it was dazzling, lighting up his whole face.

"That's right, I'm dumb and you're smart." He was so close it made her shudder, followed by a sorrow that made her frown.

"Don't condescend me."

"I would never, *cildbah*. You know that." He placed a hand over his chest. His fingers were tattooed with intriguing symbols that unlocked a deep, dark corner in the depths of Kora's mind. Like a rush of air, a memory shot through her, tearing from the darkness in the form of a single word.

"Aerion," she tested the word on her tongue.

He nodded. "That's me."

"I know you," she stated simply.

"You do. What else do you remember?" Aerion was close enough that his scent washed over her. It was spicy, making her nose wrinkle—and it wasn't the scent she *wanted*.

She moaned, her head pounding, her two selves clashing against each other as she rocked forward. Her scar felt as though it was trying to tear itself from her skin. The cacophony of battle roared around them.

"You're not him," she groaned, rubbing her head. She didn't even know who she meant, but that lingering second self—her water beast—knew. It was clawing, crying, *gagging* for him.

"No, but I got all the beauty," Aerion chuckled.

The pale-stone-armoured mercenaries closed in, and panic bubbled inside of her, cutting off her oxygen. She was trapped again. Another male had lured and trapped her. Kora's breathing quickened, her heart hammering violently as the walls closed in around her.

"Get away!" she cried, crouching down as she clawed at her hair. She needed to escape, to get away—she needed to *breathe*.

"Step back!" Aerion spread his arms out, and the mercenaries *floated* backwards. Some charged into the ensuing battle, keeping soldiers at bay from them.

Kora swiped up with her sword, positioning it over Aerion's heart. "Who are you."

He glanced down at the sword amused. He had no weapons on his person, and he tapped the blade threatening his life with a bemused snort. "You're not going to kill me."

"Why shouldn't I? Galenites are murderers."

His dark eyes flashed. "That's a lie."

Something rippled around Aerion and she leapt back. She couldn't see what it was, but she could feel it—a lingering thread, an invisible piston of power. He cricked his neck and rolled his shoulders, as if shaking off a nuisance.

"You need to come with us." He shifted and the air tremored. Kora's own power reacted, and the ship rocked violently in the ocean. Masses of soldiers flew over the sides of the ship, screaming as they plummeted to their deaths. But not a single Galenite mercenary fell. No, they were rooted to the deck, immovable.

Now, there were more Galenites than Talmon soldiers.

"No." She raised her sword again, using it as a barrier of protection.

"You're always so stubborn," he shook his head fondly, a smile dancing on his lips.

"You don't know me." A rivulet of water jetted from the ocean, aiming for Aerion, but he deflected it with a simple dismissal of his hand.

"I know a lot about you actually. I know you can command the sea. I know it reacts to you like second nature. I know you *love* daggers—more than any normal person should. I know you prefer the winter, especially when it's snowing. I know your favourite flowers are hydrangeas, and your favourite colour is blue."

Kora staggered. Even Blake didn't know these things. She was an innately private person.

"What . . . who . . ."

"Think, *cildbah.*"

Who was this male to her? Her mouth gaped like a fish, her mind splitting and fracturing as she chased a dream. No . . . a *memory.*

"*Aerion!*"

Skylar's voice travelled on the winds, winding around them as if she were screaming next to them. They faced the quarterdeck, and Skylar tumbled down the stairs, her head bloody and her body limp.

Blake was right in front of them, breaking through the barrier of mercenaries. His face was bruised, and a thick slash tore the front of his leathers. But his sword . . . it was smeared with bright red blood, silver speckles glittering within it. Kora's knees weakened, knocking together from trembling.

"Now, time for the next Windward sibling," Blake sneered.

"You'll die for touching Skylar," Aerion spat.

"Anyone who touches what is *mine* will meet the same fate."

Aerion blinked, following Blake's possessive gaze on Kora, and she reeled backwards. They were back to this *game*. He still thought he owned her. That she belonged by his side. That the façade was still *real*.

Gods spare her, what was wrong with him?

"I believe she can make her own decisions," Aerion raised his hands, his tattooed fingers twirling.

She decided she liked this male, despite his bloodthirsty lineage.

"I have paperwork that says otherwise." Blake inclined to the metal collar around her throat.

Aerion's face twisted. "You utter scum."

In an instant, Aerion waved to Kora and her body *lifted,* carrying her away to the other side of the ship. Two mercenaries followed her, and she twisted in the air, her heart lifting with elation. She was *flying*—albeit a couple feet from the ground, over countless bodies, and mounds of death. But she was flying.

Ecstasy filled her, and her mind flashed back to lavender skies and pearlescent clouds. The feeling of warm winds carrying her as she dived through the air, her laughter bouncing around her along with the inviting presence of—

Her memory cut off as she landed port side, and the mercenaries grunted as they helped her to her feet. Their armour was fascinating. From far away, it looked like literal stone, but up close it was a shining opalescent metal, resembling gold, white, and pink all at once. Both guards were tall and broad, with dark skin and deep, kind eyes.

Had they been wrong about Galen?

Had everything Barron said been a lie?

Barron.

Kora cursed herself for being distracted, and she looked back to the foredeck. He was still there, observing the crescendo of warfare between ships. His back open and exposed to the battle raging below on deck.

Fool.

Retrieving her sword, she shouldered past the mercenaries, who followed closely behind. It was unnerving that they followed, like she was their leader. She approached the foredeck, her goal in sight, sweet revenge so close she could taste it on her tongue.

All she had to do was sneak up and plunge the sword right through his back, and it would all be over. There couldn't be a war without a leader. The viceroys would fall into chaos, and the continent would amass control, silencing this nonsense. Even if it meant she'd have to go into hiding with her elemental power. But she knew, in that instant, she would never let go of it again.

"My lady, don't go up there." A mercenary tentatively obstructed her path.

"I'm not your lady. Get out of my way."

"It's not wise. Forgive me, but you won't survive."

She laughed hysterically. "You clearly don't know me." She motioned to the sword, her power rippling around it like a second blade. Flicking her wrist, a second stream of water shot from her grip, creating a three-pronged sword, and she revelled in her lethality.

The mercenary's mouth thinned, and he held up a thick arm, blocking her way. "I must insist."

"Don't think I won't kill you." She placed her sword by his throat but he didn't move. Didn't even flinch. "Very well."

She pressed the blade into his flesh, blood welling around the sword, running down his neck and—she jumped back. Something within her cried out at the sight of what she was doing.

This wasn't right.

This was wrong.

This wasn't who she was.

She knew better. She *was* better.

She . . . she . . . she was a . . . she belonged to . . .

Kora crumpled. What was wrong with her? Her mind was ready to split in two, her power frantic, and she was losing control of it too easily. Screams echoed as rivers of sea water splashed across the deck, writhing across the ship in a vice-like grip, its fingers clenching, ready to drag it down to the depths.

Panic surged. Building up and up. The ship groaned, wood cracking and splintering. Her breathing stopped and she bent over, trying to gulp down breaths, but nothing was satiating her.

Soldiers yelled, grabbing hold of ropes to abandon the vessel to nearby flanking ships. Her lungs burned for air, her mind screaming in a torrent of emotions. The mercenaries stumbled as a pool of water collected at her feet, spreading like thick tar. Her throat so dry, she was desperate for water.

She had a deep, buried, burning *need.*

A desire.

It was all-consuming, and growing, taking over her body.

Right as she felt like she was going to combust, she was hit *hard* with the scent of rain clouds and steel.

"*I'm coming!*"

The voice returned.

"*I can hear you—I'm coming.*"

He was near.

"*Scream for me.*"

She wasn't sure why she obeyed, but she released a raw scream—guttural, feral, and animalistic. With it, a second layer of her body escaped, hovering above her skin. A blue, rippling humanoid screaming along with her, calling out to the voice.

Calling him home.

It was as clear as day. Her water beast knew this voice intimately. It was the bridged connection between them. All at once, it sucked back into her, the scent so overpowering her eyes streamed. Slowly turning on her heel, she met the most handsome male she'd ever seen.

"Hello, Kordelia."

H ello, Kordelia."
     She could hear his voice out loud *and* inside her mind. When his lips moved, the familiar voice she'd listened to for a decade echoed.

Her sword clattered to the deck.

He was striking, dazzling, and her fingers *itched* to touch him. He was the water that could quench her thirst, the air that could satiate her lungs. He was the missing *piece* in her broken mind. She thrummed with desire, with an unsatisfied need she realised now Blake could never have fulfilled. He may have ignited fiery simmering in her core, but this male caused her to erupt like an inferno.

Sun rays bounced off his silver hair, and Kora's eyes roved over his rippling muscles, contained within a leather fighting suit made of the same labradorite material as Skylar's and Aerion's. The sides of his head were shaved, and silver charms pierced his ears.

"You're alive," he sighed, beaming with joy.

His voice was like *butter*. Meltingly smooth, warm, and delightful. Temptation coaxed her, and she instinctively moved towards it, intoxicated by the sound. She was distinctly aware of a growl in her throat—no, a *purr*.

Gods' sake, she was purring at this male.

His smile broke into a grin at the sound, lighting up his handsome face. He didn't approach her, remaining by the side of the railing. As she neared, his eyes came into focus, dazzlingly reflective of their surroundings. They were like crystals, and when he blinked, they turned iridescent, surrounded by dark lashes. His light brown skin was smooth, and she had the strongest urge to *lick* the beads of water dripping from his skin and leathers.

"Come to me," he lured her willingly. Her legs pushed forward without thought, and somewhere in the pits of her mind, squeaked a voice telling her to stay away.

His smile wavered, like he could hear her thoughts. "It's okay, Kordelia."

Her brow furrowed. That wasn't her name. She faltered, and the male hesitated, his movements slow and obvious. Too obvious, as if he were afraid of spooking her. A soldier neared to their left, but a Galenite mercenary intercepted. In fact, a wave of mercenaries surrounded them, protecting them in a makeshift semi-circle.

"Do you know who I am?" He swallowed, his heavy gaze flickering to her throat. His face pinched at the collar.

"You're . . . him."

"Right," he laughed. And gods-damned wasn't it *magical*, causing the symphony of battle to fade away. There was only the two of them, in this blessed bubble. "I'm him. Who's him?"

"He's . . ." she winced, pain slicing down her mind as she tried to remember. She tapped her head. "He's here."

The male reached forward at the sign of her pain and Kora flinched back. Her arm waved, rippling with a liquid, rounded shield, defending herself against his attack. He paused, shrinking back, reining in his distress.

"Yes. That's me."

"*Yes. That's me.*"

It was alarming to hear his voice simultaneously in two places, but her water beast delighted in it, curling over inside of her, purring, and clawing to connect.

"I . . ." she shuddered at his closeness, at his scent. "I'm broken."

His face softened. "I can fix you."

"How?"

She found herself stepping towards him again and, this close, she had to tilt her head to look up at him. His jaw was sharp, and on impulse she ran a single finger down its edge. He moaned, leaning into her touch, and heat collected between her legs at the sound. She could listen to him moan over and over again. Her finger sizzled at the contact.

He slowly, gently, placed a large hand on her chest, his eyes deliberately looking down to show her what he was doing. Her pulse raced as the male pushed down slightly on her chest, and Kora was propelled backwards by a flash of power, sending her into the darkness of the void.

Darkness. Emptiness. Void.

She was somehow back here—and she was awake. This wasn't a dream, it was real life. It was jarring to experience. To be in existence and to cease being, all at once. The past, present, and future converged on Kora, and she released a flare of her power.

Beautiful blue light bloomed from her core, spreading into a webbed structure all around her. It grew and expanded within the void, feathering out in intricate loops and swirls, stretching and twining. The threads echoed with sounds—voices, and when Kora touched one, a memory of her life flashed before her eyes.

She soared across her timeline, picking at the exposed threads of her mind.

Celebrating her birthday last year with Samuel and Erick.

Bree visiting when Kora caught the flu two winters ago.

Surviving the Darkoning Trials with Blake.

When she'd first defeated Erick during one of their training sessions years ago.

Her first time sailing a ship.

As she delved further into her past, peeling back the years, the blue threads dimmed, becoming infrequent and sparse. Soon, her intricate webbed structure diminished to a few frayed strands, the far ends fading from a glowing vibrant blue to a writhing shadowy black. The strands were decaying and rotting, their layers peeling away and drifting into the void where they evaporated into nothing.

"*It ends here.*"

His voice was here with her. She couldn't see him, but their connection burned brightly in her mind.

"*They have destroyed the tether to your true self—he has invaded your mind and left disease.*"

Those sickening, writhing shadows hissed, flailing in the void at the sound of his voice, and Kora grabbed onto them, her hands burning *cold.* Ice collected on her palms, cascading up her arms. Her water humanoid form began to freeze over, and she panicked.

"Help me!"

Her limbs froze solid, and the stinging chill chased up her

spine, smothering her chest, wrapping around her throat, suffocating her.

"Help me—*Raiden*!"

With a clap of thunder, Kora plummeted back into her body.

The force sent her careening into Raiden's arms, and he pulled her towards him, burying his face in her neck, inhaling deeply. The sensation of returning from the void made her head spin, and her legs gave way. He held her up, stroking the short strands of her hair.

"I've got you," he murmured.

She pulled away to look at him—at Raiden.

He frowned at her expression. "Kordelia?"

She pushed away from him, scowling. "That's not my name," she snapped.

The devastation on Raiden's face made her want to rush over to him, to comfort him, to tell him that it's okay—that *she's* got him.

It was utterly baffling, and she clenched her fists, attempting to suppress this *infatuation*.

"You don't remember," he observed.

"No. I don't know who you are."

Raiden looked away, his jaw clenching, and her chest tightened. She felt the wild, second side of herself fade away, her clarity returning. What the fuck was she doing? She was supposed to do something . . . she was supposed to kill someone.

"I'm nobody important. Now, tell me who you *think* you are." His tone riled her, and she stooped to swipe her sword from the deck.

"I'm Kora fucking Cadell. I *know* who I am."

Raiden stilled. "Cadell," he repeated.

She lifted her chin. "Yes, and?"

"That traitorous *swine*." The snarl tearing from Raiden's throat was truly terrifying and animalistic. A gust of wind whipped across the deck, and groups of bodies lifted and smashed against the masts of the ship, their spines cracking in two. The masts groaned, the already-splintered wood cracking deeper, and the iron-gated brig sprung open, metal warping from the force.

As the wind raged . . . it never touched Kora. In fact, she

couldn't feel it at all.

"*Raiden!*"

Aerion darted towards them, carrying an unconscious Skylar in his slender arms, with Aryn hot on his heels. The sight was conflicting, like two puzzle pieces that didn't fit together. Kora's spinning head threatened to curdle her knotted stomach, and she inhaled deep, ragged breaths.

Behind them, Talmon soldiers had been obliterated, and the deck was eerily quiet. Kora searched for a familiar green cape, but there was no sign of Erick, and bile burned her throat. Had he been caught in Raiden's power . . . or worse . . . hers?

"We need to go now," Aryn ordered. "Do your thing, Windward," he spoke to Raiden.

"Which one of us are you talking to?" Aerion chuckled, and Aryn rolled his slanted eyes.

The knot turned into a barbed twist. Aryn *knew* the Windward siblings. He knew their names, who were they were . . . what they could *do*. That they had magic, and it was elemental like hers.

Kora scrambled away. She couldn't be near this—them. Galen was the *enemy*. They were bloodthirsty killers, they murdered innocents, and tried to destroy the Azarian Islands in the last war. They killed Eleanore and Erick's unborn babe.

They were barbarians.

And Aryn was one of *them*. He didn't look the same, or act the same as them, but he was intimately familiar.

"Kora," Aryn hurriedly followed. "You need to trust me. I know it's scary—"

"You don't know anything!" she snapped. "You *lied* to me. Everyone *lied* to me. You're a Galenite, aren't you?"

"I wasn't born one, if that's what you're asking."

"You chose to be one—that's *worse*."

"So did you, once."

The words stunned her. They couldn't be true. It wasn't true. She wouldn't be something as awful as a Galenite.

"You need to come with us. I'm asking you to trust me one more time, Captain." Kora winced at the title. "When have I let you down before?"

It was true. Aryn may have lied about *a lot* of things—too many things to currently process—but he'd always been there. He'd always saved her, and been an ear to listen to her problems. Even his *medical field training* came in handy a couple times.

Her gaze flickered to the Windward siblings lingering behind him. Aerion smiled at her sheepishly, his features aloof, with his unconscious sister clutched in his arms. Skylar was taller, more muscled than Aerion, but he cradled her as if she were as light as a feather.

Raiden stood apart from them, his fists clenching and unclenching. His gaze wholly fixed on Kora and the world melted away, leaving just her and Raiden in their little void. She was the single point in his life, the blue light revolving around his darkness, and it took her breath away.

A light tremble shook through her, pooling in her core. Raiden's eyes dipped down, and then back up to her eyes, his lips twitching amusedly. Surely *that* was better than Talmon? Besides, they held the key to her past—to her family. She needed answers, and the truth. They could possess the power to unlock her memory.

"Okay," she shakily exhaled.

"Okay," Aryn smiled gently, his golden eyes beckoning her to follow as he turned back.

A hand reached out and grabbed Kora by the shoulder, digging into her freshly healed wound, and she yelled as she was ripped backwards, careening into a body reeking of petrichor and bitter *soil.* She writhed, confused by the change of scent, as Blake's hands clamped around her arms, and Barron stepped forward, his hands clasped behind his back.

"Raiden Windward," Barron rolled his name off his tongue. "I've been waiting a long time for you to return."

Raiden's huge form advanced, positioning his siblings behind him. Aryn nocked an arrow, aiming at Blake, who laughed in return.

"Well, being trapped by magical Mist made it a little difficult. We tried to send postcards." Raiden shrugged casually. It was a contrast to the barely contained fury on his face.

Trapped.

Kora's fingers flexed, trying to summon the ocean beneath the ship. Blake tightened his grip, his arms snaking around her body, holding her flush against him. He squeezed until she gasped, the air forcibly pushed from her lungs.

"None of that." He stroked down the side of her face to her metal collar.

Raiden growled, and an invisible hand whipped Blake, snapping his face to the side.

"Ah, now, now," Barron unclasped his hands as Blake stumbled with Kora still firmly in his grip. "Let's play nice, shall we? I do love reunions."

"Unfortunately, we can't stay. We'll take some grog to go." Raiden bared his teeth.

Aryn tightened his grip on his longbow, the bowstring so taut it shook. But it wasn't just the longbow. The entire ship was shaking, and Kora teetered as the wooden deck vibrated, shuddering up her legs.

"You see, I can't allow any of you to leave," Barron darkly chuckled.

Aerion cursed, and Kora craned her neck, locating the source of the tremor behind them. A large Talmon Empire capital vessel flanked the ship, attached with several, wide gangplanks. Rows of soldiers marched upon the ship across them. An endless stream of bodies. They all donned the black-and-malachite heavy armour, and a stale, rotted stench permeated the air, making her eyes water. Their heavy, booted feet pounded across the decked wood, the ship vibrating with every uniformed step.

There were so many. *Gods,* they were doomed.

Raiden's eyes flared, and he glanced around the ship.

"Your fleet has abandoned you," Barron gestured to the empty oceans. "You're too *weak.*"

"Shit." Aerion tightened his grip on Skylar, who moaned faintly in his arms. "*He* called the fleet back. We need to go."

Kora strained against Blake's clutches. The Galenite fleet had *vanished.* Not a single white sail peaked on the horizon. Who was Aerion referring to? Who had power to summon an entire fleet in minutes?

"I'm not leaving without her." A blast of wind circled Raiden, the thick hair atop his head wafting. She could *see* the glimmer of his magic—a sparkling, iridescent silver, like diamonds, winding around him.

"She doesn't know who you are," Barron glanced at Kora with a wink, and that sickening cold crept over her. "Why not start afresh? Leave her with us, where she belongs."

"Never." Raiden's blast of wind increased into a gale force, creating his own little cyclone on the ship. "She belongs in Galen."

The words simultaneously made her want to scream with horror and jump with joy. It was so nauseating having two selves within her, scrambling to the surface for control.

"She doesn't want you!" Blake spat. "*Kora* chose for herself already." He licked and kissed the side of her face and she wrenched her head away. *No thank you.*

The realisation dawned in Raiden's crystalised eyes, and she wasn't sure why it upset her so much—why it *mattered* to Raiden that she and Blake used to be an item. He'd said he was nobody important. But now, the sheer pain and rawness in Raiden's face at Blake staking his claim on her, was completely void shattering.

Raiden's power exploded—and Kora had never experienced anything like it. It dwarfed her own. The skies thundered, lightning bolting through clear blue sky, crackling across the ship. The air cleaved in two, split apart as a cyclone tore up into the heavens, hurtling their way.

The soldiers rushed across the deck, and Raiden faltered as his magic *bounced* off them. Aryn fired arrows at the soldiers, but his arrows snapped in half upon impact. They were outnumbered, and they were all going to die, because of her—*again.*

Raiden turned to face Blake and Kora, and he held out his hand, squeezing an invisible force. Blake stumbled, choking, releasing her. She fell to her knees as Blake coughed and choked, clawing at his neck, gasping for air.

"Run, baby. Run to me!" Raiden yelled over the torrents of his power. She was no one's *baby*, but now wasn't the time for that discussion.

Aerion stumbled onto the railing, his flight suit expanded. Skylar's unconscious body hovered in the air beside him, blood dripping from her skull.

Kora pelted forwards as Barron howled with a thunderous might. This was it. She had a chance. That tiny kernel of hope exploded in her chest, threatening to blindly consume her as the thundering neared behind her. Desperate. She was *so desperate.* Or was that Raiden?

"*Hurry!*" he screamed in her mind.

A wave of cold flashed through the atmosphere, and her back arched painfully, sharp metal slicing down her spine. Her right arm stretched out, reaching for Raiden as he frantically tried to grab hold of her. He was panicked, and it echoed deep in the recesses of her mind, his fear matching her own.

She wasn't going to make it. *No, no, no!*

"Raiden, I can't—"

Her other arm flung back, pressing into the side of her face as her scar flared with a deadly coldness that spread. It snaked down her jaw, curling under the metal collar, like frostbite clenching her windpipe, cutting off her air supply. Her body went rigid, her power fading. Raiden's grasp was mere inches away, his warmth and presence crying out to her.

"*No!*"

Raiden's cry was the last thing Kora heard as her mind and body were ripped back forcefully, dragging her into the cold clutches of death.

58

B ring her back."

"I'm trying, it's like she's holding on."

"Just do it—but not too much. We don't want her at full power."

The cold receded. Voices faded in and out. A glimmer of light bled through the crack of silent darkness, and Kora retreated.

It was all too much.

She wasn't ready to face the world—her world.

But here, she could be free. The silence was comforting, and the darkness soothed her. She floated through empty nothingness. No one telling her what to do, no one telling her what she couldn't do. No one lying to her.

No one breaking her heart.

"Are your powers waning? Bring her back *now*."

The light cracked and she hissed, scarpering further into the depths of death. Small, intricate glowing vines spread from the crack. They were lush and green, with secondary smaller black vines twirling around them. They searched the void, probing . . . hunting.

She kicked out at one and a voice jeered. "She's fighting me. I've never experienced this before."

As she descended, death's cold grip became tangible.

Multitudes of hands clawed at her body, dragging her down, down, down.

"No! She's . . . she's going to Umbra."

Ice bloomed in her lungs, her eyes, her hair turning to icicles. Her skin shone blue with death.

"What?" *A loud bang thundered through the void.* "Must I do everything!"

Invisible wheezy voices shrieked, and the hands of death shrank, dissolving. She tried to cry out, to beg death to take her, but a puff of icy smoke wafted from her lips.

Inky black tar slithered in from the crack. Something darker than night—darker than death. The vines coiled away from it, clinging to the edges of the shining splintered crack. Kora hurried, floating through the void. Gradually, the darkness faded to a hazy mist, speckled with floating ash. The cold no longer existed. Replaced by a numbness.

Sweet, numb relief.

The light of the crack began to fade.

As Kora drifted through the ashen void, her sensations dulled, and a thin, frayed cloth appeared. She floated through it, the fabric sweeping over her, until she was met with another. She floated through that. It was neither cold nor warm, nor light nor dark. It shimmered with . . . something, *leaving a trail of sparks on her iced skin.*

Layer after layer of fabric folded over her.

"It's not your time, gifted one."

She halted in the folds of the cloth. It was iridescent, shimmering from black to grey, tiny sparkles running through the weaves.

"Thanos."

"Why are you so desperate to enter my realm?"

"I . . ." she hesitated, ashamed to tell the God of Death she'd simply had enough.

"That's not a reason to die."

"Right . . . of course you can read my mind."

Her fingers brushed over the weaves of Thanos' barrier. His grey cloth, held by his very own hands. Was he above somewhere, manipulating the fabric like a puppeteer? Those individual sparkles glimmered, consuming every possible thread, tiny little dots flittering about.

"They are all of my souls."

She gasped, spinning around. Thanos' barrier stretched endlessly, folds upon folds leading to the realm of Umbra, carrying all passed souls—and they were beautiful. She had read of this in Agatha's tomes, she was in the Eternal Tryk. The passage for souls to enter the spirit realm of Umbra—just on the other side of Thanos' cloth.

Passing through it was impossible for living souls. She should've been absorbed by now, blending into the fabric of realms, finding her eternal resting place in the afterlife . . . if she were truly dead. Instead, she was caught in the swaths of the glittering, heavenly weave.

Gods' sake, she couldn't even die properly.

Somewhere, in the endless Eternal Tryk, a familiar soul drifted past. A shining star, a twinkle in the dark of night. It rippled across the folds of the barrier, and a small warmth radiated from it. The scent of wooden ash and smoke permeated the atmosphere.

"Please . . ." *Kora trembled.* "I can't."

"It pains me to see you begging for death. You possess great power, now is not the time to waste it."

"There's nothing left for me. My life is destroyed."

"Life is subjective. Do not complain because you have made mistakes."

"Mistakes?" *She swiped for the cloth, but simply passed through to the next fold.* "So many of these souls are here because of me. I condemned them. I . . . killed them. I am a murderer. I do not deserve to even be here. But please . . . I can't . . ." *The urge to weep was overpowering, but frosted ice dusted her cheeks instead.*

"Many have killed. And many will continue to do so. Do not bear the burden of the actions of others. I welcome all souls, regardless of their stain on the world. Death changes all."

"Then please . . . take me."

"All that happens, is because it was willed to do so. If you cannot enter my realm, then it is not willed."

"Then will it! Make it so!" *She'd had enough.*

"Your time is not now. Someday, you will meet your end, at the hands of your own. I cannot let you enter. Your destiny is yet to be fulfilled."

"What . . . what do you mean?"

"Calypso has more planned for you. I cannot interfere with another god's will. You have great purpose, Kordelia."

A terrifying, otherworldly force knocked her back. It enveloped her, pushing her through the depths and away from Umbra. She catapulted through the folds of the barrier, flying through the ashen void, past the frozen tunnel of lost souls.

"Stay strong until we meet again. You are one of the blessed."

The sickening, inky tar latched onto her back, dragging her towards the light.

"See? She's coming to."

"Something wasn't right. I could feel her at Thanos' door—"

"Don't speak his name. We do not worship the old gods anymore."

The vines tentatively grasped hold of Kora's limbs before winding around her body, and tears streamed down her face as the barrier to Umbra faded in the distance.

"Kora? Time to wake up."

Warmth surged through her, her bones snapping back into place, her skin regaining moisture and air as Kora sucked in a hungering, dry breath.

And then she opened her eyes.

59

G reen light blinded her. Kora's skin was sallow, and she blinked, adjusting from escaping the Eternal Tryk.

"There she is."

Barron.

Trees loomed over and all around her. Twisted, thick dark roots clawed from the ground, mud slicking her already filthy leathers. A pair of hands hovered over her body, searching, probing, and she swatted Blake away, scrambling until the rough bark of a tree scraped her back.

She was in the Emerald Forest. Just about. The path to her left led to the Citadel, and through the break of trees, she could spot the sweet, sweet ocean.

Blake paused, his green stare tracking her every movement. He wringed his hands before shaking them, as if something on them bothered him. Barron stood nearby, his oil-black hair dishevelled, donning a black longcoat and shirt. He was surrounded by *those* guards, and the reek of them made her gag. They smelled unnatural.

"Welcome back, Kora," Barron sharply smiled. "You gave us quite the scare."

"How did we get here?"

"Oh, you've been unconscious for a day. We needed to get you somewhere safe, away from those pesky rebels."

She swallowed the lump in her throat. The metal collar was still clasped around her neck—the constant reminder she was a prisoner, a slave, to this bilge rat. She used the trunk of the tree to steady herself, slowly raising to her feet. Her legs trembled. She felt *so* weak.

Blake's face was taut, lips thin, and he hovered between her and Barron, warily glancing at the latter. Last time she'd been here, she'd revealed her power to him.

Perhaps she could do it again.

In an instant, she flung her hand out, clenching her jaw as she claimed the final small dregs of her power. She was utterly drained—a trip to the Eternal Tryk would do that. A slither of water shot from the ground, spearing to her hand. It morphed instinctively, and she clasped a shimmering sabre dagger, aiming at Barron.

He stood there, his smile broadening into a grin. His dark eyes alight with amusement. "Blake!" He clicked his fingers.

Blake sighed, and with a simple flutter of his fingers, the tree behind her twisted, branches wrapping around her body, pinning her to the trunk. Vines erupted from the ground, twisting around her ankles and wrists, another circling her forehead, pulling her head back roughly against the bark.

Blake prowled slowly, his eyes *burning* a deep, green ember. A shiver rippled through him, and his dark shadow emerged, echoing his footsteps, but always a second behind. The vines clenched against Kora's skin. They were cold, and her skin turned blue from their touch.

Blake halted, and her nose wrinkled at his developing scent. He smelled like the earth, of soil and petrichor, and leaves in the autumn. He *was* the earth. Another elemental counterpart.

"I was disappointed you never noticed," he spoke quietly. "The blessed can usually recognise each other."

"Don't believe in magic then?" Kora sniped.

His mouth twisted. "I did what I had to. We live in a world where magic was forbidden. Keeping it from you was paramount to our survival."

"I shouldn't be surprised. You've kept enough secrets from me."

"I never lied. Only omitted the truth."

She barked a sharp laugh. "This is a pretty fat truth. What else have you *omitted?*"

His jaw snapped, refusing to divulge any further secrets.

"Magic is still forbidden, we're both breaking the law. The empire will kill us."

"Not anymore," Barron interjected, and Blake startled, as if remembering Barron was still there. He reluctantly stepped away. "These are *my* lands now."

"And let me guess, you're pro-mage?"

Barron's smile quirked. "You could say that."

His hand twirled in the air, and with sickening amazement,

darkness bled from his skin. It writhed like a living shadow, tendrils leaking into the air. His power permeated her skin, its strength chilling her bones and setting her scar alight. Except this time, the pain snaked down her jaw and into her neck, and she winced.

This power was new. It hadn't been recorded in any of the mage factions. No god had displayed this kind of . . . shadow wielding.

It felt familiar. She'd experienced this kind of darkness before, and Kora hissed as a memory surfaced and faded, warring against the frayed tendrils plaguing her mind. A memory of unbearable pain, blood, and a sad male telling her she was home.

"Is that what this is about? A world for mages? Just change the law, you have the power to do that."

Barron shook his head. "No. It's much *more* than that. Changing the law is not enough. We need to wipe the slate clean and start again."

Blood drained from Kora's face, as his intentions settled across the grassy plain. "This war is wrong, Barron. You're killing innocents! You can't kill everyone who isn't a mage!"

His face darkened at the mention of his name and he strode forward. She cringed away, his presence setting every nerve ablaze with horror.

"*We* are the blessed. *We* are the chosen ones. Mages are far superior to human scum. The witches are a mere copy of us. They're humans who were desperate for magic, creating a pitiful, shameful replica."

This male was insane.

"Their witch-seers are the only . . . *things* worth keeping around. They can predict the fates, the will that will be. And I have seen glory. And pirates? They're the worst of them all. They can all rot in the Tryk." Spittle flew from Barron's mouth.

"The witches' prophecy," she wheezed against the branches tightening over her lungs. Blake hovered behind Barron, observing them both intently. "You think it's about restoring the mages?"

Barron's smile returned. "You've been busy, pet. I see your amnesia hasn't stopped you." Kora flinched. "Lost to the void, power ignites. Torn across the land, harbour the vessel. And sacrifice to the rift," he recited.

That made no sense whatsoever.

"Prophecies aren't truth. That could mean anything."

"No, but they guide the hands of fate. A fate I aim to secure for myself. My power will ignite the tear in our lands, and I will sacrifice the scum to attain glory."

Kora wriggled against Blake's magic. The ends of his fingers were dusted brown, as if he'd plunged his hands into soil.

"And I want you by my side," Barron continued.

He . . . what?

Blake's magic faltered, vines loosening as he pivoted to Barron, shocked. Their words an echo of each other.

"What?" Blake snapped.

Barron barely glanced at him. "The power of the ocean is *vital*. As I said, you are the turning tide in this war."

"Is having the power of the earth not enough for you?" She glared at Blake.

"His power is . . . temperamental." Blake deflated at Barron's words. "The ocean outweighs the land. I need *your* power. With it, we will be unstoppable. We will fulfil the prophecy and restore mages. Imagine . . . a fresh, new world. No pirates. No humans. No . . . *vermin*. Not even Azaria would dare challenge us. We will use the nobles for purity. We will become new gods, in this new world."

Gods? He was more than insane.

"And if I say no?"

Barron tapped the metal collar around her neck. "Don't forget, I own you." As he walked back to his reeking guards, he clapped Blake's shoulder as he passed him. "Something I can thank my son for."

Son.

Blake's shoulders hunched as she jolted in shock against her unnatural imprisonment. *Son.* The matching black hair, the sharp features. *Son.* The similar cold demeanour and tall frame. *Son.* Their eyes were completely different, as were their powers, but now that she *looked*, they were mirrors of each other.

"*Son?*" she seethed.

"Oh, yes. I forget. You see, I couldn't let you go running back to Galen. Your memory may be impaired, but I couldn't sever your connection to them entirely," Barron waffled. "I needed to keep tabs on you, without you getting suspicious."

"You . . . no. I lost my memory from a pirate attack. I . . ." Barron's sly, darkening grin halted her words. "You! You took my memory?" Kora sagged with disbelief.

We can't lose her.

I'll see to it that she doesn't.

The memory slammed into her.

That thing *lurked in the doorway to the room. Opulence of gold and moss covered every stone wall, every crevice.*

She'd been to Mossfell Castle before—a bloody mess, with a giant gash down the side of her face. Erick had pinned her down as Barron entered the room, a living, writhing shadow that'd entered her mind.

And wiped everything away.

An endless, bloodcurdling scream ravaged her mind.

"It wasn't pirates," she whispered. Her words fell upon deaf ears as Barron rambled on.

"Getting our hands on you in the first place was difficult. Raiden and his jolly crew kept you protected on that island," he spat with vitriol. "Once I finally had you, I had to make sure you wouldn't go back. My son provided an excellent *distraction*. I couldn't lose an elemental. Not one like you."

Galen was . . . *innocent.*

The Talmon Empire was the *enemy.*

Did Erick know? Had he been spun the same lies from Barron, fuelling his vendetta against rebels for Eleanore?

She'd been hunting innocents for ten years. Trained as a weapon against her own people. She was a murderer, a reaper of her own kind. She'd single-handedly tipped the scales in the empire's favour by hunting pirates and rebels.

Her body screamed. Every nerve, every pulse, every pore cried with agony of what she'd so blindly, *willingly*, done.

And Blake was the real spy. The real enemy. Not Finlay. Not the Skytors. *Blake.*

She shot a venomous glare at him as she heaved against the vines, bark biting into her skin. With a raging cry, the earth shook, water oozing from the ground and mixing with the soil to create slick, watery mud. Droplets lifted into the air as the tree containing her cracked, and Blake flinched at the sound.

"Ah! I wouldn't do that." Barron gestured to the reeking guards, and they parted like a diseased wave, revealing a kneeling figure gagged and bound.

Erick was bleeding *everywhere.*

His face had been beaten to a pulp, black and blue with bruises. His armour had been removed, leaving him shivering, his hairy, bare chest exposed, with only trousers covering his body. Kora paled. His back had been whipped and was crusted with blood and, around his neck, was a thick, metal collar.

"Kor . . . a," he muffled around the gag.

"Silence!" A guard kicked Erick in the back and he sprawled

into the mud.

Tears brimmed her eyes. He had lied to her, kept her past and powers from her, but she couldn't bear to see him like this. Barron paused, noting the tears cascading down her cheeks.

"You feel such emotion for this male," he observed. "After everything he's done to you, and you still cry for him. I didn't expect an attachment to form between you two."

She frowned, and a sniffle followed. "He lied to me about my powers. Doesn't mean he deserves this."

Barron threw back his head and laughed. The sound truly horrified her.

"My apologies, pet. I keep forgetting how much you don't remember." *Ouch.*

Erick cried out in the mud, pushing to his knees and begging Barron to stop. The guards kicked him again, pressing their heavy boots into his back, and he spluttered, mud caking his face as he suffocated. She yelled until Barron motioned for them to stop.

"You know, Erick and I have been friends for a long time." Barron paced the grassy plain. "In fact, when we *knew* we needed you, he became my informant on the inside. He infiltrated Galen, befriended your family and the Windwards . . . and then snatched you right out from under them." Barron's slick smile sent shivers through her, his hand passing through the air, imitating the snatch.

No . . . no, he wouldn't.

"And we ensured they could never find you ever again. Placing you in his care, on the island furthest from Galen. Under *strict* instructions to keep you hidden until it was time to make our move. Allowing you in the trials, though, I was not impressed. Erick clearly has no control over you. So I had to send my son in after you. To make sure you remained loyal to us."

She stilled. Erick had vehemently begged her not to participate. Blake had been her saving grace, an unpredicted alliance, and an unprecedented win . . . but the trials had been fixed. Barron needed their power. He couldn't afford for them to die in the trials.

Even *that* had been a lie.

Barron's gaze flicked to her hair and he grunted, as if her appearance was distasteful. Erick choked on his gag, desperately seeking her attention. He had tried to hide her in plain sight . . . as a male. The haircuts. The clothes. The attitude. It was all to suppress her true self.

Everything was a fucking lie.

Erick protested through the gag, and his muffled pleas raked against Kora's ears as she looked away from him.

"What of my family?" she whispered. "Are they alive?"

Blake choked at her question.

Barron neared, until his cold breath tickled her face. He tucked a piece of hair behind her ear, the sensation icing her skin, and Erick screamed from behind.

"Your *real* father is still alive, yes. I couldn't tell you about the rest."

She glanced to Blake, his face sickeningly pale.

"Please don't tell me it's you."

Barron chuckled. "God no, lucky me." He winked and Kora gagged. Barron had no scent, only cold darkness. His presence made her muscles tense to the point of snapping, her teeth grinding, her scar screaming.

It all made perfect sense now. He was the black mark upon her soul. He was the blockage. The fraying ends of her void. He had destroyed the tether to her previous life, to her powers.

"Who is my father?"

"The question is *where*, Kora. Your father is the most famous sailor in all of history, and he currently resides at the bottom of the Black Abyss."

60

K ora was a daughter of the dark sea. She was a harbourer of
death and a siren of oceans.

"He . . . what?"

Her ears roared, and her stare helplessly snapped to
Erick as his eyes begged and pleaded with her. He'd forced lies upon
her, warping her mind to loathe pirates and Galen. Made her believe
she was acting in revenge.

He'd betrayed her, and Galen, and had the audacity to parade
as her *father*. It was the final sickening twist in her heart. To top it
all off, he'd condemned her true father to the bottom of the darkest
trench. Was he still alive down there? Nothing could survive the
Black Abyss.

Erick's conversation with Theron rang in her mind. A kraken
lived in its depths. Was it *real*? And that meant . . . her father was
Davy Jones. *Good gods.* Her father was folklore. He was legend.

He was death.

Barron's thunderous dark eyes roved over her hungrily. He
wanted her. Coveted her blessed *gifts*. He'd done everything he
could to obtain her, to isolate her, and to break her. He'd used Erick
and Blake in the process to keep tabs on her, to manipulate her
feelings and to blind her.

"Bastion!" Erick tugged his gag free, wrenching his face from
the mud. "We had a deal!"

Barron whirled, dark shadows leeching from his skin, and
writhing in the air as his voice boomed, cracking like a whip.
"You're a traitor who tried to take Kora away from me! Where were
you taking her? Back to Galen?" He scoffed. "They'd never accept
you now. You'd die in their Mist before you could reach their
wretched shores. But that's all you're good at, isn't it? Being a

traitor. You betrayed the Windwards, you betrayed Kora, and now me."

His power speared for Erick and he flipped back as black tendrils of tar wrapped around his body, squeezing, choking, draining his life. Kora screamed, the ground rumbling with her power as her heart shattered in her ears. Erick's life faded, his body paling, his eyes rolling into the back of his skull.

The ground vibrated and shook, and Blake stumbled, warily glancing at her. He shrank away from Barron's inky tendrils, cringing at the might of his father's magic.

As Erick's breaths shallowed, Barron released his power, seemingly satisfied with the torture. "Take him away. I'm done with him."

The guards hoisted Erick's limp, unconscious body, and carried him towards the Citadel. Kora panted, her heart pounding in her chest. She was well and truly fucked.

"You called it . . . *their* Mist," she spoke between wrenching breaths. "It's not from the gods?"

Barron hissed. "No," followed by a sigh. "I have spent a decade observing the phenomenon. I threw mages at it, testing their powers against it. But, alas, nothing. Whatever the source, it's coming from within. It is not external. And it's not the *gods*." He spat the final word.

"Mages," she repeated, trying to detach the vines whilst Barron was distracted. He certainly loved a show, and an audience. "You have access to mages?"

He nodded, a gleam in his eye. "Yes, but don't worry, pet. None of them are as exquisite as you."

This fucking male.

"So, you're working with the Skytors?" She took her shot and hoped it would land.

Barron stormed closer. "Those rebels will die for everything they stand for. They've been hunting you for a decade, and they nearly succeeded."

"But they didn't. Because someone intercepted their lead and killed Finlay Blackstone." She pushed against the cold vines, their grip loosening. "I see it now. I see you for who you truly are . . . *Blake*."

His head whipped up, eyes flaring.

"You were the rat!" An inch gap formed between her back and the trunk. "The letter delivered to the crew had my seal, and only the two of us had access to it. Only you and the pit guards could unlock the cells. You knew who Finlay was. That's why you were so harsh on him. And you used Silas to silence him before we made port."

"Clever." His hand ran through his onyx hair. "I tried to keep you away from it." His gaze flickered to her lips, down her body, and she halted. He had used seduction as a distraction. "But Finlay made it to the bell before Silas could finish the job. I hadn't accounted for the second twin to intervene."

Bile bubbled up her throat. "And that's why you sent the messenger hawk ahead of time to Erick," the pieces of the puzzle fit together. "You wanted Jack disposed of before he could reveal your secret."

"Their twin bond was unfortunate. But I had to protect you from the Skytors."

"Protect?" she snapped, as the vines loosened further. She could nearly reach Barron, who observed the exchange with heightened interest. "They were trying to rescue me from *you!* Doran knew, didn't he? The exiles weren't only after me, they wanted *you* dead!"

"Yes, but Samuel disposed of him for me, without realising the favour he'd bestowed. In fact, you pretty much wiped out all the exiles in one go. Saved me a job."

She scoffed in repulsion. "So much death, all so you could control me, force me to join your petty war. Samuel is in there right now! He could be dead and you don't care. Theron and Ivar, too."

"They're all traitors, they deserve their fates," Blake's eyes frosted over as Barron beamed at his son.

He'd orchestrated Finlay's death, and her essence screamed at the depths of his betrayal. And what about the remaining Skytors? John had fled the tavern. Had Blake somehow disposed of him, too? Had he stalked her throughout the town, killing any connection she created?

Gods, had he been to the Silvermaid Emporium?

Panic swelled, her skin alighting with the endless list of possible names floating in Thanos' cloth. How many souls had recognised her?

"Hmm," Barron mused, observing her. "What to do with you."

"You had your fun," Kora snapped. He had enjoyed revealing the betrayal layer by layer, his smile sickeningly gleeful. "Be done with it."

"Sending you back to the God of Death would be most

unwise." His head tilted and he signalled to Blake. "Desiccate her again, some time in the forest might make her change her mind."

Desiccate?

She needed to escape.

Now.

She lurched as the groans of the dead swarmed the forest. Blake hesitatingly stepped forward, and the ground rose to meet his foot. Knots of grass latched onto his boot, the ground coming alive and rumbling in response to him.

She shoved with her might against the tree as the groans increased. Clawed, tree-barked hands erupted from the ground, grasping for her legs, searching for a fresh body to pull under. Vines cracked around her body, and the one circling her head crumbled.

"It was you, in the forest!" she cried as he neared.

"As I said, *asterya*, I was quite disappointed you didn't recognise me then for what I was."

"You see, my son has a singular exceptional gift." Barron placed a hand on Blake's shoulder. "He can drain the life from any being, and gift it upon himself. Unfortunately, it doesn't extend to another, otherwise I'd have exceptionally smooth skin."

Blake's injuries from the battle with Skylar healed as he leeched her life, his skin knitting together, blood re-absorbing into his body and smoothing over, leaving no trace of injury. Pain spliced through her as her leg shrivelled, her trousers sagging as her muscles atrophied. She collapsed, the weakening vines holding the upper half of her body up as she lost one limb.

"*Stop!*"

"Not only that, but he can also keep someone on the precipice of death, in a state of limbo, if you will. And that's where we'll keep you. Desperate to die, unable to live. Unless you change your mind about joining us willingly." Barron flashed a smile.

She attempted to spit at him, but she only managed a couple of dried, blood-crusted teeth as the decomposition spread up her left side. Her drying tongue scraped against the hollow sockets in her mouth.

Blake flicked his wrist and the vines snapped in half. Kora tumbled, falling at his feet, and a devoid, expressionless face graced her as he directed his power across her frame. Her bag-of-bones frame tickled her mind, dragging up figures of familiar gaunt faces with rapidly thinning bodies that possessed impossible strength.

Barron applauded Kora's decaying form. "Well done, my son. You've earned a promotion. A spot for commodore has just opened . . ."

Their voices trailed off, and her mind spun. She'd be gods-damned if she died now. Not after everything that'd been revealed. With a mighty roar, she painfully pushed her decaying body up and lunged at Blake, grabbing on to his hands.

She was descendent of Calypso. He was descendent of Kaiah. And so, she called upon the gods.

Power erupted between them in a clash of green and blue, wisps of darkness leaking through. Her teeth gritted as water pooled, writhing around her body, lifting her hair into the sky. Nature exploded around Blake, leaves of all colours, vines and rocks cutting through the air as her power reached out and reclaimed what was hers.

Life slammed back into her all at once and she rocked back, her body and power invigorated. She conjured her water-sabre dagger as Blake unsheathed his golden cutlass sword. They dropped into a fighting stance, mirroring each other, and memories of the Darkoning Trials swarmed her mind.

He blinked, shaking his head.

"You went through all of *that*," she hissed. "Subjected yourself to the trials, under your father's orders to *spy* on me?"

"You've no idea what I've been through," he snapped. "I never lied about us . . . about my feelings . . . *everything*."

"Everything?" she parroted.

"Everything, *asterya*. You were the light in my dark life."

"Your life was never dark."

"There's more going on here than you know." For a moment, desperation flashed from his face and she screamed, unable to fathom the complexity of her own emotions towards him. He had betrayed her. He was her enemy.

"I don't believe you!"

Just as they lunged for each other, Barron raised his hand, a giant slab of inky tar slicing down between them.

"Enough of that! I need you both alive. It's clear we need another motive." Barron sighed, and shot a beam of shadowed power into a nearby cluster of pine trees. A moment later, a dark, malachite guard and a tall female emerged.

"Bree?" Kora faltered, her power winking out. "Don't hurt her!"

Bree was faultless. She glided in a green dress with golden embellishments, her head held high. Her long braids swished around a golden circlet placed across her head, and her bright blue eyes narrowed on Kora.

"Why is she still here?" Bree snapped. "Why is this taking so long?"

"We need some extra . . . persuasion." Barron rocked on his heels.

"What . . ." Kora staggered.

Her water beast growled viciously, her mind dizzying. Bree was . . . her power crested, surging to the surface, and she panicked. Her open palms glowed, blinding her. "What is happening?"

Bree's musical laugh floated across the air, her jewelled hand clasping something at her chest.

Kora's power welled uncontrollably, pouring from every pore of her skin, every strand of hair, and lifting in a stream that floated through the air—straight to Bree. She flung her arms out, a wicked smile on her full lips as Kora's shimmering power flowed into her chest.

Kora cried out, collapsing to her knees as a familiar numbness overcame her. As her power tapered off, leaving her completely drained, Bree hummed, her eyes sparkling . . . near glowing.

And around her neck, was Kora's talisman, brimming with her power contained in its diamond lighted core. Bree waved a hand, conjuring a few drops of water, and giggled. "This is going to be so much fun!"

Kora couldn't connect. The droplets of water twirled, but she couldn't *feel* them. She was such a *fool*. Splashes of tainted wine trickled through her memory from a hazed evening of ballgowns and tiaras.

"Why?" Kora sobbed. Bree was a snake in a ballgown. "You drugged me that night, didn't you?"

"I need the *velesma* for power," Bree snipped.

The what?

"My family are destined to rule, and we need magic to do so. I will be the conduit for yours. Seeing as you want to waste it on . . . *vermin*. As an heiress, my union with the Barron's will see us thriving and leading for generations. Leaders of the new mage world. The new gods."

"Union? You can't become gods!" Kora's world was shattering all over again. Thanos had sent her back to *this* shitshow?

Bree smiled, wrapping her hands around Blake's arm. "We are betrothed!"

Blake grimly peered down at Bree's clasped hands, his lips curling, and glanced back to Kora. His jaw clenched as his shadow-rimmed green eyes enveloped her. "It's a recent development," he added.

She's nothing compared to you.

Everyone here knows that you're nothing.

Kora glanced between them, and her gaze settled on Bree's bright blue eyes.

He's been calling for his blue-eyed beauty.

No . . . it couldn't be . . . had this been going on for *that* long? Or longer? She revulsed from the couple, nausea churning so deep that she vomited all over the ground.

"No . . . I . . ."

"He's mine now, and I'm not letting him go." Bree's grip tightened.

Rage surged within Kora, smothering her heartbreak as her eyes tunnelled on Bree's slender jewelled fingers curling around Blake. "You can have him," she snapped, and Blake flinched.

You blind, ignorant fool!

"You can't become gods!" she repeated. "You will kill *everyone.* Just because the gods are not here, doesn't mean they're not watching. You're messing with forces outside of our control! Please," she resorted to begging. "Please don't do this. These islands will die. Mages will die. Azaria won't back off. Galen won't stop. *I* won't stop."

"I have seen the future, and it is magnificent," Barron boomed. "The old gods are dead."

"You have Devani gods in your gardens!" she cried. "You still worship them, I've seen it!"

Barron paused. "Those are relics. Unfortunately, my wife insists on keeping them. And she's a hard female to say no to. Now, let's get this over with," he sighed, boredom seeping into his tone. "I have a kingdom to rule. Until you come to your senses, we will keep you in a suspended state, siphoning your power over to Lady Hydrafort."

Kora clawed at the ground, dragging her weakened body away from Blake, his green eyes burning once again as he knelt, vines trapping her in place on top of a small collection of boulders.

Her back cracked against the sharp edges, her skin slicing open, and the soil-like dust on his fingers spread to his knuckles as he conjured his power. Kora sobbed and whimpered. She couldn't go back to that state again.

No, no, no, no! Panic seized her, her mind erupting. *"NO!"*

Bree watched beside Barron, a ruthless smile pasted on her

full lips.

Blake gently placed a hand on Kora's healed shoulder, and she froze under his touch. It was soft, gentle, and reminded her too much of the male he used to be. Sadness coursed through his stare, and her shattered heart fell apart, the pieces flying to the furthest corners of the world. "Things could have been different." And then he blinked, replacing it with cold detachment.

Every inch of her life drained, seeping into him. This close, she could see a greenish light flicker in his veins—her life force. Her skin sagged once again, turning leathery and wrinkled before decomposing as her organs shrivelled, her bones protruding, pores shrinking, eyes crusting.

The pain was immeasurable.

A wrenching scream tore from her collapsing lungs, scratching up her atrophying vocal cords and past her sunken lips as the agony burned her alive.

"I told you *asterya*," Blake murmured quietly. "When I finally took you, I'd make you scream."

She screamed and screamed as he absorbed her life into his hands, suspending her into a prison of his own making. Trapped forever.

As her grasp on reality fell through her withered fingertips, Kora emitted one final flare of hope—a beacon to the only person she knew could listen.

"Raiden . . . please help me."

Epilogue

Raiden

K ordelia was alive.

She was gods-damned alive, and he'd nearly wept with fucking joy at the sight of her. She'd looked fearless—like a goddess, tearing her way through those forsaken soldiers.

He nearly took her right there and then on that deck.

Gods, it'd been so long. Ten long fucking years trapped inside the Mist. A male could only do so much with his hand. She was still as beautiful as he remembered—but her hair was short. He didn't mind, but it wasn't . . . *her.*

And that scar.

Anger spliced through him so intensely that a torrent of wind blew through the chamber, scattering papers across the long, opal table. Sun speared through tall windows lining three rectangular walls, and cheery laughter echoed from children running in the streets outside.

The Mist had receded to the seas, and for the first time in a long time, they could feel the sun on their faces. Families had been celebrating, rejoicing.

But he couldn't spare a single minute. Not when the Galenite War was back on the table. Literally.

"Stop brooding," Aerion muttered, as he used his power to reorganise the papers on the shining surface.

"I'm not brooding," Raiden snapped.

He folded his arms across his chest. He'd been planning everything he was going to do to the Talmon Empire for stealing Kordelia away from him. He'd had ten years to think about it.

But now . . . it was much worse. So much fucking worse.

He was going to kill them off one by one—slowly. Maybe Kordelia would join in. His cock twitched in his trousers at the thought of them together again, enacting their revenge.

"They stole her memories," Raiden sighed. "She doesn't know who I am."

Aerion's deer-like gaze softened. "She will. It's in there somewhere. No one could break your bond."

"And that scar. What have they been doing to her? What has *he* been doing to her?" A snarl ripped from Raiden's throat.

He could smell that earthy mutt all over her body, and it positively sickened him. But beneath all that *stench*, was their connection. That twining of steel, slicked in ocean spray, cool air basked in vanilla.

"Rai," Aerion shuffled some papers. "She remembered me, okay? She's in there somewhere. We'll figure it out. As for that *creep*, I don't want to know."

Aerion had a point. Despite being trapped here in Galen, by the Mist, unable to leave for ten years, he'd still managed to distantly connect to her through their void. He'd caught glimpses of her life through her eyes, and he'd been able to send her his voice on the winds. There was still a chance. Hope pressed its harsh blade to his throat.

If their connection still existed, then there was hope.

Sometimes . . . Raiden had regretted it. Some of the things he'd seen Kordelia do and experience had been horrible to witness. And he'd been unable to help, stuck here in their city, useless and helpless when she needed him. Especially when that royal prick—

"*Stop it.*" Aerion waved a hand, reorganising the papers once again. "These are our strategies for the war. I need them in order. We can't lose again, Rai. We really need to win this thing."

"I don't care." Raiden stood, the chair flipping back. "They've taken Kordelia *again*. I fucking left her there! I'm going to get her back. There's no winning without her."

An arched, opal door slammed shut on the far side of the wide chamber, the sound bouncing off the citrine-painted walls.

"If it makes you feel better, I made you leave." Aryn strolled in, his boots echoing on the polished, pearlescent tiled floor.

He crossed the space in a flash, which was large enough to

host two hundred people. They had sealed off half the castle during the Mist, and this ballroom had become a common space. Even city residents would sleep in here during especially dark winters, when the smallest of sun rays couldn't pierce the Mist.

"Yeah, blame him," Aerion complained.

"Maybe I will. You were supposed to protect her!"

Raiden stared down at Aryn. His golden eyes always made Raiden on edge. They were not of this world, and spoke volumes about what lay hidden beneath his youthful skin.

Aryn glared back. "It's not easy. She's not exactly hazard-free. It took an age to find her in the first place. Erick had hidden her well, and getting past him onto the ship was harder than you may believe."

"Well, you're not short on time, *skildaj.*"

Aryn's ethereal gaze flashed, his shoulders hunching from the pressing force crushing the air in the ballroom. They were all tense.

Raiden's hands clenched into fists. He needed to break something—or snap. That nature-loving mutt's neck would do. Or perhaps a visit to Erick Cadell. He shuddered with violence. He couldn't even unpack the list of revenge he had planned for Erick fucking Cadell.

"I nearly got her back," Raiden choked out. "And we fucking *left* her. Gods know where she is now, or how we'll find her again."

It wasn't a possibility to him. There was no world that existed for him without Kordelia. He'd rather die in the pits of Umbra.

"Trust me, we wouldn't have survived, and Barron would have taken her regardless. We need to plan." Aryn approached Aerion, glancing over the papers. "You need a better system, Aerion."

"I had one," Aerion moaned. "Rai's full power reawakened now the Mist is broken, and this is what I'm dealing with."

"Barron will regret ending the Mist. Now we can attack. In fact, right now would be good." Raiden smacked his fists, rolling his shoulders.

"Erm . . . Barron has nothing to do with the Mist," Aryn rubbed the nape of his neck. "We all assumed it was the gods."

Well that didn't make an ounce of fucking sense.

"Why would the gods punish us like that? We were fighting to keep the old ways alive. To end the empire's oppression," Raiden snapped.

"Maybe they thought you were too violent," his brother joked. "Either way, we can come and go now, including Cassidy,

Hector and Leto."

"Shame Skylar isn't awake to keep Raiden in check," Aryn snorted, and Aerion's lips quirked.

Raiden growled in response, the sound resonating through the arched chamber. The towering, black-paned windows vibrated, and crystal chandeliers rocked, twinkling glass chiming.

"What do you propose we do? Just sit and wait it out for him to attack first?" His voice grew fervent, and his power rippled around him like a constant shield—a shimmering diamond layer. "What if they're taking her memory again? We'll have to start from square one and—"

"*Raiden* . . ."

He released a sharp breath, air escaping his lungs as he stumbled into the table. Aryn jolted as Raiden's hands slammed down onto the surface, steadying himself. Deep in his mind—a flutter of a connection. A gentle breeze carrying salted ocean, and warming vanilla.

"*. . . please help me.*"

"Kordelia." He glanced up, meeting Aryn's gaze, whose golden eyes were so wide, his power leaked into the edges. "She needs me."

To be continued . . .

GLOSSARY OF TERMS

DEVANIA

Devanian Language:

Asterya / a-stir-ya / – a shining star.
Ayterni / a-ter-ni / – eternal.
Cildbah / kild-bar / – affectionate term for kid, child, or kiddo.
Sehwani / sir-va-ni / – a deep expression to say hello, to say you see into one's soul and essence.
Skildaj / skill-dah-j / – a shield or protector.
Velesma / vel-es-ma / – talisman.

PIRATES

Food/Drink:

Grog – alcoholic spirit beverages, commonly mixed with water.
Sea biscuit – a type of bread or biscuit, usually hard but can be soaked in water and flavoured.

Currency:

Bits – a bit is equivalent to one eighth of real-world dollars.
Two-bit – equivalent to a real-world quarter. It's a dollar coin cut into two pieces.
Pieces of eight – a dollar that cannot be cut into eight bits, so it's equivalent to eight bits.
Doubloon – a golden coin worth double currency.

Pirate nomenclature:

Aye – affirmation, saying yes.
Belay – a command to stop.
Bilge rat – insulting term describing the lowest ranking crew

members who work in the lowest parts of the ship where the rats are.

Come about – to bring the ship full way around in the wind.

Davy Jones' Locker – a deep place at the bottom of the ocean where sailors' souls go to rest.

Dead men tell no tales – a phrase to leave no survivors.

Grog blossom – redness in the nose and/or face from drinking too much alcohol.

Lad/Lass – young boy/girl.

List – to lean to one side.

Scourge (Scourge of the Seven Seas) – a pirate known for his violent and brutal nature.

Three sheets to the wind – intoxicated, highly drunk.

Wench – young woman or girl referred as a prostitute.

ACKNOWLEDGEMENTS

Oh. My. God. I can't believe we're at the acknowledgements. Thank you so much for reading my story. I've poured my heart and soul into it, and I hope certain themes have resonated with yourself, dearest reader. This has been a long time coming from the idea first sparking in December 2023, all the way to publication in September 2025. I want to say thank you to the following people, who have helped me along the way. You all deserve so much recognition.

First and foremost, my best friend April. If it wasn't for a spontaneous walk in the summer of 2024, you wouldn't have directed me into the world of self-publishing, proposing the idea that I could achieve my dreams. You opened the door for me, and I am forever grateful. Not only that, but you were also my amazing cover designer, and took my chaotic ideas, and turned them into something beautiful, as well as helping the marketing side. You can find April on Instagram with the following handle: @april.wardesigns.

Meg, you've been a star. If it wasn't for your advice, I don't know if I'd be at this final stage. As a fellow indie author, your insight has been invaluable. From explaining the process to me multiple times (sorry!) to taking me on as a client to turn my story into a real-life formatted book. On top of that, you connected me with valuable professionals in this industry, especially my editor. Thank you so much.

Thank you to Lauren, my editor at Wonderporium Ink. You've been so kind and caring, and your excitement for my novel spurred me on during times where I was losing hope. Thank you for being so accommodating, for listening to my random ideas and queries, and guiding me through this process—especially when I wouldn't put the manuscript down!

To all the author friends I've made along the way—Meg, Amy and

Trish—your support means so much to me, and your infinite wisdom and feedback. Thank you for listening to my endless questions, even when they were silly.

Thank you to my friends, family and partner. Your support is the foundation that stopped me from giving up. I couldn't have carried on without your encouragement, and excitement for me. Even when my rattling and venting didn't make much sense—Eden I'm looking at you—you listened regardless and helped me see the bigger picture. Mum, your constant joy and pride for me achieving my dreams knows no bounds. I love you all.

Finally, thank you dear reader. If you're reading this, thank you for taking a chance on my book. Your support means so much to me, and you have made my dreams come true. If any of you have engaged with me online, please know every like, comment or message fills my heart with joy, and reminds me why I'm doing this. If you enjoyed Daughter of the Dark Sea, please take the time to leave a review, it would mean the world to me!

ABOUT THE AUTHOR

G. E. Smith is a marketer full time, and a fantasy writer in her spare time. When she isn't working or writing, she loves reading with the same songs on repeat or playing sci-fi games. She enjoys working on her fitness—despite eating lots of biscuits—to support her scoliosis and has a passion for swimming and being around water which may bleed into her writing (got to calm the anxiety somehow!). G. E. Smith currently resides in the southeast of England with her fluffy, hyperactive dog, Rolo, and her favourite place to be is curled up with her partner, Eden, with lots of snacks and trashy TV.

She enjoys writing about fantasy with dark themes, and challenging societal norms along with exploring concepts related to anxiety. She loves to weave in plot twists, with shattering revelations that'll leave readers gasping with shock . . . or horror.

If you enjoyed Daughter of the Dark Sea, and are seeking to whet your pirate fantasy appetite, keep up to date with G. E. Smith here:

Instagram: @gesmithauthor
TikTok: @gesmithauthor
Email: gesmithauthor@outlook.com
Website: https://gesmithauthor.my.canva.site

Printed in Dunstable, United Kingdom

67194303R00251